"Land of Alw

an

"Mad Mesa"

TWO CLASSIC ADVENTURES OF

DOC SAVAGE

REG. U.S PAT. OFF.

by W. Ryerson Johnson and
Lester Dent writing as "Kenneth Robeson"

with new historical essays by Will Murray

Published by Sanctum Productions for
NOSTALGIA VENTURES, INC.
P.O. Box 231183; Encinitas, CA 92023-1183

This Nostalgia Ventures edition is an unabridged republication of the text and illustrations of two stories from *Doc Savage Magazine,* as originally published by Street & Smith Publications, Inc., N.Y.: *Land of Always-Night* from the March 1935 issue, and *Mad Mesa* from the January 1939 issue. These two novels are works of their time. Consequently, the text is reprinted intact in its original historical form, including occasional out-of-date ethnic and cultural stereotyping. Typographical errors have been tacitly corrected in this edition.

ISBN 1-932806-28-8   13 DIGIT 978-1-932806-28-1

Series editor: Anthony Tollin
P.O. Box 761474
San Antonio, TX 78245-1474
sanctumotr@earthlink.net

Contributing editor: Will Murray

Copy editor: Joseph Wrzos

Proofreader: Carl Gafford

Cover restoration: Michael Piper

The editor gratefully acknowledges the contributions of Tom Stephens and Scott Cranford in the preparation of this volume.

Nostalgia Ventures, Inc.
P.O. Box 231183; Encinitas, CA 92023-1183

Visit Doc Savage at www.shadowsanctum.com
and www.nostalgiatown.com

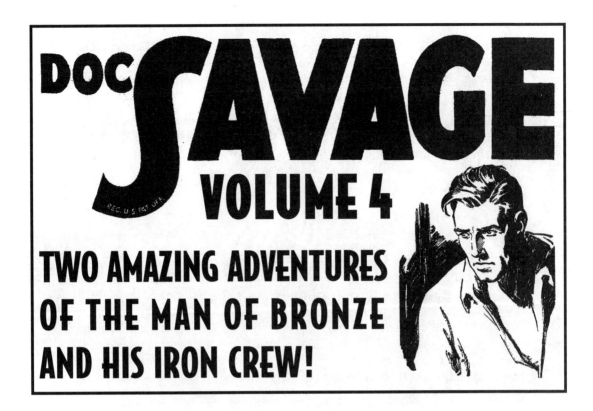

DOC SAVAGE VOLUME 4

TWO AMAZING ADVENTURES OF THE MAN OF BRONZE AND HIS IRON CREW!

Thrilling Tales and Features

Cover art by Walter Baumhofer, Emery Clarke and Robert Harris

Interior illustrations by Paul Orban

Again Doc Savage and his men head for the icy wastes beyond the Arctic Circle, to pierce the mystery of eternal blackness that was the

Land of Always-Night

A Complete Book-length Novel

by KENNETH ROBESON

Chapter I
THE BUTTERFLY DEATH

IT is somewhat ridiculous to say that a human hand can resemble a butterfly. Yet this particular hand did attain that similarity. Probably it was the way it moved, hovered, moved again, with something about it that was remindful of a slow-motion picture being shown on a screen.

The color had something to do with the impression. The hand was white, unnatural; it might have been fashioned of mother-of-pearl. There was something serpentine, hideous, about the way it strayed and hovered, yet was never still. It made one think of a venomous white moth.

It made Beery Hosmer think of death. Only the expression on Beery Hosmer's face told that, for he was not saying anything. But he was trying to. His lips shaped word syllables and the muscle strings in his scrawny throat jerked, but no sounds came out.

The horrible white hand floated up toward Beery Hosmer's face. The side street was gloomy, deserted except for Beery Hosmer and the man with the uncanny hand. The hand stood out in the murk almost as if it were a thing of white paper with a light inside.

Beery Hosmer went through a convulsion of fright. Beery was a rather unusual fellow. He was a crook who looked the part. At best, he was rather a sickening specimen, and now his aspect was doubly unwholesome. He managed to pump words out.

"Naw, naw, don't!" he choked. "I dunno where it is! So help me, I don't!"

The other man made no answer. His fantastic white hand—the other one never moved, as if it were dead—was not his only unusual characteristic. His eyes were unnaturally huge and so very pale as to be almost the color of water, and he had a thin face, a thin body. When occasional distant automobile headlights caused him to cast a shadow, the shadow was skeleton-thin.

Beery Hosmer broke out in gibberish.

"I don't know," he gulped. "I wouldn't kid you. I don't know anything about it!"

The other man's white hand kept moving.

"Where is it?" he asked. His voice was utterly flat; it held the mechanical quality found in the speech of persons so deaf that they can hardly hear themselves talk.

Beery Hosmer tried to back away. He was already pressed against the darkened window of a candy store.

"Wouldn't I tell you if I knew?" he whimpered. "Lookit, Ool—"

The hand of the man called Ool seemed to move a little slower.

"You have it," he said tonelessly. "You were on your way to endeavor to sell it to this man Doc Savage. It is in the money belt which you carry around your waist."

Beery made choking sounds. He was almost sobbing.

"Take it easy!" he blubbered. "We can fix this tip. Gimme time! Lemme think!"

"You," said Ool, "will have all infinity in which to think."

The white hand darted. There was no slow-motion effect this time. No onlooker could have told whether or not the hand actually touched Beery Hosmer.

ALL of the pent-up terror of the last few moments burst from Beery Hosmer's slack lips in one animal scream. He wrenched violently backward. Head, shoulders and elbows rammed into the plate glass of the candy store.

The window collapsed. Glass crashed to the cement walk with a jangle.

Beery seemed to be trying to get a gun out of an armpit holster. But he thrashed about like one suddenly stricken mad. He kicked trays of chocolates and mints out on the sidewalk. Great shudders began to course over his scrawny body, but did not persist for long, because he gave a vast, wheezing sigh and slumped over, becoming as inert as the chocolate creams crushed beneath him.

Ool leaned into the window. His left hand remained at his side, as if lifeless. His right hand drifted to Beery Hosmer's shirt, wrenched. Two buttons flew and clicked far out in the street, then chamois of a money belt tore with a rotten sound.

The object which Ool brought into view resembled a pair of goggles, more than anything else. But as goggles, they were peculiar, for the lenses were as large as small condensed milk cans, and their glass—the stuff did not look like true glass—was almost jet black.

One thing was striking. The workmanship was exquisite.

Ool put the goggles on, and they contrasted grotesquely with his chalky face. Then he made a disgusted sound, took them off hurriedly and pocketed them. A psychologist would have called the little incident strange. It was as if the donning of the goggles had been an instinctive action.

There was nothing hurried about the man's movements. He reached down, picked up a chocolate, tasted it and smacked his lips. Then he took off his hat and scooped chocolates into it until it was nearly full.

Walking away, he ate the candy avidly, as if it were some exquisite delicacy with which he had just become acquainted.

At the corner, Ool passed under a streetlight, and a peculiarity about his hair became apparent. It was little more than a golden down, like the fine fur on a mouse.

One man saw Ool go under the streetlight. The man was a janitor in a nearby building.

It was inevitable that the breaking glass should have attracted attention, and within a few moments, a uniformed policeman came running. He stood looking at the candy strewn over the walk, at first not noticing the human form in the window. Then he saw it, swore, and leaned in to make an examination. When he backed away, he looked puzzled.

"Guy must've had a fit, fell in the window and died," he muttered.

That was the story the next editions of the newspapers carried, after a medical examiner had expressed the tentative opinion that death was due to natural causes.

Moreover, there had been over a thousand dollars in the chamois money belt, and since this was intact, it did not seem that the motive was robbery.

It was some hours before the police got a different slant on the story. It required that long for the janitor who had seen Ool go under the streetlight to make up his mind. The janitor was a timid soul. His story created quite a furor when he decided to talk.

The janitor had seen the whole thing.

Chapter II
PLANS

EARL MAURICE "WATCHES" BOWEN stood in his modernistic Park Avenue apartment and poured eighty-year-old Napoleon brandy into a fragile glass, tested its bouquet long and pleasurably, then took a sip and blotted his lips with a silk handkerchief.

He was a big man, with some surplus around the waist. His dress was immaculate, his manner suave. He did not look the part of one of the smoothest crooks in the big time.

Watches Bowen leaned back in the exquisitely molded chair and absently fingered the thin yellow gold chain which connected the two lower pockets of his vest. There was a watch on either end of the chain. There was a jeweled timepiece on each of his slightly thick wrists.

Watches Bowen had two loves. One was his watches, of which he always carried four or more, and kept them perfectly in time. The other love was his Napoleon brandy.

It was possible also that he might be considered to have a third affection—his liking for other people's money.

Watches said, "And so Beery Hosmer is dead?"

Ool sat a dozen feet away on another delicately modernistic chair, his hat held on his knees. From time to time his pearl-colored right hand drifted into the hat and transferred a chocolate cream to his forbidding slit of a mouth. The hat was almost empty, but he still ate avidly.

Ool swallowed, nodded, "That is what I came here to tell you."

"Unfortunate, very unfortunate," Watches said dryly. "What happened to the damned fool?"

Ool removed a chocolate from the hat and eyed it lovingly.

"These are delicious," he said. "What do you call them?"

"Candy," said Watches. "Chocolate creams. What about Beery?"

Ool ate the chocolate with much smacking of lips.

"No one will trace me here," he said. "I am sure of that."

Watches looked, acted as if he had been slapped. He had idly detached one of the watches from the gold chain and it all but slipped from his fingers; his mouth sagged roundly open.

"*You!*" he exploded. "You got Beery?"

"These chocolate creams, as you call them—I must have more of them," Ool said tonelessly. "Yes, I killed Beery."

Watches Bowen sagged back, reached for the brandy and did something which was very rare for him—he drank a slug without sampling its bouquet.

"Whew!" he muttered. "And you sit there gobbling down candy! Oh, I know you're only about half human, but—"

"My people had a civilization greater than yours some thousands of years ago!" Ool said. For the first time, there was some slight feeling in his voice.

"All right, all right." Watches spread his hands. "We won't go into that. Would you mind telling me why, particularly, you decided to scratch Beery off?"

"He knew our plans," Ool said.

Watches scowled. "Now look here, if you're gonna start bumping—"

"Beery Hosmer knew our plans and he was greedy," Ool stated, interrupting. "He thought he saw a way to gather unto himself much money."

"This begins to make sense," Watches grunted. "What was Beery up to?"

"The device which you call my goggles—" Ool paused.

"Yeah?"

"Beery stole them," said Ool.

"The hell!" Watches polished the back of the timepiece he was holding. "But how in the devil did he plan to make a buck from that? He knew how things stack up. He knew—"

"He knew there was one man in your United States who might make use of the goggles," Ool interposed.

Watches shook his head slowly. "I don't get this. Who was Beery going to?"

Ool evidently knew something of dramatic effects. He allowed just the proper pause before answering.

"Doc Savage," he said.

"WHAT?"

Had someone shot him unexpectedly, Watches might have been more surprised, but only slightly more so. He whipped to his feet. He did something he had not done in years—he dropped one of his watches, the one he was fingering at the moment. And after his one blasting exclamation, he tried to speak and the words stuck somewhere down in his chest.

Ool ate chocolate peacefully. Electric lights were on in the apartment, and under their glow, several points about the man were noticeable which would have escaped casual observation. His white skin was given the mother-of-pearl appearance by an interlacing of fine blue veins. It somehow had the aspect of a tropical flower doomed to live its life among venomous insects and more venomous serpents, cut off from the sun in the depths of some swamp.

With a perceptibly shaking hand, Watches

poured himself a hooker of the Napoleon brandy, downed it, once more without sampling its aroma and flavor. The rare liquor seemed to open a channel for his words.

"Did Beery get to Doc Savage?" he asked hoarsely.

"No," said Ool.

Watches let out a gusty sigh of relief.

"That's a break for us," he said fervently. "I'm telling you that I'd rather fight the United States army than this Doc Savage. A guy can at least run from the army."

"This Doc Savage must be a remarkable individual," Ool said, his dead voice making it seem that he had no interest in the matter.

"'Remarkable' is putting it mild," Watches snorted. "That bird Savage is a wizard! They say he knows all about electricity and chemistry and psychology and engineering and them things. They say he's a mental marvel. On top of that, he's supposed to be able to bend horseshoes in his hands, and things like that."

"Dangerous?" Ool murmured.

"You mean to guys like us?" countered Watches.

"Exactly."

"Poison!" Watches said vehemently. "Doc Savage makes a profession of mixing up in unusual things. He's what the newspapers call a big-time adventurer. He's supposed to travel around over the world, helping people out of trouble and punishing wrongdoers."

"That hardly applies to us," said Ool.

"Oh, yeah?" Watches grinned wryly. "From what I've heard, this thing is right up Doc Savage's alley."

Ool said nothing. He took the last chocolate out of his hat, ate it, licked his fingers, shook a few chocolate crumbs out in his hand, ate them, then stood up.

"You will get me more of those chocolate creams," he said.

Watches scowled as if he resented being given an order, then said hastily, "Sure! Sure!"

Ool went to one of the large windows and looked out upon the amazing display of lights which is New York City after nightfall.

Watches Bowen asked curiously, "How did you kill Beery?"

"I merely looked at him," said Ool, "and he dropped dead."

"O. K.," Watches growled, "if that's the way you feel about it."

Ool was looking steadily through the window, his head back as if he were eyeing the sky rather than the lights.

"How are our plans progressing?" he asked.

"Rotten," said Watches.

"WHAT do you mean?" Ool asked, not turning.

"I've canvassed all of the big airplane factories," Watches explained. "They can build us a true gyroplane, sure. This true gyro will rise straight up and hover. It can be controlled fairly well. But here's the rub. The damn things won't carry more than two men, and they won't lift hardly any fuel at all. The things are still in the experimental stage."

"Then you think we are doomed to failure?" Ool asked. He was still peering steadily at the sky.

"We're stumped," Watches said. He looked at the other curiously. "Say, what're you looking at?"

"Come here." Ool lifted an arm. "Look."

Watches Bowen came over and stared out of the window, not at the lights, but at the black abyss of the sky. A moment later, he saw that which Ool was indicating—a short string of lights suspended in the heavens. He watched these, and they came closer; and it became apparent that the lights were strings of luminous letters.

It was an advertisement, a flexible electric sign pulled behind a small dirigible.

Watches snorted. The thing was a common sight over New York City.

"What the hell?" he sniffed.

"An idea that I have," Ool said mechanically.

"Idea?"

"Which may enable us to quickly consummate our plans," Ool said. "We will make use of this Doc Savage."

Watches wet his lips, shuddered. "Don't crack wise."

"You think I am joking?" Ool asked.

"Either that, or you're crazy!"

Ool turned away from the window. "I know a great deal of this Doc Savage. I have studied him. I know his characteristics, and the characteristics of the five men who aid him. I even know that each of those five men is a specialist in some line. One is a chemist, one an electrical engineer, one a lawyer, another a civil engineer and the fifth a geologist and archaeologist. I know what mechanical equipment Doc Savage uses. I know—"

Watches gulped, "A minute ago, you acted as if you didn't know much about the guy!"

"I wanted to see if you were afraid of him," Ool said.

"I *am* afraid of him," Watches snapped. "I'm not ashamed of it, either. No man in his right sense will buck Doc Savage."

"Nevertheless," Ool murmured emotionlessly, "we are going to use him."

Watches all but yelled. "Don't! I tell you that Doc Savage and his five helpers are poison! We can find some way without mixing with them!"

But Ool wheeled and stalked out of the apartment.

HALF an hour later, Ool was on the Hudson River, in a small rowboat. He had the oarlocks muffled with rags, and the only sound penetrating the darkness was the occasional slap of a wave against the side of his boat. These small noises did not matter, being lost in the rhythmic lappings of waves among the pilings of the piers along the nearby waterfront.

Ool peered intently into the darkness. It was very black, yet the man with the strange mother-of-pearl complexion seemed to have some slight ability to see in the darkness, for he soon pulled in toward one particular pier.

This pier was roofed over, and it bulked large in the darkness. Across the outer end, after the fashion of piers, a name was lettered:

HIDALGO TRADING COMPANY

Most of the building was smoke-stained, old-looking, but there was a part, a higher addition to one side, which was obviously quite new. The end of this was closed with enormous doors.

Ool pulled his rowboat close to the pier warehouse and made the painter fast to a piling. For an instant, he stood looking up out of his flat, water-colored eyes at the blackly looming hulk of the structure. Then he grasped the nearest piling.

He did not look like a strong man, yet he shinned up the smooth timber with squirrel agility, and reaching the top of the piling, he continued his ascent up the warehouse wall, employing a steel girder, a number of which formed the outer structure of the wall.

A moment later, he squirmed over the top of the hangar.

He listened for a time. There was no sound, except small water noises. Ool crept forward, making for a large ventilator. He rounded this. Then things happened.

A squat, bulky form hurtled from behind the ventilator. Tremendous arms enwrapped Ool in a grip that forced air from his lung with a sharp roar. The stocky attacker wedged a head under Ool's chin, and Ool's stringy neck was bent until it creaked.

Ool tried desperately to bring his right hand into play, but it was pinned to his side. He lifted his feet in an attempt to overbalance his assailant. The apish attacker did not upset. Ool's mother-of-pearl face began to take on a purplish hue. He was entirely helpless.

Chapter III
THE MAN WHO WAS NOT HUMAN

A FLASHLIGHT spiked a white beam out of the darkness and another man came from behind the ventilator.

"You do have your moments, eh, Monk?" he asked.

"Frisk 'im, Ham," grunted the apish man who had seized Ool. "See if he's got a gun."

The newcomer, "Ham," placed his flashlight on the roof, then stepped forward to search Ool. This put him in the flash glow. He was lean, of about average height, and attired in remarkably dapper fashion. He carried a slender black cane.

Ool stared at him.

"Brigadier General Theodore Marley Brooks," he said emotionlessly.

Ham did not look surprised. Courtroom training had taught him that, for Ham was one of the most astute lawyers ever to be matriculated from Harvard. He was also by way of being the male fashion plate for New York City. His other and major claim to distinction was that he was a member of Doc Savage's group of five remarkable aides.

Ham tucked the cane under an arm and began searching Ool.

"Hurry up, you overdressed shyster!" "Monk" grunted. Monk had a small, childlike voice.

Ool tried to move his right arm. Monk put on pressure. A faint, strangely piteous cry came from Ool's lips and he subsided. Monk's strength was fabulous.

Monk had other abilities too, although a stranger would not have dreamed it after one look at his bullet of a head. There did not seem to be room for even an ample spoonful of brains above Monk's eyebrow line. Yet, as Lieutenant Colonel Andrew Blodgett Mayfair, he was among the half dozen greatest living chemists.

Monk was also a member of Doc Savage's group of five aides.

Ool revived slightly and spoke, his voice weaker, but still retaining its mechanical quality.

"How did you discover me?" he asked.

Monk grinned. The grin had the effect of making his incredibly homely face very pleasant to look at.

"A bird can't light on this building without us knowing it," he said. "Boy, you should see our alarm system."

"I see," Ool said. "I should have thought of photo-electric eyes and magnetic fields."

Ham, conducting his search leisurely, said, "The man seems to know something of electricity."

"Will you hurry up, you fashion plate?" Monk requested.

Ool lifted his left foot and stamped with all of his might on Monk's toes and instep. Monk bellowed—he liked to yell at the top of his voice when he was getting hurt. He released Ool suddenly.

Ool, so unexpectedly released, staggered. Monk swung a fist. Ool had no time to dodge. The fist hit him and he slammed down on the roof. Almost instantly, he sat up, but did not try to get to his feet.

"Blazes!" Monk grunted. "He's tough. When I hit a guy like that, he generally sleeps."

HAM studied Ool's face. Ham had withdrawn a pace and tugged his black cane apart near the handle, disclosing that it was in reality a sword cane with a long, thin blade.

"He is a strange one," Ham said wonderingly. "Look at those eyes, and that mouse-fur hair on his head. And the color of his skin! Say, he's almost as funny-looking as you!"

Monk scowled at Ham.

Ool chose that instant to lunge, and his right hand drifted out with a moccasin speed. Monk jumped. Only his agility, fabulous for one of such bulk, saved him.

"Watch it!" Ham yelled. "He's got something in that right hand!"

"You're telling me!" Monk circled warily.

Ool was up on all fours now. He scuttled backward, spider fashion. Ham, circling swiftly, menaced the pale man with the tip of his sword cane.

Ool, staring at the cane, saw that the tip was coated for some inches with a sticky-looking substance.

"Poison?" he asked. His voice was still utterly flat.

Ham, startled by the calmness of the question, started to say something, then reconsidered and was silent.

"Shut up!" he snapped. "Show us the inside of that hand!"

Ool hesitated. Then he turned the hand over, and both Monk and Ham bent over to examine it.

There was nothing in Ool's hand.

"You search him," Ham told Monk. "If he gets funny again, I'll tickle his ribs in a way he won't like."

While Ham threatened with the sword cane, Monk went through Ool's pockets.

"Nothing!" Monk said disgustedly. "No gun, no knife—wait a minute. What's this?"

He pulled the strange goggles out of Ool's pocket and held them up to get better light on them.

Ool stared blankly, but his right hand, held high above his head, started wavering like a butterfly's feeble fluttering when it feels the first warm rays of the morning sun on its wings.

Monk pressed the goggles to his eyes.

"Can't see through 'em," he growled, then addressed Ool: "What are these things?"

Ool did not answer. His right hand kept up its weird shifting.

Monk pocketed the goggles.

"What did you come here for?" he asked Ool.

Ool said nothing, but his right hand continued its butterfly fluttering.

Ham watched the motion, frowned, then pressed the point of his sword against Ool's ribs. The chalk-faced assassin quieted his hand and kept it motionless.

"We'll take him to Doc," Ham said.

IN the center of New York City, the skyscrapers jut up like silver pines, each seemingly striving to overshadow the other; but there is one building taller and finer than all the rest, an astounding mass of polished granite and stainless steel towering nearly a hundred stories into the sky, a structure that is possibly man's proudest building triumph.

The entire eighty-sixth floor of this building was occupied by the man whose name was lettered in modest bronze on a door:

CLARK SAVAGE, JR.

Monk and Ham took their captive to Doc Savage's headquarters by way of Doc's private speed elevator, a lift especially designed by Doc, one which swooped the eighty-six stories in about the time it took an ordinary express elevator to rise half a dozen floors. Almost invariably, a man, riding in the speed elevator for the first time, was forced to his knees by the shock of starting.

Monk and Ham watched Ool amusedly when the elevator started. But Ool's knees gave slightly, and that was all. At no time was he in danger of losing his balance.

"I told you he was tough," Monk grinned.

"And funny-looking," Ham reminded. "Funnier looking than you."

Monk ceased grinning. "Listen, shyster—one of these days I'm gonna make you put on a sword-swallowing act with that trick cane!"

The pair glared at each other the rest of the way up. A stranger, from their manner, would have thought they were on the point of coming to blows, when, as a matter of truth, they were the best of friends.

They stepped out on the eighty-sixth floor, crossed the corridor and passed into a large room, plentifully furnished with huge, comfortable chairs. A deep-piled Oriental rug lay underfoot. Between the two great windows stood a solid-looking table inlaid with ivory of exquisite workmanship.

A shortwave radio receiving set squatted inconspicuously at the back of the table, and a voice was droning from the loudspeaker as the men entered with their captive. It was a police broadcast.

"—all cars will be on the lookout for Dimiter Daikoff," the radio droned. "Daikoff is a very large man, with black hair and dark eyes. Officers will use care, since Daikoff is reported to be dangerous. Daikoff recently escaped from a Chicago jail and is reported to have been seen in New York—"

Monk raised his voice over the drone of the radio.

"Doc!" he yelled. "We found a guy on top of the waterfront plane hangar! Thought you'd want to talk to him! He must've been up to something!"

Doc Savage came through a door into the room.

PERHAPS the reaction of Ool to the appearance of Doc Savage was the thing which best indicated what a remarkable physical specimen the bronze man presented. Ool, who had murdered a man that evening without showing the slightest excitement, stared and let his jaw down slightly; his water-colored eyes became quite wide.

Doc Savage was a giant of bronze. As he came through the door, his stature was tremendous, but when he was beyond the door and there was nothing by which to compare his size, he seemed to grow smaller in stature. That was because of the symmetry of his development; his corded muscles meshed under his skin in a manner which made their tremendous size scarcely noticeable, except for the tendons on his hands which were like cables.

But the compelling thing about the bronze man was his eyes. Strange eyes, they were, like pools of flake-gold, hypnotically compelling in their power, stirred continuously with a weird life.

Doc Savage was quietly dressed. The bronze of his hair was but little darker than the bronze of his skin.

"What's this?" he asked.

The bronze man had a voice of remarkable modulation, and his tone, while not loud, carried to the corners of the room.

Monk explained what had happened.

"The photo-electric alarms on the roof gave the guy away," he said.

Then he went on to tell of the capture, of the weird way in which Ool moved his hand—the hand in which they had found nothing. He finished up by producing the goggles with the black lenses as thick as condensed milk cans.

The bronze man eyed the goggles closely.

There came into existence an eerie trilling sound. It welled up and pervaded the room, tuneful yet tuneless, mellow and so soft that it might have been the whispering note of an evening wind seeping through palm fronds, or the distant murmur of glacial ice on its ponderous way to the sea.

Monk and Ham watched curiously. They knew that sound. It was part of Doc Savage, although they could not see his lips move as he made it. The note was a small, unconscious thing which he did in moments of stress, or when surprised, or puzzled.

Doc Savage asked Ool, "What are these?"

Ool replied promptly, tonelessly.

"Just a toy," he said. "They are of no value, no importance."

There was nothing in his voice to show that he had killed Beery Hosmer earlier in the night because Beery had taken the strange goggles with the intention of selling them to this same remarkable bronze man.

DOC SAVAGE watched Ool intently.

"Why were you prowling over our waterfront hangar?" he asked.

Ool smiled. It was the smile of a man not accustomed to showing emotion in that manner. The smile was slightly horrible.

"I went to the hangar for the purpose of contacting you," Ool said.

"Why did you not come to me here?" the bronze man asked.

"You are a busy man—I know your reputation—I despaired of being granted an interview." Ool spoke by spurts.

"The interview was an urgent matter?"

"Tremendously urgent."

"So you went prowling about the hangar, knowing it would be guarded, knowing you would be captured and brought to me?"

"Precisely."

Monk blurted: "Bunk! This lug was up to something."

Doc turned the curious goggles over slowly in

his cabled hands. Again came his low trilling sound, more felt than heard, flooding the room with its tremulous quality.

Police broadcast continued to issue from the shortwave set, flooding the room with droning. "Calling all cars—calling all cars—"

Then the announcement concerning the Chicago criminal came through again:

"—Dimiter Daikoff wanted for murder. A big man, walks with a limp; black hair; small, dark eyes; a scar that starts from the lobe of his right ear and slants across his neck—"

Doc Savage's compelling voice broke in upon the radio droning.

"Who are you?" he questioned Ool.

"Gray Forestay is my name," Ool said promptly. "In Mongolia my name, as nearly as can be translated, was Lleigh Foor Saath."

Doc Savage's features remained undecipherable, but the flake-gold which seemed always alive in his eyes, swirled a bit faster.

Monk muttered: "The yahoo is lying, Doc."

Ool kept his flat-eyed stare centered upon Doc. "I am not lying," he said. "You are judging from my appearance that I am not a pure Mongol. You are correct. I am only part Chinese."

He paused. "My unnatural appearance is not entirely the result of a mixture of bloods. It is the result of hardships more grueling than you would believe a man could endure, and live."

"Go on," Doc said.

Ool spoke monotonously. "I hesitate to speak lest I be disbelieved, and yet I know you to be a man of such mature intellect as to realize that there are strange things in the world, things so strange as to be utterly discredited by the conventional mind."

Ool paused again. After fully half a minute, he continued:

"You have heard of the Lenderthorn Expedition, lost in the pack ice north of Canada? I, Gray Forestay, was the only member of the expedition to escape. In recent months, as perhaps you have read in the news, I headed a rescue expedition to search for the lost men. We found that airships were utterly impractical in that region. We could not effect a landing upon the rough ice. But where an airship has failed, a dirigible would succeed."

"So?"

"You have a dirigible. That is one reason why I have come to you. There is also another reason."

"And this other reason?" Doc queried.

"You control, so I understand, what is perhaps the most superior aggregation of brains and brawn in the world. I need your help."

Monk squinted at Doc. "Is this dope about a Lenderthorn Expedition straight stuff?"

"It is," Doc nodded slowly. "It was in the newspapers, but not prominently so. Lenderthorn was not a famous man."

Ool spoke suddenly, dramatically:

"The Lenderthorn Expedition was not lost through natural causes, as was reported."

Ool stared with his flat, water-colored eyes while he let an interval of silence pass.

"We encountered what I can only call mysterious 'things,'" he went on. "These came in the night, and I know only that they were black, shapeless and utterly horrible, and that they carried off members of our expedition one at a time, until only I escaped."

Chapter IV
THE MOCCASIN DEATH

OOL paused after making his unusual proclamation, and eyed Doc Savage and his two aides, as if endeavoring to learn how they took it.

Monk and Ham registered an admixture of doubt and surprise. Doc Savage's regular bronze features portrayed no emotion at all.

On the inlaid table, the radio droned on and on, the police announcer reciting descriptions of stolen cars, of lost persons, of petty crimes and emergency calls.

"—emergency call to all cars," the loudspeaker droned unexpectedly. "Pickup order for a tall, slender man with very pale skin. Man wanted for the murder of Beery Hosmer, a man with a police record. Killer's most pronounced characteristic is his short, very fine hair, which looks from a distance somewhat like the fur on a mole. Man was wearing dark suit and dark hat and—"

Monk, watching Ool intently, breathed, "Blazes!" in soft comprehension.

Ool began to sidle toward the door.

MONK

Doc Savage ripped out a few words in a softly musical, but unintelligible, jargon—a language known only to himself and his aides. It was the language of ancient Maya, the speech of a civilization which had supposedly vanished from the earth centuries ago. Doc and his men used the tongue to communicate orders.

Monk and Ham, reacting to the order in Mayan, rushed on Ool. Things happened quickly. One moment, Ool was under their fingertips. It seemed impossible that they could miss seizing him. But the next instant, Ool eluded them, his speed blinding, and Monk and Ham found themselves clutching each other.

"You dumb fashion plate!" Monk choked.

"Ape!" Ham retorted.

Jerking around, Doc's aides charged Ool again. Carefully this time, with grim purpose. Doc was barring the door.

"That guy is greased lightning," Monk muttered.

Ool made a snarling sound and advanced on them. His right hand was weaving about in its peculiar weird fashion.

"Look out!" Doc called sharply. "Get back!"

Monk and Ham retreated, but in uncanny fashion Ool was within striking distance of them. His weird right hand floated out. There was no dilatory butterfly flutter about the motion this time.

Straight at Ham, the hand drove. The hand was bent at the wrist, the bony fingers extended.

Then, suddenly, Ool was off his feet, falling to the floor.

Doc Savage had whipped out a foot to kick hard against the side of Ool's leg.

Ool should have been stunned by the shock as he struck the floor. But the white-faced murderer bounced up immediately. His moccasinlike hand drifted out viciously.

"Monk—get clear!" Doc Savage's voice was a crack of authority.

Monk hurled his simian bulk to one side. Ool's hand went short. The hand jerked back. It was like a snake's head recoiling. It struck again, at Ham.

"Ham!" Doc Savage rapped. "Don't let him touch you!"

Ham, dropping to the floor, evaded the hand. He rolled to one side, got his feet under him, whipped upright.

Ool glared at them.

"The goggles," he said flatly. "Throw me the black goggles or I will kill you all!"

Doc Savage spoke in Mayan. His hands went into his pocket, came out and were clasped behind him. He took a single step backward. After that, he stood still. A surprising thing happened.

The long, skeletal frame of Ool went down like a bag of bones collapsing. His flat eyes blinked shut; the gaunt head flopped forward on its stringy neck; the legs bent at the knees, and he lay as still as if in death.

DOC turned, walked over and hoisted a window. For a space of about forty seconds neither he nor his aides said anything, but simply stood and regarded each other.

Monk went over and, with a foot, reached out exploringly and stirred a few fine particles of glass on the floor where Doc Savage had been standing when Ool went down. There were crystal-glinting particles, such as might have been made by the shattering of a very small electric light bulb.

Doc said, "All right."

He, as well as Monk and Ham, breathed deeply; it became apparent that from the time Doc had uttered the words in Mayan, they had all three been holding their breath.

As a matter of fact, Doc's words had been a warning to Monk and Ham that he was going to break a tiny glass anaesthetic bomb on the floor. The anaesthetic was one developed by Monk, disseminating almost instantaneously into the air, and powerful enough to produce unconsciousness at the first whiff.

The gas became ineffective after mixing with fresh air, but the effect upon one who had already breathed it would not wear off for some time.

"Well, that's that," Ham said. He adjusted his necktie and brushed his trousers which had collected dust when he rolled on the floor to elude Ool's weird right hand.

Monk pawed his own jaw. "The guy sure wanted that black goggle doo-dad. He had a chance to get away, but he wouldn't leave without 'em."

Doc walked across and stood looking down at Ool's prostrate form. Monk and Ham pressed close at his side.

Ham remarked, in a voice heavy with disbelief: "Yes, sir, he's even uglier than you are, Monk. I don't know how it's possible, but he is!"

"You clothesrack!" Monk growled. "You don't know masculine beauty when you see some. I exude virility, I do! I'm an example of the dominant male."

As Doc leaned over Ool, that apparently senseless individual became charged with appalling vigor. Ool's knees doubled under him and he sprang furiously to his feet. At the same split-second his deadly right hand moccasined out toward Doc.

It was something absolutely new to the experience of Doc Savage and his aides. Never had a man who had gone down under the spell of the anaesthetic bombs, risen so soon.

A bronze flash, Doc backed to avoid the

mysterious touch of Ool's mother-of-pearl fingers. He succeeded in hurtling clear, and in doing so, his corded arms, sweeping out, thrust Monk and Ham behind him to temporary safety.

"Get in the other room," Doc ordered Monk and Ham, his flake-gold eyes remaining fixed on the crouching Ool.

"Aw, Doc—" Monk started a protest.

"Get in there and shut the door," Doc repeated; and when his aides did not move fast enough, he lunged, using both mighty arms to shove them through into the next room.

He tossed Ool's strange goggles in after them. Then he slammed the door behind them.

INSIDE the other room, cut off from Doc, Ham and Monk reared to their feet and tried the door. The force of their combined body-jolts shuddered, but did not open the chromium-ribbed door in its steel frame.

"He's locked us in here!" Monk bellowed. "Hey—Doc!"

He banged his gnarled fists against the unyielding door.

"He's in there alone!" Ham shouted.

"That white-skinned, mouse-haired guy ain't human!" Monk roared. "The anaesthetic gas never even fazed him!"

From the outer room, Ool's flat voice came clearly.

"One man already tonight I have killed for these goggles," he intoned. "Now I kill another."

Ham and Monk quit pounding, numbed momentarily by a flesh-crawling dread.

Following Ool's pronouncement, muffled sounds came under the door. Feet padded. A body thudded. A chair overturned. Then there was a chilling sound, unnameable a dry clacking more than anything else.

Ham clutched Monk by the arm. "That sound— It's that—that ghoul—laughing!"

"Yeah," Monk said thickly. "Yeah."

The eerie clacking laugh faded away. Feet pattered. The patterings grew quickly fainter. The hall door slammed.

Ham and Monk commenced furious fist-batterings against their own door.

"Doc!" Their voices crashed together. "Doc! Are you there?"

The only sound now was the interminable police broadcast coming in over the shortwave set. The announcer was repeating an earlier broadcast.

"—Dimiter Daikoff, murderer, escaped from Chicago jail, believed to be in hiding in Manhattan. His description: A big man, walks with a limp, a scar slanting downward across his neck from the lobe of his right ear—"

The radio voice crackled on and on, while Monk and Ham endeavored to get out of the room.

Chapter V
THE MYSTERIOUS MURDERER

SIXTH AVENUE by day is a working man's street. The children who scamper there between the wheels of automobile traffic, the men and women who swarm over its grimy sidewalks, give it a degree of friendly warmth.

But late at night, denuded of its human adornments, the avenue lies stark and ugly. Occasional rats haunt its sidewalk garbage cans. And another breed of rodent, more vicious, comes to life in curtain-drawn back rooms.

Ool was the only human figure in sight on the dim street. A lean cat, dirty-furred, claw-scarred and with most of one ear missing, leaped down to the sidewalk from a sour-smelling garbage can and slunk into shadows at Ool's approach.

The cat was hardly more sinister than Ool as the white-faced assassin moved along through the night with his characteristic animal prowl, gaunt head hunched far forward, spidery arms dangling.

He slowed his pace as he came to a spot where a sickly glow of light seeped over the sidewalk from the half-curtained windows of a barroom. Dingy yellow lettering on the window glass proclaimed the place to be "Bill Noonan's Tavern." Ool paused long enough at the door to flash covert glances in both directions, then entered, scuffed through gray sawdust covering the floor and approached the bar.

A fat Negro, his head seemingly a ball perched on his multiplicity of chins, dozed on a stool near the cash register. He opened one red-rimmed eye as Ool approached.

"Are you Ham-hock Piney?" Ool questioned.

The Negro betrayed no surprise at Ool's appearance or voice.

"Dat's right, boss," he said. "Ham-hock Piney, dat's me."

"I want to see Watches Bowen," Ool stated.

The Negro yawned cavernously, said nothing.

"Did you understand me?" Ool snapped.

"Cou'se I understan'," the Negro grinned. "What you want me to do about it—put a fly in your beer?"

Ool expressed quick anger. As though propelled without volition, his right hand started drifting about.

The Negro laughed sleepily, said softly, "All right. Ah see yo' knows de pass sign. Yo' can go on up. Take dat door in de back. Go up de only steps yo'll see."

A MINUTE later, facing Watches Bowen in the mobster's top-floor hideout, Ool said, "You had better give your watchdogs more explicit instructions concerning me."

"Ham-hock?" Watches laughed, and his thick hand hovered near the gold watch chain which sprawled across his vest. "He's all right. Slicker than you'd think."

A man hunched in a nearby chair, rattled the pages of a racing form which draped across his lap. He was a mouse of a man, small. He seemed intent on doping out a possible track winner, when, in reality, his ferret eyes never left Ool. Concealed by the form sheet, his right hand gripped a flat automatic.

At an oilcloth-covered table on the opposite side of the room, three men killed time with cards. Occasionally, they flashed curious glances at Ool and Watches. These men were all young, sleek, barber-shop groomed. Each smoked, and there was a hard calmness in their manner.

Watches jerked his head at Ool. "Let's talk private," he said.

The suave mobster moved to the far corner of the room, Ool following closely.

Ool questioned blankly, "Are you not afraid he might miss me at this distance?"

"Who?"

"The little man in the chair."

Watches' bleak eyes slitted, and his hand swerved instinctively back to his watch chain.

"You don't miss much, do you?" he grunted.

"Not much," Ool said. "You do not trust me?"

"It's not that," Watches said. "We were afraid a cop might tag you in. I don't take chances."

"Who is the man with the racing form and the gun?" Ool asked.

"Honey Hamilton," Watches said proudly. "He can shoot fly specks off a hundred-watt bulb."

"That is an exaggeration?"

"A little, maybe." Watches grinned. "What've you been up to?"

"I have," said Ool, "suffered a misfortune."

"Didn't I tell you not to monkey with Doc Savage?" Watches unclipped a timepiece and fumbled it. "Just how bad is the situation?"

Ool began to speak. His voice was like the intonation of a phonograph which possessed no qualities of tone whatever; his words were so flat that at times they were hardly understandable. He told of his going to the waterfront warehouse-hanger, of his capture, of exactly what had happened thereafter.

"This Doc Savage locked his two men in an inner room in his headquarters," he finished. "The bronze man and I fought. For a time, he evaded my right hand. He pursued me down to the street.

His speed is almost unbelievable. Then I touched him and he staggered back and collapsed. I came here."

Watches swallowed twice. "Doc Savage is dead?"

"He is," Ool said, emphatically.

WATCHES seemed to be thinking deeply. His breathing was heavy. He polished the watches on both ends of the chain, then compared their time with that shown by his two wrist watches, found one of the wrist watches a few seconds off, and made a correction.

"What was the idea of the song and dance about the Lenderthorn Expedition?" he asked.

Ool shrugged. "It is part of my plan."

Watches put out a disgusted jaw. "*Your* plan! Say, don't I rate on this? You go ahead with a scheme that's as wild as hell, and you don't give me a gander at it. I don't like it! Who's running this, anyway?"

"You," said Ool, "and I."

Watches put the timepieces back in his pockets and began to curse. He swore in a low voice, but venomously and without repeating himself.

"What a sweet mess," he finished. "Doc Savage has those goggles?"

Ool began, "I have a plan—"

Somewhere in the room a buzzer whizzed twice, loudly and jarringly.

Watches stiffened. The three men playing cards pushed back from the table with such quick violence that the stacked chips washed over the oilcloth and spilled on the floor. Even mouselike "Honey" Hamilton snapped from his tilted chair, forgetting to keep his gun concealed beneath the form sheet.

Ool, alone, showed no perturbation.

"What is it?" he asked.

"That buzzer's never been rung before," Watches clipped. "It's an emergency—worked from a button behind the bar where Ham-hock can reach it with his toe."

"Maybe," Ool ventured, "Ham-hock went to sleep and kicked it accidentally."

"Not a chance! That fat devil is never sleepy, and not as harmless as he looks."

Then color faded out of Watches' florid face.

"What is the matter?" Ool asked. "You look sick."

"Listen," Watches Bowen demanded hoarsely, "did you go dumb and let Doc Savage's men trail you down here?"

"I did not. I was careful to come in a roundabout way."

"You sure? You'd have to be good to shake those men who work with Savage."

From the hall, behind the closed door, sounded the scrape of numerous feet. A single fist pounded heavily on the door.

"Open up!" a voice bawled.

Honey Hamilton had been stationed at a cleverly concealed loophole in the wall. The loophole looked out upon the hallway and was of a size to permit insertion of a gun snout.

The mouselike little man cupped his hand to his mouth and hissed back to Watches, "It's coppers!"

"JOHN LAWS!" Watches mumbled incredulously, then wheeled upon Ool. "This is your doing! They've got you tagged for the Beery Hosmer job! You let them see you come in here!"

Ool shrugged. "That is impossible."

"Then some stool tipped them." Watches shook his head violently. "Nix. No pigeons get a line on me. I'm careful about that. How in the devil did they know you're here?"

The pounding on the door continued. The hollow, metallic quality of the sounds was an indication that the door was in reality an armored panel.

"Let's blow," Honey Hamilton suggested uneasily.

Watches nodded, and leaped to a side door. This gave into a narrow hall which in turn led to a flight of steps angling downward. They started to descend these steps.

"Shure, and you can come r-right down," said a strong Irish voice from below. "But it'd be healthiest if you'd throw your guns down first."

"Damn!" Watches gritted. "They've got the back way blocked. Now we *are* in a jam!"

The men retreated to the room and closed both doors. Honey Hamilton pried up a cleverly hinged floor board and lifted out a submachine gun. He posted himself at the loophole.

Watches ran over to the window and looked out. There was another building some thirty feet distant. There were windows in the wall. But no man could jump that distance.

Then Watches snapped back hastily. He had glimpsed a uniformed policeman in the court below. The officer was looking up, balancing a heavy service revolver suggestively in one hand.

"You birds had better get wise to yourselves," the cop called. "We've got you surrounded!"

Watches looked at Ool speculatively.

Ool seemed to read his mind.

"You can turn me over to the police," he said slowly. "No doubt they will then hold you on no charge more serious than that of possessing weapons."

Watches shook his head. "I'm not that kind of a guy. Anyhow, think I wanta lose my cut in a few millions?"

Ool shrugged. "It seems there is nothing for us to do but fight."

Honey Hamilton said nervously, "They're gonna use torches on that door, Watches."

Watches yelled, "Well, are you gonna stand there and let them?"

Honey Hamilton spread a benign look over his face as he shoved the submachine gun snout through the loophole and his finger sought the trigger. But he never discharged bullets.

There was an ear-splitting crack. Steel splinters flew like shrapnel over the room. A screaming fragment crashed a bottle of whisky, went entirely through the tabletop and sank into the floor. Another ripped Watches' coat sleeve from wrist to elbow.

Honey Hamilton tumbled backward off his chair; blood began to well from gashes on his face and shoulders. He lay prone, pawing at his bloody face.

Watches squawled at him, "What happened?"

"They cut loose at the loophole from outside!" Honey gulped. "A bullet must have walked into the muzzle of my typewriter. Jammed in the barrel. Blew the breech all to hell!"

He slumped down on the floor. Watches let him lie, and glared wildly at the loophole. Then he scuttled to one side. One of the policemen in the hall had thrust a gun barrel through the loophole from the outside. He could not fire and do any damage, because the angle was not right, but the loophole was effectively plugged.

Watches pulled helplessly at his gold vest chain. "What a lulu we're in," he groaned.

They stood there, nerve-taut, anxious. Outside in the hall, a soft roaring began and grew louder, and after a bit, the inside of the door started smoking. The police were using a cutting torch on the armor plate panel.

Watches groaned, "We ain't got a chance to fight—"

"Hey, there!" called an entirely new voice.

FOR a moment, they could not locate the voice; then they spun, and after that they stared unbelievingly.

Across the thirty-foot space between the two buildings, a window was open. A man leaned from that window. He was a dark-skinned man, very big, smooth-shaven, with very dark eyes, black hair and a scar which started at the lobe of his right ear and slanted down across his neck. His appearance was utterly villainous.

In his hands, the man held a coil of fire hose of the type often affixed to reels inside office buildings.

Watches ran to the window, looked out and down cautiously. He could see the policeman in

The hose sagged and groaned as, hand over hand, the dark man pitted his gigantic strength against the sagging.

the alley below. The bluecoat was sprawled out, motionless on the grimy concrete.

"Get a move on, you birds," snapped the big, scarred man across the alley. "Or are you interested?"

"Hell, yes!" Watches exploded. "Toss us the end of that hose!"

The big man hurled the hose, missed the first time, but on the second try, Watches seized it, drew it inside and knotted it to a radiator.

Hand over hand, the men started coming across. They were not interrupted. The policeman below in the alley did not stir. The large, dark man with the scar voiced only a single word.

"Hurry," he said, and led the flight.

The swarthy fellow had a pronounced limp.

Like rats deserting a sinking ship, Watches Bowen's gang swung gingerly across the hose span and through the window. Honey Hamilton, the last to attempt the crossing, suddenly discovered that, due to his wounds, he was incapable of making it.

"Go on," he growled. "I'll keep the cops entertained."

"Don't be a fool!" snapped the big, dark man.

He swung out over the span, grunting and straining with the effort, and got his legs around Honey Hamilton. Then began the return journey.

It was a remarkable feat, for the dark man held Honey gripped in his legs, suspended in the air above the alley. The hose sagged and groaned as, hand over hand, the dark man pitted his gigantic strength against the swaying. But slowly, like a cable car over a quarry, he finally made the other side with his wounded burden.

Honey Hamilton, weak with relief now that the trip was over, made a wry grin. "Thanks, guy. Remind me, if I should happen to forget that sometime."

AN hour or more later, Watches Bowen was relaxing in another of his numerous hangouts—a fifty-foot cabin cruiser tied up at a City Island dock. A bottle of Watches' eighty-year-old Napoleon brandy contributed substantially to his relaxing; by the time he had drained a third glass, he had recovered much of his old suave manner.

Slumped near Watches, on an over-stuffed berth, the three sleek, hard, young gunmen were engaged with a fresh deck of cards.

In the same room, the big, dark stranger who had come so mysteriously to their rescue was doing an excellent job of bandaging Honey Hamilton's wounds.

Ool sat on another berth, as motionless as if he were dead, except for an occasional twitch from his weird right hand.

From forward in another cabin came the soft drone of a shortwave radio loudspeaker. It was giving police broadcasts.

"—repeating pickup order number one, naught, naught, seven, two," said the radio. "Dimiter Daikoff, who escaped two days ago from a Chicago jail and is believed to be in New York. Daikoff is a large man with a limp. Has dark skin and eyes, and a scar on his neck, on the right side. Reported to be dangerous."

Watches Bowen, in the act of drinking more brandy, made an explosive sound and shot a fine spray of the stuff through his teeth. He choked and coughed.

"So *that's* who you are!" he gulped, eyeing the dark, bulky man who had saved them from the police trap.

The stranger looked up from his bandaging.

"Right," he said quietly.

Then the man stood up. He held his head proudly. His black eyes flashed with an almost fanatical glitter. The light from the overhead electric bulb glowed on the smooth skin covering his high cheek bones. Like many of his race, this man's cheek bones were so prominent that his cheeks looked hollow. They were thrown into shadow.

"I am no murderer!" he proclaimed tragically. "I simply liquidate one who was traitor to our party. I, Dimiter Daikoff, am no criminal. In my country, I would be honored, receive a medal. But here, they hunt me like animal."

Watches shrugged tolerantly. "That's all right by me, brother. One turn rates another. You can hang around if you want to."

"Thank you." The big man bent again to his task of mercy. "I am no killer. I am a patriot."

"One thing I'd like to know, though," Watches continued, "is how in the hell did you happen to show up just when we needed you."

Dimiter Daikoff smiled gravely. "That is simple. I was hiding next door. When I heard the shots, I thought it was myself that the police were after. I struck unconscious the officer who was on guard in the alley. Then I saw it was you that they sought. I do not like policemen. They do not know the difference between a patriot who came here to the United States and eliminated one who had been a thieving government official of his own country—the police do not know such a patriot from a common murderer. I hate them for it. So I help you."

Watches stretched luxuriantly and grinned.

"What a swell thing hate can be sometimes," he said.

DURING the course of the next several hours, the men loitered aboard the boat. Dimiter Daikoff fitted into the situation as naturally as a big house dog. He came and went about the boat, administering to Honey Hamilton and preparing drinks and sandwiches.

Eventually Watches and Ool went into a huddle in the forecastle.

Honey and the two younger gunmen were sleeping and Dimiter Daikoff, the self-claimed patriot, was washing dishes in the galley, so there did not seem to be reason for undue secrecy, but Watches and Ool, nevertheless, kept their voices lowered.

Several times the name of Doc Savage, and the phrase "black goggles," was audible, however. It would have been apparent to anyone interested that they were carefully planning a move against Doc Savage's men, believing Doc to be dead.

When they finished their conference, they awakened the others and departed. Honey Hamilton could walk.

"You can stay here and play admiral until we get back," Watches told Daikoff.

The instant the gunmen were out of sight, Daikoff strode to the forecastle where Watches and Ool had held their whispered conversation, and from the ventilator removed a small compact dictograph device which had been lowered there. Then he proceeded to wind up a length of fine wire attached to the dictograph, wire as fine as hair, and hence practically unnoticeable. It ran back to where Daikoff had been dishwashing in the galley.

Watches and Ool might have been worried, certainly they would have been surprised, if they had known that their whispered plotting against Doc Savage's men had been overheard by the big man.

Stowing the dictaphone device away in his pocket, Dimiter Daikoff hurriedly left the boat.

Chapter VI
THE SCARED EXPLORER

FIVE men stood in the early morning sun which streamed through the "health glass" windows of Doc Savage's eighty-sixth floor headquarters. Two of the five were Monk and Ham. And for once in their lives, the hairy chemist and the dapper lawyer were finding themselves aligned on the same side of the argument.

The men on the other side of the argument were Doc Savage's other three aides, familiarly known as "Johnny," "Long Tom" and "Renny."

"Holy cow!" Renny roared. "You mean to stand there and tell us Doc may be dead?"

Renny, or Colonel John Renwick, as his engineering associates knew him, had a long, puritanical face. He was inches over six feet tall, and weighed in the neighborhood of two hundred and fifty pounds. His great frame gave the appearance of being composed mostly of bone. But the really remarkable thing about him were his fists. Each was composed of fully a quart of bone and gristle.

"Locked in a room while Doc went up against this guy with the funny white hand, were you!" Renny boomed. "Why didn't you bust out?"

He swung one of his huge fists as if by way of demonstration. It was Renny's boast that no wooden door was made with a panel so strong that he could not shatter it with one blow of those fists.

Monk and Ham squirmed.

"Blast it, we did!" Monk groaned. "It took time. When we got out, both Doc and this guy were gone!"

A mildly scholastic voice put in, "Not an empyrean collocation of circumstances."

The speaker was Johnny, or William Harper Littlejohn, a man who never used a small word when he had time to think of a large one, and also a man who was one of the greatest living archaeologists and geologists. Johnny was very tall, and thin as Old Man Death himself, and he carried, on a ribbon, a monocle which was in actuality a powerful magnifier.

The fifth of Doc Savage's aides was a thin man with a skin the color of a mushroom. He looked about as unhealthy as a man could look. As a matter of fact, he had never been ill in his life, and could, if occasion called for it, whip nine out of every ten men he chanced to meet on a street.

He was Major Thomas J. Roberts, electrical wizard extraordinary. He was more often known simply as "Long Tom," a name he had annexed long ago after a disastrous experience in trying to make use of a rusted "long tom" cannon of buccaneer vintage.

Long Tom shook his head. "This strange white-skinned man you caught at the warehouse-hanger, he claimed to be Gray Forestay, a member of the Lenderthorn Exploration party?"

"Exactly," Monk agreed.

"He gave no logical explanation of why he was prowling around the hangar?" Long Tom persisted.

"He said he knew he'd get caught and brought to Doc, if you call that logical," Monk snorted.

"That man," Long Tom pointed out, "answers the description of a fellow who murdered a gangster named Beery Hosmer last night. He is supposed to have waved his right hand at Beery Hosmer, and the man dropped dead."

"He was great at waving that right hand," Monk agreed gloomily. "I dunno just what kind of devilment was connected with the way he did it."

Suddenly, from somewhere outside the reception room door, came a burst of scuffling. Then a long-drawn screech of terror reached them. There was something about the screech which put a strange feeling around the roots of their hair.

"I'll be superamalgamated!" exploded big-worded Johnny.

"Holy cow!" echoed Renny.

Each had used his pet exclamation for moments of great excitement.

ALL lunged for the door. Ham, with his sword cane, was first outside, with big-fisted Renny and the others crowding him close. The corridor was empty. All elevator doors were closed, and the indicators showed that no cages were on that floor. They ran for the stairs.

Halfway down, at the turn of the flight, they encountered a man who was scuttling upward.

"Help!" the man screeched. "Help!"

The fleeing man had no hat. His thick gray hair flopped over his forehead. He had a close-cropped gray mustache, and was wearing smoked glasses.

To all appearances panic-stricken, he flung himself upon Ham, who was still leading. The man was larger than Ham, but he cringed close to the lawyer, like a whipped dog.

"Who's after you?" Renny swung his huge fists.

He did not have long to wait for an answer. Men charged around the corner of the stair landing, coming from below with such speed that they piled up the first few steps before they noticed Doc's aides.

The speed with which they stopped was ludicrous. Evidently they had expected to find one fear-crazed man. Now they were confronted by five men, not at all scared.

Wheeling back without warning, those in front collided with those who pushed close from behind. Three of the men fell, sprawling in fantastic fashion.

"Keep them away!" the fleeing man pleaded. "They'll kill me!"

Renny bellowed, and pitched his two hundred and fifty pounds of brawn down the steps.

His fists flailed. One man went back under his pile-driver blows. His sheer hurtling weight downed another. Renny bored on. A man on his back drove a vicious kick at the inside of Renny's knee. Renny fell heavily, adding his own thrashing limbs to the writhing tangle already on the floor.

Doc's other four aides, lunging after Renny, smacked blows in all directions. They did not, however, do all the battering. They took terrific jolts from fists. The foes knew how to fight.

But they had been taken at a disadvantage. They were forced back along the corridor—all except one bent-eared man who was rolling on the floor, locked in a gorilla-grip with Renny.

When the fighting reached the region of the elevator shaft, one of the men swerved, jammed a thumb against the button which brought Doc Savage's speed elevator up.

"Back of me, men!" he yelled. "Lemme take 'em!"

The other men quit fighting, leaped back.

The man who had pressed the buzzer wrenched a revolver out of his pocket and leveled down at his crowding enemies. His fellows were out of the way, backed up against the elevator door, so the gun could cover Doc's aides.

"Stand back!" the gunman yelled, "or I'll blast the pack of you!"

Doc's aides stood tense and glaring. There was nothing they could do. Any move might draw bullets from that menacing revolver. It would be hard for the gunman to miss.

A soft *click* announced the arrival of the elevator. The doors fanned open.

"Inside!" the man with the gun ordered his men.

But the men did not get inside.

A BRONZE cyclone seemed to boil out of the elevator. The man nearest the door was engulfed. Yanked shoulder-high, he was hurled shrieking, upon his companions. He crashed into the gun wielder, knocked him down.

The bronze cyclone moved on. There was blurred motion. Men went down like shingles wind-whipped from a barn.

Doc Savage, who had been riding the elevator up, waded through them with his cable-corded fists.

Sprawled on the floor, the gun-toter jerked up his revolver an instant before the bronze man crashed through to reach him. The gun belched thunder. The slug creased an ugly red furrow along Doc's muscle-rippled neck, slammed on to hiss over Monk's rusty nubbin of a head and spanged into the corridor wall.

Doc froze in his tracks.

"All right," he said quietly. "Don't shoot again. You win."

Doc's self-possessed manner seemed to have a miraculously quieting effect on the gunman. He held his fire and threw an order to his men.

"In the elevator—quickly!"

He saw them all inside while he held Doc and his five aides off with the gun. With a last menacing flourish of the weapon, he leaped inside himself. The door slid shut. The elevator sucked, swishing, downward.

Monk leaped to ring the buzzer for one of the regular elevators.

"We'll ride this down," he roared.

Doc waved him away. "Let them go, Monk."

Doc's aides stared, completely mystified. It had baffled them enough when Doc quit fighting, and now for him to calmly allow the assailants to get away was—

Renny cracked his huge fists together.

"Holy cow!" he boomed. "What's the idea? Where you been, Doc? We thought you were dead."

The bronze man answered with a question. "What started this?"

"A fellow let out a bellow and came charging up the steps," Monk explained.

"Where is he now?"

"Hiding in your office, Doc," Long Tom volunteered.

"We will talk to him," Doc said. "Ham, you stay behind here and tell a straight-sounding story to any office workers who might investigate the shots."

"That shyster," Monk grunted, "can talk fast enough to make anyone believe them shots was just a stenographer popping her chewing gum."

Ham flourished his sword cane and glared at Monk.

THE bronze man and his four aides filed into the eighty-sixth floor headquarters. They looked around.

Carefully calculated training had rendered Doc Savage capable of concealing all emotion. He showed no emotion now. That was not true of the others. They showed a vast surprise.

"Well, I'll be superamalgamated!" Johnny gasped.

"Where is your stranger?" Doc questioned.

Monk blinked small eyes. "He *was* here!"

"He *must* be here!" Johnny put in.

The only time Johnny used little words was when he was excited.

Doc strode across the deep-piled Oriental rug and threw open the door to the adjoining room. It was spacious, lined from floor to ceiling with crammed bookshelves. It was Doc Savage's scientific library, a collection of tomes almost without equal.

Beyond was another room, larger, a room of fantastically shaped glass flasks and beakers, banked test tubes, brightly colored chemicals in bottles. Massive electric furnaces, testing machines, and chemical apparatus crowded the floor space. It was the bronze man's workshop-laboratory.

Doc and his men entered quietly. Their feet on the acid-resisting composition floor gave off no sound. This fact enabled them to make a discovery.

Beside an opened glass case, his broad back toward them, stood the man who had fled from the thugs. He was bent over, examining something.

"Find something interesting?" Doc questioned, in a quiet tone.

The man whirled so quickly that a shock of his gray hair cascaded down over the smoked glasses which he wore. His left hand went behind him.

Doc Savage strode forward. He did not seem to walk with undue speed, yet so perfectly did his huge muscles coordinate that he reached the man's side with startling suddenness. The gray-haired man was heavily built, but Doc brushed him aside with one movement of his hand.

The stranger was holding at his back the goggles which Ham and Monk had taken from Ool, the skeleton-thin prowler on the hangar roof the night before.

Doc held the goggles loosely.

"Were you interested in these?" he asked.

"Yes—no!" the man stammered.

"You will notice that they are unusual," Doc went on. "The lenses are fully two inches in thickness, and black—so black that no light penetrates them."

"I—I picked them up by mistake," the man said, a little hoarsely. "My own smoked glasses fell off. I don't see well without them. The light hurts my eyes—snow blindness. I picked these of yours up by mistake. For a minute I thought they were mine."

Doc turned the black-lensed goggles over in his great sensitive hand.

"This flexible material in which the lenses are imbedded—can you identify it?" he asked the stranger.

"I don't know anything about them," the man declared. "I picked them up by mistake—"

"The material seems to be fish skin," Doc said.

"It somewhat resembles the skin of a species of deep-sea fish with a habitat in the Arctic Ocean."

"I'm not interested in the goggles," the man reiterated earnestly. "I'm only interested in my life. I came here to get away from men who would have killed me."

He peered intently through his own smoked glasses at the faces of Doc's men. "Are they gone now—those men in the hall? Are they gone?"

"They decamped," Renny boomed sourly.

"Your perambulations are imperspicuous," said big-worded Johnny.

"He means," said Monk, who could seldom resist interpreting Johnny's verbiage, "that we want to know what you were snooping around in here for?"

"Please don't mistake my intentions, gentlemen," the man said earnestly. He steadied his nervous gaze on Doc. "I confess I was terror-stricken. When I ran in here, my only idea was to get as far as possible from those thugs. When they attacked me, I was on my way to see Doc Savage. You are Doc Savage?"

"Right," Doc said. He replaced the black goggles on the shelf and closed the glass door.

The stranger cast one brief glance at the goggles. His thick hand waved out toward them.

"If they're so valuable," he said, "I should think you'd put them in a safe place."

Doc shrugged. "They do not look valuable. Who would want them? They are safe here— Come on."

Through the impressive laboratory, through the library with its smell of paper, Doc led the way.

The stranger settled back in a comfortable chair in the outer office.

"YOU may have heard of me," he suggested. "I am an explorer, Gray Forestay—"

"Gray Forestay!" Long Tom ejaculated.

"Now don't tell us," Monk cut in sarcastically, "that you are the sole survivor of an attack by *black things!*"

The gray-haired stranger stared blankly.

"Now how did you know that?" he exploded.

Now that the man had control of himself, his voice was no longer hoarse, but softly resonant, smooth.

Doc explained. "Last night a man came here who represented himself as Gray Forestay, only surviving member of the Lenderthorn Expedition. He stated that his party, on the pack ice north of Canada, had been set upon by weird shapeless things—black things."

"But *I* am Gray Forestay!" the other wailed. "I accompanied the Lenderthorn Expedition! And that is precisely what happened!"

"Black things and all?" Monk demanded skeptically.

A shudder coursed over the man's sturdy bulk. "The mysterious black assailants, I assure you, gentlemen, are very real and no joking matter."

"You saw them yourself?" Monk demanded.

"I saw them." The man gripped the arms of his chair. His tone was rather desperately defiant.

"What did they look like?"

The man seemed to be searching for words. He spoke finally. "They were—shapeless, black, like ghosts. There is no other way to say it. There is nothing to compare them with. They are not real. And yet they *are* real. I saw them. They came from nowhere."

"From nowhere?" Monk scoffed.

"They just appeared. They stayed only for a moment. Then they disappeared. Maybe I went out of my head. I don't know. The first thing I realized was my comrades were gone. All of them gone. *And no trace*—"

The man reached up to clutch fiercely at his thick mop of gray hair. His pudgy fingers brushed over his gray mustache.

"I am not old—only thirty-six. I got like this all in a single day—in a single hour!"

A tense silence followed the impassioned account. Even Monk was impressed.

The man reached in his inside coat pocket. There was a crinkling sound as he drew out a sheaf of papers. He got up, walked across and handed the papers to Doc Savage.

"Here are some letters—documents," he said. "They establish my identity."

The bronze man examined the papers.

His expression remained enigmatic. But his decision was apparent when he looked up and said:

"Forestay, do you know who it was that came here last night representing himself to be you?"

The man shook his head. "I haven't an idea in the world who it could have been."

"Who were your attackers in the hallway?"

The man turned up the palms of his hands in an instinctive gesture of helplessness. "I haven't an idea in the world about that either. The attack came as a complete surprise."

"Somebody, obviously, who sought to keep you from seeing me."

"Obviously. But who, I do not know. They attacked me first in the lobby of the building. I got away and ducked into an elevator. They took another elevator. I got out two flights below this floor, thinking to elude them. They got out after me. I finally escaped them again when your men came to my rescue."

Doc asked, "You can add nothing more that might be of help?"

"Nothing—except, now that I have collected my wits, I do not believe they meant to kill me," the man said slowly. "Not then, at any rate. They had chances to kill me. But they seemed to be trying to take me alive."

"A kidnaping?"

"So it would appear."

Doc Savage fixed his gaze upon the man. "And you came to see me, Mr. Forestay—why?"

"To get your aid in a search for my comrades of the vanished Lenderthorn Expedition," the man said. "To solve the mystery of the black assailants in the Arctic, whatever they were. With your dirigible, it would be possible to land on the ice pack and make an extended search."

"You know I have a dirigible?" Doc asked.

"It was in the newspapers," the other replied. "It is a new and quite remarkable ship, only recently delivered to you."

Doc was silent a moment. "You think your fellows on the expedition still live?"

"I am not sure," the other said soberly. "But there is a chance. Something happened to them. I do not know what. A search should be made. I owe them that."

"I see," Doc said slowly.

The gray-haired man became very earnest.

"I am only doing what any other man would do," he said levelly. "If such a thing as I have described happened to your own comrades, you would leave nothing undone to find out what occurred, and to help them, if possible. Is that not true?"

"It is," Doc admitted.

"Will you help me?" the other asked bluntly.

"We will help you," Doc said just as promptly.

The man rushed across to seize Doc Savage's hand.

"Thank you!" he exploded fervently. "Thank you!"

He wrung the bronze man's hand.

"My men and I—the six of us," Doc stated, "are having lunch this morning at eleven o'clock in the Cafe Oriental downstairs. We would be glad to have you join us. We can go over the details."

The man bowed respectfully. "I appreciate the honor. I regret I cannot be there. Later—"

"If you change your mind," Doc said, "you'll find us at a table near the door."

After the man had gone Monk blurted, "Hey, Doc, what's the idea? You know I don't like chop-suey?"

"I doubt that we will do much eating," Doc told him

WATCHES BOWEN and his men had returned to the cruiser moored at a City Island wharf.

They went into a huddle. Watches included

them all—Ool, Honey Hamilton, the three sleek, hard young men, the obese Negro "Ham-hock" Piney, and several newcomers, members of the organization.

The tragic-faced dark giant, Dimiter Daikoff, was back aboard.

Watches, when he came in, greeted Daikoff with loud good humor, an indication that things had gone well.

"You're good luck for me, my patriotic friend," Watches said, and gave Daikoff a friendly slap on the back.

Daikoff's tragic black eyes rolled their gratefulness for this comradely consideration; in the manner of a dog delightedly fetching its master's slippers, he eased swiftly around the place, repeatedly filling glasses for everybody from Watches' supply of Napoleon brandy.

This conference was not quite so secretive as that held earlier in the night. Snatches of conversation had to deal with "Doc Savage"—"black goggles"—"laboratory"—"glass case."

Dimiter Daikoff, easing around unobtrusively, filling glasses, emptying ash trays, heard much.

Chapter VII
BLUE LIGHTNING

TWO hours following the boat conference, a hard-lipped, ferret-eyed young man stood on a busy New York street corner in front of the Cafe Oriental. He casually stretched his arms and allowed the five fingers of one hand to stand out, widespread. The other hand he kept closed, except for a single finger. It was a cautious signal.

A black sedan which was rolling along through the traffic, angled to the curb. The man next to the driver was a husky Negro, whose chunk of a head seemed perched atop his numerous chins.

The sedan driver said, "O. K.?"

Ham-hock Piney muttered softly: "Dat Doc Savage and all five o' his outfit must be in de eatin' house. Swell-elegant, Ah calls it."

Ham-hock got out. Three other men piled out of the rear. The driver wheeled back into the traffic stream. The overdressed young man who had stood in front of the restaurant joined them as they walked briskly along the pavement and turned into the impressive skyscraper of gleaming metal and granite, which towered nearly a hundred stories into the air, and which housed Doc Savage's headquarters.

They entered the express elevator.

"Eighty-six," Ham-hock said.

"Doc Savage's floor?" the elevator operator queried by way of verification.

"Dat's right."

At the eighty-sixth floor stop, one of the men shoved an automatic in the operator's ribs and said, "We stay here and wait, you and me, with the elevator."

Ham-hock led the other men across the corridor. They stopped in front of the door to Doc Savage's office. There was a note pinched in the door. It read:

Lunching downstairs in the Cafe Oriental.
Doc Savage

Doc's visitors stared at each other.

Ham-hock shrugged ponderously. "Come on."

They opened the door and pushed inside. Ham-hock led the way over the deep carpet to the library door. He pushed experimentally on the chrome-steel panels.

"Here's where trouble starts," he grunted. "Ease that soup and soap out your pocket, Squirrel, and we'll get busy."

"Squirrel" Dorgan—so-called because of his long, pointed frontal teeth—took a phial of nitroglycerine and a piece of yellow laundry soap out of his pocket. He went to work expertly preparing to blow the door.

Just before he was ready to pour the nitroglycerine, he tried the doorknob with more force.

The door swung open.

Squirrel stared stupidly. One of the others cursed softly. Ham-hock thoughtfully massaged his many chins.

"Hell! Looks like a plant!" Squirrel Dorgan breathed.

"Somethin' fishy about it," another agreed. "This Doc Savage ain't sap enough to go 'way and leave a setup like this open to the public."

SQUIRREL DORGAN peered inside the library. The utter silence of the place, the thousands of solidly shelved books, seemed to oppress him. His pointed teeth nipped his slack lips.

"I'm for blowin'," he said nervously.

Ham-hock growled. "We come heah to get dem black goggles, an' we gwine get 'em. Come on."

He heaved his fat bulk through the doorway. Across the ominously silent library they trailed, moving warily, guns out, fingers close to triggers. Ham-hock himself turned the knob of the door which led on into the laboratory. This panel opened as readily as the others.

The Negro stared inside. The array of fantastically shaped glass tubes and retorts, the chemical and scientific devices, invested the place with an air more sinister than that of the library.

"How Ah figures it," Ham-hock muttered, as though to convince himself by the sound of his own words, "is dat dis Doc Savage, bein' a big shot, can't imagine anybody am gwine come triflin' 'round. Dat's why he don't bothah 'bout lockin' no doahs."

One of the hard-faced young men blinked furtive eyes. "Well, let's get this thing over."

"Yeah," another rasped. "The things I've heard about this guy, Savage!"

Squirrel Dorgan's teeth chattered. "Brother, what I could do with a bottle of the chief's brandy!"

"You-all shut up," Ham-hock grunted. "Come on."

Through the doorway he eased his fat frame. The others followed, single file. Down the long aisle they trailed, between ceiling-high scientific equipment which mushroomed weirdly from the floor, and which seemed to exude a ghostly aura of unreality.

"Right ahead theah," Ham-hock whispered, and indicated by pointing his gun muzzle at a tall glass case.

"Look!" Squirrel Dorgan gulped when they had approached a few steps closer. "There's the goggles! This ain't gonna be tough after all!"

They stopped in front of the case. Ham-hock, with a gloating in his eyes, sent a sepia paw toward the goggles which lay unprotected on a glass shelf.

His hand passed through the goggles. Through them, as though they were air. His clawing finger nails scraped the glass of the shelf.

Ham-hock jerked his hand back as if it had touched flame. His hand had not been able to grasp the goggles, yet he could see them clearly, still lying on the shelf. An uneasy rumbling sounded from deep within his throat. His chins shook as he tried to swallow.

"What in hell's the matter?" one of the hard-eyed young men asked, in a voice suddenly gone shaky.

"How de hell does Ah know!" Ham-hock gulped. His hand snatched out again toward the black goggles so plainly visible on the shelf.

As before, he could not clutch them. He could not even feel them. His fingers seemed to pass through them as easily as they would pass through thin air. His nails scraped, grating, on the glass of the shelf.

Ham-hock's whitish eyes rolled. His breath came faster. Sweat oozed from the creases of his many chins.

"What the hell, Ham-hock?" Squirrel Dorgan gritted. "Have you got butter fingers?"

Squirrel shoved forward and snatched out his own hand for the goggles. He had no more success than had Ham-hock. His hand seemed to pass through the goggles as though they were of no substance. His finger nails scraped futilely on the glass shelf. His face blanched. His rodent teeth started chattering.

"They're there," he grated. *"But they ain't there!* Hell! I've got enough of this place."

He wheeled to start for the door. Cursing, clutching their guns tightly, the others turned also. They stopped as suddenly as they had turned, then cringed back in slack-lipped terror.

DIRECTLY in front of them, beside the door and barring their path to it, a weird blue flame, pencil-thin, had leaped from a shiny plate embedded in one wall, across the door opening to another plate.

The flame remained suspended, a lance of crackling, hissing blue. It rippled up and down. Other blue lances zigzagged like chain lightning until there was a whole pattern of blue flame leaping and rattling, barring an exit from the door.

"We all goin' be electrocuted!" Ham-hock bawled fearfully.

He recoiled, swerved, started to run in the opposite direction. The others, shaking off the paralysis which held them, turned with him—only to stop again, so fear-struck that one of them dropped his gun.

Grimly barring their way down the narrow aisle in that direction, stood Doc Savage and his five men.

They held strange-looking weapons which, in appearance, resembled overgrown automatics.

Ham-hock was the first to recover his wits.

"Don't shoot!" he croaked, raising his voice to make it sound above the crackling roar of the blue lightning which continued to feed out of the machine behind them. In token of submission, he allowed his gun to sag until it pointed at the floor.

One of the hard young men at Ham-hock's elbow went haywire and tried to level his automatic.

Doc Savage's finger tightened on the trigger of his weapon. The gun emitted a single ear-splitting hoot. It was a machine pistol with a tremendously fast rate of fire.

The hard young man's automatic dropped from his hand. He pitched forward and lay huddled on the floor.

"Don' shoot no moah!" Ham-hock pleaded.

"Take their guns, Monk," Doc directed.

Monk went forward and relieved the prisoners of weapons.

"Long Tom, turn off the high-frequency current," Doc directed.

The thin electrical wizard pressed a button on a near wall board. The blue electrical display subsided.

"NOW," Doc said, "talk is in order."

His flake-gold eyes bored into the faces of the prisoners.

"The first question," he said slowly. "Why are you here?"

None of the captives answered. They were trying hard to look ugly.

"You can imagine the effect," Doc said dryly, "if you were to be tied to a chair which happened to stand between those door plates. That high-frequency current would do some remarkable things to you."

Squirrel Dorgan's pointed teeth had sunk into his lip, drawing a little scarlet. But he remained silent with the others.

Monk, a great grin on his simian features, suggested, "They all gotta be electrocuted anyway, judging by their looks. Whatcha say we save the State some money? We've got an electric furnace over there big enough to cremate their bodies, and we can scatter the ashes out of a window."

Monk looked utterly earnest as he made this callous suggestion; no one, watching him, would have dreamed but that he meant it, unless they had known Monk, in which case they would have recognized the bluff.

The captives took it in various fashions. Ham-hock Piney remained rigidly silent, too scared to even tremble as lustily as he would have liked. The matter of the goggles which he had reached for repeatedly had upset his superstitious soul, and the display of high-frequency electricity had finished the demoralization.

Doc gestured at Squirrel Dorgan. "Put him in a chair in the door, Monk."

Squirrel Dorgan was not without nerve. He bit holes in his lips with his long teeth as they seized him and tied him in a chair, but he did not talk. Monk positioned the chair in the door.

"Wanta talk?" the homely chemist demanded.

"Go to hell!" Dorgan gritted.

"After you, my friend," Monk said, his small voice utterly unconcerned. He reached up and turned on the current.

There was a terrific burst of blue flame, a sheeting, blinding mass of it—ahead of Squirrel Dorgan. It did not quite touch him. But it ripped horribly in front of his face.

"Just a slight error," Monk said cheerfully. "I'll slide the chair up a little."

He moved the chair, stood back, studied its position, then moved it again. Then he leered at the sword-cane-carrying Ham.

"I'll bet you five bucks that his hair bursts into flame when the sparks touch him," he offered.

"Nothing doing," Ham refused. "I know how that current works."

Monk shrugged and ambled for the switch.

Squirrel Dorgan broke down.

"Whatcha wanna know?" he screamed.

"Shut up, you yellow fool!" one of the hard young men grated.

Dorgan snarled at him: "If you think this bronze guy is kidding, you're nuts! I've heard of guys who went up against him and were never heard from again."

Ham-hock Piney bawled out, "I tell you-all, dis place am got a hoodoo. Ah could see dem goggles, but dey wasn't dar!"

"Who sent you here?" Doc asked Squirrel Dorgan.

"Watches Bowen," Squirrel snarled.

"What did he want?"

"The goggles," Dorgan mumbled.

"Why?"

Dorgan blew scarlet off his lips. "I don't know."

"That high-frequency current," Monk suggested.

"All I know," Squirrel said shrilly, "is that the black goggles have something to do with black things in the Arctic. That sounds goofy, but it's all I know."

"What are the black things?" the bronze man queried.

"I don't know," Dorgan insisted. "I heard Watches and—and Ool mention them. They're supposed to be somewhere in the Arctic. That's all I know. That's all any of us know. Watches and Ool didn't spill their plans to us."

"Who is this Ool?" Doc questioned.

Squirrel's teeth started chattering. "He ain't quite human."

"What do you mean?"

"He can kill you without even touching you! I ain't makin' this up. It's the truth!"

The bronze man frowned. "This Ool is very tall and very thin and he has a skin which somewhat resembles mother-of-pearl. Is that right?"

"That's the guy," Dorgan agreed.

MONK grunted loudly in comprehension. "That's the egg we caught on top of the hangar—the bird who claimed to be Gray Forestay, survivor of that Lenderthorn Arctic Expedition."

Doc Savage asked Squirrel Dorgan, "Where did this Ool come from?"

"He showed up one day with Watches Bowen. That's all I know."

"Is he the one who brought the news of the black—things?"

"I guess so," Dorgan mumbled. "They didn't tell us much."

"Is Watches Bowen planning a trip with Ool to the Arctic?"

Dorgan squirmed. "Yeah."

"Where?" Doc demanded. "Name the exact spot."

"Can't!" Dorgan shook his head. "Watches don't talk to us, I tell you."

"How soon is he leaving?"

"Just as soon as—" He did not finish.

"Spill it, guy!" Monk rumbled.

"As soon as he—he makes arrangements about using your dirigible," Squirrel wailed fearfully. "And he'll croak me for spillin' that!"

Doc Savage said dryly, "He intends to arrange, I presume, in the same raggedly individualistic manner in which he went about securing the goggles."

Squirrel ran the tip of his tongue along his sharp teeth. "I—I wouldn't know about that."

"Think carefully and do not lie," Doc said. "Who was the second Gray Forestay?"

Squirrel fidgeted, but did not answer.

"You know who he was?" Doc persisted.

Squirrel was silent.

The bronze man leaned forward and his eyes, gold pools, seemed alive, possessed of a weird power.

"Who was the second Gray Forestay?" he asked.

Squirrel Dorgan suddenly gave in.

"Watches Bowen himself!" he wailed.

Monk started and exploded, "Blazes!"

Ham flourished his sword cane.

"We want a description of that Watches Bowen!" he snapped. "Was he wearing a disguise when he played the part of Forestay?"

"He grayed his hair and put on a pair of smoked spectacles and a trick mustache," Dorgan mumbled.

Doc Savage had shown no perceptible surprise at the revelation. His bronze features seemed incapable of showing emotion.

"What was Watches Bowen's purpose in pretending to be a man named Forestay?" he asked.

"Ool tried it first," Dorgan muttered. "Then Watches gave it a whirl. They wanted to trick you into taking them north in that airship of yours."

"But the attack here in the corridor?" Ham put in. "Was that genuine? I mean, when the men attacked this Watches Bowen while he was pretending to be Forestay?"

"A play put on by some of Watches' boys to make it look good," Dorgan said.

Doc Savage said, "I am to gather that you men do not know more than you have told me, because your chief failed to take you into his confidence?"

"That's it," Dorgan gasped.

At this point, big, fat Ham-hock Piney spoke up. He had been staring at the case which held the goggles.

"Dem black specs," he mumbled, eyes rolling. "Why couldn't I pick 'em up? Dat's what Ah wants to know."

Doc did not answer.

Monk snorted mirthfully. A series of mirrors had been employed to cast a lifelike reflection of the goggles—a trick magicians sometimes use to make an article seem where it is not.

But Ham-hock Piney remained in the dark about the phenomena which had so baffled him.

THE victim of the machine-pistol blast suddenly got to his feet. The slugs which the weapon discharged were so-called "mercy" bullets, pellets which were merely composition shells filled with a chemical concoction which produced almost instant unconsciousness. The period of insensibility thus induced would last only a short time.

"What are we gonna do with these birds?" Monk asked.

"The usual thing," Doc said.

That statement, to Monk, was explanation sufficient; for it concerned the strange institution which Doc maintained in upstate New York.

Grinning widely, Monk went forward to take his victims in charge.

Ham-hock Piney, who had been standing in stupefied silence, spun suddenly and lunged to get past the plates from which the sparks had jumped. The other criminals, seizing that bare chance, and moved more by animal instinct than anything else, leaped after him.

"They're getting away!" Renny yelled.

It is not the creed of Doc Savage and his five men to kill. Rather, they look upon criminals as people diseased and sick mentally—and on this theory plan their cure. Against crooks Doc Savage employs the use of fingertip hypodermic needles, attached to small caps on the ends of his fingers. A slight scratch—and the crook is unconscious.

Then, rather than turn him over to the law, Doc Savage sends the individual to an institution he maintains in upstate New York. There, the lawbreakers are subjected to a delicate brain operation, which eliminates all knowledge of their past lives. On recovery, the criminals are given a course of training which converts them into upright citizens, with a useful trade for gaining a livelihood.

RENNY

Ham-hock and the others were charging wildly across the laboratory. They were in such a mental state that only physical violence sufficient to incapacitate would stop them.

Doc Savage, strangely enough, was making no move to halt the exodus.

As the frenziedly fleeting men lurched through the doorway into the library, Ham clipped: "We can go down on the speed lift. Beat them to the bottom!"

"Let them go," Doc Savage said.

That stunned Monk. His large mouth hung open.

Big-worded Johnny was the first to find speech. The lack of big words indicated how surprised he was.

"You let them escape!" he murmured. "But why?"

"Yeah," Monk gulped. "Explain that."

Doc Savage said, "It is a rather long story and, unfortunately, there is not time for it right now."

Chapter VIII
DEATH IN A TELEPHONE

AFTER scuttling breathlessly out of the skyscraper which housed Doc Savage's headquarters, Ham-hock Piney, Squirrel Dorgan and the others walked more slowly down the street. They would have preferred to run, but that would have attracted attention.

Within a block, they sighted their sedan. It was circling the block to pick them up. The driver pulled into the curb near the corner and waited for them.

Watches Bowen and Ool were now in the machine.

Ham-hock Piney eyed Squirrel Dorgan.

"Ah sho' hates to think what de boss am gonna do when he finds out what yo' done tell dat Doc Savage," he muttered.

Squirrel Dorgan stopped.

"Lookit, you guys," he said grimly. "We know how Watches cuts up when something goes wrong. He's liable to throw sonic lead into somebody. We'd better oil this up a little."

"What yo'-all mean?" Ham-hock questioned.

"Tell Watches we didn't get in, and got chased out," Dorgan suggested. "Let it go at that. What he don't know won't hurt him."

"Ah favors dat idea," said Ham-hock.

The hard young men nodded.

"We got trouble enough without Watches ridin' us," one of them said.

Their story agreed upon, they advanced and entered the sedan.

Watches Bowen extended a hand.

"The goggles," he requested.

Ool, awaiting the answer, fixed his water-colored eyes on Ham-hock. The fat Negro was still wheezing from the exertions of his escape; sweat had flooded his banked chins. And now Ool's appraisal threw him into a fresh perspiration.

"We didn't get the goggles," Squirrel Dorgan told Watches Bowen.

"What the hell?" Watches snarled.

"We was lucky to get out of there alive," Dorgan continued. "Say, I thought you had things fixed! We walk into that place and there was Doc Savage!"

Watches Bowen scowled blackly. "You are crazy," he snapped. "Doc Savage is in that restaurant right now and has been for the past thirty minutes."

Squirrel Dorgan gaped. The hard young men looked surprised. Ham-hock Piney breathed noisily and watched Ool as if he were looking at a spike-tailed devil.

Watches Bowen snapped a command, and the car swerved back and passed the Cafe Oriental. They all peered into the restaurant. Plainly visible inside, six men sat around a table, dining in leisurely fashion.

"Doc Savage and his five aides!" Dorgan exploded. "But, hell, it can't be! Them guys in the restaurant must be actors that bird Savage fixed up."

Ham-hock rolled his eyes.

"Ah tells yo' dat bronze man am more'n half spook," he declared.

Squirrel Dorgan was obviously doing some fast thinking in an effort to make their defeat seem logical.

"Doc Savage knew that bird Forestay was you in disguise," he told Watches Bowen.

Bowen yelled, "What?"

"That probably explains it," Squirrel said, with the air of a mastermind. "Doc Savage told you when he was gonna be out of his place in the restaurant, figuring you would take a whirl at getting the goggles. Then he arranged some actors or somebody down there eating to look like himself and his men."

Bowen swore fervently and fumbled with the two watches on the gold chain.

"Maybe that explains it," he admitted.

"Ah still claims dat Savage man is worse dan voodoo," proclaimed Ham-hock Piney.

ARRIVING at their yacht alongside the City Island dock, the gang trooped aboard in surly silence.

Dimiter Daikoff came out of the galley to meet them, bringing coffee and some of Watches Bowen's favorite brandy.

His ministrations were not received kindly. Watches gave him a round cursing on general principles, and the big, dark, scarred man who claimed he was a patriot instead of a murderer, retired to a corner of the cabin and sat with his arms folded, a look of utter tragedy on his swarthy face.

Watches Bowen kept pulling one timepiece after another out of his pockets, and juggling them in his hand.

"We've got to rub this Doc Savage out," he growled.

"It is true," Ool agreed. "And we must have that dirigible. We must get those goggles also."

Watches nodded. "It's a job I hate to tackle, but it's got to be done."

"It is more dangerous trying to trick that man than to kill him," Ool said. "We will kill him."

"Ah ain't cravin' no prominent part in the killin'," Hamhock put in.

Ool's cold glance fixed upon Hamhock.

The fat Negro's temerity oozed. "Dat is," he qualified weakly, "Ah hopes us can dope out some shoah-fire scheme."

Watches restored his timepieces to his pockets, and his thick hand slid up and down the gold vest chain.

"I've got an idea," he purred. Turning, he walked to the far corner of the room, nodding for Ool to accompany him.

The two talked together earnestly for several minutes. They were careful to keep their voices lowered. No word reached other ears than their own.

Dimiter Daikoff remained glowering in the opposite corner of the room, entirely out of earshot.

Dimiter Daikoff was not out of eye-shot, however, and both Watches Bowen and Ool would have been vastly surprised had they known that the big man whose dark eyes watched them so intently, was making those eyes serve as ears.

Dimiter Daikoff was reading lips as Bowen and Ool talked.

SOME three hours later, in Doc Savage's fabulous library of scientific tomes, Monk was pacing as restlessly as a newly caged ape.

Ham sat watching him, an overdone expression of pity on his handsome face. He made clucking noises of pity with his tongue.

"No imagination," he said. "He just don't know what to do with himself."

Monk snorted, seemed to try to think of a suitable retort, gave it up and turned to watch Doc Savage, who stood before a large globe of the world.

Doc was studying the Arctic regions, and drawing a line with a colored pencil. Nearby was a stack of newspapers dating some months back. They carried stories of the lost Lenderthorn Expedition. The mark on the globe indicated the route of the Lenderthorn Expedition, as given by the newspaper accounts.

"Doc," Monk said.

The bronze man looked up. "Yes?"

"Where were you the past couple of hours? Getting those papers?" Monk asked.

Doc nodded. "That, and otherwise trying to find out what this is all about."

"You got any idea what those goggles are?" Monk asked.

"The lenses are very peculiar," the bronze giant stated. "They seem to be composed of a material similar to quartz. Yet this quartz—and I am not quite sure it is quartz—is not of natural formation. The crystalline structure indicates an artificial source."

Monk scratched the bristles atop his bullet of a head.

"At least, we know they're after our dirigible," he said, "even if we don't know why those goggles are so valuable and what is behind all this finagling."

Doc turned back to the globe.

Monk grinned as he watched the bronze man concentrate on the Arctic longitudes. The apish chemist pulled his coat collar tight about his chin and executed an elaborate shiver.

"I feel in my bones," he said, "that we're due to shove off for the land of the midnight sun."

A buzzer sounded faintly. It was one which warned of approaching visitors—a contact was closed automatically when an elevator stopped at the eighty-sixth floor level.

The bronze man pressed a button. Electrical mechanism whirred, and on one wall of the room, an inset television scanning panel of frosted glass was suddenly flooded with light. A picture appeared of the corridor outside. A uniformed policeman was stepping from an elevator.

"Now what?" muttered Monk. "Have we got the police after us, too?"

"I hope this isn't another Gray Forestay," pale Long Tom put in.

The door buzzer rang.

"I'll let him in," Monk said.

THE policeman whom Monk ushered into the room removed his cap when Doc Savage nodded in greeting. The officer seemed to have an instinctive feeling that the giant bronze man was entitled to special respect. It was not an unnatural feeling shared by everyone who met Doc Savage.

"I'm Lieutenant O'Malley," the uniformed man said. "I am on detached service working out of the chief's office. I'm here to interview Doc Savage."

"This is Doc Savage," Monk said, nodding in the direction of the world-renowned man.

"I know." O'Malley's eyes showed open admiration as they rested upon the bronze giant.

"Brother," he said, hesitating as if doubtful of the propriety of the term of address, but unable to resist its honest expression, "I'd sure feel safe with a man like you walking a beat with me."

Doc Savage turned the conversation away from himself.

"What can we do for you?" he questioned.

"It's a routine matter," the policeman said. "The office is checking up on the murder of a Watches Bowen mobster—Beery Hosmer. The suspected murderer seems to be a sideshow freak, if the descriptions that have come in are any good. White-faced, water-colored eyes, gold mustache, and a fine fuzz on his head. That's the way the description—"

"And why are you interviewing me?" Doc interposed.

"This man was reported seen around your office," the officer said.

Doc nodded. "Such a man did come to see me."

"When?"

"Late last night."

"What did he want?" O'Malley asked excitedly.

"There is more to this than shows on the surface," Doc said. "You make an appointment with your chief and we'll go over the matter together."

O'Malley's face clouded. Plainly he disliked the idea. But the bronze man's words had held a note of quiet finality.

O'Malley shrugged. "O. K.," he said. He turned, started for the door, then stopped and looked back.

"Say," he grinned, "mind if I use your telephone to call my wife? She's got corned beef and cabbage cooking tonight. It looks like I'm going to be late. I want her to keep it hot."

Doc waved at the desk phone. "Help yourself."

O'Malley spun the dial and got a number. He talked briefly regarding the conservation of corned beef and cabbage.

After he had spoken, he listened. He listened a much longer time than he had spoken. The sound of a high-pitched, querulous voice could be heard from the receiver. O'Malley squirmed; looked sheepish. His free hand went into his side pants pocket and out again.

Finally, he banged the receiver in a show of temper. The receiver missed the prongs, struck the phone, rocked it on the desk top. His right hand reached out to steady the instrument. With the right hand gripping the inside of the mouthpiece, he hooked the receiver on the fork and stepped back.

"There's a woman for you," he muttered, flushed. "She says if I don't get home on time I can eat it cold."

After the policeman had left, Doc said: "Monk, follow him."

"Tail that cop?" Monk asked, surprised.

"Right. Report all he does."

BY riding Doc's speed elevator down, Monk reached the lobby before the policeman arrived on a slower cage. Monk trailed O'Malley down the crowded avenue.

O'Malley walked fast, almost ran. He went only half a block, then turned into a cigar store and walked to the back where phone booths were arrayed. He paused in front of one of the booths.

A man came out of the booth. O'Malley crowded in.

Monk started violently when he saw the man who had come out. The man was Watches Bowen.

Monk recognized him, although he had seen Watches only in the characterization of Gray Forestay.

Monk's hand dipped into his pocket, came out with small change. He dropped a coin on the news counter and grabbed a newspaper, jerked it open, held it before his face, and advanced on the phone booths in the manner of a man absorbed in the day's news.

He stopped at the phone booth adjacent to the one the policeman had entered. But the booth was occupied. He caught a glimpse of the occupant through the glass window. It was the strangely white-skinned man who carried death in his right hand—Ool.

It had been Monk's intention to ease into the booth and listen in on O'Malley's telephone conversation. Occupied as the booth was, Monk pushed ahead to the booth on the other side of the policeman's. He had to pass so close to Watches Bowen that he almost scraped elbows with the gangster.

Monk grimaced as he saw his plan of overhearing the policeman's conversation going to smash. The booth on the opposite side was occupied also.

Monk got a quick look at the occupant. The man was small, inoffensive appearing; mouselike, in fact. A wide bandage swathing his head made him look more harmless than ever. It was Honey Hamilton, although Monk had no way of knowing that.

Monk started on, intending to enter one of the other booths and put a call through to Doc Savage for reinforcements. But he never made the call.

A sudden sharp pressure came against the small of his back. A voice purred, "Take it easy. You sure have pushed yourself into bad company."

MONK stood unmoving, saying nothing, a policy he considered excellent when the muzzle of an automatic was gouging into his back.

"So you tailed our fake copper here," Watches Bowen purred. "You boys are very, very bright, aren't you?"

Monk said nothing.

Watches Bowen laughed with an oily softness, and said, "All right, you wanted to know things. Get your ear against that booth."

Monk retreated, the muzzle of the gun barrel making steady pressure against his back.

Watches laughed unnaturally. "This is too good to keep," he said. "I'm going to let you in. Our fake copper is going to call Savage. *And when Savage answers his phone it'll be his last minute on earth.*"

"Huh?" Monk grunted, startled by the cold confidence of Watches' tone.

"Were you in Savage's office when 'Officer' O'Malley was fumbling around with the telephone?"

"Sure." Monk growled.

Watches grinned. "'Officer' O'Malley's thumb smeared poison in the telephone mouthpiece in Doc Savage's office."

"Huh?" Monk said again.

"A very unusual poison," Watches elaborated. "One which vaporized when moistened by the breath. The gas kills!"

"Hey, listen—" Monk growled, suddenly alarmed.

The gun barrel jabbed into his back. "*You* listen, ape! That's all! You're just in time!"

Monk listened, suffering all the tortures of the damned. A whirring and clicking could he heard from within the booth as the fake policeman dialed Doc Savage's number. Doc, Monk knew, would be called to the telephone in case he did not answer himself. There could hardly be a slip-up.

There was an interval of silence inside the booth, then the fake policeman spoke: "Hello … Doc Savage?"

Monk, the homely, loyal Monk, did a magnificent thing. It was not his fault that it was a useless thing.

It has been long accepted that "greater love hath no man—" Monk did the best he could to lay down his life for his brother.

There was only one way he could have managed it. With that automatic nosed into his back, he could only yell, warn Doc Savage of the poison danger by the roar of his great voice—and by the roar of the gangster's gun as it blared its lead through flesh and bone.

Monk opened his cavernous mouth to yell. It was not his fault that no sound came.

Before he could utter so much as a murmur, the barrel of a submachine gun crashed against his temple and felled him to the floor.

"HONEY" HAMILTON, anticipating the hairy chemist's intention of shouting a warning, had stepped out of the door of his telephone booth and struck the blow. The mouselike fellow eased back inside the folding doors of the booth like a snail writhing into its shell. He pretended to be talking into the phone.

Monk's collapsing bulk could not help but attract attention. Several men raced back from the cigar counter.

Watches thrust his flat automatic into a coat pocket and bent over Monk with an appearance of solicitude.

"Help me with him, will you?" he asked the first clerk who came up.

The man bent to help Watches lift Monk. "What's the matter?" he wanted to know.

"Fainted," Watches said briskly. "He gets these spells."

"Look at the blood!" the clerk gasped. "He's hit his head."

"Afraid so." Watches made a *tsk-tsk* sound and looked concerned.

"We better get a doctor."

"I," Watches said in a suavely authoritative voice, "am his doctor. Help me with him, some of you fellows. We'll put him in my car."

They carried Monk outside to the car. Watches drove away with him.

At the telephone booth inside the cigar store the fake policeman's conversation with Doc Savage had proceeded according to plan.

"I'm O'Malley," he had said.

"I recognize your voice," Doc Savage had replied over the wire.

"Will you speak a little closer to the mouthpiece, please?" the gangster requested. "This connection is not good."

Doc Savage raised his voice.

"I still can't hear you," the gangster lied. "Maybe if you'd talk a little closer still—"

"How is this?" Doc Savage's words were blurred, as if his lips were against the mouthpiece.

"That's better," said the fake officer. "Now, about this Beery Hosmer killing—there is a point or two that I forgot—"

He talked on, making conversation concerning the murder of Hosmer, going over some of the points which he had already discussed with Doc Savage.

He heard a crash. It was loud, brittle, such a sound as the telephone at the other end might have made if dropped. The man in the blue uniform broke up his monologue and called sharply, "Doc Savage!"

There was no answer.

"Doc Savage!" the man repeated.

Silence replied. Then there were excited shouts coming over the wire, the noise of men moving about rapidly in Doc Savage's office. Finally, there was a cry, hoarse and filled with horror.

"He's dead!" a voice shrieked. "Doc Savage is dead!"

The fake policeman hung up hastily and left the booth. Ool came out of the adjacent booth.

"Did it succeed?" Ool asked.

"It did," the other grinned.

Chapter IX
FROSTED DEATH

WITHIN the hour Watches Bowen, transporting the unconscious Monk, was back at the boat at the City Island dock. He looked around irritably for Dimiter Daikoff.

"Where is the patriot?" he asked of Ham-hock Piney.

The fat Negro shrugged ponderous shoulders. "I donno, chief."

The big, dark, scarred man came in a few minutes later.

"Where were you?" Watches snarled.

"Out for some air," Daikoff said gloomily.

"Well, see if you can start some air circulating in this." Watches indicated the still unconscious figure of Monk.

The big, dark man scowled ferociously. When he did this, the scar on his neck tightened like something alive.

He said, "Violence I do not like, except to traitors and political foes."

Watches regarded him bleakly. "You might call this guy a political foe of ours. You did a good repair job on Honey Hamilton. See if you can fix this one up, too."

Daikoff clicked his heels, bowed, then commenced expert ministrations to Monk.

Watches produced his eighty-year-old brandy and poured his own drinks. Ool and Honey Hamilton, and the fake policeman, O'Malley, came in a few minutes later. Ool's face was as dispassionate as usual, but Honey Hamilton's cherubic features were beaming.

"What's the dope?" Watches asked. "Did it work?"

"You tell it, Ool," Honey sighed.

"Doc Savage," Ool announced, "is dead."

"You sure?" Watches frowned.

"I know my poisons," Ool said flatly. "This one, in my land, is known as *ssl-yto-mng*. That name means 'the poison that cannot fail.'"

"He's dead, all right," said O'Malley. "I heard his men howling that he had croaked."

Watches breathed heavily and reached for the brandy. "So Savage is out of the way. Maybe that ain't a load off my chest! Ool, you're smart enough to be president of these United States!"

Ool nodded. "I have thought of that. Perhaps I shall be."

Watches stared. "Well, for—"

"What," Ool questioned, "is to prevent me?"

"Sure," Watches muttered, a strange gleam coming into his bleak eyes. "You took me off my feet for a minute by being so casual—"

"It is not too much to hope for," Ool said.

"Sure— Why, sure," Watches said slowly, "if we put this deal across—hell, anything is possible!"

Watches gulped his drink and his hand trembled on his glass.

"Your hand," Ool said, "is not steady."

Watches cursed softly. "You'd shake too, if you were half human. When I think about what we can do if this goes through—" He reached for another drink.

"Now that Doc Savage is out of the way," Ool said, "we have only to appropriate his dirigible— and the goggles—and leave. Right?" He made a gesture indicating simplicity, with his pale hands.

THERE was a series of five sharp raps at the door. They were insistent.

"That's Squirrel's signal," Watches said. "Sounds as if something is on him. Let him in, Ham-hock."

The corpulent Negro waddled over and opened the door, and Squirrel landed inside like one of his furry namesakes tumbling out of a tree.

"Watches!" he jabbered, "I seen Doc Savage and—"

"When?" Watches cut.

"Since that poison was supposed to have got him!"

"Where?" the crook leader's word was a crash.

"I been shadowin' his place like you told me. He come out and I followed him. He turns in at a cable office and sends some radiograms—"

"Radiograms?"

"Yeah—"

"Who to?"

"How would I know?" Squirrel asked in an injured tone. "I couldn't walk in and look."

Watches jerked savagely at his watch chain.

"Get me a copy of those radiograms. Stick up the place, or blow the safe, or anything. But get 'em!"

Ool's right hand floated out in Squirrel's direction in a loathsome moccasin motion. His flat voice said ominously: "If you do not manage better with the radiograms than you did with the goggles—"

He left it unfinished for effect.

Squirrel Dorgan shuddered, mumbled, "Aw, I done my best." Then he went out hastily.

Watches turned, frowning, on Ool.

"The poison which never fails—" he began with biting sarcasm.

Ool silenced him with a fluttering of his right hand.

"It was not the poison which failed," he said. "It is your stupid men."

The fake policeman, O'Malley, protested desperately: "I smeared that poison in the telephone mouthpiece!"

Watches rasped, "There was a slip somewhere."

Ham-hock rolled his whitish eyes. "Yassuh, an' de way things turned out when we all went foah dem goggles—Ah done mah best to pick 'em up, but dey just wahn't dere, even if'n Ah could see 'em."

Ool's voice crashed flatly. "There is another poison from my land, a sister poison to this one which has failed. We call these poisons the 'twin sisters.' The one which has failed is volatized by moisture. The other one is turned into a deadly gas by the application of heat. I shall prepare the heat poison."

The golden-fuzzed assassin paused. "I suggest you, Watches, yourself, arrange that Doc Savage meet the other of the twin sisters. We do not want another failure."

Watches glowered. "I'll arrange the introduction, all right."

Watches absent-mindedly pulled a timepiece from his coat sleeve. There was evidently a special pocket in the sleeve. The watch was very large, of silver, and looked ancient.

Watches looked at it, appeared to see it for the first time, seemed startled, and hastily returned it to its concealed sleeve pouch.

A DEEP and melancholy voice at Ool's elbow asked: "What is the time, please, Mr. Bowen?"

Watches looked around, startled. He had not heard big Dimiter Daikoff approach.

"Damn it!" he snapped. "That's a good way to get yourself a lead vaccination—slipping up behind me like that!"

"What is the time?" Daikoff asked again, unperturbed.

"That watch doesn't tell time," the mob chief growled. "Some of my watches tell time—some of 'em I carry for other reasons." He held out his wrist where Daikoff could see the minute and hour. "That one keeps time."

"Thank you," Daikoff said. He turned and started away. Even bent over, and limping as he did, he looked enormous. There was an aura of quiet power about him.

"How's the patient?" Watches called after him.

Daikoff paused. "You mean the man who resembles a huge monkey? The one who seems to have been hit over the head?"

"Sure." Watches nodded. "Is he gonna croak?"

"It is too soon to tell," Daikoff's deep voice boomed. "He must remain quiet for a while."

EARLY that evening, Squirrel Dorgan returned to the moored yacht and put copies of four radiograms in Watches' hands.

"They're the ones Doc Savage sent," he said. "I just walked into the cable office, showed a clerk the noisy end of my gun, and he coughed up."

Watches scanned the radiograms quickly, then cursed with soft deadliness and called Ool.

Ool's hand, after he had read the radiograms, crept out instinctively in a butterfly movement. But all he said was, "We have no time to lose."

"We'll finish him tonight!" Watches rasped. "That's no pipe-dream, either!"

One of the radiograms was addressed to the Royal Canadian Mounted Police detachment at Aklavik, at the head of the Mackenzie River on the Arctic coast. The other three were addressed to United States government authorities in settlements on the mainland of Alaska and on the Aleutian Islands. The text of all four radiograms was the same:

PLEASE SEND AVAILABLE INFORMATION REGARDING GRAY FORESTAY EXPEDITION

OR ANY OTHER EXPEDITION OPERATING THROUGH YOUR TERRITORY WITHIN LAST SIX MONTHS STOP HAVE YOU ANY RECORD OF SHRUNKEN-FACED ABNORMALLY WHITE-SKINNED MAN FINE GOLDEN HAIR TALL BONY REMARKABLY STRONG FLAT UNNATURAL VOICE WHEN SPEAKING ENGLISH KNOWN PERHAPS AS OOL STOP THIS INFORMATION OF UTMOST URGENCY.

CLARK SAVAGE, JR.

"Yeah," Watches growled, after reading the messages again. "We've got to nail him before he gets a line on you, Ool."

SHORTLY before ten o'clock that night, Doc Savage and his four aides were gathered in the reception room of the bronze man's eighty-sixth floor headquarters. Talking little, they were waiting with some impatience—except for big-fisted Renny, who frowned at the telephone from time to time.

"How'd you ever get wise to that trick poison, Doc?" he boomed. "The stuff was colorless, and it didn't look wet like a liquid."

"Did you watch that fake policeman, O'Malley, when he was here?" Doc asked.

Renny nodded. "Sure."

"He was not very clever in fumbling the telephone," the bronze man said dryly. "That made me suspicious. There was only about one thing he could have been doing. So, immediately after the man who called himself O'Malley had departed, I disconnected that instrument and substituted another."

Johnny, the big-worded archaeologist and geologist, fumbled his monocle and murmured, "I wonder if your chicane histrionics were consummative?"

"He means that he wonders if that was a successful act that you put on over the telephone, when you had one of us yell that you were dead," Renny rumbled.

Doc evidently intended to answer, but there was an interruption. The telephone rang. The bronze man got up and swung toward the instrument.

"Holy cow!" Renny thumped uneasily. "Watch it! Maybe there's been some more poison smeared in that mouthpiece!"

It was noticeable that the bronze man stood well away from the instrument as he answered it. A shrill, whining voice came from the receiver.

"Listen, guy," it said, "I know who I'm talkin' to, see. I know your voice. That ain't all I know, either."

"Interesting," Doc said without emotion.

"Beery Hosmer was my pal," the voice whined. "He got it dirty, see? He didn't have it comin'. So I'm layin' a finger on the guy that done it."

"All right," Doc Savage said sharply. "Who are you and what do you know?"

The voice quickened over the telephone.

"Think I'm a sap?" it demanded. "All kinds of troubles have a way of lightin' on guys like me, so I ain't tellin' no names. But you go to that warehouse thing owned by the Hidalgo Tradin' Company down on the Hudson River waterfront. Look for a green coupé, see?"

"How did you get this information?" Doc asked.

The other hung up.

IT was half past ten that night when Doc Savage and his four aides approached the great warehouse hangar. The car in which they rode eased along with the silence of an electric lift. The bronze man was at the wheel.

Ham, Renny, Long Tom, and Johnny were all a little glum because of the absence of Monk. The fact that Doc did not appear worried did not cheer them much, because the bronze man rarely showed the emotions which he felt.

Ham tried to cheer himself. "After all, Monk don't often get into a spot that he can't get out of."

"Yeah," Renny said. "Monk'll come through all right. What I'm worried about is this call from the party who claims to be a friend of Beery Hosmer."

"Right," Long Tom concurred. "It's got some of the earmarks of a phony."

The car rolled silently, a perfectly balanced motor virtually eliminating vibration, expert filling of the heavy body and chassis parts assuring no creakings. One of the individual features of the car was the fenders of chrome construction, able to withstand a terrific collision.

Long Tom's voice cracked, "There's a green coupé!"

The green coupé, a large one, was a block distant and under a streetlight.

A man leaned out, looked behind, then turned swiftly and seemed to be giving directions to the driver.

"It's that white-skinned scamp, Ool!" Long Tom barked.

"We'll pull alongside," Renny began, "and—no, we won't."

The green coupé, with a throaty snarl from its exhaust, leaped from the curb, gathered speed. Within a very few seconds it was breaking speed limits.

Doc fed more gas. His own car eased silently up to keep pace with the other. It began to close the gap between the two machines.

The green coupé began to rocket through night traffic. The car needed no warning siren to secure a right-of-way. Its exhaust roar was ample. It cannoned the night with a pounding thunder which would have drowned out a fire siren. Taxis scurried to the curb. Pedestrians flattened back against shop windows.

Holding close behind the roaring green coupé, Doc's low sedan was still almost silent.

Renny flourished his supermachine pistol.

"Shall I let 'em have a dose?"

Doc shook his head. "Traveling too fast!"

Doc fed more gas—and more. His car drew up alongside the other. His intention was obviously to get around the green coupé, cut in front, and force the machine to the curb.

But the other car also had speed. The driver circumvented Doc's maneuver by putting on a burst of speed as great as the bronze man had managed. White lights, green lights, red lights streaked past, blurred.

Doc commented, "They have quite a motor under that hood."

"Wait until we get on an open road!" clipped Johnny, reverting to few syllable words in the excitement of the pursuit.

In anticipation of violent action, he took his monocle from his pocket, wrapped it in his handkerchief to protect it from breakage, and thrust it back in his pocket. The monocle was not an affectation with him. In the past, before Doc Savage had exercised his surgical skill to restore complete sight to the wiry geologist's left eye, injured in the World War, Johnny had worn eyeglasses, the left eyepiece carrying the magnifying glass. Needing eyeglasses no longer, he insisted that he needed the magnifier in his work, so he still carried it in the monocle.

SUDDENLY the air in front of Doc Savage's hurtling car was choked with smoke. Beams from the powerful lamps were absorbed as completely as the sun's rays behind storm clouds.

The driver of the green coupé was spreading a smoke screen from his exhaust in the fashion devised long ago by ingenious criminals. Doc's car was coursing blindly at nearly a hundred miles an hour.

The bronze man drove a hand under the instrument panel and touched one of an array of switches concealed there. Then he wrenched out large, somewhat clumsy eyepieces. He peered through one of these.

A fantastic change was wrought. A weird light seemed to have suffused the pall of black smoke. To a layman, it would have smacked of black magic, but an electrical engineer would not have been more than surprised at the efficiency of the apparatus for projecting invisible infra-red light rays, which have the faculty of penetrating smoke and fog to a great degree.

The eyepieces, highly ingenious, for making the infra-light visible would have been even more interesting to an electrical expert.

"Watch out!" Renny shouted suddenly.

Directly ahead, crosswise of the street, loomed an abandoned truck. Someone, working in collusion with the driver of the green coupé, had driven the truck out of a side street and left it, anticipating that Doc would crash into it, head on, in the smoke.

Tires squalled on pavement as Doc swerved the sedan in an attempt to clear the obstruction. No ordinary car could have made it.

There was a sickening skid. They vaulted the curb. Metal crashed, rasped. They had glanced off a wall. Brick dust cascaded. The machine rocked, nearly went over. Then it jarred back on the street, beyond the truck.

"Holy cow!" Renny gasped.

Long-winded Johnny blinked his eyes. "I vouchsafe a kindred articulation!"

The speeding cars were beyond the region of traffic lights now and streaking on open boulevards. Doc's sedan crawled up immediately behind the other car. At their terrific speed, telephone poles were almost like pickets in a fence. The green coupé lurched a good deal, but Doc's scientifically weighted car held the road smoothly.

Doc's cabled bronze hands eased the wheel over. The car swung around the green coupé, came up abreast. Plainly, Doc meant to wedge the other car in, force it to stop.

A submachine gun nosed out of the green coupé and a burst of bullets flattened harmlessly against the steel plating and bulletproofed glass of Doc's vehicle.

With the speeding cars side by side, Doc and his men could get a look at their adversaries in the coupé.

"Hey, that's not Ool!" Long Tom said tersely. "They've chalked somebody's face up to make him look like Ool!"

"Ool would hardly risk his neck with a driver like that one," Doc said.

"Well then, what—" Long Tom never finished his sentence.

THERE was a bump, a terrifying swerve, a crash, a crazy sword-slashing of lights in the night as the two cars collided and one of them turned up end for end and rolled like a barrel off the road, over a ditch, through a hedge of trees and far into a plowed field.

The insanely reckless driver of the green coupé had tried to shove the other car off the road.

The trick backfired. The other driver had not

calculated on Doc's reinforced fenders. It was his own car which went over.

Doc's machine held the road. It weaved, but not dangerously. Doc eased down on the brakes, cut the lights, and brought the car to an abrupt stop.

What he did then was a surprise.

"Slide over here in the driver's seat, Ham," he directed. "Take the car back to town. You will hear from me at the office."

He opened the door, swung out, glided across the road and disappeared in the shadow of a high hedge.

Ham hesitated, then drove away, carrying with him a puzzled and disgusted Long Tom, Johnny, and Renny.

At the scene of the disaster, Doc Savage ascertained that both the driver and gunner were dead, killed instantly.

He was examining the bodies, when a peculiar rhythmic drone of a sound assailed his ears. Doc looked up.

Clearly against the starlit sky he could see a huge shape poised against the night, resembling, at first, a bird with grotesquely whirling wings. Even as he looked, the object settled lower. It was a plane, an autogyro.

Doc exploded in a burst of furious energy, and barely reached the shadows of a grove of trees as a sharp clatter sounded from above and machine gun bullets rapped the ground.

Doc was not carrying one of the machine pistols so much relied upon by his men; he preferred to depend for defense on ingenuity and various scientific devices carried in pockets of a specially constructed vest.

Since the autogyro was not flying low enough for him to take any effective measures against it, he contented himself with outguessing the machine gun bursts. Repeatedly bullets snarled through the massed leaves, tracing patterns of death. But the bronze man kept clear.

After a few minutes of ineffectual firing, the autogyro lifted and skimmed away to the west, still flying low.

Not more than two minutes later, Doc saw it poise, then drop lazily to the earth in almost vertical decent.

Leaving his evergreen shelter, Doc ran for the spot where the autogyro had landed. The distance was not great and, eventually, he located the windmill plane.

The craft had settled in a farm lot, in a shallow valley not far off the road. There was a house close by. Doc approached cautiously. The moon added to the brilliance of the stars.

He heard a man curse, then heard his own name spoken—"Doc Savage!"—in evident alarm. A window went black in the farmhouse. A man ran out and was joined by another outside. The two started racing across the farm lot in the direction of the autogyro.

Then one of them stopped, caught the other by the arm and pulled him in the opposite direction.

"Nix!" The arm-puller's words wafted clearly to Doc. "We can't land in the gyro where we wanta go! The hell with it! We'll take the car!"

THE men ran, stumbling, to the road. Doc following them, heard the whine of a starter, then the silence-wrecking roar of a motor and a clashing of gears as a car got under way.

The headlights switched on. Doc was able to recognize the two men. Ool and Watches Bowen!

The car droned away, blurring into black distance.

After satisfying himself that he was alone, Doc Savage ran toward the autogyro. He examined it carefully. He devoted particular attention to the controls.

He found a bomb attached to the starter in such a way that it would have exploded at the first revolution. The bomb explained the "act" which Watches Bowen and Ool had put on in the farm lot. The performance had been calculated to decoy the bronze man into following the fleeing car with the autogyro. It was just one more murder attempt.

Doc Savage entered the house and began a searching examination of the rooms. It seemed to be a small tenant farmer's house, deserted now, used, judging from the litter about, as an occasional hide-out by Watches Bowen.

The white beam of his flashlight poked everywhere. In the room where he had seen the light go out, papers on the floor and more papers on a time-scarred desk made it look as if the criminals, in their haste to clear out, had been forced to leave documents behind.

Doc picked one of the papers from the floor. Light from the hand flash washed over it, revealing a maze of handwriting and figures— apparently some of Watches Bowen's calculations.

Doc gathered all papers on the floor and carried them to the desk. There was a lamp on the desk, with an electric bulb in it. Evidently there was an electric plant on the farm.

For greater convenience, Doc laid down his flash and turned on the electric light. It was a dim bulb, heavily frosted.

Doc bent close to the light while sorting over the papers. So intent was he upon the documents that he did not see the faint vapor which crept out from the frosted bulb as it warmed.

He did notice it, finally. His arm slashed out.

He smashed the bulb in his bare hand. But the vapor was already in the air.

The bronze man took two staggering steps, then keeled over, to lie inert on the floor.

Chapter X
THE PATRIOT UNMASKED

OOL and Watches Bowen did not drive into town when they fled the farmhouse, but turned into a nearby side road, from where, after parking their machine, they circled back to the farmhouse on foot, arriving in time to watch from a distance as Doc Savage turned on the lamp at the desk.

When they heard the solid *thump* of his body as it struck the floor, they came charging in. They stared triumphantly at the bronze man's prostrate form.

"The second of the twin sisters got him," Ool spoke tonelessly.

Watches' voice had a rasp in it. "After this, Ool, I vote for you and your fancy poisons every time. When that fool coupé driver got himself wrecked, I was ready to quit."

Watches collected his personal papers which had formed the lure. Then he approached the body of Doc Savage.

"Let's lug it out to the car," he suggested.

Together the two bent over Doc's heavy frame.

What happened next neither Ool nor Watches could have correctly detailed. There was a nightmare sensation, as though the roof had fallen on them and a tornado had funneled its way into the room.

Vaguely, of course, they knew that Doc Savage was not dead. The corded muscles of the bronze man, which had been slacked in apparent helplessness as he lay upon the floor, had suddenly become galvanized with uncalculable force.

Both Ool and Watches Bowen were strong men. But they were helpless the instant a metallic hand closed over the throat of each. Their blood seemed to turn to water, their muscles got limp as rags, their eyes bulged in purpling faces, their tongues ran out.

Doc, with an unexpected movement, cracked their heads together. They lost consciousness.

Searching the pair, Doc relieved them of weapons. Then he devoted much time to an examination of Ool's right hand, the hand which the thin, strangely white-skinned man seemed never to keep still.

He found nothing peculiar about the hand.

The bronze man dragged the two senseless forms to the autogyro and calmly detached the bomb from the starting mechanism.

He flew his two captives back to the city, landing in a vacant lot conveniently near his own waterfront warehouse hangar. He took a closed car from the big building and loaded the captives aboard.

IN the skyscraper headquarters, Ham, Johnny, Long Tom, and Renny stared as Doc issued from his private elevator with his two prisoners in tow. Doc slumped the pair of limp forms on the floor.

Long Tom, the electrical wizard, was first to speak. "You sure did a heavy night's work, Doc," he said.

"Let us hope it is all over but the questioning," Doc said.

Big-fisted Renny handed over a sheaf of radiograms.

"These came in answer to the radiograms you sent up North," he told the bronze man. "They give us something to go on when we start questioning these two."

The messages were all very long, and all alike in one respect—they all conveyed the information that no expedition other than the Lenderthorn party had left the Arctic-American coast in recent months.

One message carried a surprise. It described the members of the Lenderthorn party. The descriptions were unmistakable.

Lenderthorn, the explorer, had been no other person than Watches Bowen himself. Assisting him had been a lieutenant who resembled Ool to perfection.

The expedition had taken off by plane and had not been heard from since, the message stated.

One radiogram, from Point Barrow, on the north Alaskan coast, contained additional information regarding Ool.

The weirdly white-skinned man, so the radiogram informed, had arrived mysteriously into the settlement some months ago.

Ool had carried a strange pair of black goggles. He had been acting strangely, seeming to have not the slightest idea of what modern life was like, and being unable to speak any intelligible language. But during the short time he had remained there, he had learned language and customs with amazing rapidity.

He had refused to divulge much information about himself except to infer vaguely that he had come from off the Arctic ice pack, which obviously was a lie, it being regarded as an impossibility. He had disappeared from the settlement as mysteriously as he had come.

Several strange deaths among the Eskimo population had been credited by them to Ool, but this was thought to be superstitious fancy on their part, since no direct evidence of Ool's guilt could be obtained and fatalities in each case having been attended by severe local inflammation and swelling, and no autopsies having been performed, death had been credited by settlement authorities to pernicious infection, or simple blood poisoning.

Renny jarred his huge fists together restlessly. "What say we take a trip, Doc, over—"

"—over the Arctic ice pack," Long Tom supplied. "We can use—"

"—the new dirigible." Ham added.

"For the specific purposes," Johnny finished grandly, "of investigating the mysterious origin of one malicious malefactor having golden hirsute adornment, not to mention delving into the mystery of a certain pair of goggles—and alleged mysterious *things*."

"HAM—jump!" Doc's voice was a crash of sound.

Ham jumped, suddenly, without question. The dapper lawyer leaped a yard in the air.

Ool clutched his ankle at about the half-yard level.

Ham fell violently, sprawling his full length on the floor, his sword cane clattering out of his hand. He kicked, but he could not shake Ool's relentless grip from his ankle.

"Hold it, Ham!" Doc rasped. "Do not move!"

Ham lay still.

Ool spoke.

"You have done well to order him to lie still," he droned. "Now listen to me. You have witnessed my strength. I did not stay long unconscious, like this other one." He indicated Watches Bowen's limp form.

"I could give you," he continued, speaking with his sepulchral lack of tone, "a more deadly exhibition of my powers. If I had reached for your man with my right hand, instead of my left, he would now be dead. So try no tricks on me, bronze man. You could kill me—yes; but not before I could kill this man of yours."

"What do you want?" Doc asked quietly.

"First, the goggles."

Without further argument, Doc went into the laboratory and returned with the goggles. He tossed them to Ool.

"You have discrimination," Ool said, flatly. "I could wish I had you for a partner instead of Watches Bowen."

"What else do you want?"

"Escape—that is all." Ool spoke like an ineffi- cient phonograph. "I am not greedy. I might bar- gain with you for your dirigible. But that would incur complications. I prefer to consolidate my gains, and strike another time."

"You propose to do what now?" Doc asked.

"I am going to move back and enter your elevator," Ool said. "I shall drag Watches Bowen, and I shall drag your man also. My right hand is death. Understand! But you have my word that it will function only if you interfere with my escape."

"What do you intend doing with Ham?" Doc demanded.

"I do not want him. Nor do I wish to encourage reprisals from you by killing him. If you do not interfere with my escape, I shall leave him at the bottom of the elevator shaft unhurt. Is it agreed?"

Above everything else, Doc Savage was solicitous about the safety of his aides.

"It is agreed," he said.

Without further words, Ool backed out of the door with his human burdens, entered an elevator, and sank the eighty-six stories to the ground.

Eventually the elevator came back to the eighty-sixth floor. Ham was in it, lashed with his back to the handrail.

"Let's go after that scut!" Renny roared, crowding into the elevator.

Doc vetoed the proposal. "Not now. I have other plans. You men wait."

The bronze man got them out, then went down alone in the cage.

Doc's aides crowded about Ham, firing queries.

"That while-faced, death-fingered fellow isn't human!" Ham shuddered.

ABOARD Watches Bowen's moored yacht, Dimiter Daikoff, the big, dark, scarred patriot, moved swiftly to bring out more eighty-year-old brandy as Watches Bowen and Ool tramped aboard and shoved noisily through the door.

Watches was in a savage mood. His neck was swelling from Doc Savage's choking, and his head felt like a thousand steel mallets were knocking on it. He gulped the brandy greedily.

"Some stuff, them twin sisters of yours," he snarled at Ool.

"There is no known poison in your world more deadly than the twin sisters," Ool replied.

"Then how come Savage snapped out of it so quick?" Watches demanded.

"He did not come out of it."

"What do you mean?"

"He never was under the influence of it. No man can embrace either of the twin sisters and live."

"You mean he faked it—pretended to be knocked out in order to get us in there and nab us?"

"Obviously."

"Then something's gone screwy as hell!"

Watches snarled. "There's a leak somewhere. Savage has been tipped off to every plan we've made." The mob leader's hand clawed at the front of his vest, jerked fiercely at his gold watch chain.

Dimiter Daikoff came forward silently, proffering cigarettes, but Watches knocked the package out of his hand.

"You're beginning to get under my skin!" he rasped.

"Hold onto your nerves," Ool cautioned. He produced the goggles from his pocket. "We have these—that is one important thing."

Watches continued to stare malevolently at Dimiter Daikoff, at the scar on his neck, the tragically-glowing dark eyes, the high cheek bones, hollow cheeks, the superb muscular power that even the swarthy man's ill-fitting suit could not hide.

Shortly afterward, Dimiter Daikoff found occasion to leave the cabin.

Watches Bowen jerked a thumb after him.

"Savage knows too much; he evidently finds out our plans," he said. "I wonder if the leak could be that damned patriot?"

Ool showed no emotion, but asked, "Need we take chances?"

"Hell, no!" Watches growled.

"I will shake hands with him when he returns," Ool said emotionlessly. "I will use my right hand."

Dimiter Daikoff came back after a time and Ool stood up.

"I wish to compliment you on the excellent serving of the brandy," he said. "Shake hands with me, if you will."

Dimiter Daikoff was standing very close. He reached out readily to take Ool's proffered hand.

But at the last instant the big patriot's forward-reaching hand swerved, but down toward the goggles in Ool's left hand. His flashing grab was accurately directed. He got the goggles.

All in the same motion, it seemed, he lunged to one side and his other hand clawed out and caught Watches by the throat. He jerked the thick-waisted gangster clear off the floor.

For the second time that evening, Watches Bowen thought a tornado had funneled into the room and was stirring splintered timbers about his head.

The big, dark man's throat grip tightened until the room was a red blur in Watches' bulging eyes. Then Ool sliced toward Dimiter Daikoff with his right hand fluttering. Watches felt himself lifted, hurled. He crashed against Ool, knocked him down.

Watches worked his jaw spasmodically, trying to talk. When he wrenched words out, they came in a hoarse rasp.

"It's Doc Savage!" he choked.

"Yes," came the tragic-voiced patriot's affirmation. "It is Doc Savage."

UPON hearing the struggle, Monk came charging in from the other cabin where he had been lying on a bed in pretended convalescence.

"Grab a chair, Monk," Doc called out. "Hold it in front of you. Ool's touch is death!"

Ool scrambled to his feet ahead of Watches. Crouching, he sidled in toward Doc, with his right hand weaving like the head of a coiled moccasin.

Doc did not wait for an attack. He hurled forward, avoided the moccasin thrust of the assassin, and thudded bronze knuckles on Ool's jaw.

Ool reeled back, collapsed against the wall. But he sprang up, cat-quick, and sidled in again. Had Doc been able to throw more weight into the jaw punch, Ool, unnaturally strong though he was, would have caved in then.

As Ool slunk in for a second attack, Doc drew out one of the small glass bulbs which were his anesthetic bombs. He snapped it to the floor. It shattered. Doc held his breath.

"Hold your breath!" Ool yelled at Watches Bowen.

Doc had half expected this, recalling that in his office Ool had survived one of the bombs in similar fashion.

Doc made a pass at Ool, dodged the assassin's finger thrust as before, and planted a clean blow to the face.

An ordinary man would have been knocked out. Ool was only flung back against the wall, badly shaken. His endurance was tremendous.

At the same instant Monk, with his chair, rushed Watches. The gangster had gained his feet and was whirling the watch which had been in the secret pocket up his sleeve. Since escaping with Ool from Doc Savage's office, Watches had not re-armed himself with an automatic. He did not appear to be concerned about it. His lips writhed in a killer's snarl as he opened his hand and let the watch fly.

The watch was one of Bowen's pet weapons. The mechanism had been removed from the case and a quantity of molten lead inserted. Bowen could hurl the watch as accurately as he could aim a revolver.

The leaded watch plummeted toward Monk with the speed of a projectile. Monk ducked as the missile struck his chair. The watch splintered entirely through the thin wicker of the boat chair and struck Monk lightly on the chest.

Monk bellowed, came in with the chair as a battering-ram. The gangster lurched to one side. The chair scraped his shoulder and went into the wall with such force that the legs splintered the cabin sheathing.

The gangster's hand dipped to his wide coat pocket. It whipped out clutching another leaded watch. There was a chain attached. It was the gangster's habit to use the weighted timepiece as a substitute for a blackjack. He swung the unique weapon at Monk's head.

Jerking the chair around, Monk sideswiped the clumsy weapon in a vicious swing at the gangster. The chair knocked the leaded timepiece from Watches Bowen's fist, and went on to thud heavily against his shoulder.

The gangster reeled back. There was a jangle of breaking glass as his heavy bulk crashed into a porthole.

At the same moment, Doc Savage, eluding Ool's fourth successive moccasin jab, sent the tall pale man crashing to the wall. Ool struggled up again, but now noticeably weakened.

Watches Bowen's voice roared in savage desperation. "The hell with the goggles, Ool! Let's get out of here!"

The gang chief hurled his heavy bulk backward out the broken, oversize porthole, jangling the rest of the glass pane to the floor. Ool made a gangling lunge to the door.

Outside, they tumbled head-first into a speed-boat which was moored under the stern.

"Give her the gun!" Watches yelled frantically.

There was a sudden roar as the speedboat engine came to life. A machine gun stuttered out. It must have been lying in the boat. The rain of slugs drove Doc and Monk flat on the deck.

The speedboat, running without lights, roared swiftly away with water piling up in its wake. Doc and Monk stood on the deck and stared after it.

Before Monk's admiring eyes, Doc Savage obliterated the Dimiter Daikoff disguise. He gouged from his mouth the wadding which had produced the effect of high cheek bones. A deft movement of his thumb and finger removed a pair of dark glass cuplike lenses which had fitted snugly over his eyeballs. A chemical paste cleared the last trace of blackness from his bronze hair. He peeled off the collodion-manufactured scar which slanted from the lobe of his ear down across his neck.

Monk grinned. "The patriot unmasked," he said. "I didn't know you myself at first as Dimiter Daikoff. Say, was there sure enough a Dimiter Daikoff?"

"The police radio calls were legitimate," Doc supplied. "I merely took advantage of them to gain Watches Bowen's confidence."

AN hour later, from an obscure Long Island airport, there sounded the multiple drone of airplane engines as a big ship, massive of hull and with a wide wing spread, barely cleared the twinkling line of lights marking the edge of the landing field.

Under its heavy weight of men and fuel, the ship rose sluggishly, circling the field and gaining altitude, then it put on speed and throbbed away into the northwest.

For passengers, the ship carried Watches Bowen, Ool, Ham-hock Piney, Honey Hamilton, Squirrel Dorgan, and four other men. Nine of them, and a pilot. As vicious an assortment of criminals as had ever disgraced a good plane.

It was some hours before Johnny, checking the airports and railway stations at Doc's suggestion, learned of the plane's departure.

Chapter XI
ARCTIC PROCESSION

LIKE a moonbeam caught up, congealed, and set adrift again, a cruising dirigible, a silver sliver against the bleak, sub-Arctic sky, droned over the Canadian northwest at a rate of speed highly unusual for such ships. The speed of the dirigible— almost two hundred miles an hour—was achieved through improved propulsion power and lessened wind resistance.

Doc Savage had personally developed the alloy motors, and Doc, with help from Monk, had succeeded in synthesizing an inflating gas, noninflammable, with substantially greater lifting power than helium or hydrogen.

At the settlement of Resolution, on Great Slave Lake, the silver dirigible nosed down for refueling. Doc and his five inquiring aides learned there that a two-motored transport plane carrying ten men had touched for gas and oil two hours before them.

"Ool and Watches Bowen," Monk muttered.

"Deduction corroborated," Johnny agreed.

In the air again, boring into the northwest, the slender dirigible was like a bright needle thread-ing together a thousand-mile line of tall spruces and black monzonite ridges. Hour after hour, the craft drilled over the great, lonely land, rising higher as it approached the Alaskan border, in order to clear the Yukon Rockies.

In the cabin, enclosed in the hull, Doc and his aides were comfortable. Ham was at the controls. Long Tom, in charge of radio communications, kept in regular contact with ground stations for the purpose of determining weather conditions over their intended line of flight.

There was no great need for this however, since the streamlined bag cut down wind resistance greatly over conventional designs, rendering the craft easily manageable in any wind less than a hurricane.

Appointed by Doc as navigator for the trip, Renny spent much time looking over charts.

Monk did nothing more creative than to recline in his bunk and tickle the ear of his pet pig with his toe.

The pig, Habeas Corpus by name, had missed the hostilities in New York. The reason was unusual. A certain famous psychologist, amazed at the intelligence which the porker seemed to possess, had requested, in all seriousness, permission to seclude the pig for study.

Not less than fifty times, Monk had told all who would listen of the learned man's findings.

"The guy said Habeas was a wizard of a hog," Monk repeated. "He said that Habeas—"

Ham snarled, "Will you shut up about that porky freak, you missing link!"

Monk only grinned.

Habeas Corpus was a remarkable sight to behold. He was a runty razorback, with the snout of a possum, legs of a stag, and great flapping ears that took the wind when he ran and looked like they were going to fly away with him.

Habeas Corpus, reacting contentedly to Monk's foot massaging, emitted soft grunts.

Whenever Monk went on a trip, he took Habeas. Habeas Corpus was an intelligent porker; Monk had trained him until he could perform things which amazed those whose acquaintance with porkers had been limited to a slab of bacon.

MONK shifted his administrations from Habeas Corpus' left ear to the right, then asked, "Doc, have you any idea where we're gonna run into that gang?"

"Yes," Doc answered, "I have."

"Huh?" Monk squirmed. "After we leave Point Barrow, I thought we were going to run blind."

"We will cruise over the ice pack, using our radio direction finder in an attempt to locate specific static disturbances," Doc said.

"Where in blazes did you get onto that hunch?"

"The information," Doc supplied, "was contained on some papers of Watches Bowen's which I examined while playing the part of Dimiter Daikoff. It was not a clear clue exactly. The paper was a bill for such a direction finder that had been built for Watches Bowen."

"Maybe it's a phony?"

"Maybe." The bronze man made a slight gesture. "We have no better clue."

"Learn anything else?" Monk asked.

"Very little as applies to this case."

"You didn't find out what the goggles were for?"

"Regrettably, no."

Habeas Corpus made insistent gruntings. Monk resumed his lazy rubbing of the porker's ear.

"I'd give the curl out of Habeas' tail," the homely chemist declaimed, "to know what those goggles are good for."

Big-fisted Renny looked up from his charts.

"Listen, Doc," he said, "have you the slightest idea of what is behind all of this?"

The bronze man shook his head slowly.

"That is not yet clear," he said.

AT Point Barrow, on the north Alaskan Coast, the silver dirigible settled down for its last refueling. As in Resolution, Doc learned here that Watches Bowen's plane had preceded him by a short time.

And, since it was from Point Barrow that the radiogram had been transmitted to Doc concerning the original appearance into civilization of Ool, Doc made further inquiries. In particular he contacted an old Scotch fur trader, who had harbored Ool for a time in his cabin, and who knew the North Alaskan coast as few men did.

"I understand," Doc said, "that it is considered an impossibility for Ool to have come off the ice pack, as he claimed."

"Aye, 'tis that," the rosy-cheeked old Scot replied, pleased to have the famous bronze man coming to him for information.

"Why?"

"On account of nae mon could wi'hstand the exposure," explained the trader.

Doc nodded. "I know. No food, no fuel, chunked-up ice to make hard traveling, open leads where a man might slip into the water, a wind like rawhide—it would be beyond human endurance for a man to make the trip, you think."

"Aye. 'Tis self-evident, mon. The Arctic pack lies unexplored tae this day, a dead white space on the map."

Doc nodded again. "What is your idea about it? Where do you think Ool came from?"

The old Scot shrugged gnarled shoulders. "In my life, I ha' seen strange things, but Ool be the strangest."

Doc held up the goggles. "Have you seen these?"

The old Scot's face lighted with recognition. "Ool had such things. The sun, he said, hurt his eyes. He lay in my cabin for a solid week, not venturing out. That was when first he came off the ice pack—"

"But I thought you said it was impossible for him to have come off the pack."

"Aye," the old Scot replied imperturbably, "but where else could he ha' come from?"

Doc, looking intently at the man, said nothing.

The trader met Doc's gold-flecked eyes without flinching. He said: "I know not. Certain 'tis, there be more of the devil to Ool than of mon or the heavenly speerit. At first, this Ool were not like a human being."

"What do you mean?" Doc asked.

"There were such things like this: Fire—Ool tried to catch it in his hand, as though it were a bird. When he got so's he could talk a bit, he said he had never before seen fire! Such things as that."

"Why did he leave you?"

The old Scot's face grimaced. "I drove him out at the end o' my shotgun."

"Why?"

"I was afeered a' him. One day I picked up his goggles, bein' curious. Worthless things they be. You canna see through them. But he came at me wi' sech a unholy look in his flat eyes, and his hand—the right hand, I mind 'twas—reachin' out for me somehow like a snake. It gave me the shudders. I tossed him the goggles and drove him out."

TAKING the air again, Doc headed his silver dirigible out over the sea at Point Barrow in a northerly direction. After a few hours above the desolate Arctic pack, which looked, from their great height, like a sink full of chipped ice, he turned on his radio direction finder.

A hodge-podge of noises, conventional static disturbances, came through the loudspeaker. There were buzzes and burrs and whines and crackles. But they could have been duplicated at almost any point on the earth.

Suddenly, the dirigible filled with a soft low note which throbbed and ran high up the musical scale and back again; the sound was not new static disturbance, but Doc Savage's trilling, that weird sound, so unconsciously a part of him, which he made in moments of surprise or puzzlement.

The bronze man's inordinately sensitive ears, conditioned by intensive training to catch sounds above and below the usual range considered possible for human reception, had identified a peculiar static sound coming from the finder.

To Doc's aides, the finder continued to pour out the usual din of static. But Doc, turning the loop device, gave steering directions to Johnny at the controls. Johnny swung the dirigible in a more westerly direction.

Within an hour the eerie static disturbance, which at first only Doc had heard, was audible to all. It came over the loudspeaker in a high, rhythmic thrumming, each note being throttled off in an entirely unearthly manner, only to swell again in a fashion even more unearthly.

As Johnny drove the dirigible toward the sound, the noise grew louder, filling the gondola with its strange pulsing clamor. It grew so insistent that Doc cut down the loudspeaker volume control to almost the absolute minimum.

There came a moment when Monk let out an excited bellow. Standing in the rear of the gondola, looking out behind, the pleasantly ugly chemist had been experimenting with the strange goggles, trying them on his eyes, squinting, ogling, attempting in every way possible to see through the thick lenses of obsidian blackness.

"What's eating you?" Ham clipped, startled at Monk's show of excitement.

"Down here—everybody—look!" Monk clamored without turning around.

"Look where?" Renny complained. "I don't see anything."

"Are you blind?" Monk blared. "Right below us!"

"You're crazy!" Long Tom put in. "There's nothing there but ice."

"Don't kid me at a time like this!" Monk howled. "See that pillar of fire? It must be a hundred feet high! What is it?"

"Fire! Fire on the ice?"

"Yeah! Comin' out of the ice. It's kind of weaving—not like regular flame—more like liquid fire!"

Ham laughed derisively. "A column of liquid fire a hundred feet high coming out of the ice! Nuts! There's nothing there at all—only ice and some fog."

Monk turned around angrily to face Ham in the gondola. He could not see Ham. He became conscious then, that he was wearing the black goggles. He pawed off the goggles and pointed downward.

"Right down there—look." He stared himself. His jaw fell.

"Blazes!" he ejaculated. "Gone now!"

DOC'S compelling voice broke in. "Let me have those goggles, Monk."

Monk handed them over. Doc adjusted them quickly to his eyes, looked down. His weird trilling note throbbed through the gondola. One after another, the bronze man had his aides look down through the goggles. Expressions of confused surprise and awe came from each.

"Well, I'll be a pork chop off Monk's pig!" Ham exclaimed.

Each man, when he looked through the goggles, saw precisely what Monk had seen—a tall writhing column of what was apparently liquid fire issuing from the ice. When the goggles were removed from the eyes, the column of fire disappeared.

"What is it?" Monk gasped.

"I do not know," Doc said flatly. "It certainly is not a gas flame." He continued studying the phenomenon through the black goggles. "Nose the dirigible down, Johnny. Slack speed and float in as close as you can."

"It looks like this clears up the mystery of the black goggles," Renny said excitedly. "Ool needed them to locate this place."

"I think there is more to it than that, Renny," Doc answered.

At closer range, the thing which seemed to be fire took on more detail. There seemed to be a living, liquid, white-hot core swelling out smoothly in a golden blush, tinged with flashes of opalescence-glazed yellows, purples, reds, greens, and blues. The predominating tone, however, was golden; not so much the gold of solid flame, but as of a thick fog in which every separate particle of moisture was a floating globule of gold.

At about the hundred-foot level, the writhing pillar, in a thinning golden haze, blurred into nothingness.

Johnny had nosed down to a hundred feet and drifted in as close as he dared. From the low height it was apparent that the pillar—whatever it was—issued from a rock crevice. A long, black rent in the dismal welter of pack ice was clearly identifiable as rock.

"Work the dirigible in closer," Doc directed. He adjusted the black goggles to Johnny's eyes to make the mysterious flame visible to him.

"Yeah, but Doc, we'll burn!" Johnny objected in quick dismay.

But he did as Doc suggested. Closer and closer the silver dirigible floated until, in Johnny's eyes, it was very close to the weirdly writhing flame.

With motors idling, and the dirigible's silver sides bathed in the living golden glow, Doc pointed to the sensitized thermometer visible on the outside of the gondola wall.

"Heat!" Monk squalled. "Then it is a fire!"

"It is only up to room temperature," Doc corrected. "There is no flame, as we know it."

"Enough to give a guy the jitters!" Monk grunted. "A flame a hundred feet high, making no noise, giving off no more heat than a hot-air register, and not even visible unless you're looking at it through black goggles."

Johnny lost his trepidation and sent the dirigible directly into the mysterious light which was visible only through the goggles. Nothing happened. They flew down lower, seeking to examine the cleft in the ice from which the thing came. This, it developed, was larger than had at first appeared. It was many feet wide, more than a half a mile long.

So interested were the occupants of the dirigible in examining the source of the fiery plume that the new development all but took them by surprise.

"Here!" Doc Savage said sharply, and lunged for the controls. "Let me have them!"

"What's wrong?" Johnny demanded.

Doc pointed. "Look!"

The big-worded geologist stared.

"I'll be superamalgamated!" he exploded.

A PLANE was hurtling toward them. It was a gray machine, against the leaden sky. It came on swiftly. Details became distinguishable.

"Watches Bowen," Doc decided. "It answers the description of the craft in which he came from New York."

"Holy cow!" Renny exploded. "It's gonna be tough if they're carrying much artillery."

"They will be careful not to cripple the dirigible," Doc said positively. "Remember, they have wanted this ship from the first."

"And the only way they can get it," Long Tom said, "is to cripple us."

Renny bounced his big fists together. "That's a job they won't find easy."

Doc settled the dirigible downward.

"Hey!" Johnny gulped. "You're going down into the crack that flame is comin' out of!"

But to all except Johnny, the landing process appeared to be merely an expert maneuvering job in clear air. To the gaunt archeologist, wearing the black goggles, the silver sliver carrying its freight of human lives was nesting down in a bath of fire.

As softly as a leaf falling through a golden autumn haze, the dirigible came to rest on the crevice floor.

Chapter XII
THE GOLDEN GODDESS

THE crevice made a snug shelter for the dirigible. They tied down the bag. Doc, with Long Tom's assistance, removed a few delicate parts from the silver craft's ignition system, parts necessary for the operation of the dirigible; since there were no other similar motors in the world, the removal of these key parts rendered the dirigible positively theft-proof.

Overhead, Watches Bowen's plane wheeled slowly, like a huge buzzard hung between the pale glaze of the sky and the leaden gray of the far-stretching ice pack.

"They must be waiting for us to move away from the dirigible," Monk decided.

Johnny had been busy studying the rock formation with his monocle magnifier. The wiry geologist was an expert field man as well as a theoretician. His geological experience now bore fruit.

"The configuration of this rock cleft indicates a substantial cavern opening may be expected at about that point." His lean hand indicated.

Doc agreed. "We seem to be on an uncharted island or rocky reef thrust up through the ice pack. The steady current of warm air along this crevice is of sufficient volume to indicate the presence of an underground labyrinth."

Doc's gold-flecked eyes squinted up at Watches Bowen's circling craft. Now and again the plane, wheeling above, was momentarily obscured.

Doc eyed his men. "You have your emergency packs?"

They nodded.

Monk said, "I'll put Habeas Corpus under my coat."

"The next time their plane is out of sight," Doc warned, "we will make a break. We might as well look this place over while we are here."

A plane was hurtling toward them. It was a gray

They watched tensely. The plane drifted out of sight.

Doc said: "All right!"

They made their dash. The plane sliced into view before Doc and his aides quite reached their objective. They were sighted by the flying crooks. Machine guns cut loose from above with a macabre cackle; gun sound pummeled against the sides of the rocky crevasse.

Rock chips mingled with spattering lead as Doc and his men lunged for the safety of a great overhang. They made it safely, but at the last instant a flying rock chip struck sharply against Monk's coat. Habeas Corpus was on that side. The ungainly shoat squealed in pain, flounced and fell out, landing heavily. He rolled about, squealing under the leaden hail.

MONK, from his position of safety within the cavern entrance, called frantically, and when the

machine, hard to distinguish against the leaden sky.

animal, dazed, did not respond, Monk leaped out like an anthropoid ape springing from a tree.

Bullets slashed around him. One went through his coat. He paid no heed. With the ease of an anthropoid picking up a coconut, the homely chemist swept up the pig and lunged back for the cavern mouth. He made it.

Ham groaned in pretended disappointment. "For a minute," he said, "I thought we were going to have pork chops for supper."

Monk glared, breathing heavily. "Some day, you two-bit shyster, you'll make one crack too many against this hog!"

Above them, the noisy airplane motors cut out. The sudden stillness seemed to press down like something tangible, alive. The Arctic hush, which lay interminable over the desert of ice, was broken only by the soft complaining whine of wind in struts and wires as the huge plane dipped down and leveled off.

"They're going to crash!" Ham exclaimed.

"Yeah!" Monk growled. "But they're comin' down in the cleft."

There was a cracking as the undercarriage of Watches Bowen's plane was wrenched from the fuselage by contact with up-rearing ice cakes frozen into position as solidly as though they were cement.

The plane nosed half over, poised like an off-balanced bird, then flopped back, tilting on one crumpled wing.

The door in the side of the cabin burst open. The mobsters spilled out, half leaping, half falling. All carried submachine guns.

"It's dog eat dog now," Renny rumbled, and his long puritanical face grew more mournful than ever in anticipation of the fight.

"Yeah," Monk agreed. "Notice where they landed? We gotta smear 'em to get back to our ship."

"They would not have risked landing if we had not come down first," Doc said. "They probably have been aware that we were trailing them across Canada."

Long Tom nodded. "Their radio receiving set could have picked up our communications with ground stations."

Doc whipped out his flashlight and turned it on the darker recess below the ledge.

"Hey!" Renny boomed. "That looks like that cavern Johnny was predicting!"

THAT Watches Bowen had not acted without forethought soon became evident. One of the men was carrying a wooden case. He opened this and produced a weapon resembling a shotgun. He charged the barrel with a slender rod to which was attached a cylinder resembling that on a skyrocket. He aimed at the ledge and fired.

The results were cataclysmic, for the man had shot a rifle grenade. There was a tremendous concussion. Rock fell. Frozen ice and some snow clouded up.

"Holy cow!" Renny boomed. "We'd better get back inside. They've got us in a spot!"

"We'll see how far back this goes," Doc agreed. "But wait. We'll insure that they don't entomb us in here."

In a loud voice, the bronze man now yelled at Watches Bowen and his followers, conveying the information that important parts had been removed from the dirigible.

"They won't blast the roof down on us now for fear of damaging the parts," he said.

They moved back into the cavern. It was small at first, and gave indications of playing out.

"I sure hate to leave that dirigible," Ham said anxiously.

"It is perfectly safe," Doc assured. "Since they expect to be the ones to ride back in it, they will be careful not to cripple it."

"Doc," Monk said, "let's stay here and fight it out."

"Nothing would be gained by making a stand," Doc pointed out. "They would use those grenades, if they could do so without burying us."

"O. K., Doc," Monk said, resignedly, "but I'm craving heavy action."

"You may get it," Ham reminded, "if we run into a pack of the black *things* back in here."

Ham spoke half jokingly, with no inkling that the time was close when he was to take the black *things* in anything but a joking way.

THE relatively narrow granite cleft which they had entered led into a limestone labyrinth. They produced flashlights. The caverns progressed down at a sharp angle, and widened out into rooms of awe-inspiring proportions.

It was suddenly not at all cold.

Stalactites and stalagmites looked like massive ivory columns. There were whole domes of crystalline formation which glittered like massed diamonds under the prying glare of the flashlight beams. Some of the rooms were cathedral arched, and so high that the white pencil paths of light from the hand flashes could not delineate them.

Monk craned his bull neck in rapt admiration.

"King Solomon's temple must of been like this," he said, and turned to call to Habeas Corpus, who was lagging behind. "Yeah." he continued soulfully, "this sure would be a swell setup for a harem."

"You would think of that," Ham said dryly, aware of Monk's weakness for women, singly or in numbers.

Echoes bounded back and forth between the cavern walls in a bewildering and oftentimes frightening manner, foot scufflings and voices going out into the air and being wafted back in distorted sound splashes.

Doc, in a low voice, called a halt.

"Nobody talk," he ordered.

No one did talk and no one moved; yet, disturbingly, the echoes of foot scufflings and garbled conversation did not cease. In fact, as they waited there, listening, the echoes grew alarmingly. They welled to a veritable clamor.

"I thought so," Doc said guardedly. "The echoes are not all our own."

"From the sound of them," Long Tom whispered, "Watches Bowen and his gang must have stumbled onto a shortcut. They sound close."

"They *are* close," Doc affirmed.

The bronze man conferred for a moment under his breath with Johnny on a question of geology. Although Doc, as a result of his exhaustive studies, his self-imposed mental, physical, and emotional discipline, had accumulated a store of knowledge greater in every case than that of his five aides, he nevertheless consulted frequently with them on questions involving their specialty.

He did this because he was a thorough man who preferred to check his reasonings. On the present geological question, Doc and Johnny came to quick agreement.

"Come on," Doc called out, and whipped his light ahead as he led off into a cavern which narrowed rapidly as they hurried along.

Renny, casting backward glances in the darkness, caught a glimpse of a flashlight carried by one of the pursuing gangsters.

"They are close," he rapped. "Look behind!"

THE others looked. They were not quick enough to see the white beam of the flashlight, but were quick enough to see the saffron flare which coughed from the muzzle of an automatic.

Pursued by roaring echoes, the bullet slammed down the narrow entry past the heads of Doc and his aides, making musical sounds against hanging stalactites.

"Down on the floor!" Doc ordered. "Douse the lights!"

More saffron flashes bloomed at gun tips and more bullets slammed with echoing thunder down the narrow stone corridor.

"Back up," Doc called to his men, "around the bend here! Find cover before you open with your superfirers!"

As they felt around in the dark and flopped behind protecting rocks, the saffron blobs which marked the exploding pistols of their enemies became obscured by slow angry streaks of red, as the gangsters opened up with their machine guns. Lead and flying rock chips sprayed the rock tunnel. Echoes resembled close thunder.

Loud above everything else sounded the bull-fiddle bellow of Doc's supermachine pistols, as his aides returned the fire. Pale greenish-gold flares fanned out from the heavy snouts of the strange mercy weapons. The efficient superfirers, manned expertly by Doc's men, were having an effect.

Back at the crooks' end of the rock corridor, Watches Bowen cursed savagely and gave his men word to hold up their fire until they could determine the extent of their injuries. His words were plainly audible.

Doc's men quit firing, also. Slamming echoes settled down like thunder rolling away.

The attackers counted up their losses.

"Three men knocked out by their damned mercy bullets!" Watches Bowen grated. "Find better cover, you birds—no, wait!" His voice stabbed with soft intensity.

Speech echoes of Doc and his men were wafting clearly to the attackers from down the tunnel. They were echoes of alarm.

Long Tom was talking.

"I've been back a few rods with Doc," he barked. "We examined the rock walls—and this is a dead-end tunnel!"

"You mean it don't lead nowhere?" Monk demanded loudly.

"Right!" Long Tom agreed. "The only way we can get out is the way we came in."

"And that gang has that opening blocked with machine guns!" Ham clipped.

"Holy cow!" Renny's huge voice roared. "Ain't there no way out back here at all?"

Even Doc's cautioning voice was picked up by the malicious echoes and carried back clearly to Watches' avidly listening mob.

"Do not speak so loud!" Doc warned. "They will hear us. We will have to keep them from knowing the jam we are in."

Back at the open end of the tunnel Watches Bowen became galvanized in action.

"THIS is our chance," Watches purred. "Ham-hock, you're carrying that grenade gun. We'll blow this opening shut."

The fat Negro's appreciative voice echoed back.

"Lock dem in dar foah a hundred yeahs, huh?"

"Lock 'em in, hell!" Watches whispered. "We'll close it up, then give 'em a day or two to think it over. They'll be ready to say 'uncle,' when we blast it open again."

Watches selected a crack, rupture of which

would cave in the entry. Ham-hock took careful aim.

Careful though Watches and his men had been to speak in undertones, the cavern echoes had carried their voices.

Monk's reckless voice sounded. "Let's charge 'em, Doc. I ain't cravin' to be locked in here."

"Do not be a fool, Monk," echoed Doc's chastising voice. "We could never get through in the face of half a dozen machine guns."

"We could clip some of 'em with our super-firers!" Monk pleaded desperately.

"What good would that do," Doc reasoned logically. "In the end, they'd wipe us all out."

"What are we gonna do then?" Renny bawled.

"Do nothing. We will stay here and take our chances with the explosion. It is the only thing we *can* do."

Watches Bowen's malignant voice crashed loud in the tunnel. He was not speaking to his men this time. He was speaking to Doc.

"This is the payoff!" he yelled. "Savage, you can come out, or stay there! Take your choice!"

Doc made no reply.

A thundering detonation came as Ham-hock used the grenade gun. There was a blaze of flame. Tunnel ceiling came down. The walls heaved.

All the way to the far back end of the tunnel the rock crashed down, choking the passage so completely that an object so small as a rat could not have escaped crushing destruction. The cataclysm was far greater than Watches Bowen had expected.

Watches Bowen and his men were thrown off their feet by the terrific forces of the explosion. Sound throbs assailed their ears with a force almost strong enough to crack their eardrums. White limestone dust billowed.

The sound salvos wafted away finally. Dust settled. The crooks' flashlights streamed over the piled rock wreckage.

"Choked from floor to roof," Watches shrieked. "Those dirigible parts—they're buried!"

Ool spoke up quietly, "We are dumb fools, if, given sufficient time, we cannot fashion new parts. But it would be much better if we had the black goggles."

"We'll get by," Watches muttered. "Let's get away from this dust. We might as well go in it, Ool?"

"Yes," Ool said. "We will go in now."

GUIDED by Ool, Watches and his men, carrying the three men made temporarily unconscious by the mercy slugs, turned into another of the caverns and stumbled hastily along the rock-strewn floor. Their flashlights cut fantastic white swaths in the Stygian gloom.

Ool was following certain trail marks, vague scratches, a pile of rocks here and there. His manner, his sureness, indicated he himself had placed the guiding marks.

The labyrinthian chambers were empty, dead, devoid of all life or living matter. Everywhere, under the flashlight glare, the walls, floor and roof showed coldly with a kind of leaden glaze.

"Dis heah place give a man creeps," Ham-hock Piney asserted, rolling his eyes uneasily. "Dat's accordin' to any man's figurin'!"

"These particular caverns," Ool said enigmatically, "are known as the Land of the Lost. No man penetrates them far and comes out alive."

"But yo'-all done dat very t'ing," Ham-hock insinuated plaintively.

"I did," Ool agreed. "I was the first to do so."

The crook party continued onward for hours.

SUDDENLY, Ool paused in mid-stride. He stood looking down. Watches Bowen, coming close behind, bumped into him before he could stop.

"What's the matter?" the crook leader asked.

Ool's long arm pointed to the floor.

Watches looked, then cursed nervously. The others crowded about, staring.

Clearly defined in white rock dust on the floor were footprints. Small footprints, delicately formed. The maker of the prints had apparently been wearing skin-tight moccasins. The indentations showed a firmly modeled heel, high arch, and five toes as uncramped and rounded as a child's. But the mature spacing of the footprints as they led off into one of the side chambers, revealed clearly they were not the prints of a child.

"What could Sona be doing here?" The white-faced man's flat voice actually carried a modicum of emotion.

"Sona?" Watches questioned.

Ool indicated barely discernible webbed markings in the footprints.

"It is Sona," he stated positively. "She, and she only, is privileged to wear footgear with the imperial design in the weaving."

"Who in the hell is Sona?" Watches wanted to know.

Ool, flashing his light in the direction of the disappearing footprints, did not answer. Instead, he said, "She passed a few minutes ago."

His arm waved out to call attention ahead, to a fine haze of rock dust which hung in the air with a crystalline glitter.

"Yes, she was here very recently. Come. We will get her."

He turned in the direction taken by the footprints.

He loped along in an ungainly manner. The others followed closely.

It was a mere matter of minutes before they sighted their quarry—a girl.

She ran at their approach. She had long flowing hair, gold in hue, and she was clothed in some sort of gossamery stuff which clung close, moulding lithesome curves as she ran. She wore goggles with enormously thick lenses.

At Watches' direction, Honey Hamilton chopped a few machine gun bullets over the girl's head. The caverns had narrowed down at this place; the gun thunder was terrific.

The girl did not stop, and it was evident that bullets and gun thunder were something strange in her experience.

"Outrun her!" Watches rapped.

Eventually, they did that. They seized her, held her.

Ool approached with his deadly right hand fluttering in butterflylike motion. The girl recoiled. It was evident that the butterfly gesture was not new to her.

Ool said something to the girl in an unintelligible gibberish. The goggles which she wore were similar to the ones which Ool had possessed. Their grotesqueness contrasted oddly with the softly exquisite curve of her cheeks, with her natural blond complexion.

JOHNNY

Ool snatched the goggles from her eyes with such ferocity that he left a red scratch on her smooth cheek.

Then Ool turned to Watches. "To have run across her is such luck as I could never have hoped for," he said.

"It's as clear as Manhattan mud to me," Watches growled. "Who the hell is she?"

"She is—Sona," Ool said. "In your so-called civilization, she would be called Princess Sona."

The gang chief's mind began to work along his conventionally lawless pattern.

"Say!" he exploded. "Somebody oughta—"

"Exactly!" Ool interrupted. "We will hold her hostage to guarantee our own safety, and to bargain for that which we want."

"Sure," Watches emphasized, tugging at the gold chain which sprawled across his vest. "That which may make you boss of the U. S. A., in a manner of speakin'."

Ool turned to Sona with a harsh order.

Then suddenly a vast roaring filled the tunnel with so terrific a noise as to make past sounds seem, in comparison, a feeble murmur.

Watches cursed.

"An attack from some of your blasted countrymen, Ool!" he rasped.

But Ham-hock Piney had another idea.

"Dat's Doc Savage's spooks a-shootin'!" he wailed.

Chapter XIII
FLASHLIGHT TERROR

HAM-HOCK PINEY was correct, but only partially so. The bludgeoning sound echoes could be identified as they crashed closer.

They were the hooting sounds of Doc Savage's supermachine pistols.

"Dat Doc Savage dead!" screamed Ham-hock. "Dey got to be his ghosts firing dem hoot guns!"

As the crooks doused their lights and scattered, leveling automatics and machine guns in confused haste, one of them dropped his gun and crumpled to the ground, a victim of one of the machine pistol mercy slugs.

Ham-hock stooped and dragged the unconscious man around a right angle turn into a blind-end tunnel. The other crooks made a desperate stand. Their thundering guns stabbed wild flame spurts.

The attack, coming unexpectedly and from such an unexplainable source, had disorganized them and they did not even realize for several moments that their guns were the only ones roaring; that, after the first bullfiddle fusillade, the superfirers of Doc Savage and his men had stopped firing.

Then, swooping from out of the darkness, a giant of bronze, by this time a familiar phenomenon to Watches Bowen, invaded the cavern. Doc's aides were close behind. Frenzied yells mixed with gunfire. Fist blows thudded. The last flashlight went out. Darkness was intense.

"Don't shoot!" Watches screamed to his men. "You'll kill each other!"

The gang chief's hand, wielding his leaded watch by the end of its stout chain, chopped down, swinging the deadly weapon against a human bulk which thrust up close against him in the dark.

"Hey, don't do dat to me," bleated Ham-hock's aggrieved voice.

Ool, throughout the fighting had remained silent, holding onto Sona with one hand, and with the other trying to adjust her goggles to his eyes. Suddenly a flashlight blazed not six inches from his face. Before his right arm could moccasin out, the light disappeared and a metallic fist crashed into his face, knocking him down.

He lurched to his feet again and pawed frenziedly for the girl, Sona. She was gone.

Doc Savage had developed a faculty of judging distance almost to the inch. As the last of the flashlights had blacked out, Doc had fixed Ool's position in his mind. Flattened close against the side wall of the tunnel, the bronze man had worked forward.

Then he battered his way through Watches' men. When he flashed his light, he was close upon Ool. His fist blow had followed. At the same instant his other arm streaked out to catch the girl around the waist.

HOLDING her firmly, Doc leaped to one side in the dark and deposited the girl in a position of safety behind a pile of rock fragments which in some past age had fallen from the roof.

By giving a sibilant signal in the Mayan tongue, Doc indicated to his men that the girl was safe. His aides responded by unleashing new blasts from their superfirers.

This new attack demoralized Watches Bowen's crew completely. They broke and ran, slamming against each other in the dark. They got around the right-angle turn into the blind-end tunnel. Here, Watches and Ool, screaming orders, managed to rally them.

Doc directed a cessation of fire. Quiet settled down except for the wrangling of Watches Bowen's mobsters as the gang chief verbally beat them into line. A horrified silence followed.

Then a new voice sounded. It was Monk's hoarse bellow.

"So long, Bowen!" he taunted. "I'll tell 'em you died brave! We got you right where we want you now!"

Desperate as was their situation, Ham-hock Piney could not throttle a natural curiosity.

"How yo'-all done come to life?" he shouted. "We done dynamite a million tons of rock on yo'-all!"

"You never dynamited any rock on us!" Monk bellowed down the entry.

"We did so!" the Negro yelled back.

Monk's laughter rolled down the black passageway.

"That wasn't a dead-end passage you blew down," he advised. "We went out through the back of that tunnel. All our talk took place a block away. You can't tell about voices in this place."

"All right, Monk," Doc called tolerantly. "Let's get stationed. We have these plotters bottled up. Our next job is to smoke them out."

Doc flashed on his light and wandered the white beam quickly about, seeking good vantage points for his men to crouch behind in a supermachine pistol bombardment of the dead-end tunnel.

There was no danger of the light attracting enemy bullets, since Watches Bowen's men were around an angle. Doc's aides added to the single searching beam by switching their own lights on. Monk curiously turned his beam on Doc. What Monk saw in the glare caused him to drop Habeas Corpus from under his arms and stare. He sighed.

"I ask you," he said at large, "ain't it perfect?"

He was referring to the picture which the bronze giant made, standing beside the golden-haired girl Sona—she whom Ool had called princess. The girl clung to Doc with the instinctive trust of a child.

"Do you," Doc asked, "want to get us shot at?"

The homely chemist grinned and removed the light from them. Doc stepped to one side to examine the tunnel opening.

"Who is she?" Monk called after him.

"She has not offered that information," Doc replied. "She responds to none of the languages I have spoken with her. Nor can I understand a word of hers."

Monk suggested, "As soon as you find how to talk to her, put in a good word for me, will you?"

From somewhere in the darkness, Ham snorted loudly.

Monk said angrily, "What'd you mean by that hoot?"

THE two growled at each other, warming up for a battle which never extended beyond the verbal stage, no matter what the provocation.

Monk came over and thrust this face close to Ham's. Then, suddenly, Monk's flashlight was knocked from his hand. The knocking was done with deftness. It went out from the impact.

"You lowlife!" Monk gritted at Ham. "Pick up my flashlight."

"Pick it up yourself," Ham retorted. "You dropped it."

"You're a liar!" Monk bellowed. "You knocked it out of my hand!"

"Who's a liar, you hairy—" Ham broke off as his own flashlight was knocked to the ground and extinguished.

"You bush-ape," he began again, with new vehemence, "pick up *my* flashlight!"

"Pick it up yourself!" Monk blustered. "You dropped it."

"Dropped it nothing! You knocked it out of my hand!"

"Hey, one of us is nuts!" Monk said.

Both were silent. Ham's grip tightened spasmodically on his sword cane. Monk clawed absently at his bristling red hair.

Then the cavern resounded with Renny's great bellow.

"Something got my flashlight!" he howled.

The cavern was now absolutely dark.

Doc had felt the golden-haired girl, Sona, leave his side. She went suddenly, as if torn away by a terrific force. Doc reached out for her in the blackness. His metallic hands closed only on air. He leaped to one side, then the other, groping furiously. He found no trace of the girl.

He paused to pull out an emergency flashlight. But it was smashed from his hand by a terrific blow. Its mechanism was shattered.

Doc called a sharp warning to his men.

"Hold onto your machine pistols," he rapped. "Do not shoot until we get light. You might hit each other."

"It's the *things!*" Ham yelled shrilly. "What in the devil are they?"

"We'd better get together," Doc advised. "Come over here, all of you!"

The bronze man's aides never reached him. There, in the cavern of unknown horror, something soft and slimy enveloped them, an odious material at which they tore helplessly, accomplishing nothing by their most desperate efforts. They could not use the machine pistols.

The material, whatever it was, pressed closer and closer to their faces with a softly insidious force which burned their eyes, seared their throats, and imparted weakness to their limbs.

One by one, they fell to the floor of the cavern, tumbling down and squirming grotesquely, to grow weaker and weaker and eventually became slack.

Doc Savage himself did not escape the fantastic terror, although the bronze man did last longer than the others. He held his breath for minutes in an attempt to escape the noxious substance which, he believed, exerted its effect by suffocation, and, during those minutes he rammed about, straining his cabled muscles to their utmost capacity, seeking to free himself from the slimy encompass. But the material molded about him, hemming in his movements and, in the end, utterly restraining them.

He had to breathe finally. And when he did, he crumpled to the floor, as completely overcome as the others.

Chapter XIV
BLACK THINGS

DOC SAVAGE and his five aides, reviving, found themselves lying on a smooth, hard floor in utter darkness. Doc, first to recover, called the roll of his men, finding them all to be with him, with no one seriously damaged.

"*Ugh!*" gasped the fastidious Ham. "When I think of that slimy stuff—"

"Save it," Monk growled. "We know all about it. Boy, I'd trade Habeas' left ear for some good daylight."

"Where do you figure we are, Doc?" Ham questioned.

"Judging from the pressure against my drums, and from the change in the temperature, we are a great deal farther down in the earth than when we were captured."

"We're not even tied," Long Tom remarked, hope in his voice.

"That is not necessarily a good sign," Doc reminded.

"Why not?"

"It probably means that whoever or whatever is responsible for bringing us here considers escape so impossible that binding us would be a needless precaution."

"They frisked our clothes," Renny rumbled. "My pockets are as bare as the Arctic ice pack."

"And our machine pistols are gone," Renny clipped.

"Did they get the goggles, too, Doc?" Ham asked.

"Yes," Doc said thoughtfully.

"I wonder what happened to Watches Bowen?" Renny rumbled.

"Hey!" Monk howled suddenly. "Where you suppose my pig is?" He pursed his lips and whistled, then called: "Habeas! Habeas!"

There was a squeal and a pattering rush in the darkness, and the pet pig, answering Monk's call, rammed against his legs. Monk was sitting up on the floor. The pig climbed over him like an excited terrier. Then the pig romped in the darkness, his sensitive snout feeling out the others of the party.

"Stay away from me, hog!" Ham warned in a positive manner. "The only way I'd welcome you is on a platter with an apple in your mouth. And brown gravy over you, and maybe mashed potatoes."

Doc had been feeling over the floor. Now he stood up, groped out, contacted a wall and started feeling along it.

"We are in an artificially constructed room," he decided aloud. "The floor and walls are tiled. And not a bad job. The surface is very level."

Ham, feeling a light jar against his back, as if Habeas Corpus had touched him, struck out behind him. He hit nothing, but there was a squealing sound.

"Ham! You hurting my pig?" Monk yelled ominously.

"No, but I will if I get hold of him!" Ham promised enthusiastically.

Ham, sitting in the dark, next felt a cold, wet contact against the back of his neck, the kind of touch that the pig's inquisitive snout might have made.

Ham struck out again, felt nothing, but as

before the quick action of his hand evoked from out of the darkness a strange, small squeal.

"Monk!" the fastidious lawyer rapped angrily. "Get your hog away from me!"

"Nuts!" Monk called inelegantly. "Habeas is over here."

SOMETHING tweaked Monk's ear. He slapped at what he thought to be Ham's offending fingers; his slapping hand sliced empty air, then, suddenly, Habeas was lifted away.

Monk reached for his pet; his hand encountered nothing, but he could hear the pig's frantic squealing. Monk pushed his simian bulk up from the floor and lunged forward in the darkness, groping. The pig's squeals sounded apparently at his fingertips, as though someone held the animal shoulder-high.

"Ham!" Monk grated. "Dang your soul! Put that pig down!"

Stumbling about, Monk fell over Ham who barked wrathfully at him.

"Gimme my pig!" Monk thundered in Ham's ear.

Ham jerked away. "I haven't got your pig! I don't want your pig! I hate your pig! Can you get that through your dumb skull?"

"Yeah," Monk said in a voice suddenly gone very small, "I think I get it. Ham—you other guys—" He did not finish.

"Elucidate specifically—" Johnny began, then dropped his big words. "Which one of you just now grabbed my monocle? I call that carrying a joke too far."

"Johnny," Monk questioned, in a voice ominously calm, "how could anybody *see* to take it?"

"I'll be superamalgamated!" Johnny exploded. "It's the *things!*"

Some distance away in the jet blackness, Habeas Corpus commenced squealing again.

"They took my pig!" Monk bellowed, his voice welling up.

"Something tried to yank a ring off my finger!" Ham shouted. There was the sound of his furious groping. "I can't get hold of anything!"

Suddenly bedlam broke out among Doc's men. From all sides their clothing was plucked as though by tiny pinchers, and tiny, hammerlike blows rained on their faces and bodies. New sounds broke through the blackness, strange, unintelligible sounds—squeaks, hushed whistlings, harsh clackings.

Doc's men fought, shouting, groping and clawing. Each time they collided or got their hands on a moving object, it turned out to be one of their own number.

"If I could only hit something," big-fisted Renny boomed.

Monk, hearing renewed squealing, clearly recognizable as coming from Habeas Corpus, appointed himself a one-man rescue party and plunged forward. With his second step he rammed solidly against the wall. A shock sent him back to the floor, stunned.

"Doc!" he called.

"He was over here, the last I knew," Long Tom jerked out. "Ouch!"

The thin electrical genius had been probed sharply by an invisible bedeviler.

"TAKE it easy!" the bronze man's voice was a welcome sound.

"They're like air!" Renny roared. "You can't hit 'em. You can poke your fist clear through 'em, and you can't even feel 'em!"

"Utterly denuded of tangibility!" Johnny concurred.

"I doubt it," Doc answered. "More likely they are creatures with strong muscle reflexes. They can quickly dodge out of our way."

"But how can they see?" Ham demanded. "This darkness is absolute."

"It is a puzzle," Doc said.

From out of the terror-taut darkness the protesting squeal of Monk's pig sounded again.

"They're devilin' Habeas!" Monk raved.

"Maybe," Ham said, sarcastically, "they're human, after all. I've had the same itch for a long time."

Doc's voice began issuing crisp orders. "Over here with me, everybody! There is a corner here. It marks one end of a long, narrow room."

Doc's aides came jostling toward him in the darkness.

"String out," the bronze man directed. "You will be close enough together that you can touch hands on either side."

They lined up at the end of the room with their backs against the wall.

"All right—now forward, slowly," Doc commanded. "I will keep talking. Keep pace with my voice and with each other. Bend low. Keep sweeping your fists to each side. *Do not let anything get behind you!*"

Under Doc's guidance they started grimly forward, a human broom that started at one end of the dark room and swept forward. Just as it is the function of a broom to keep all debris in front of it, so this human broom strove to push ahead of it the mysterious inhabitants of the darkness.

Forward they moved, slowly, fists swinging fast. Nothing opposed their progress; it was as if the weird bedevilers were falling silently back before them, impressed by the cooperative attack.

But suddenly there was a *thup* of a fist against some substance.

"They're real!" Renny boomed. "I hit one!"

"Good!" Doc said. "Pick up whatever you hit and keep moving ahead."

"There's nothing to pick up," Renny complained. "But I sure slugged something."

Thup! Thup! Johnny and Long Tom connected simultaneously with solid objects.

"Grab hold of anything you can!" Doc directed.

Then his own metallic fist hit a soft, yielding object. He grasped with lightning speed, but found nothing to pick up.

"They are fast," he said grimly. "Try to catch one. Concentrate on forcing them back."

Ham's sweeping fist was the next to find a target.

"Hey!" he called excitedly. "I got hold of this one!"

"Stand in your places!" Doc ordered. "Do not let anything pass us! Can you handle it alone, Ham?"

"I—think so! Ouch, it bites!"

There were brief and furious struggle sounds. Then came taut silence.

Ham's disgusted voice said, "It's that damn pig!"

Then they were assailed with a furious battering.

From out of the dark, high and low the blows drove. All in the advancing line were subjected to the same violent treatment.

"Hold your positions!" Doc's voice called sternly. "Keep driving. We are nearly at the end of the room."

THEY fought stubbornly on, pummeling, kicking, sometimes butting with their heads. Not once did their fingers clutch on an assailant.

But all at once the darkness emptied before them. They bumped heavily against a wall.

There was a loud grating sound.

"A door!" Doc rapped. "Here! They got out and are trying to close it!"

"Wonder where they got wood down here for a door?" Renny muttered, doors being one of the heavy-fisted engineer's interests in life, since it was his boast that one did not exist that he could not break down with his fists.

"It is not wood." Doc informed. "It is some unfamiliar substance, apparently of artificial composition."

They managed to force the door open and get through. Once outside the room, they were not, for a time, molested. They felt their way forward carefully in the darkness, and their feet found well-formed steps, while exploring hands located walls which were intricately ornamented in places, and perforated by man-size openings shaped in accurate geometric designs.

They found other geometric objects which rested solidly on the floor—evidently articles of furniture, and all in the shape of circles, oblongs, squares, and triangles.

The articles were strongly made, but out of extremely light materials. Monk, lumbering around, knocked over one object that seemed as big as a piano. It did not break, and he righted it with one hand.

"What a life!" he groaned.

Doc Savage said, "One peculiar feature is that everything seems to be constructed of the same unfamiliar substance as that door. If these people—or *things*—have learned the art of synthesizing building materials, we are pitted against no mean intellects."

"What have they got down here to make anything out of?" Ham wondered.

Doc pushed at a triangular-shaped panel which he encountered. It was a ponderous door, but it opened readily. A dank, near-suffocating smell came through, engulfing them.

Doc slammed the door. He hesitated. Then he opened the door again, stepped through and called his aides.

"Use your hands," he told them. "I think you will find answers to several puzzles."

They explored, and their hands came in contact with a satiny object—smooth, curved, cool to the touch, and soft.

"Now do you recognize the odor?" Doc questioned.

"Mushrooms!" Monk exploded.

"Cultivated fungi of a gigantic and unknown variety," Johnny seconded. "I'll be superamalgamated!"

"I guess this must be what the—the *things* eat," Long Tom commented.

Doc said, "The fungi may be the basis for the lightweight composition material out of which everything here seems to be constructed."

AS they turned to go back to the door, something slapped their faces wetly, and they recoiled; then their heads were enveloped in a soft, slimy grip.

"Throw it off before it gets a firm hold!" Doc shouted. "And hold your breaths! I think this is the same thing which got the best of us the other time."

Doc rammed forward to the door. The door was closed. All the bronze man's prodigious strength could not bulge it. Renny came lunging alongside in the dark, but the combined battering of their four fists evoked only sodden echoes.

The insidious stuff which wrapped their heads pressed softly tighter. They tore at it frenziedly. Then, from all sides, Doc and his aides were assailed by battering blows.

Clawing at the unseen enemy, they could find nothing to seize except the slimy horror. Their enemies were as elusive as they had been in the long prison room.

Reacting to a sharp blow against his face, Doc finally grabbed something. His great hand clutched a moving object. His cabled fingers closed down with the precision of a steel trap.

His fingers got it. A small, hard article of peculiar shape. Doc's inordinately developed sense of touch made him instantly aware of what he had snatched from the dark.

A pair of goggles with amazingly thick lenses.

Backing up, pawing at the mysterious substance which sought to envelop his head, Doc fitted the goggles to his eyes.

Instantly, to his gaze, the air became filled with a weird, golden yellow haze. The blackness vanished! In its place there was the fantastic golden aura, shot through and through with a faint opalescence.

After the first moment or two, Doc began to identify objects in the uncanny light. He saw the ghost-stuff which his aides were fighting. He recognized it for what it was—a gigantic species of the fungus growth which dangles like soft moss from decaying overhead timbers in coal mines. This fungus, Doc knew, thrives on a total absence of light.

This particular growth, revealed to Doc through the black goggles, had obviously been cultivated in the exotic cavern, and had attained gigantic proportions, reaching tensile strength.

Doc's aides were dimly revealed to him through the golden haze. They were black forms, seen through the goggles. They were engaged in a terrific grapple with the enveloping fungus.

Doc leaped to aid them, but from all sides shapeless forms converged toward him. In the uncanny yellow light, the figures stood out in vague black. The black *things!*

The black creatures were about the height of men. Some of them clutched long poles with which they were jabbing the noxious fungus into the faces of Doc's men. Others moved as free agents. Rushing Doc, they pummeled him from all sides.

The bronze man's scientific paraphernalia had been taken from him at the time of his first capture; he had no means of defense now, except his superb fists, and these he used with all the effect possible, causing the black assailants to fall in rows under the flailing of his fists. But always, new rows took their places.

From front, back, and from the sides they hurled upon him, and in the end, the bronze man fell. The fantastic attackers piled over his prone body like ants onto a stricken beetle.

Chapter XV
GOLDEN BLACKNESS

THE sound of a compelling voice of pleasing musical quality caused the black assailants to stop their attack. The voice sounded again, apparently issuing an order, and the foes withdrew from Doc, standing back around him in a thick ring. Then, at another order from the haunting voice, the cotton fungus was removed.

Doc's five men each felt deft fingers about their eyes; when the fingers were removed, they discovered they had each been equipped with strange goggles.

They were slower than Doc had been in accustoming their eyes to the weird golden light, but gradually, through the all-pervading golden shimmer, they were able to make out hazy outlines in black.

"You see what I see?" Monk gasped.

Doc Savage's voice sounded: "Focus your eyes steadily on the object. They will soon take on detail."

They did this, and the black monsters stood out as individuals.

"They're men!" Renny boomed.

"Keep looking," Doc advised. "You'll develop a color sense."

"Sure," Long Tom gasped. "I'm getting it. I can see the mushrooms. They look pinkish."

"Look behind you," Doc requested.

They turned their goggled eyes. There, standing a pace in advance of the black monsters, was the girl, the Princess Sona.

She stood there like a fairy-book figure seen through a golden autumn haze. The curves of her youthful body were alluring, revealed by a clinging robe. Her golden hair, silken heaps of it, hung down to her waist and seemed a part of her diaphanous garb.

Her lips were perfect, her features exquisitely chiseled. Her appearance was marred only by the presence of a pair of the grotesque goggles.

In pardonable feminine vanity she removed the goggles for a moment while she flicked imaginary dust from their thick lenses. The effect to the battery of admiring masculine eyes was annihilating.

"Holy cow!" Renny breathed.

"I'll be superamalgamated!" Johnny intoned.

"I'm in love," Monk advised.

Doc Savage's calmly analytical words brought them back to earth.

"You are witnessing an amazing phenomenon," he expounded. "You are seeing where there is no light, as we know light. Air particles have apparently been treated in a way to make them luminous when viewed through the black-lensed spectacles. Objects, which first appeared black to our unadjusted vision, now stand out in something near natural colors, tempered slightly by the effect of the golden haze."

Monk said dreamily, "It's like when the sun is slanting rays over the earth in the autumn. You know, just before twilight, how it is, with the sun's rays filtering through the trees in a kind of soft golden blush—"

"What are you doing?" Ham cut in sourly. "Waxing poetical?"

"Nuts to you, you shyster," Monk suggested.

LONG TOM

DOC SAVAGE was not affected by the charms of the girl. But the bronze man, in his inflexible resolve to spend his life helping those who needed help, punishing those who deserved punishing, had made bitter enemies, unscrupulous foes who would stop at nothing to end his career.

The bronze man was able to care for himself, but if adversaries struck at him through someone he loved, his hands would be tied, and hence he had steeled himself against thought of attachment with one of the opposite sex.

"Can you talk to them, Doc?" Renny asked.

"I'll try," Doc said.

As a linguist, the bronze man was probably unsurpassed. He now spoke rapidly, using different languages. But to every tongue he articulated the girl only stared, smiling, and replied in soft tremulous tones, as stirring to the senses as violin music—and as analytically unintelligible.

She came forward finally and took the bronze man by the hand, indicating that he and his aides were to accompany her. She then led the way through the ponderous triangular door—and her followers, now revealed clearly as goggled men, closed in behind.

Immediately outside the door two goggled men, apparently guards, made gestures—their right hands drifted up from their sides with an eerie movement, like the flutterings of crippled butterflies.

At a sharp word from Sona, the hands subsided.

"Get that!" Johnny said excitedly.

"Ool had that habit!" Ham gasped.

Monk came close to the two whose hands moved so peculiarly.

"These even look like Ool," he decided aloud. "Not so shriveled up and flat-eyed, maybe."

He scanned the faces of the other male members of the escort. "These others don't look so bad."

"This seems to solve the identity mystery of Ool," Doc said. "He came from this underground world. But why he returned and brought Watches Bowen with him is still something we do not know."

Long Tom took a deep breath which expanded his deceptively hollow chest to an amazing extent. "I'm sure glad to get out of that mushroom house and get some fresh air."

"Judging from the way the place is guarded," Doc offered, "we were probably correct in assuming that the mushrooms are of vast importance to both the economic and physical life of these people."

"I wonder what they eat?" Monk pondered.

"We can try to find out," the bronze man said.

IN the spacious outer room, Doc made motions indicating hunger to which the girl, Sona, gave understanding smiles and nods, and clapped her hands sharply. Then she motioned Doc and his aides to be seated.

They reclined on geometric-shaped, padded divans, not uncomfortable, they discovered, with a yielding fiber remindful of sponge rubber.

Monk's small eyes popped when he saw the array of dishes set before him, an amazing assortment, artistically prepared. The food was as tasty as attractive.

All ate lustily. But Monk, in particular, gorged himself.

"I don't know what I'm eating," he said, "but I can take more of the same for supper."

Doc waited until Monk had finished, then he said, "You were eating only one thing, Monk."

"Yeah? What?"

"Mushrooms."

"Holy cow!" Renny grunted.

"They have devised ways of disguising appearance and flavor in order to avoid monotony, I presume," Johnny commented.

"But how can you live on mushrooms alone?" Monk demanded.

"Undoubtedly these people have had to build up a unique economy," Doc suggested. "Probably they have plants other than mushrooms, but of a kindred nature. Chemicals from these and from natural deposits, perhaps, furnish fertilizer for their specialized culture. Since these people are living, and with rather astonishing vitality, it is safe to assume they are able to extract from their surroundings all the elements necessary to sustain life."

"This air smells funny," Renny added.

"I think we will find out they manufacture, or at least purify their air, too, possibly out of oxygen extracted from water."

Monk blinked. "These birds are not dumb. They seem to take things which we can accomplish only as laboratory experiments, and employ them in everyday use."

The girl, Sona, had waited patiently, but now she came close, plucked at Doc's sleeve and led the way out of that cavernous room.

Outside, Doc's men stood and stared. Doc

... between smoothly-rearing walls, along a lane spotless and clean, Sona guided them.

himself gazed intently. On all sides, bathed in the soft golden haze, smooth walls towered. They were white, and shimmered in the golden atmosphere. Just as inside the room they had left, everything was laid out in strict geometrical conformity—here straight lines and broad sweeping curves were beautiful in their gaunt simplicity.

"It—it's plenty modernistic!" Monk stammered.

"The most striking example of functional architecture I have ever seen," Renny, the civil engineer, said in admiration.

Doc said, "They had to build within the limited confines of this underground cavern. Also, being cramped as to quantity of building materials, they have abandoned all frills and false fronts. In every instance, they have used the least amount of material possible for the purpose."

AS they stood there, they became aware of a faint, steady clicking sound. It was very regular.

"What's that noise I keep hearing?" Long Tom questioned.

Monk looked around, puzzled. "Yeah, I been noticing that. It sounds like a big clock ticking."

"The kind of a noise you wouldn't notice after you got used to it," Renny offered.

They were quiet for a time, listening to the sound which tremored in the golden haze with a muffled cadence like the beating of a slow pulse.

Then, between smoothly-rearing walls, along a lane spotless and clean, Sona guided them.

They began to see the living apartments of the weird metropolis. These towered through the golden air to the dome of the arched cavern, each separate apartment set back from the one below, in the fashion of skyscrapers. The quarters looked as efficient as an electrical switchboard in a dynamo room.

Monk pointed out a many-windowed structure, obviously a manufacturing plant of some type, built over a rushing stream.

"What's that?" he asked. "Looks like a modernistic fish design over the door."

"It is," Doc said dryly. "Here, probably, they process fish taken from the river. They evidently have something besides mushrooms."

Long Tom also pointed. "That building over there with what appear to be modernistic mushrooms on it, must be the fungus processing plant."

"Some factories!" Renny boomed in appreciation. "No smoke, no dust, no smell!"

"There is no waste anywhere, apparently," Doc commented. "Factories as efficient and scientific as a technocrat's dream."

They moved on and their group was joined by more goggled figures who dribbled in from all sides, attracted by the amazing spectacle of men

from another world. Women, too, dressed in robes only slightly less lustrous and diaphanous than Sona's, joined the throng.

Long Tom called attention to a set of structures built in a large open court. These he inferred to be government buildings. The structures were as rigidly functional in design as the others.

The most spacious structure of all was one in the heart of the metropolis, and which seemed to contain scientific laboratories, and possibly housed machinery for processing air for breathing and illuminating purposes. At least, the air was fresher, brighter near here. It was a high, circular building, topped with a complicated array of weirdly curved pipes and conduits. This was called in the local language, they learned later, the equivalent of "Central Mechanical Plant."

"Hey," Monk called out, "that pulse beat that keeps ringing in our ears—doesn't it sound louder here?"

"Yes," Doc answered, "that is undoubtedly the source of the noise."

They stood listening. Like the muffled beatings of a giant heart, the sound permeated the golden air.

Doc decided, "The noise must be in some way incidental to the manufacture of the luminous air. The sound might truly be called the heartbeat of the metropolis."

Without warning, yells ripped out; a loud, malignant clatter burst on the air. Echoes rebounded fearfully under the vast cavern dome.

"Hey," Monk shouted, "that ain't no heart beat!"

"Machine guns!" Ham ejaculated.

Sona recoiled close to Doc Savage in quick dread of the unaccustomed noise. Her escort, their strange, loose garments fluttering, commenced milling about in panic.

"Sounds like an attack on the Central Mechanical Plant," Doc said quickly.

Gently and firmly, Doc removed himself from Sona's vicinity, then made signs to the milling underground men that they should surround her with a protective guard.

"Come on!" He called to his five aides.

Chapter XVI
COLD LIGHT

AT the Central Mechanical Plant, machine gun bullets mauled the smooth, rounded surface of the walls, making a flat drumming noise. The gunners were bunched—and working toward the structure, endeavored to get to the big doors.

The latter had closed at the first outburst of firing. The doors were enormous, clumsy appearing, but they had operated smoothly.

Doc Savage caught sight of the gunners.

"Watches Bowen and his gang!" he said grimly.

In front of the Central Mechanical Plant, perhaps half a dozen limp bodies were sprawled—cavern men who had no doubt discovered Watches Bowen and his gang approaching the plant, and had given an alarm that had cost them their lives.

These slain cavern men were without their goggles.

Doc Savage veered to one side, toward what was apparently a storehouse for a type of pressed fibre tile. The tiles were in squares measuring some six inches across and an inch thick. The bronze man picked up several of these and tossed them to his aides.

"Hold them as you would guns!" he ordered. "This yellow light is tricky. We may fool them into thinking we have our machine pistols."

The ruse was more successful than they had expected. Watches Bowen and his men, already unnerved by the failure of what must have been intended as a surprise attack, saw Doc and his five approaching.

"Dey got dem hoot guns!" Ham-hock Piney bawled.

Yelling loudly, Watches ordered a retreat into one of the nearby tall habitation buildings. There was much uproar and more shooting inside, but soon Watches and his gang appeared on top of the structure.

From the roof, they could direct an uninterrupted stream of machine gun slugs at the Central Mechanical Plant and at the same time be immune to attack from above.

Machine gun lead drove Doc and his party to shelter; more bullets hammered at the walls of the Mechanical Plant, making a patter like the insistent chatter of hail.

"The slugs don't seem to be penetrating the Plant walls!" Long Tom shouted as they ran along, keeping undercover and heading for the circular plant itself.

They were running alone, the inhabitants of the vast underground domain of weird yellow light having sought cover because of the uproar. There were, it was later ascertained, strong, buried chambers to which the populace fled on the rare occasions when there were roof cave-ins—although the latter had become rare through the last few centuries, due to the strengthening, by scientific means, of the populated portions of the subterranean labyrinth.

"What is their idea of the attack on that Mechanical Plant?" Monk pondered aloud.

"Some scheme of Watches Bowen," Renny rumbled. "Guess they must've got goggles through Ool."

They were fired at by the machine gunners. The distance was too great for effective shooting. A few moments later Doc Savage, in the fantastic golden light, issued orders.

"We'll try this," he said quietly. "You five men endeavor to gain entrance through the rear door of the Mechanical Plant and organize those inside into an emergency defense unit."

Monk exploded. "But we can't talk their lingo!"

"Make signs," Doc said. "They are adept at understanding gestures."

"What you gonna do, Doc?"

Doc said grimly: "I will see what I can do about stopping the machine guns."

DOC glided away, and before his aides could protest had disappeared among the modernistic maze of unusual buildings.

"Watches Bowen has nine men with machine guns," Long Tom muttered doubtfully. "Doc is unarmed. He may have some trouble."

"Don't sweat about that!" Monk snorted. "My bet is that he'll stop 'em."

At the door of the Central Mechanical Plant on the opposite side of the bombardment, Doc's aides pounded for admittance.

A black-caped observer from a position in a pill-box turret on top of the plant had obviously noted their approach, and had seen that they came from the Princess Sona's party. He evidently thought they must be all right, for he signaled that the door be opened for them.

Silently, the door opened wide enough for them to squeeze in, and one by one they crowded through, Ham being the last to enter.

As the door was closing upon the heels of the dapper lawyer, a black-caped figure charged frantically to the plant building, shouting something in flat-voiced gibberish unintelligible to Doc's aides, but not, however, meaningless to the cavern men controlling the door to the Mechanical Plant.

The door slid shut with a silent fury that caught the always impeccably dressed Ham and ripped off the entire rear of his coat.

The one who had raced up was left outside.

Remarkably enough, Ham was not in the least concerned about his wrecked appearance. Just before the door closed, a backward glance had disclosed something which concerned him infinitely more.

"Ool!" he barked. "That was Ool who just came running up. He was dressed in the garb of these cavern people. Bet they didn't recognize him!"

Figures began to close in on Doc Savage's men. Their attitude was anything but friendly.

"Now what's eatin' these birds?" Monk muttered uneasily.

"It must have been what Ool shouted," Ham said.

The dapper lawyer's fears were justified, for inside the gleaming plant harsh orders were shouted in the same unfamiliar language Ool had used. Unexcited orders, they seemed. Like Ool, all these other cavern people seemed to have achieved a high state of emotional control.

"Betcha," Monk barked, "Ool told these boys we were in with Watches Bowen!"

Renny knocked his big fists together. "Yeah, he probably told 'em we were trying to bluff our way in here and take the place."

The next instant, the cavern men had stalked forward and surrounded Doc's aides in a tight ring. They made a grim appearing circle with their dark capes, black goggles, and white, emotionless faces that, because of the mother-of-pearl texture, did not seem quite human.

"Now what?" Long Tom grunted.

His answer came soon. The right hands of the cavern men began drifting out from their sides in a vague butterflylike fluttering.

"Blazes!" Renny gasped. "I wish Doc was here to help out!"

AFTER Doc Savage dispatched his men toward the Central Mechanical Plant, he himself hurried through a maze of modernistic passageways and circled to reach the rear of the fantastic home-cell house on top of which Watches Bowen and his men were ensconced with their machine guns.

He looked up through the shimmering golden haze. The bronze man could catch glimpses of the mobster men as they chopped bullets in the direction of the Central Mechanical Plant.

The home-cell house, which Watches Bowen had chosen as his machine gun nest, was high, pressing its roof close to the arching dome of the gigantic cavern. There were no fire escapes on the building, such as a dweller in American cities might have expected, for the reason that the construction was probably absolutely fireproof.

Due to the lack of fire escapes, Watches Bowen and his men seemingly believed themselves secure from a rear attack, and therefore concentrated all their attention on firing at the Central Mechanical Plant.

A professional human fly, accustomed to scanning the walls, would no doubt have eyed the sheer surface lifting upward story after story to the cavern dome, and would not have attempted the climb. According to the discussions which took place later, not even the cavern people, for all their strength and agility, thought it possible of accomplishment.

But Doc Savage ascended the first hundred feet in a flat two minutes. After that, his pace was considerably slowed. The structural indentations which marked the lower part of the building became less pronounced as the height became greater. But although the bronze man's pace was slowed, it was not stopped; up and up he climbed, depending entirely on precarious finger-holds that at times seemed non-existent.

The windows were not closed by glass, since there was no rain or cold to keep out of the building; there were only shutters for privacy, hinged in the window frames.

The bronze man might have made better time if he had used the window ledges for extra purchase, but not wishing to attract attention to himself, he scrupulously avoided the windows. As things turned out, he might as well have used them.

A cavern dweller, looking out, sighted the bronze man. The observer was a woman, a housewifely sort of person who looked as if her life might be devoted to the care of her man and her children. The spectacle of the great bronze man mounting the side of the building unnerved her, and she clutched her children closely and screamed shrilly and repeatedly. This occurred only a few stories from the top of the building.

One of Watches Bowen's crew, attracted by the screams, looked over the edge. He wore goggles. He sighted Doc, yelled.

Ham-hock, also wearing goggles, dived swiftly to the mobster's side. The latter pointed.

"Dat's ol' bad luck hisself!" the big Negro stuttered.

He seemed too paralyzed to swing down his submachine gun. The other man leaned over with his and bore down grimly on the trigger. A leaden thread of death streamed downward.

Then a startling thing occurred. The golden haze went out of the air. Utter blackness clamped down on the cavern metropolis.

"Mah goggles done gone bad on me!" Ham-hock shouted.

"Hell," rasped the other. "Something's happened!"

The man did not let the darkness interfere with his job at hand. He hosed machine gun lead along the side of the building where last he had seen Doc, using an entire drum of ammunition to make a thorough job out of it.

"HE'S gone now!" the gunner shouted loudly in the darkness.

"Sure he doan swing himself in t'rough a window?" Hamhock mumbled.

"There wasn't a window in thirty feet of him."

"Good work, you two," Watches Bowen called. "That's a load off my chest, and I don't mean maybe!"

"You won't be havin' no use now for that special gold watch, chief."

The special gold watch Ham-hock referred to was a new addition to the mob chief's collection, one especially reserved for the annihilation of Doc Savage. Bowen had even indulged in a whim, and had engraved Doc Savage's name on the case.

He had not revealed wherein lay the deadly nature of the watch, boasting only that this watch would finish Savage off if the proper chance came.

"She sho am dahk," Ham-hock mumbled. "Ah done think my trick specks done gone wrong. Only Ah guess dey ain't. Dat yaller light done just plumb gone out'n de sky, ain't it?"

Watches Bowen's curse rasped through the pitch blackness. "This wasn't on the program. Ool's bungled down below, or this couldn't have happened. They've done something at the Central Mechanical Plant. That's where their cold light comes from."

"Ah don' lak dis place," Ham-hock grumbled. "Dis heah dahk—it don't seem like regular dahk. Dis dahk—it sorta jams down on yo', if yo' know what Ah mean?"

Came a sharp, chattering noise in the blackness nearby. Watches cursed.

"Squirrel," he snarled, "keep them teeth still, or I'll knock 'em down your throat."

A certain quaver in the mob chief's voice showed he was more than a little jittery himself.

"I ain't scared!" Squirrel Dorgan insisted in a false voice. "It's just a habit."

"Break the habit, or I'll break your neck!" Watches promised.

In spite of Watches' warning, Squirrel's teeth kept chattering. Then suddenly they quit chattering. There was something unnatural about the way they stopped.

"Squirrel!" Watches Bowen called sharply.

There was no answer. The darkness seemed to press closer, so blackly intense that it appeared thick enough to handle. Watches cursed nervously and called again. When there was no answer, his hands pawed out, feeling in the darkness.

They found Squirrel Dorgan, found him slumped over the rooftop railing—dead.

Watches Bowen cursed savagely, and Ham-hock mumbled some vague incantation to his personal mistress of luck, this being the way each had of keeping his courage up. The other mobsters crowded close together.

"It must've been heart failure," one of them growled. "Squirrel always had a chicken heart."

His voice broke off sharply, and there was a soft *thump* in the darkness, as of a body striking the rooftop. Watches and his men hurriedly groped, and encountered a silently huddled body.

"Dis am Joe!" Ham-hock wailed, naming a member of the gang.

"Joe never had a weak heart!" Watches rasped. "Say, what the hell's goin' on—"

THERE was taut silence, graveyard silence, while the gangsters huddled closer together, as though, in the darkness, an unseen menace was tightening an invisible noose about them.

"I found something!" Honey Hamilton's mild voice stated.

"What is it?" Watches exploded. "Where?"

"Sticking in Joe's neck. It pulls out hard. Feels like a little weighted ball, with a kind of webbed thorn stuck through it—"

"Drop it, Honey!" the mob leader's voice slashed. "Don't scratch yourself on it! Whatever it is, it must be poisoned to kill Joe like it did."

There was a noise in the darkness behind Watches, a sound not unlike a load of rock unloaded suddenly and heavily.

The gang chief whirled.

"Ham-hock!" he yelled, "has it got you?"

There was no answer.

"Ham-hock!"

This time there was an answer. "Ah—Ah'm all right, chief!" the big Negro stuttered the words out. "But-but Ah wouldn't uh been if it had come any closer."

"If *what* had come closer?" Watches demanded.

"One uh dem things lak what Honey pulled outa Joe's neck, Ah reckons," said the Negro. "Ah could feel it come past mah face in de dahk."

"Why in the hell didn't you say so?" Watches snapped, unreasonably.

There was a faint hiss in the air above Watches' head. He ducked instinctively, cursed, and followed Ham-hock to the floor to get the protection afforded by the low parapet.

"Flatten out!" he ordered. "They're filling the air with poison darts. Shootin' 'em up with air guns or sling shots or something, I guess."

Flat on their stomachs on the roof, the men listened in near-panic as the air above them was filled with the whirring of the death missiles, many of which struck with sharp *clicks* against the protecting parapet.

Ham-hock Piney howled dolefully, "What Ah wants to know is why we done mess wit' dat Meck-a-nickel Plant foah, anyhow?"

"It was Ool's idea," Watches snapped. "If we get that Plant, we can take over this place. It's the heart of their existence down here. The roof above is reinforced so it cannot come down. It's the strongest place in the cavern."

"Ah wishes we had nevah come up heah," Ham-hock stated.

"Well, what could we do?" Watches yelled angrily. "Doc Savage's men cut us off. Say, you rascal, are you criticizing my way of running this?"

"No, suh," Ham-hock denied. "Ah thinks things am goin' jes' fine."

THROUGH it all, the "heartbeat" of the processing machine at the Central Mechanical Plant had been throbbing through the blackness, a slow, muffled cadence which impinged on their ear drums with ominous insistence.

Ham-hock breathed heavily, taking three quick inhalations in succession. Then he gasped, "Don' it seem like dat tickin' am slowin' down?"

Watches listened.

"Yeah, it is," he agreed. "And they're not shooting up so many of those darts. They probably figure they've rubbed us out. Wait'll they turn on their screwy yellow light again. We'll fog somebody plenty with lead."

Ham-hock's ponderous wheezes were getting so loud now that they even drowned out the insistent clicking emanating from the air machine in the Central Mechanical Plant. Nor was the fat Negro the only one who was breathing hard. All were wheezing. It began to sound like a contest.

Honey Hamilton's mild voice inquired between gaspings: "Doesn't it seem—to anybody else— like it's getting hard—to breathe?"

Honey got an emphatic agreement from everything on the roof.

Ham-hock gasped, "Could dis have—somethin' to do—with dat clock-tick business? Dem ticks am soundin'—mighty slow now."

Watches Bowen ripped out short volleys of profanity. He seemed to lack the breath for as extended profanity as he would have liked.

"You hit it, Ham-hock," he gasped. "That clock-tick controls the air down here. What they're doing is—thinning it out on us—high up here—under the dome—where we are—It's worse than—below—"

He gagged, made awful hacking noises.

"Takin' de bref right out our mouths," Ham-hock's frightened voice sounded. "What kind people is these? Le's get out'n heah."

They pulled off their black goggles—they had taken them from the cavern men they had shot down near the Mechanical Plant—and used their flashlights. Access to the lower level of the great house-cell was by a moving stairway similar to an escalator, and riding down on this, they kept their flashlight beams playing, and several times shot at inquisitive heads.

REACHING the floor level of the cavern, they set off swiftly, using their guns freely. Ham-hock Piney, more courageous now, fired the grenade rifle several times.

The air was better down here.

Watches Bowen seemed to have a very definite idea of where he was going. He veered sharply to the right and came to a very steep wall. He stopped and called upward.

"Lower away!" he shouted. "And don't show a light!"

An answer wafted from above. "O. K.!"

Watches moved about, groped, got his fingers on the rung of a rope ladder which had been lowered. He tried his weight on it, then swung on and started climbing up.

"Come on," he hurled back to the others. "Don't forget to bring Joe's and Squirrel's machine guns."

Twenty feet up, Watches squirmed through a narrow rock opening in the cavern. He stood by at the aperture while the others climbed, one after the other, up the twisting, dangling ladder. He counted the men as they arrived at the top and scraped past him in the darkness, puffing and blowing.

"What the hell!" he exploded. "I counted one too many!"

He ordered the ladder hauled up. Then he flashed his light, slithering the white beam around in the low limestone passage.

"Where's Ool?" he asked.

"Not back yet," said the man who lowered the ladder. "Say, what went wrong?"

"Everything!" Watches snarled.

This natural passageway led around some distance in an indirect connection with that labyrinth of tunnels, the so-called Land of the Lost, which straggled underground for miles to the surface cleft where the dirigible was moored.

This passage was fed by the same sluggish current of air as circulated through the Land of the Lost—in a sense, exhaust air from the city in the domed cavern.

Watches' flashlight revealed the faces of his men. All were here except Ool and the two who had been killed on the rooftop. The nervously poking light revealed no one else.

"My mistake," Watches muttered. "I'd have sworn I counted one too many."

But Watches Bowen's first hunch was right, for he had counted one too many men in his outfit. The third to mount the ladder behind the mob chief had been the extra man.

It was Doc Savage. Doc had not been shot off the side of the building by machine gun fire. When darkness clamped over the cavern, and the bullets sliced toward him in a leaden stream, he had let go his finger hold, leaped twenty feet down and ten feet to one side and landed on a thick conduit pipe which entered the building from another across the way.

Out of the tail of his eye he had photographed the position of that aerial conduit in the last glimmer of the failing golden light.

His leap was gauged precisely. In utter darkness, he caught the conduit against his steel-thewed thighs, breaking his fall sufficiently for his cabled arms to wrap around and drag up his dangling legs.

In silence, he had recommenced his climb up the side of the building, and eased over the parapet in the darkness. He had been present, lurking below the roof opening, when Watches' two men were killed by the poisonous darts hurled up by the outraged cavern inhabitants.

He had followed the gang chief to the dangling rope ladder. And he was present now, in the passageway, crouched behind a pile of broken rock fragments just outside the range of flashlight beams.

Chapter XVII
RENDEZVOUS TRAP

UTTERLY unaware of the crouching presence of Doc Savage in the passageway, Watches Bowen brought out a flask of the eighty-year old Napoleon brandy which he had brought along; he killed half the flask in two greedy swigs, then passed the rest to his men.

The slow fire of the liquor did little to sweeten the mob chief's temper. His pudgy hand tugged continually at his watch chain, and he prowled about, cursing everything in sight, and many things not in sight. Most particularly he cursed Ool.

Honey Hamilton put up a mild defense of the maligned assassin.

"It wasn't Ool's fault that we bumped into them men near the Central Mechanical Plant, chief," he pointed out.

"Yeah, I know," Watches growled, "but he might've stuck around and helped us out."

One of the mobsters, a man with small, overly bright eyes, scowled and muttered, "There's a lotta screwy things about this place."

Honey Hamilton cleared his throat gently.

"Watches, the boys been wantin' me to ask somethin' for 'em," he said.

"Yeah?" Watches growled. "Shoot! Who's stopping you?"

"It's only that this is working up into a plenty bloody business," Honey Hamilton said apologetically. "That's all right. We ain't backin' out. But we figure it's time we know exactly what we're takin' the risks for."

"Didn't I tell you we come after a treasure that will set the richest guy in the country way over the other side the tracks?" Watches demanded.

"Yeah, you told us that," the other agreed. "But it don't mean a hell of a lot to us."

Watches laughed harshly. "So you want details?"

"That's right," Honey said in his mouselike voice.

Watches shrugged. "All right— We came after light."

There was a stir among the men.

"Light—hell!" someone snorted.

Watches continued, "The yellow light that's in this air down here—to be more specific."

"Dis golden stuff what we see with dem goggles?" Ham-hock questioned. "Yo' wouldn't fool us, boss man!"

"Go on, Watches," Honey Hamilton urged. "You're still way ahead of us. Where does that stuff make us a buck?"

"You dope!" the mob chief retorted. "Don't you see that the formula for this golden air is worth more than all the heavy gold that ever came out of the ground?"

"No," Honey's gentle voice stated. "Damned if I do!"

"THE way I get it from Ool," Watches continued. "His ancestors came underground here thousands of years ago, to get away from the cold. It used to be hot country up here a few hundred thousand years ago or so. Then everything started freezing up, like it is now. It didn't happen overnight. Took thousands of years, I guess.

"Anyhow, the ancestors of these people developed ways of takin' care of themselves," Watches continued. "They had to make their light to see by. But by the time the ice closed in for good, they were all set. They had learned to make their air, too. Ool says they've got tanks of liquid air at the Central Mechanical Plant that would refrigerate all of New York City."

"What do they do with it?" Honey questioned.

"I've read about that stuff. It'll freeze a rubber ball so bad that it'll break like glass," Watches said. "They use it to make breathing air out of— something like we do in submarines, I guess."

"Yassuh!" Ham-hock interrupted. "Dey put me in one of dem submarine things in de war. Ah know about submarines."

"Shut up," Watches growled. "The yellow, or

golden color in the air down here is nothing more than a kind of phosphorescence. It's caused by treating the air somehow, then turning a form of X-ray, or something on it. In other words, these cavern dwellers have realized a dream of modern science. They have perfected a method of getting so-called 'cold light' on a practical basis.

"At their Central Mechanical Plant they treat the air particles in a way to make them luminous when seen through specially-devised goggles. That's the long and short of it."

One of the men stirred restlessly. "It's a nice history lesson. But where does the treasure come in?"

"You mug!" Watches rasped. "You haven't got the imagination to dodge a bullet! Don't you see what it would do back in America, in Europe—everywhere—if we showed up with a formula for making cold light? It would put every electric light company in the world out of business. We'd make them power pirates pay plenty! I mean plenty!"

Honey Hamilton's awed voice sounded insistently. "Ool—according to the way I been hearing him talk, has got even bigger ideas than that," he said.

"Nothing the matter with Ool's imagination," the mob chief chuckled.

He pulled a watch out of his pocket by the end of the chain and started swinging it around unconsciously.

"There's nothing the matter with my imagination either," he said. "I'm stringing along with Ool. We'll go just as far as money will take us. And that's plenty far."

"Yo' sho' nuff goin' have a knob on somebody's head, too," Ham-hock protested, "if'n yo' don' quit swinging dat watch so wild."

Watches quit spinning the watch. His thick fingers shoved it back in his pocket. "You're right, Ham-hock. We're a little ahead of ourselves. We've got to make a successful raid on the Central Mechanical Plant, first."

Honey Hamilton, lost in a mental consideration of what he had just heard, had wandered off to one side humming to himself. He was not sure that they could hold up the electric power companies—either in selling them the secret, or by getting them to pay to keep it from being used, and thus damaging great utilities investments. But Watches must be right. Watches had a business head.

Watches turned a flashlight on one of his timepieces.

Then Honey Hamilton stopped dreaming. He kept humming, however, and continued on a few steps farther, then turned and walked slowly back to the group. He said something to Watches

Bowen out of the corner of his mouth, barely opening his lips. But Watches heard him.

The crook chief's face went plaster-white, but there was no illumination on his face, so no one noticed. He did not answer Honey, but kept on talking to Ham-hock.

He paused, looked at his wrist watch for the time.

"I'm supposed to meet Ool in an hour and a quarter, down the passage here, in that little room off to the right," he said. "I'm going to sit down and rest."

He sat down. The others sat down also. At his order they crowded together in a close circle with their flashlights ready and machine guns across their knees.

"You never know when somebody may come snooping around," Watches growled in explanation.

Ham-hock's mountainous bulk shivered. "De way dem fellers move them hands of their'n makes dis baby t'ink of dem ol' cottonmouth snakes dot used to go fo' mah bare feet when Ah was a boy down in Gawgia. Ah wonder how Ool kills by touchin' you?"

"I'd give plenty to know that myself," Watches admitted sourly. "He never has explained it."

They talked on. Then Honey Hamilton, at a nudge from Watches, got up and wandered a short distance away. He was humming to himself again as he retraced the course he had taken before.

He came back, and said in a voice audible to all this time: "O. K."

"What's O. K.?" Ham-hock demanded. "What yo'-all talkin' about?"

Watches Bowen turned on the fat Negro viciously. "Not you, Ham-hock! You told me you'd bumped Savage, didn't you?"

"Ah sho did not! Dat was Joe, de boy dat got hisself killed."

"Doc Savage was right here, listening to everything we said!" Watches grated. "Honey saw him a little while ago when one of the flashes went on. He came back and whispered the dope to me."

NOBODY said anything. Their tongues were frozen, for they held the bronze man in greater dread than they did the dart killers of the cold-light cavern. Watches laughed grimly.

"Take it easy," he purred. "That appointment I claimed I had with Ool was faked."

"Lawsy me!" Ham-hock moaned.

"Savage doesn't know it's faked," Watches went on. "He thinks he's got straight dope. He's on his way now to trip up Ool. But Ool will be here soon. We'll fix it for Ool to get Savage. And no guesswork about it this time."

One of them said sullenly, "Watches, I don't want no part in it. This bronze guy is a jinx for us. Hell! We've tried to kill him twenty times."

"Going canary?" Watches sneered.

"Yeah, when it comes to him, I am. And I ain't ashamed to admit it."

"Me neither," another sullenly defiant voice agreed.

Watches Bowen did not get angry. He did not even swear. He surprised everybody by laughing quietly.

"That's all right, boys," he said. "I know how you feel. We won't any of us take any more chances with this baby. We'll leave all the dirty work to Ool and any of these cavern guys he can get to take a risk."

He paused.

"You see, Ool has some friends down here," he said.

IN the small rendezvous room, Doc Savage waited. Watches Bowen's act had been convincing; the bronze man held no suspicion of the trap which had been set. He stood silently in a man-sized niche in the rock-cluttered cavity.

He did not have long to wait, for the little room soon caught up the shuffle of approaching feet on the rocky tunnel floor. The sound came closer, and Doc flexed great muscles and waited.

He tried his goggles, found them ineffective still, and pushed them up on his forehead. No doubt the ray device which caused the air to become luminous was still shut off.

As the steps came closer, a sudden aura of light danced on the roof a stone's throw distant, such a display on the pitted roof as might have been the work of a flashlight beam. The person who approached had rounded one of the final curves in the crooked passage.

The next instant the flash beam was spurting into the rendezvous room itself. The one who carried the light approached within a few feet of Doc, stopped, shook the flash, pounded it with a hand as though he thought a jolting would make it function better, and finally turned the white rays toward his face while he examined the reflector.

It was Ool's face that was revealed in the flashlight glare.

Doc sprang.

With the precision of a leaping puma, the bronze man's hurtling weight landed immediately behind Ool. His hands clamped Ool's arms just below the shoulder joints; his thumbs dug into the flesh. Ool became helpless; the whole maneuver having taken the bronze man only split-seconds.

Adjusting the flashlight in a wall niche, Doc Savage examined Ool's hands, particularly the

right one. He found nothing. Ool spoke, and in spite of the pain he must be suffering, his tone had changed little from its normal expressionlessness.

"My right hand interests you, does it not, bronze man?" he asked.

Doc Savage did not answer.

"You are due for a surprise," Ool said quietly. "You were interested in capturing me, so interested that you did not hear my men come close."

Doc Savage became slightly tense. The other felt the stiffening.

"There are at present a *vaex* of men surrounding you," Ool said. "In your language, that number is equal to the total of all the toes and fingers which a normal man has. Twenty!"

The bronze man suddenly picked up his light and streamed it about, cutting a white path in the close-pressing blackness. It was true. The mouth of the room was literally packed with white-faced, dark-caped figures.

THESE newcomers moved forward slowly, purposefully, closing in on Doc and his prisoner. And as they approached closer, their right hands drifted up from their sides in vague butterfly gestures which seemed as natural as nature itself.

"You had best not resist," Ool warned. "You are not, at this time, to be killed."

There was a cold certainty about Ool's actions which said he was not bluffing, and Doc Savage did the only thing left to do—he allowed himself to be taken.

Ool stood clear and worked his arms experimentally. In his long black cape he looked very grotesque. He gibbered an order to the cavern men, and they moved down the passage, conducting Doc Savage in their midst, until they came to a smooth wall completely blocking the passage. Here, one of the men gave signal knocks on the wall, and a wide door slid slowly open.

Doc and his captors passed through. The door closed softly behind them. That he might walk more easily, the bronze man slid down his goggles—for the cold light was working again—and donning them, found himself once more in the metropolis of fantastic buildings.

The throbbing which was the heartbeat of this city under the dome permeated the "cold light" realm more strongly, and the place seemed to have settled back to its accustomed routine.

Many of the populace came to stare at the bronze man. They did not seem friendly.

Doc was conducted to a chamber in one of the government buildings, a room that was obviously a prison cell; he was left alone with the door locked behind him, and was allowed to keep the black goggles.

The room was large, with a wall-like partition at the opposite end. Beyond the partition, he discovered other prisoners—his five aides.

"And Habeas Corpus," Monk muttered, after the first excited greetings were over. "They put him in their dang jail, too."

THE meeting of Doc Savage and his men would have been considerably dampened in spirit could they have listened to another meeting which was taking place in the executive palace. There, Ool faced the dictator, Anos.

Anos, father of the girl Sona, wore a red cape as mark of high position. The girl, Sona, had acquired her name by a simple reversal of the letters of the male parent's name, a custom in all father-and-daughter relationships in the cavern metropolis.

Anos, the dictator, occupied a low, thronelike affair which stood near a design on the throne-room floor, a mammoth fourteen-pointed star inlaid with an opalescent substance. Around the points of the star were arrayed the chairs of the government council, the *Nonverid*, the members of which wore slightly less gaudy capes.

Ool stood in the middle of the star and faced the dictator.

"My repentance is great," he said.

"That is fitting," the dictator replied slowly. "You have been noted in the past for your greed and treachery, and for your insane thirst to take over the government here. It was for attempting to take over the government that you were banished to the *Stor*, the working squadrons. When you tried to lead the *Stor* in revolt, you were sent to the Land of the Lost."

Ool spoke contritely.

"I have repented," he said. "And I have proved it by bringing you the giant man and the other five, and the strange insect with fur upon it which they call a 'hog.'"

"You say these five are allied with the others who attacked us with their carrying-rods which roar and kill?" the dictator asked.

"They are," Ool lied solemnly. "I saw them together in the Land of the Lost. I joined them and learned their language, which is simple. And for days, I tried to keep them lost in the desert caverns. But finally, they no longer heeded my counsel, and found this place."

At that point the girl, Sona, spoke up vehemently.

"Those are not true words," she said. "This man Ool, who has always caused trouble, is one of the leaders of the men with the carrying-rods that make noise and death. The six whom we now have prisoners—the big man with the strange skin

and the other five—are not our enemies, but foes of Ool and the others."

Ool said in an injured manner, "It is true that I was with these men when you were seized in the outer caverns, and acted as one of them. But have I not told you that I was deceiving them."

Anos, the dictator, said, "We will deliberate over the matter of the truth of your statements."

Ool threw his head far back and became rigid for a moment, eyes upcast. This seemed to be the local method of kowtowing.

"I wish a boon, a favor, for my services," he said.

The dictator did not seem very enthusiastic.

"What is it?" he asked.

"The formula for the 'cold light,' which only your scientific men know," Ool said.

"You could not understand it," Anos pointed out. "You were not trained in that branch of science. In fact, I recall you as a very stupid, unruly youth who learned little."

Ool made a faint scowl under the rebuke. "What about doing me the honor of giving me the formula?"

"Why do you wish it?" the other countered.

"I thirst for knowledge," was the best excuse Ool could offer.

"It is a strange thirst, considering your record," he was told. "Your request is denied. We suspect a trick, to speak without falseness."

Ool did not have much success masking his disappointment. He bowed.

"I have another boon to ask," he said.

"What is this one?"

"The giant bronze man and his five companions—" Ool said. "They are dangerous. For the common good of my people, I ask that they be put to death. That is the boon I ask."

Anos, the dictator, considered.

"It is a matter for the *Nonverid* to deliberate and pass judgment upon," he said.

Ool had brought one bad habit back with him from the outer world. He swore a good mule-skinner oath, one he must have picked up among Watches Bowen's men.

Then Anos, the dictator, added something which made Ool feel much better.

"It would appear that this giant of a man and his five companions are our enemies," Anos said. "It is equally probable that the *Nonverid* will decree their death."

Ool, to hide his delight, put back his head in the strange kowtow, for his deadpan features were showing more emotion than usual.

"How will death be decreed?" he asked.

"In the traditional manner," said Anos.

"It is well," Ool said, and walked backward

from the audience chamber with his head bent stiffly, eyes upturned.

Chapter XVIII
TERROR IN GOLD

BACK again in the desert labyrinth of the Land of the Lost, Ool conferred with Watches Bowen and his gang.

"We will have to fight," Ool said.

Watches objected. "But you said their whatcha-call-it—*Nonverid*, could be persuaded—"

"That old fool, Anos, put his foot down," Ool said. "They will not give up the formula without a fight."

Watches Bowen jerked nervously at his watch chain. "Our guns didn't do much good last time."

"We will plan more carefully," Ool stated. "We will capture the Central Mechanical Plant with the help of the *Stor*."

"*Stor?*" Watches grunted. "What's that?"

"Workers," Ool explained.

"Ah didn't see nobody workin' much," Hamhock Piney put in. "Most of 'em was jus' restin' around. Ah would like a job like dey-all got."

"The *Stor* are not great in number, but bitter, vicious," Ool explained. "We will use them. It is what I had in mind."

"Just who are these birds in the *Stor?*" Watches persisted.

"In your country, they would be called criminals," Ool told him.

"When do we start this?" Watches Bowen questioned.

"Savage is to be sentenced to death by the *Nonverid*, I hope," Ool said bluntly. "That will make it simple. We will wait until Savage has been disposed of."

"I hope it ain't long," Watches offered.

"It will not be," said Ool. "It is probable that the bronze man is being sentenced now."

IN the prison cell where Doc Savage and his five aides were confined, gloom was thick, both physically and spiritually. The gaunt Johnny paced steadily—as Monk had expressed it a moment before, "Like somebody's lost skeleton." The fact that they were listening to a dire pronouncement did not deter him, for he could understand no word.

Anos, the dictator, was speaking.

"And so our ruling council, the *Nonverid*, has deliberated fairly and found you to be enemies of ours," he was saying. "It is further considered that you were responsible in whole or in part for the deaths of certain of our population and that, as is customary only in cases of murderers, you shall receive the death penalty, wielded in public, for all to witness and be warned."

With that, he turned and walked out.

Anos had spoken the local language, of which Doc Savage and his aides understood nothing. The bronze man, usually able to acquire a smattering of strange tongues within a short time, had found this one especially obtuse. But he hazarded a guess.

"It was something serious," he said. "The man's expression showed that."

Monk said, "That pretty girl we helped out, the one they call Sona, or some thing—you'd think maybe she'd help us out. I think she took a fancy to Doc."

"I guess there's nothing she can do about it," Ham said shortly.

There was a ventilating opening to one side of the room, a large square, closed by a stout lattice of pressed fibre. Doc and the others now cooperated in trying to break the lattice down, but with no perceptible success.

They were straining at it when, as though wafted in on the soft, aureate air, the girl, Sona, appeared noiselessly on the other side of the lattice, then went to the door.

"Am I a prophet!" Monk grinned.

The girl's voice made music as she spoke in low tones to the guard, who answered in brief gutturals, occasionally shaking his head vigorously, but finally nodding, mumbling under his breath. He opened the door. The girl entered.

She went directly to Doc, hesitated, then rested a hand on his arm. Her exquisite face was serious. She took the bronze man's right hand and made motions as though she were attaching something to the hand. She went through the same motions with each of Doc's aides.

"It feels swell when she holds my hand," Monk chuckled. "But what in the devil is she trying to show us?"

The girl now seized Doc's right hand and moved it in the butterfly manner characteristic of Ool.

"Holy cow!" Renny boomed.

Without a word, the girl left their cell.

DOC SAVAGE stood up suddenly. "I think the girl was trying to tell us how we would be killed," he said. "But that suggests an idea."

He drew his men together. They whispered.

Doc Savage approached the lattice. He made gestures for the guard to come close. The latter did so, having no idea of how far Doc could leap. When the bronze man's left hand streaked through the grating to pin the guard's arm, the guard's eyes bulged with fear. When Doc made a butterfly motion with his right hand, the guard's capitulation was sudden, complete. He opened the lattice.

Doc and his aides, swarming out, were sighted almost immediately by cavern men down the shimmering golden corridor. These rushed forward to cut off escape, but Doc and his men, pushing the mysterious power of the right-hand phenomena to its utmost, made horrible grimaces as they hurtled forward.

Their right hands they held out in a manner dreadfully familiar to the "cold-light" people. These gave way.

Back in the prison building, a penetrating gong started clanging, apparently an emergency signal audible far out in the fantastic cavern. People began filling the streets.

"We can't make it into the outer caverns," Doc said suddenly. "We'll try for the Central Mechanical Plant."

They made it nearly all of the way to the Central Mechanical Plant without their progress being seriously threatened, but were sighted by many persons. Occasional poisonous darts, of the type which had brought death to two of Watches Bowen's mobsters, were sent against them, the lethal bolts being fired from peculiar compressed air tubes.

Nearing the Central Mechanical Plant, Doc's aides fell in on each side of him to form a flying wedge. On they hurtled, with Monk slightly behind the others, carrying his pet pig.

Those in the Plant apparently considered it impossible that six men could make it to the doors, and they had not closed the panels.

Before they awakened to the possibilities, Doc was almost in the aperture. He lunged, drove a fist out and knocked a foe away.

If Monk had been satisfied with Doc's blow, the thing which happened next might never have occurred. The homely chemist, fired with fighting fever, expressed himself by shoving the stunned victim out of the way. This occupied a fractional moment—long enough to allow another enemy to lunge in with one of the deadly darts held knife-fashion.

Monk swerved toward the open door. The dart raked along his arm, barely missed it.

It did not miss Habeas Corpus, gripped securely under Monk's arm. Before Monk's horrified gaze, the poisonous dart sank deep into the pig's neck.

Habeas Corpus emitted a shrill squeal. Almost instantly, the porker became limp.

DOC dragged the raging Monk inside, then got the door closed. With his right hand, he kept a grip on Monk. The few cavern men inside the plant offered only shouts by way of resistance.

They mounted steps. Monk still carried the limp pig. They came to large rooms which seemed to be laboratories.

"Lookit!" Renny boomed.

Through the welter of strange scientific apparatus, Renny had sighted various articles of equipment which they had brought along from the dirigible. Obviously the equipment had been brought here by the cavern men for analyzing and study, some of the things no doubt being as strange as implements from another world.

Gathering their duffel, gripping their recovered supermachine pistols, they left the laboratory. Doc rested a hand on Monk's shoulder.

"Better leave Habeas," he advised. "You'll need both hands for fighting."

"Leave Habeas for these heathens to dissect?" Monk snorted. "Nix!"

Doc said no more about that.

"Get set," he told his aides.

He opened the door a crack, looking out into the corridor which led to another part of the plant. Instantly, a sizzling jet of something streamed inside. Doc slammed the door, leaping far back inside the laboratory and dragging the others with him. The air seemed to be filled with a sudden, bitter cold. Gray stains appeared on the fiber door and spread outward over the surface.

"*Br-r-r!*" Renny exploded. "What's happened to the heat?"

"I'll be superamalgamated!" Johnny barked. "Liquid air!"

"Huh?" Renny ejaculated.

"Air compressed to a liquefied state," Johnny said seriously. "Permitted to vaporize, it has the effect of producing terrific cold."

Long Tom looked toward Monk. "Bad?" he questioned.

"Liquid air is cold enough to freeze dang near

anything," Monk muttered. "They probably use it in their air-conditioning system, and have pipes close to this door."

Doc Savage's strange flake-gold eyes roved the room. The door was the only exit. The windows gave on a sheer surface that even the bronze man himself could not climb. This wall was not like that of the home-cell structure, being of infinitely finer workmanship.

Ham went over to Monk, who still clutched the form of the pet pig. Monk was hit harder by what had befallen Habeas than by any misfortune he had encountered in a long time.

Ham dropped a hand on Monk's arm.

"Monk," he said slowly, "I'm damned sorry. Guess I never really meant all I said about that hog."

"Sure," Monk muttered. "I know."

Ham reached out a hand and ruffled the stiff bristles on Habeas' back. And then an unexpected thing happened. A shudder coursed over the body of Habeas Corpus. His big ears flapped feebly; from his long snout came a faint grunt.

Doc and the others crowded about. Monk's eyes were staring in disbelief. Habeas Corpus shook his head, commenced to kick ungainly legs.

"He's comin' to life!" Monk said hoarsely.

WITHIN a few minutes, Habeas Corpus was able to stand alone on the floor. His little eyes in their fat pockets sighted Ham. He grunted a friendly recognition and trotted toward him.

The dapper lawyer glared. "Monk, keep that strip of bacon away from me!"

"You said you liked Habeas!" Monk snorted.

"When did I ever say that?" Ham questioned belligerently. "Keep this flea garage away from me!"

Doc Savage had been keenly observant of Habeas Corpus' revival, and now he commented on the phenomenon.

"Break out your chemical pack, Monk," he suggested. "Let's do some experimenting."

While the others stood guard at the doors and windows, Doc and Monk worked over Habeas Corpus. They worked for a long time, surrounded by an array of tiny test tubes and extremely small phials of chemicals which had come from Monk's chemical pack, which was in itself a marvelously compact and remarkably complete analytical laboratory.

There was much angry shouting from the cavern people, and this kept up steadily, but nothing drastic was done.

Doc Savage worked steadily. Needing certain chemicals, he surveyed the big laboratory, noting the multiplicity of apparatus in view. The purpose of many of the devices, he recognized; although they differed greatly in appearance from those, for instance, to be found in Doc's New York City headquarters laboratory, their functional process was similar.

Other devices baffled him in the brief moments he devoted to examination, and carried conviction that in many respects these strange cavern people were far ahead, scientifically, of the so-called civilizations on the outside of the globe.

The cavern people apparently had no system of writing, or if they had, did not use it, for there were great filing bins to one side, and these held spools of stiff, thin, bright wire; while nearby were apparatus resembling phonographs. The bronze man recognized this as mechanism for recording speech magnetically on wire.

As time passed, the cavern men became more impatient. The violence of their assaults increased. They drilled holes in the walls; and although Doc and his men fired mercy bullets through some of the apertures, the cavern men eventually managed to insert nozzles which began spraying liquid air.

Vaporizing, the stuff condensed the moisture in the air, causing clouds of steam.

Most of the liquefied air was forced in through holes in the ceiling. Some of it fell on a large wad of soft cottonlike fibre which Doc had used in his ministrations to Habeas Corpus.

The fibre was knocked off the table, struck the floor with a sharp rap and, frozen incredibly solid, broke into a myriad of particles.

"I'll say that's potent stuff!" Ham said grimly.

Doc tried the doors. These were locked from the outside now, it developed.

"Br-r-r!" Monk shivered. "Surrendering means they'll probably croak us."

Doc's face was bleak and he continued to pound on the door, signifying their readiness to surrender.

"We cannot stay here," he pointed out.

THE bronze man produced a bottle of fair size and handed it about, ordering each of his men to drink. They did so, making faces over the vile green contents; then Doc drank some himself.

The men did not ask questions. They knew that the bottle was filled with some substance which the bronze man had mixed in the laboratory. It was awful stuff to the taste.

The door was opened shortly, but only wide enough to let them out one at a time, and they were seized by a number of cavern men, which made resistance futile. They were disarmed, searched thoroughly.

Their captors spent much time examining their right hands and seemed puzzled when they found nothing.

"They really thought we could kill people by waving our right hands like that bird Ool," Monk muttered.

Ham said, "What worries me is what they'll do with us now."

There was a great multitude in the streets, a throng which was ominously uneasy, and it spread around Doc Savage and his aides in waves as they were conducted toward the executive buildings.

They did not enter the buildings, but circled to a vast amphitheater in the rear, the center of which held a platform of considerable areas. This was raised just sufficiently to be in view of the throng.

"Holy cow!" Renny rumbled. "Kinda looks like they're gonna make a public example of us!"

Chapter XIX
EXECUTION

THE ceremonies following were unpleasantly meaningful. Unbound, but ludicrously helpless simply because they were held and led by leash-like cords attached to their necks, wrists and ankles, Doc Savage and his five men were hauled ignominiously to the rostrum and boosted upon it.

As they were thus put within view of everyone, an insistent drone went up to the high roof of the weird cavern, the multitude calling out in their unintelligible tongue and, judging from the insistent tone, demanding the events be hurried.

The babble of talk drowned out completely the throbbing of the processing machine from the Central Mechanical Plant, which ticked so interminably through the golden haze; but as the time for the climax came close, the hubbub of talk quieted, although for another few seconds, echoes haunted the luminous cavern. Then these, too, sank into nothingness, so that silence settled, broken only by the throbbing from the Central Mechanical Plant, which was now audible and accentuated the grisly quiet.

Six cavern men, stalwart, half a head taller than the average of the "cold-light" people, stepped out, one beside Doc Savage and one beside each of the bronze man's five aides. Attired in hooded capes, and with their black-goggled white faces grimly emotionless, they looked the very personification of death itself.

Each of these six gripped a flat fibre case in one hand.

Anos, the dictator, came on the scene at the head of a procession which included his own daughter, Sona, the members of the *Nonverid*, or governing council, and various minor functionaries. These took up a position on the rostrum.

"Damn it!" Monk growled. "If we could only talk to these people!"

The dictator, attired in a blood-red cape, stood facing the prisoners, the *Nonverid* flanking him on either side, and the girl, Sona, standing directly behind the father.

The young woman seemed to be arguing. She had been arguing as they entered. Her speech was vehement, but to it the dictator returned only a gesture which seemed to be the local equivalent of a headshake. This was a quick convulsing of the shoulders.

Then the girl tried to move forward to Doc and the five others, crying out loudly, angrily. She was grasped and drawn back.

"Good kid," Renny rumbled. "She's doing her bit."

Anos, the dictator, shouted out, and the six large men grasping the fibre cases stepped even closer, opened the cases and took out slender, shining objects. These were poison darts.

"I'll be superamalgamated!" gulped Johnny. "The executioners!"

ANOS cried out again. The executioners leaped suddenly.

Doc and his men were taken, in a way, by surprise. They had expected more preliminaries. They struggled, struck, wrenched about. But several men were on each leash, and they were spread-eagled in a trice, helpless.

The darts were plunged into their flesh.

The results which followed were much like those that had accompanied the death of Beery Hosmer, long ago, in front of the candy store in New York. Doc and his men flounced about, struggling feebly, and their movements became weaker, less violent, so that, finally, when the leashes which held them were slackened, they did not move at all.

Anos, the dictator, said in his native tongue, "Justice is done."

The girl, Sona, wailed shrilly.

On the outskirts of the multitude, a man detached himself and scuttled away. So great was the interest in the execution that his action was not noticed.

THE man who had departed so furtively went by devious ways to a spot where he encountered Ool, Watches Bowen and his men, who were gathered with a considerable number of vicious-looking members of the *Stor*, or forced labor squadrons.

"The giant man and his five are dead," advised the messenger, addressing Ool.

"It is good," said Ool. Then Ool spoke his stilted English to Watches Bowen.

"The bronze man has been executed," he said.

"We will rush the Central Mechanical Plant now. Once we reach it, members of the *Stor*, who are working with us, will admit us. The plant is strong; we can hold it. And by cutting off the warmth from the air, and the 'cold light,' as you call it, we can make our own terms."

"Let's go," said Watches.

They advanced. Showing no scruples, no human feeling, they cut down the first cavern man to discover them, using a blast from a submachine gun. At the terrifying roar of the gun, bedlam broke loose in the multitude gathered to witness the execution.

Anos, the dictator, kept his head, and dispatched squadrons of men to take up positions in various buildings commanding approaches to the Central Mechanical Plant. These were equipped with the little air tubes launching the poisoned darts.

Watches Bowen defeated the menace of the darts by a simple device. He and his men, according to a prearranged plan, rushed a certain building and got large sheets of the compressed building fibre. This material was light, and the darts would not penetrate it. They served as shields. The advance on the Central Mechanical Plant began.

Complications developed to aid them, complications which they had planned. Members of the *Stor*, who were at work—not having been permitted to witness the execution—began revolting. Somehow they had gotten darts and the air guns, and they proceeded to wreak destruction of their own.

From the fabrication plants, they ran along ramps toward the home-cells, or habitation structures. On top of one of these, Honey Hamilton had established a machine gun nest.

The cavern men released repeated barrages of poisoned darts, but these had little effect, since the ramps were protected by waist-high walls, and Honey Hamilton was sheltered by a parapet.

Closer and closer, the raiders came to the Central Mechanical Plant. Honey Hamilton, shooting expertly, kept down the worst of the opposition.

Those of the *Stor* in the Central Mechanical Plant, having overcome their guards, got the doors open and stood in the apertures, howling a welcome, as well as advice.

It seemed that Watches Bowen and his crew would soon enter.

But there was an interruption.

ANOS, the dictator, had himself taken charge of a picked squad in a desperate effort to stem the raid. He had bunched his men, and they rushed in a body, striving by superior force to beat down Watches Bowen and his shielded party.

Honey Hamilton, that he might not be cut off on top of the home-cell, had descended, and with his guard was rushing along the street. Fortune brought him in directly behind the dictator's squad. The next instant, they were embroiled in a hand-to-hand fight.

Yelling, Honey Hamilton managed to fight clear of the fray. He jacked a fresh ammo drum into his machine gun, and, in order that its recoil would not get the instrument away from his control, he snapped it to a large belt which encircled his middle. The bit of delay was his undoing.

Anos, the dictator, himself, rushed Honey Hamilton. Anos gripped one of the darts, and was endeavoring to get it into a pneumatic tube. He gave that up as being too slow, and hurled it, spear fashion, at the mouselike killer.

Honey Hamilton dodged, but just a little too late, for the dart caught him in the face and clung there, flipping up and down as he jumped about.

But he did not jump for long. His eyes lost their glitter; for a fleeting instant, they held a bewildered expression as if the brain behind them were groping for something. Then the eyes blinked shut. The machine gun fell and hung by the belt fastenings. Honey Hamilton upset on the smooth stone.

Anos, the dictator, lunged and tried to pick up the machine gun, but the belt fastenings, being unfamiliar, baffled him, and instead, he lifted the dead thug up bodily, using the lifeless form as a shield. Anos had some luck then, or perhaps it was not luck, for he had observed closely the position of the hands when the gun wrought its havoc. He found the trigger.

The weapon's bawl wrought havoc on friend and foe alike. Shrieks arose. Men went down. Misdirected slugs streamed up to the roof, flattened, and came back like slow leaden rain. Cries from both sides pierced the uproar.

The effect of having one of the guns turned on them was unnerving to the rebelling *Stor* members. They wavered, milled. Then they began to retreat.

"Hold it!" Watches squawled, forgetting his command could not be understood.

Ool put the same orders into the cavern dialect, but without perceptible results. The *Stor* men fell back. The matter of personal safety dictated that Watches, Ool and the others keep in their midst, for men of the *Stor* were being used as human shields to a degree.

The dictator's seized machine gun stuttered to emptiness.

That changed the situation. Watches Bowen roared and rushed forward. He had his peculiar watch out, whirling it on the end of its stout chain. With hoarse cries, the *Stor* lunged to help him.

The end came quickly, for the darts were no match for the machine guns.

Anos, the dictator, was taken prisoner, and along with him, various members of the ruling *Nonverid*, who had been with him. This had the effect of breaking the backbone of the entire defense. These cavern people were not a fighting race, and with their leadership shattered, were virtually helpless.

The raiders went on and took the Central Mechanical Plant.

TWENTY minutes later, in a latticed chamber of the executive building, Anos, the dictator, his daughter Sona, the entire membership of the *Nonverid*, and certain other dignitaries, stood prisoners.

"They must be executed," said Ool. "That will insure us having no more trouble."

Members of the *Stor*, who packed the room, roared their approval of that suggestion.

"Sure," said Watches Bowen. "It's jake by me."

Ool translated, and the roars of fierce approval from the *Stor* echoed to the cavern roof.

"I got an idea," Watches said. "Get the bodies of Doc Savage and his men and bring 'em here. We'll bury the whole crowd together."

Ool agreed, and dispatched men to bring the bodies.

"We will hold off the execution for a time," he said.

"Why?" Watches wanted to know.

"The secret of the 'cold light' may not be on the voice wires in the laboratory file bins," Ool explained. "We can get the secret by studying the machinery, of course, but that will take much time. We may find it convenient to make some of these prisoners tell us, that we may be saved the labor of a search."

The men sent to bring the bodies of Doc Savage and his five aides, returned unexpectedly soon. They were excited, and stuttered out excitedly to Ool.

Ool swore one of the oaths he had picked up in association with Watches Bowen.

"What's wrong?" Watches demanded.

"The bodies have disappeared!" Ool explained gloomily.

Chapter XX
COLD FATE

THE failure to find the bodies of Doc Savage and his aides worried Watches Bowen and the others, but they did not let it interfere with their desires. They left the prisoners under guard and headed for the Central Mechanical Plant and its laboratories to search the voice wires in the file bins in an endeavor to locate the formula for the making of the "cold light."

"The absence of the bodies means nothing," Watches snorted. "Somebody took 'em away. That's all."

"Ah done feel bettah if Ah see dat bronze man put in de ground wit' mah own eyes," Ham-hock Piney advised. He shook his knob of a head on its many chins. "Ah don' know if Ah would feel plumb safe even den."

"Nuts!" said Watches.

Ham-hock moistened thick lips. "Watches, yo'-all nevah did get to give dat Doc Savage man de special watch what yo'-all been carryin' foah him."

"I'll bury it with him," Watches said.

The mechanism of the Central Mechanical Plant was throbbing steadily, monotonously, as they approached the wide doors. Although the excitement was seemingly over, Watches and his party had brought along a group of the *Stor*, in the center of whom they walked, in order to be safe from an unexpected attack.

They had sought to gather up the poison darts and the pneumatic tubes used to discharge them, but many of the darts, they knew, were still at large.

When they were very close to the Mechanical Plant entrance, things happened. There was a sudden hooting roar, a tremendous sound that blasted up a million echoes.

Watches and his men had heard it before.

"Ol' bronze bad luck ag'in!" Ham-hock Piney wailed. "Ah knowed he wasn't dead!"

The outer fringe of *Stor* was collapsing, mowed down by mercy bullets from the rapidfirers.

"Back!" Watches roared. "Get undercover!"

In the uproar, it was impossible that many could have heard, but hearing was not necessary. Shrinking instinctively before the devastating hail of chemical-charged lead slugs, the men poured backward around the nearest corner. Not all made it. Fully a score of the *Stor* had gone down.

While Ool was getting some sort of organization, Ham-hock muttered to Watches, "Ah reckons yo'-al goin' have a chance to use dat special watch, huh?"

Watches could only moan, "But I thought he was dead!"

They retreated on around to the other side of the building, a home-cell habitation structure, and took up positions behind a low ramp where they could not be reached by the supermachine pistols.

Ool and Watches conferred earnestly; then Ool, who knew the metropolis well, pointed out a route whereby they could gain the nearest door of the Central Mechanical Plant.

Watches ordered fresh drums in the submachine

guns. He planted himself and his men in the midst of the remaining Stor, and the charge started.

They reached the door of the Mechanical Plant with no losses in Watches' group, and with only a loss of about a third of the Stor allies. This was because the hooting of the supermachine pistols ceased when it was evident Watches and his party could not be kept out of the Plant.

The reason for that interruption in firing was soon evident. Doc Savage and his men had retreated and also entered the Central Mechanical Plant, but by another door.

Shots began to crash in the confines of the great plant.

Over and over, Ham-hock Piney muttered, "Dat bronze boy jes' ain't human."

ACTUAL explanation of how Doc Savage had maneuvered the escape from the dart death would probably have been incomprehensible to Ham-hock, for it entailed the use of numerous chemicals—the concocting, in short, of an antidote.

The fact that Habeas Corpus had not perished from the dart venom had indicated it was not necessarily as fatal as they had at first thought. The survival of Habeas was simple—hogs are frequently immune to snake bites, due possibly to their fatty structure. Doc's work in the laboratory, while besieged, had been for the purpose of concocting the antidote which he had persuaded his men to drink just before their capture.

As a matter of fact, the inoculation had not been as effective as was hoped, Doc and his aides all having lost consciousness at the execution. But the serum had prevented death, and they had revived after a time. The confusion during the thick of the fighting had covered their escape.

"Ah wishes Ah was back home!" Ham-hock Piney was wailing somewhere.

Big-fisted Renny rumbled, "He'll wish it even more if I can get hold of him!"

The Watches Bowen party were below, behind a fabulous tier of pipes which seemed to be heavily insulated and very strong.

"We will try to get above them," Doc said grimly.

There was a series of rungs, hardly a stairway, but intended as such, to the right. It worked up through more tubes, past tanks. The ticking of the plant was a sound of enormous volume here. They reached a spot where they could look down in a machine room, and there they saw the source of the ticking.

It was a huge compressor which worked with rhythmatic strokes, actuating tremendous pistons.

They went on. Twice, Watches Bowen's party saw them. Bullets rained. Doc got a bad scratch over one leg. Then Watches Bowen and Ool whipped their Stor allies into a compact group and forced them to charge forward.

Up the stairs, the Stor men came, realizing they were being used simply as shields, but more afraid of the raging threats behind than the possible death in front.

"Holy cow!" Renny stuttered. "They're liable to head us off!"

The crash of shots inside the Plant was terrific. In various spots, cavern men not engaged in the fighting were yelling out. Some seemed to be battling scattered members of the Stor.

Doc Savage and his men reached a narrow ledge which had a parapet that offered some shelter. They crouched behind it, unlimbered their machine pistols. The hooting blasts brought Watches Bowen's gang up sharp.

The Stor shields were more reluctant now. They milled about, hung back. Watches cursed them. Ham-hock Piney was too scared to be of much aid. Ool was making fierce darting gestures with his mysterious right hand, menacing the Stor men.

Watches Bowen fell to glaring at the ledge where Doc Savage and his men lay. Below the ledge was a sheer drop of fully fifty feet, and then moving machinery.

"Here's where I deliver that special watch!" Bowen gritted.

He dived a hand into a pocket.

THE timepiece which Watches Bowen brought out was the one which he had repeatedly assured members of his gang was a special gift destined for Doc Savage. The watch was unusually large. Bowen drew back an arm to throw it.

Doc Savage saw the move.

"Don't!" His remarkable voice was a crash of sound.

"Sure!" Watches yelled. "I'll do that!"

With a quick twist of thumb and forefinger, the mob chief turned the stem of the watch as if he were winding it. There started a faintly audible whir. His arm arched back, and he prepared to throw.

It was doubtful if Watches Bowen ever fully comprehended what happened next. Ool, apparently sensing Watches' intention, clawed out desperately to stop the throw. Their arms collided.

The watch flew forward and upward and landed in a maze of pipes almost over their heads.

Watches screamed, "Damn you! What—"

"Fool!" Ool said. "The pipes are carrying what you call liquid air—"

Whoo-o-m! The watch was a small, violent grenade, and it let go. Steel fragments rained from above. There was a shrill roar, not of powder unleashed, but of something else—something gray and smoking that boiled down in great sheets from rent pipes.

"The liquid air!" Ool screamed. "Run!"

His words were in the cavern language. Watches and the other thugs did not understand, at first—and when they did, it was too late, for the liquid air was spilling upon them and vaporizing, causing unearthly cold.

It engulfed Ool and Watches Bowen, and seemed to congeal them where they stood, for the insidious stuff came down in tremendous quantities, by hundreds of gallons.

Ool, having brief advance knowledge of what was going to happen, leaped and gained a little distance, but he fell down trying to wedge between pipes, and he lay there, his right arm outstretched through the pipes so that it was visible to Doc Savage and his men where they stood on the balcony. Doc had a pistol which he had seized, intending to shoot down the watch grenade in the air, were it thrown, a trick he could have accomplished, having done so on other occasions.

Ool's hideous right hand weaved, twisted for a time, then became still, for he was in the path of the flood of liquid air.

Vapor, like steam, was coming from the flood of liquid air in tremendous quantities, filling all of the Mechanical Plant.

Doc Savage and his men, able to see nothing, retreated, taking up positions at the doors, lest Watches Bowen or some of the others come out.

None came.

SOMETHING like ten hours saw the end of the *Stor* revolt which Watches Bowen and Ool had fostered—the men of the *Stor* did not stand up for long against the machine pistols of Doc Savage and his aides.

Anos, the dictator, Sona, his daughter, and members of the council were released, unharmed.

Since sufficient time had elapsed for the liquid air to vaporize in the Central Mechanical Plant, Doc Savage and his party entered to examine the remains of Watches Bowen, Ool and the others. The sight was not pleasant. The incredibly low temperatures of the liquid air had done strange things to the bodies; one, apparently freezing while sprawled over a pipe, had later upset, and being brittle, had broken as if it were glass.

It was Monk who first made an examination of Ool's right hand, which had not been affected greatly by the liquid air, projecting as it did through the pipes.

"The light dawns!" he exploded. "Lookit!"

The secret of Ool's hand-waving death was a bit complicated, but simply understood. It was a tiny pneumatic cylinder, discharging a dart, and this, being of a color almost identical with his hands, would escape ordinary eyes. It was held in place by a particularly strong adhesive which did not harden, and thus being quickly detachable, could be removed and hidden quickly.

That last, it was evident, accounted for Doc Savage not finding it on the occasions when he had searched Ool.

Ool's particular dart was very small, and driven with such force that it entered, bulletlike, entirely under the skin, leaving a wound that was perceptible to no ordinary examination.

Although Doc Savage and his men had not been equipped with the minute hand darts when they escaped from the latticed-windowed jail, it was evident that the guard, after seeing Doc's hand wave in butterfly fashion, had surmised the girl Sona had given Doc one of the small hand darts. It was this ruse which had caused his fright and allowed Doc and his aides to escape.

THE final fight in the Central Mechanical Plant marked the end of Doc Savage's trouble with the cavern people, it being demonstrated that he was a friend.

Learning their language, so that he could speak it even passably, required the expenditure of nearly a month. Not the entire time was spent learning the speech, however. There were other things— experiments with the strange "cold light," for instance. Those were not so encouraging.

It developed that the manner of illuminating the cavern air was not efficient where there was any considerable amount of moisture in suspension. That made it virtually useless for the outer world. The cavern air was fully as dry as that over the Sahara, and even it was a bit damp for efficiency at times.

"It works nicely here," Long Tom expressed it. "But it's no good outside."

Monk snorted. "Too bad we didn't know that. Watches Bowen and Ool could have had it."

The question of the population of the cavern came up. Doc offered them transportation to the outer world. It was feasible, using the dirigible.

The cavern people asked many questions about the outer world. Doc told them. They learned of blizzards, of summer heat, tornadoes, snowstorms, of modern transportation. Then they talked it over.

"We stay here," Anos, the dictator, advised Doc Savage. "Yours does not sound like such an attractive world. But we do have one boon to ask."

"What is it?" Doc questioned.

"Keep the existence of this place secret," said the other. "Revealing its existence can accomplish naught but trouble for us."

Doc Savage agreed. It was not the only fantastic secret he was keeping. Fantastic things had a way of coming in his direction, he reflected.

BEING no clairvoyant, the bronze man had no inkling of the next fantastic adventure which was to come his way, a thing more amazing, more inexplicable than any puzzle connected with this fabulous cavern land.

The Spook Legion was the fantastic foe next to confront Doc Savage. Horror came with this *Spook Legion,* and a terror that threw a nation into panic and fear. It was a foe which no man could oppose, this *Spook Legion,* for no man could see it. Yet it fell upon Doc Savage to go against the new terror, and in doing that, he was ordained to find a foe beside whom past enemies were mere tyros.

It was not true that the departure of Doc Savage from the cavern land was unmarked by regret. The remarkable bronze man had made an impression, especially among the members of the scientific groups, who found his knowledge surprising.

The girl, Sona, was reluctant to see him go. That was evident. And out of that, there grew a parting complication as Doc Savage and his aides, having been guided to the outer cleft where their dirigible still rested, and having gotten it ready for the air, prepared to take off.

Habeas Corpus could not be found.

There was an uproar. Departure was delayed while Monk charged about, hunting his porker. Eventually, he appeared with Habeas.

"Where's Ham?" he howled. "I'll wring that shyster's neck!"

Ham was, prudently, not in sight.

"The princess wanted a souvenir of our visit," Monk roared angrily. "What did this Ham do? I ask you? The shyster up and gave her Habeas!"

The homely chemist grinned.

"Now, if she had wanted *me* for a souvenir, I might have stayed," he chuckled. "But leave this hog? Nix!"

THE END

A TALE OF TWO GHOSTS by Will Murray

Land of Always-Night was one of the most celebrated Doc Savage novels ever. For years after its publication, *Doc Savage* editor John L. Nanovic claimed that readers still talked about that one. Once and awhile, he and one of the other "Kenneth Robesons" would try to work out a variation of the story, hoping to catch lightning in a bottle a second time. But they never did. Good as they were, only Lester Dent had the magic touch.

But Dent was not alone responsible for this Doc Savage classic.

Sometime early in 1934, he made the acquaintance of a fictioneer named W. Ryerson Johnson at one of the American Fiction Guild dinners for pulp writers. Dent may have been struck by the fact that Walter Johnson was known as "Johnny," which surely reminded him of the Doc Savage aide, Johnny Littlejohn. Although Johnson had grown up in Illinois coal country, he had briefly gone to medical school, where he had picked up the serendipitous nickname of "Doc."

Ryerson Johnson

Dent and Johnson hit it off right away.

"When you're talking about Les Dent," Johnson once said, "you're talking about one of my favorite people on this earth. A completely genuine honest person; not a phoney pore in his body—and it was a big body, big and gangling and awkward. I used to wonder how he could fly a plane with his rough coordination. But he did. Man, yes. A stunt pilot... Doc Savage. I sometimes halfway thought of him in those terms."

They were a contrast. One big and bluff, a giant of a man. The other was small and spry. Johnson had once bummed around the Balkans, earning his way by playing the musical saw. After he saved a local man from drowning, Johnson became a feted hero, and gave a musical saw concert on the Bulgarian National Opera stage. He was a Bohemian soul who during the early days of the Depression rode the boxcar tops in the company of hobos, seeing America and searching for story ideas.

"Johnny is one guy who never lets anything interfere with the pleasant ambling business of grazing through life," Dent once observed.

Dent was on the prowl for help writing the monthly Doc Savage novels, and he liked to pick the brains of prospective Kenneth Robesons for unique treasures.

"It often started with 'something of value to be attained,'" Johnson once recalled. "'Can you think of any new treasure Doc can go after?' Les would sometimes ask me. 'Something nobody would think of? The farther out the better. I get the treasure, I've got the Doc.'"

As Johnson's roommate, Mort Weisinger, recounted:

"These treasures ran the spectrum. I remember one novel where the treasure was—bat shit! Guano droppings. It was used for fertilizer—a very valuable fertilizer. There were caves of the stuff. Thousands of tons of the stuff. Since time immemorial bats have been feathering the nest, so to speak."

From Johnson, Dent learned about a unique gold-mining scheme up in Maine, where the little pulpster had a summer home. Dent soon spun a Doc Savage yarn called *The Sea Magician* out of that anecdote.

Before long, Dent approached his new friend about ghosting a Doc. Although Johnson had broken into the pulp fiction field writing tales of the Canadian Mounted Police, switching to Westerns when the Mountie subgenre went out of fashion, he was a fan of the science fiction pulps. They paid too poorly for Johnson's tastes, but *Doc Savage* presented an opportunity to do an adventure yarn with a strong fantastic element against the backdrop of the Far North he wrote about so vigorously.

Together, they brainstormed an idea about a weird individual who appears in New York, and may or may not be entirely human. Ool, as he was dubbed, made a worthy foe for the superhuman Man of Bronze.

Johnson remembered Dent saying, "Doc Savage looks human, acts human, but he's just a slightly little bit more. Not enough to make him freaky. It takes delicate handling...."

With Weisinger at his side, Johnson concocted an outline titled "The Always-Night Land." It began:

> In ancient days, a highly civilized people—perhaps an off-shoot of the Chinese—dwelling on an island off the Alaskan coast, were forced, because of encroaching glaciers, to go underground to live. These people have built up a complete underground economy.

Lost civilizations were a recurring Doc theme, but here was unexplored territory—an excursion into the "hollow Earth" myth popularized in speculative fact and fiction. Many writers had postulated that the earth was hollow and inhabited. Some thought entrances to this inner realm lay at the poles. Now it was Doc Savage's turn to plunge into this ultimate unknown land.

Dent reworked the outline, making many changes. Where Johnson had Doc Savage travel to the North Pole by trimotor, Dent took this opportunity to outfit the Man of Bronze with a personal dirigible. It was the first of Doc's mighty airship fleet, each one of which got bigger and more futuristic in succeeding adventures. Rarely did they survive an adventure, but this prototype did.

Once Street & Smith approved the idea, Johnson tackled three chapters, which Dent punched up. Then Lester handed the book off to his friend to complete.

"Just blast it out," Dent instructed, "just get the action flow and the plot down... I'll do the prettying afterwards."

Johnson wrote for some of the top pulp magazines, including *Argosy* and *Adventure*—markets Dent had yet to crack. So he encouraged Johnny to introduce stylistic touches of his own. One was the colorful new descriptions employed for Doc's signature sound.

"The business of trying to be fresh in every story," Johnson recounted, "trying to find new ways to describe the faintly-more-than-human power, was a hoodoo. He scoured the dictionary to find synonyms: humming, evanescence, trilling. I think I may have 'sold' the word 'evanescence' (in relation to Doc's trilling) to Les. Every writer

Lester Dent

absorbs a few out-of-the-way words that he slots in here and there. Evanescence was one of mine.... I seem to remember his pleasurable acceptance of the word when I mentioned it in relation to the trilling, after he told me to try to think up some fresh words to use in describing it."

Johnson slipped a few personal touches into the tale. Dent had set up the story so that Doc operated in the guise of an unnamed American Indian, an escaped murderer from Sing Sing. Johnson changed him to Dimiter Daikoff, named after the man whose life he had saved in Bulgaria.

"I didn't know Les too well at that time," Johnson explained, "... and now looking back, it seemed childishly important to somehow have some identification with the book....I dreamed up a governing body for that underearth world, named the Nonrevid. 'That's a screwy name,' Les said, when he first looked over the story. But a little to my surprise, he left it in. I never told him until years later that it was the name of my hometown in Illinois spelled backwards: Divernon."

Dent did modify it slightly, to "Nonverid." The story title was changed to *Land of Always-Night.* Ool was also toned down. Originally, he was described as "...a strange man covered with a growth of golden fur," which Johnson recalls stood up in the presence of danger like a tomcat arching its back.

Another Dentian touch was Watches Bowen's headquarters at Long Island's City Island dock. This is where Dent moored his schooner *Albatross* before relocating it to Miami later in 1934.

A Socialist sympathizer, Johnson meant this yarn to be a commentary on the ruling class versus the workers. Dent's view was far from that.

Johnson drafted this story in September 1934. Intended as the 24th Doc novel, *Land of Always-Night* took Johnson an entire month to produce, forcing Dent to write *Red Snow* to keep the magazine on schedule.

When it was finished, the two pulpeteers decided to visit their families in the midwest. So they headed west together in Dent's red LaSalle convertible. Dent picked Johnson up on a New York street corner.

"He met me with his fist full of 10 and 20 dollar bills—$500," Johnson reminisced. "'Okay, chum,' he said, 'now if we get robbed on the way home, remember I paid you.'"

Land of Always-Night received a typical Lester Dent polish in October, and ran in the March 1935 issue of *Doc Savage Magazine.* It had the distinction of being the first Doc novel penned in La Plata, Missouri, where Dent was born and where he would finally settle down. It stands with the very best of this legendary series, and Nostalgia Ventures is pleased to re-present it.

Strange events which changed people into
other identities bring Doc Savage into

MAD MESA

BY KENNETH ROBESON

Chapter I
HONDO WEATHERBEE

THE life of Thomas Idle had been an ordinary
one. Nothing fantastic had ever happened to him.

Nor, unfortunately, was Tom Idle a well-known
young man. Had he been a person of importance,
the newspapers might have blazed up about his
disappearance, and perhaps this would have

focused attention on the utterly incredible thing
that happened to him.

Still, the thing was so strange that no one might
have believed it, even if it had happened to Hitler,
or Mussolini, or someone equally well-known.
No one believed Tom Idle. No one believed him
in time, that is, to stop the baby monster of horror
which began to grow when it took its first bite and
swallowed Tom Idle.

Tom Idle was born on a Missouri farm, soon orphaned, went to high school, then worked on a farm as a hired man. A few weeks ago, he had become tired of farming, and, seeking greener fields, had vagabonded westward on freight trains and by hitchhiking.

Now he was trying to find a job in Salt Lake City, Utah.

So far, the nearest he had come to an adventure was the time old Jinn, the farm mule, kicked him; but old Jinn kicked him on the leg, not the head, so the incident in no way explained what occurred in Salt Lake City.

Tom Idle was using the city park for his hotel.

He awakened on the same park bench he had occupied three nights running. He carefully folded the newspapers he had used to keep the dew off, and placed them in a trash can—he had learned that the park cop, Officer Sam Stevens, did not mind you using the place for a hotel, but resented having the grass littered.

Officer Sam Stevens passed. Tom Idle gave him a grin, and the policeman grinned back.

"Today's a lucky day, kid," Officer Stevens said. "I been feelin' it all mornin'. Today, you find that job."

"Thanks!" Tom Idle said.

The officer's hunch made him feel better. He was no clairvoyant, so he could not know what a phantasm the near future held.

Morning air was bracing, the sunshine was bright, and the sky had that remarkably healthful clarity peculiar to Salt Lake City. It did look like a lucky day, at that. Tom Idle went to Skookum's lunchroom.

"Sinkers and java, Skookum." He deposited his last nickel on the white counter.

He tried not to remember this was the third day he'd subsisted on coffee and doughnuts.

Skookum said, "This monotony'll get you down, chief."

"It'll have to, then," Tom Idle answered wryly, "because I'm broke."

Skookum's name wasn't Skookum; it was something which nobody but a Greek could pronounce. Everyone called him Skookum because he was always using slangy Indian expressions when he talked. Skookum was liked.

A few moments later, Skookum unexpectedly put a plate of ham and eggs in front of Tom Idle.

"I can't pay for that," Tom Idle said.

"Pay when you land job, chief."

"What makes you think I'll land one?"

"Don't kid yourself. Heap plenty job. You catch."

Tom Idle's eyes became suddenly damp with gratitude.

"Thanks, Skookum," he mumbled.

Physically fortified with Skookum's unexpected ham and eggs, and mentally perked up by Officer Sam Stevens' statement that this was a lucky day, Tom Idle did his best—but did not find work that day. He visited all the employment agencies, and even solicited from door to door; but as one man put it, "Jobs are as scarce as hen's teeth!"

Tom Idle slept that night on his usual bench in the park.

Ever afterward, it seemed to him that this was the last really normal day that he ever spent.

THE next morning, a strangled rasping sound caused Tom Idle to awaken. He jerked erect, scattering his newspaper blankets. Because he had really starved for several days, he at once felt nervous and shaky.

He batted his eyes in the morning sun, looking around.

He saw the horrified man immediately.

The man stood beside the park bench. He was past middle age, looked seedy, might have been a professional bum. There was much of the furtiveness and insolence of a confirmed hobo in his face.

The man had obviously made the strangled sound which had aroused Tom Idle. There was utter horror on the man's face.

"Hondo Weatherbee!"

"What?" Tom Idle said. "What'd you say?"

"Hondo!"

Tom Idle looked blankly at the man's shocked, terrified expression, and came to the conclusion that the fellow was a drunk. He was some souse who'd mistaken Tom Idle for someone named Hondo Weatherbee. That must be it.

"Better sit down," he suggested soothingly, "and get your eyes uncrossed."

The horrified man acted as if the devil had asked him to come down and sample the warmth. He started back. Whirled. Fled. He ran wildly away, not looking back.

"I'll be darned!" Tom Idle said.

He gazed after the fleeing man—the fellow looked so comically ridiculous in his flight. But Tom Idle somehow could not smile, because there was something unnerving about the whole thing. He had a creepy feeling.

"Snap out of it, guy," he told himself. "The bum was only plastered to the gills."

Trying to get rid of the creeps, Tom Idle made an elaborate business of stretching and scratching himself, then of retying his shoestrings and necktie, for loosening shoestrings and necktie were about the only bedtime preparations he'd made since a park bench was his hotel.

Again this morning, the world was full of beautiful sunshine, with birds singing in the park trees, and the air pleasant with the fruity odor of the orchards surrounding oasislike Salt Lake City, while a few clouds were sitting like big white rabbits on top of the black mountains to the eastward.

But Tom Idle was in no frame of mind to enjoy a balmy morning.

He was looking at his shoes.

They were not his shoes! They were gaudy yellow shoes—his shoes had been black and scuffed. He dropped his eyes and stared at the necktie he was wearing, and it was not his necktie; it was flashy green and yellow in color, whereas his necktie had been a subdued brown. Nor was the shirt his, nor the suit. All the clothes he was wearing were *different.*

He stared in horror at his hands—for they were not his hands either, it seemed; they looked pale, and on one finger was a ring he had never seen before, a big, ugly, yellow gold ring with the top carved in the shape of a skull.

Tom Idle stood up, feeling like a man having a bad dream, and walked out of the park.

He did not see Officer Sam Stevens just then.

Since the incredible thing had already started to happen to Tom Idle, it was doubtful if it would have made any difference had he seen the cop at this juncture.

Tom Idle was partially rid of most of his creeps by the time he entered Skookum's lunchroom.

But he got them again when Skookum grabbed a gun and began shooting at him.

THERE were some brief preliminaries.

First, Skookum saw Tom Idle and jumped up. Skookum was eating his own breakfast, and he knocked his cup of coffee to the floor.

"Hondo Weatherbee!" Skookum yelled.

Tom Idle began to think this was all some kind of a gag. They must be having some fun with him.

"Hey, cut it out!" he said. "Heap much is enough."

But Skookum stood so rigidly and stared with such ghastly fixity, that Tom Idle suddenly saw that it could not be acting. Skookum was not that good an actor.

"Cut it," Tom Idle muttered. "You know me. I'm Tom Idle, the guy you staked to ham and eggs yesterday. Some darn fool swapped clothes on me."

Skookum licked his lips.

"Who you trying to kid, Hondo?" he snarled. "I know that nice kid. You're not him."

Tom Idle then did something which he habitually did when he was ill at ease; he put his hands in his coat pockets. In thinking it all over later, he realized that Skookum might have thought he was reaching for a gun.

Skookum made a wild dive, got down behind the counter, came up with a sawed-off shotgun. He blazed away.

Gun roar was ear-splitting. The blast blew a hole in the lunchroom wall so close to Tom Idle's head that he could have put his arm through it.

There was no joke about this. That shotgun was real, and Skookum was trying to kill him.

Tom Idle wheeled, ducked, dived out of the lunchroom. He ran. It was only a short distance to the park. He turned into the park. Behind, the shotgun slammed again. Shot cut leaves off the trees, and frightened birds flew up all over the park.

The Officer Sam Stevens met Tom Idle for the first time that morning.

Officer Stevens was a tall young man, a year or two older than Tom Idle. He came racing through the park to see what all the shooting was about, rounded a clump of bushes, and almost bumped into Tom Idle. Tom Idle never forgot that meeting.

"Hey help me!" Tom Idle panted. "That fool, Skookum, is trying to kill me!"

Officer Stevens stared at Tom Idle.

"Damn!" he barked. "It's Hondo Weatherbee!"

He struck with his club, swung a blow at Tom Idle's head. Tom Idle's reaction was instinctive. He dodged, and the club hit his head a glancing blow; he grabbed the club and they fought over it. Idle got the officer's billy.

Then the cop reached for his revolver.

Tom Idle struck the officer down with his own club. There was nothing else he could do. Something fantastic had happened, and he wasn't a young man named Tom Idle in search of a job; he was a sallow-skinned, garishly dressed man named Hondo Weatherbee, and everyone was either afraid of him or wanted to kill him. He could not understand it.

Officer Sam Stevens fell senseless.

Tom Idle dropped the club, whirled and ran. He did not know how long Officer Stevens would remain unconscious, and he had no idea at what instant Skookum might haul into view with his shotgun.

"The thing is to get out of here!" he thought.

Professional humorists claim that anything so unbelievable that it is preposterous constitutes a joke. Tom Idle was bewildered, frightened, horror-stricken; but one thing he did know—that no part of the last few minutes had been a joke. Everybody had been in dead earnest, from the seedy bum whose gasp had awakened him on the park bench, to Skookum and his shotgun and Officer Stevens and his pistol.

Probably the most incredible thing of all to Tom Idle was that he had gone to sleep wearing black shoes and a neat, if worn, blue suit—and had awakened with strange yellow shoes and a gaudy

Tom Idle struck the officer down.

suit. And his skin! His tanned brown skin! It had become pale! He was completely bewildered.

The appearance of the black-gloved man did not clarify the situation, either.

Chapter II
THE BLACK-GLOVED MAN

THE black-gloved man was in a car, and the machine apparently had been cruising around and around the park in search of Tom Idle. The car was a touring model, the top down. The black-gloved man drove, and he was craning his neck as though hunting someone. Apparently, it was Tom Idle he sought, because he sent the car to Idle's side.

"Hondo!" he yelled. "Get in!"

Tom Idle did not like the looks of the man. Probably he would never have gotten in the car, except for the fact that Skookum appeared in the distance, fired a shotgun blast, and two or three shot stung Tom Idle's skin. He decided to get in the car after all. The stranger at least looked friendly.

The moment Tom Idle landed in the car, the vehicle leaped into motion. Within two minutes, it was breaking the speed limit; and in five minutes, it was going faster than Tom Idle had ever before ridden in a car.

"What in the hell happened?" asked the black-gloved man.

"I don't know," Tom Idle said truthfully.

"You went in the park with that bottle of stuff," the stranger snapped. "That was over two hours ago. You told me to cruise around and be ready to pick you up. While I'm doing that, I see Seedy Smith come tearing out of the park as if a devil were after him."

Tom Idle stared blankly. Here was another man who thought he was someone else.

"Who—who is Seedy Smith?" he asked uncertainly.

"Why, Seedy used to belong to your gang, Hondo. Don't you remember? He double-crossed you, and you've been promising to croak him when you saw him."

Tom Idle swallowed.

"Croak him? You mean kill him?"

"Sure," said the black-gloved man calmly.

"Am I—am I the kind of a man who would kill Seedy Smith?" Tom Idle asked, feeling strange.

The black-gloved man laughed harshly.

"You're Hondo Weatherbee," he said. "You'd do anything!"

TOM IDLE looked at the speedometer, and got such a shock that he decided not to do it again. The needle was kicking close to a hundred. The car felt as if it were a skyrocket, running on the earth only part of the time. They had left the city behind and were now climbing mountains, traversing the first of what promised to be a series of dizzy curves from which sheer precipices fell hundreds, in some places thousands, of feet.

"Not so fast!" Tom Idle said hoarsely.

The black-gloved man stared at him in surprise.

"What the hell, Hondo? It ain't like you to be made jittery by a little speed."

Tom Idle didn't think it safe to startle the man by saying he was not Hondo Weatherbee. Not at the speed they were traveling, and on a road like this.

Clutching the door of the speeding car, Tom Idle examined his companion. The fellow had a long, well-stuffed body that was remindful of a number of large sausages. His face was distinctly uninviting. It was evil. The mouth was vicious, the nose thin, the ears pointed, the eyes small and discolored, like bird eggs that hadn't hatched. He wore his black gloves, on both hands.

This unsavory personage was in turn eyeing Tom Idle at such times as he was not busy wheeling the thunderbolt of a car around awful mountain curves.

"There's something strange about you, Hondo," he said.

Tom Idle thought of a way in which he might perhaps get a clue to what had happened to him without startling this stranger.

"I must have got a bump on the head," Tom Idle said, untruthfully.

"So that was it!"

Deciding the man seemed satisfied with the explanation, Tom Idle ventured, "You say I went into that park two hours ago with a bottle?"

"Sure," the black-gloved man said. "Don't you remember that."

"I don't recall it. What was in the bottle?"

"The stuff you got from a nut chemist."

"What kind of stuff?"

"You didn't tell me, Hondo."

"Who was the chemist I got the bottle from?"

"Well—hell, you never told me that, neither. It was a big secret."

Tom Idle felt defeated and desperate. More and more he was being gripped by the feeling that something frightful, and something he couldn't possibly prevent, was happening to him.

"Didn't I tell you anything at all?" he asked wildly.

The black-gloved man grimaced in a puzzled way. "You talked like you were drunk."

"What did I say?"

"Something about if you could only find a bum asleep in the park, your troubles would be over." The man gave Tom Idle a blank look and added, "Damn it, Hondo, I'll never forget your exact words, just before you walked into that park with the bottle."

Tom Idle shuddered. "What were they?"

"'If I can find a bum asleep in the park, the cops will never get their hands on the brain of Hondo Weatherbee!' That's exactly what you said, Hondo."

THE touring car continued its headlong speed. The engine must have special power, because the steep grades did not seem to bother it. They had climbed so high now that the air was already much cooler, and the clouds, the great clouds that seemed like white rabbits, were close overhead.

Tom Idle sat so tensely that every muscle in his body seemed to ache. He was trying to make his mind grasp the situation. It was *his mind*. But his body—and his clothing—were the property of an outlaw named Hondo Weatherbee. His black-gloved companion apparently belonged to a bandit gang ruled by Hondo Weatherbee. And the bum, Seedy Smith, had been a man whom Hondo Weatherbee had promised to kill. And Skookum, the lunchroom man, and Officer Sam Stevens, had both known Hondo Weatherbee by sight, and had tried to capture him. Tom Idle took his head in his hands. It was too impossible to believe!

A violent start by his companion aroused him. Tom Idle realized the car had slowed, and that they were traversing a series of terrible curves.

The black-gloved man wiped his forehead.

"That one was close!" he croaked.

"What's wrong?" Tom Idle gasped.

"Cops!"

"Huh?"

"They're after us. Whatcha think we been drivin' like a bat for? They've got high-powered rifles. They're shooting at us."

"Police shooting at us?"

"Look back, if you don't believe me!"

Tom Idle was turning to look back when the inside of his head seemed to explode in a flood of blackness—and the blackness, spreading, washed completely through his body until all of him, mind and flesh alike, was composed of nothing but darkness, empty and still.

Chapter III
THE FINGERPRINTS

THE penitentiary had high stone walls, and they were gray. The summer sun beat down on the place; hot desert winds blew across it and heated the interior like a furnace. In the winter, the same winds were as cold as solid ice, and refrigerated the place thoroughly. The penitentiary had a reputation as being a place of which to steer clear—the kind of a reputation a penitentiary should have—in spite of the fact that it was modern, and had a warden who was perfectly fair to every inmate.

There was a cell block to itself where the desperate criminals were confined. This was isolated. The cells were bare. No luxuries were allowed. There were no windows, but plenty of light came through the cell doors. There were great frosted windows across the corridor, and light from these fell through the cell doors and cast bar-checked shadows across the cell floors.

It was the shadows of these steel bars which Tom Idle saw when he regained consciousness.

He had the sensation of something being wrong about the way he regained consciousness. Back in Missouri, he had once fallen out of a tree while trying to twist an opossum out of a hole with a forked stick, and it had knocked him senseless. He recalled how he had felt when he regained consciousness. This awakening was different. He felt as though he had been ill for a long time. But then, everything that had happened had been different.

He stared at the bar shadows on the cell floor until his eyes hurt.

"Hey!" a voice said. "Wake up!"

Tom Idle turned his head to look at the speaker.

The man was big; he was incredibly huge—and as long as Tom Idle knew him afterward, the man appeared to get each day a little bigger. Maybe it was the increasing evil of the man that made it seem so. Each day that you knew him, you realized he was a little more vicious than you had thought he possibly could be.

"Who . . . who are you?" Tom Idle stuttered.

"Big Eva," the man growled. "Who'd you think it'd be, Hondo?"

There was nothing distorted about Big Eva's size; he was not puffy, he did not seem to have a thick neck—just big. He was about seven feet tall.

"Where am I?" Tom Idle demanded.

Big Eva chuckled. "If it's not the Utah State Penitentiary, I've wasted three years in the wrong place."

"How long have I been here?" Tom Idle asked.

"Eleven years and three days." Big Eva showed large snaggle teeth in a grin. "Mean to say you don't remember?"

Tom Idle was stupefied.

"I've been in here eleven years?" he croaked.

Big Eva pointed at the cell wall beside Idle's bunk. On the wall was a series of marks made with a pencil, marks in groups of seven, as if they represented days and weeks.

"Count it up on your calendar, if you don't believe me," the giant convict said.

Tom Idle gripped the rail of his bunk. His head ached, felt as if shingle nails were being driven

BIG EVA

into his skull. His self-control slipped, and suddenly he was on his feet, gripping the barred cell door, rattling it madly.

"The warden!" he screamed. "I want to talk to the warden!"

A burly man in uniform appeared before the door. A penitentiary guard, Tom Idle presumed.

"How'd you like solitary confinement?" the guard asked harshly.

Then Big Eva had Tom Idle by the elbow and was pulling him back.

"I dunno what's got into you, Hondo," Big Eva growled. "You're startin' the day wrong."

THAT day was a nightmare for Tom Idle, and it was the first of a series. Because there seemed nothing else to do, he went to breakfast with the rest of the convicts, and later to work in the overall shop. As Hondo Weatherbee, it developed that he was supposed to know all about operating one of the sewing machines; but since he knew nothing about the device, he at once got the thread snarled, then accidentally did something which broke the machine. For this, he was put in solitary confinement the rest of the day, the guards thinking he had broken the machine maliciously.

He took off a shoe and beat the steel door of the cell. He also kept up a steady shouting, demanding to see the warden.

Later in the afternoon, they took him to the warden's office.

The instant he entered the warden's room, Tom Idle yanked to a stop and stared.

There was a huge mirror on the wall. Tom Idle was seeing himself for the first time since things had started to happen to him.

His face *was* different—and yet, not completely. It was sallow. The cheeks seemed lumpy. He brought his hands to his face and explored, discovered that there were indeed lumps in his cheeks that felt as though they might be old scar tissue. But his eyes were the same. Bloodshot with strain, it was true; but still his eyes.

"Ahem," said a voice.

Tom Idle realized he must seem a lunatic, staring at the mirror in that fashion.

"Are you the warden?" he asked.

"Yes."

The warden was a lean, weatherbeaten man who resembled the movie version of a cowboy sheriff. The squint that came from looking at far places was in his eyes, and he had a jaw built like the device they once put on the front of railway locomotives to knock cows off the tracks.

To this quiet, determined man, Tom Idle told his whole story exactly as it had happened, from his awakening in the Salt Lake City park to his becoming unconscious, presumably from the effects of a bullet, on the mountain road.

To all this, the penitentiary warden listened with intent interest.

"Let's feel the top of your head," he said.

Tom Idle let the warden's fingers explore in his hair.

"This where the bullet hit you?" the warden asked.

"Well, it hit me on the head."

"There's no scar there," the warden said.

"But something hit me!"

The warden's voice had turned cold, and now he got to his feet, put his capable hands on his lean hips, and looked Tom Idle up and down without sympathy.

"I don't know what your game is, Hondo Weatherbee. But you'd better not try to put anything over."

"I've told you the truth!" Tom Idle said desperately.

The warden snorted. "Do you remember how you were captured eleven years ago?"

"No! Of course not!"

"You were found asleep on a Salt Lake City park bench, and you were pursued by a policeman and a lunchroom man, and you were captured fleeing up the mountains in a car driven by an accomplice."

"I … but—"

"In other words," the warden snapped, "you've just been telling me the story of how you were captured eleven years ago. Only you trimmed the story up a bit."

Tom Idle was stunned.

"What date is this?" he wanted to know. "What day and year?"

The warden told him.

Tom Idle repeated the date under his breath. Five days had elapsed, somehow, into blankness. Only five days. Five days ago he had been in that Salt Lake City park, and he couldn't remember anything about how the ensuing interval had gone; that was just more of the incredible mystery.

"But I'm Tom Idle!" he said wildly.

The warden sighed. "I'm a patient man, Hondo, and a fair one. Nobody can say different and talk truth. What do you want me to do? What will satisfy you?"

"Have you got Hondo Weatherbee's fingerprints here?" Tom Idle asked.

"Yes."

"Compare them with mine."

The warden had Hondo Weatherbee's fingerprint card brought from the files, and he inked Tom Idle's prints onto a white paper and put it side by side with the fingerprints of the outlaw.

Even Tom Idle could see that his fingerprints and Hondo Weatherbee's were the same.

If it were possible, Tom Idle was more stunned.

BEING a young man with a perfectly normal mentality, Tom Idle realized that the best thing for him to do now was to settle back and get himself accustomed to the position in which he found himself. Rushing around screaming that he was Tom Idle, a Missouri farm boy, would not help. The mental agitation might even drive him insane.

He behaved, kept his eyes open, and tried to work out some way of helping himself.

He learned that Big Eva was afraid of him. So were most of the other convicts. Or rather, they were afraid of the man they thought was Hondo Weatherbee, which gave an idea of the kind of reprobate Hondo Weatherbee must have been. There were some tough jailbirds in that penitentiary.

He obtained but slight information about Hondo Weatherbee. The man had been a prospector at odd times when he was not in assorted penitentiaries. Eleven years ago, he had stood trial for murdering his partner, and received a life sentence.

It was a tribute to Tom Idle's character that he did not sink into a black abyss of despair. He could not, no matter how much he thought about it, understand how he had become another man serving a life sentence in a penitentiary, and the desperation of that situation might have broken his will. But Tom Idle bore up.

He took to reading a great deal.

That was how he happened to learn about Doc Savage.

TOM IDLE started reading the magazine feature about Doc Savage without much interest. But halfway through the article, he became so excited he had to stop and let off steam.

"Say!" he said. "Say, boy!"

He was seeing the first ray of hope that had come his way for days.

When he had calmed himself, he continued reading about Doc Savage.

The article stated that Doc Savage was a man who had one of the most remarkable scientific minds of the day. The item added that Doc Savage made a business of solving unusual mysteries— but he did this, it was stated, only if a wrong was righted or someone was helped as a result.

Since a career of righting wrongs was an unusual one for a man to follow, the author of the magazine story went to lengths to explain that this was Savage's most spectacular activity, hence got the most attention, but that his real career was that of a scientist.

The author of the magazine article waxed enthusiastic about the "Man of Bronze," as he called Doc Savage; he wrote that the Man of Bronze was really a man of mystery, because he avoided publicity, and very little information concerning him came to the attention of the public.

Tom Idle realized that here was exactly the kind of man he needed to help him. But the author of the article made Doc Savage out to be such a combination of scientific genius, mental marvel and physical giant that Tom Idle was skeptical about such a super-person existing. The magazine item said that the name of Doc Savage was enough to strike terror into the heart of the most hardened crook.

Tom Idle decided to test this out. He made his experiment on Big Eva, who was a hardened crook if there ever were one.

"Doc Savage!" Tom Idle said unexpectedly.

The effect on Big Eva was impressive.

He dropped the pencil with which he was marking up the day on his own wall calendar across the cell. He whirled. His expression was stark.

"What about Doc Savage?" Big Eva snarled. *"Is he mixing in this—"* The huge, bestial crook swallowed two or three times. "But hell, he couldn't have gotten wise. There's no way—"

At this point, Big Eva appeared to realize he was saying too much.

"What about Doc Savage?" he growled.

"I was just reading about him in this magazine," Tom Idle explained.

Big Eva took several large gulps of relief.

"What the hell do you mean," he exploded, "by scaring people that way?"

SEVERAL days later, Tom Idle learned about the prison grapevine. This was an important event, because indirectly it saved thousands of lives.

But in the meantime, Tom Idle had given some thought to the blurtings of Big Eva when he had been so startled.

"What did you mean," he asked, "by what you said?"

"Said when?"

"When I told you about Doc Savage," Tom Idle explained. "You seemed worried for fear he'd found out about something."

Big Eva stood up. He doubled his huge fists.

"Shut up!" he snarled. "If you ever breathe a word about that to a soul, I'll kill you!"

He meant it. Nobody could doubt that.

The prison grapevine is a furtive thing. All penitentiaries have them. This was how it functioned:

Tom Idle was served four pancakes for breakfast, ate two of them, and left two on his plate with a letter secreted between them. In the kitchen, the convict dishwasher was careful to put the two pancakes, still with the letter between them, on top of the garbage can. The driver of the garbage wagon mailed the letter.

The magazine article had not given Doc Savage's address.

But Tom Idle had a sister in Missouri. The letter was addressed to his sister. It told Tom Idle's story, and asked his sister to get Doc Savage to investigate.

The letter got off successfully, and on its way to Missouri.

But two nights later, Tom Idle talked in his sleep, mumblingly, and told about the letter he had mailed to his sister asking her to appeal to Doc Savage for aid—and Big Eva listened in open-mouthed horror.

Chapter IV
THE MYSTERIOUS PILOT

SUE CITY, Missouri, is a settlement that can be found on the larger maps. It does not have a reputation for size, but it is a lively place, supplying the needs of the agricultural community, and on Saturday nights staging square dances and boxing matches, as well as holding, once a year, a homecoming that is an event.

Samantha Nona Idle lived near Sue City, in the big white house on the gravel road. She kept house for her Aunt Annie and her Uncle Herm, who had raised her.

Nona was a striking girl. She was tall and firm and streamlined, and bore some resemblance to her brother, Tom Idle. She had managed to drop the Samantha from her name by carefully telling nobody about it for a number of years. She was intelligent, and was specializing in voice at the State University in Columbia. The boys liked her looks, and her college professors liked her determination to make something out of herself.

The mail carrier left Tom Idle's letter in the galvanized mailbox under the big elm tree at the gate.

Nona did not mention her brother's letter to anybody. He had requested this. He did not want the neighbors to know he was in the penitentiary.

The next day, Nona left for New York to see Doc Savage.

She went by bus because it was cheaper. Money was a scarce commodity around there.

That evening, the airplane landed at Sue City. The plane was piloted by the man with the black gloves.

THE plane came wabbling down out of the sky as if something was wrong, and landed in a cow pasture on Nona Idle's farm. The pilot climbed out and doubled up on the ground.

NONA IDLE

"Damn, but I'm sick!" he croaked. "Must be somethin' I ate."

His condition improved quickly when there was talk of taking him to a hospital. He stated that all he needed was a rest, and he managed to persuade Aunt Annie and Uncle Herm to put him up for the night.

"You seem depressed," remarked the pilot, at the supper table that evening.

"I reckon as how we're gettin' old and lonesome," said Uncle Herm. "Anyhow, we sure hate to see one of the family leave."

The pilot had not removed his black gloves to eat, but he did explain that he intended to consume only a bite or two because of his upset stomach. He was suave, effusively friendly, and his manner had overcome Uncle Herm's first dislike for the fellow. His body—like jointed sausages—was dressed in an expensive, neat suit, and dark glasses concealed the evil character of his eyes, which were like bird eggs that hadn't hatched.

"One of your children leave recently?" the pilot asked.

"Not exactly. It was Nona Idle. We raised her." Uncle Herm sighed regretfully. "That's sure gonna be a long bus trip, all the way to New York."

"Nona Idle has gone to New York?"

The pilot barely kept a rasp of anxiety out of the question.

"Yep," said Uncle Herm.

"Why?"

"That's what kinda worries us," Uncle Herm explained. "She didn't say. Ain't like the girl not to tell us, neither."

The pilot took off in a hurry in his airplane. His stomach was better, he said—but as a matter of fact, he looked sicker than when he had landed.

He flew toward New York.

Mixed with the motor fumes in the wake of his plane was a sulphurous haze of curses which the pilot flung at the Idles, brother and sister, at Big Eva, at himself, but most of all at a man named Doc Savage. He swore himself into such a stew that he began talking aloud to his plane.

"What if I don't manage to stop that girl?" he yelled at the plane.

The possibility was good for several minutes of anxious snarling.

Later, he settled down grimly to the business of flying to overtake Nona Idle.

NONA IDLE reached Columbus, Ohio, with a conviction that bus travel was almost as comfortable as railroad. She had the good sense to resist the impulse which seems to seize bus patrons to fill up on hamburgers and ice-cream cones at every hot-dog stand. When she reached Columbus, she was hungry, but she felt well.

Beyond Columbus, on U. S. Highway No. 40, the bus swung into one of the comfortable roadside stations, and Nona Idle, noting the clean-looking restaurant in connection, decided to have her first meal.

A man wearing black gloves slid onto the adjacent seat shortly after she started eating.

The man did not say anything, did not appear to as much as notice the tall, very pretty girl at his side. When a waitress came, he spoke in a loud voice.

"I am Dr. Joiner," he said. "Has anyone called for me?"

"Dr. Joiner. No; no call," the waitress replied.

"I am a medical doctor, and I was supposed to receive a call here," the man added, a bit unnecessarily, Nona Idle thought.

Nona noticed the man's black gloves, and thought it curious that he did not remove them. She wondered what was wrong with his hands— or did he wear gloves to keep his hands soft and supple? Incidentally, she was aware that he did not once look at her. Men who did not notice Nona Idle were scarce.

Suddenly, the man whirled and pointed out of the window.

"Look!" he exploded.

Nona Idle naturally turned on the stool—they ate on white stools in the lunchroom—and stared. But she saw nothing except a car passing.

"I'm sorry," the black-gloved man said. "I guess I'm seeing things. That car looked just like an elephant when I first saw it."

Nona went back to her chicken-fried steak, French fried potatoes and buttermilk. "He's a goof," she thought.

She had not noticed the man empty a small bottle of amber liquid into her buttermilk while her attention was diverted by the imaginary elephant.

Nona finished her meal, got off the stool, took one step and buckled to the floor.

"Here, stand back!" barked the black-gloved man. "I'm Dr. Joiner!"

He made a phony examination of Nona Idle. The waitress pushed people back and told them to give "Dr. Joiner" some room.

The black-gloved man straightened and made a weighty pronunciation.

"This young lady has compound pulmonary palpitation," he said.

He gave the bystanders a look of heavy seriousness.

"I must rush her to a hospital!" he added.

Nona Idle was carried out and placed in the black-gloved man's car. No one happened to notice, due to the excitement, that this was a rented machine. The man drove off with his unconscious passenger.

When he had left the roadside dining room behind—he was not driving toward a hospital— the man spoke grimly to himself.

"That," he said, "keeps Doc Savage out of it."

Chapter V
THE DUMB WAITRESS

DOC SAVAGE had often considered changing the location of his headquarters. Too many people knew that he could be found on the eighty-sixth floor of the New York skyscraper that came near to scratching clouds, and not all of these people wanted to see the "Man of Bronze" go on living.

That was why Doc Savage, or one of his five assistants, always X-rayed the incoming mail. The X-ray would show which packages contained bombs. The bomb percentage in the mail had been high during the last year. Also, all the mail was subjected to a spectroscopic analyzing device which detected such clever ruses as perfume on a letter, to invite one to sniff, coupled with a subtle poison to bring death with the sniff.

In fact, the headquarters was a maze of scientific gadgets to protect the bronze man and his five aids.

But in spite of these irritations, Doc Savage had maintained his establishment on the top floor of the skyscraper, an aerie which could be seen from any part of the city, and on a clear day, from far out to sea. He wanted certain kinds of people to find him.

Doc Savage had been trained from childhood for the strange avocation which he followed—that of righting wrongs and punishing evildoers in the far corners of the earth. It was an unusual profession. In medieval times, knights in armor went around following the profession, but it had been out of fashion for several hundred years. The knights helped others for the glory of it, whereas Doc Savage did all he could to avoid the glory. He had a genuine horror of publicity; as a result he almost never went to a theater, a prize fight, or walked the streets any more than he had to.

But his avocation was helping other people out of trouble, so he used the skyscraper in order that persons with trouble would not have difficulty finding him.

People's troubles came to him in many fashions.

Tom Idle's trouble—which had now become that of his sister, Nona—came in the form of a letter.

The letter was X-rayed, tested for poisons, then passed on to Doc Savage on the theory that it was a safe letter—no one dreaming that it was going to cause more excitement, terror and bloodshed than all the bombs and poison letters they would ever receive.

The letter was lying on the big inlaid table in the reception room when Doc Savage came out of the laboratory. Doc was a physical giant with a handsome but not a pretty face; and he had strange flake-gold eyes which had been known to give an enemy a large case of the creeps, but which could be very persuasive and friendly when the bronze man wished. A peculiar aspect of Doc's size was that he appeared to be a man of normal build when seen from a distance; it was only on close examination that one realized here was a physical phenomenon, a man who could probably tie a knot in a horseshoe.

Doc Savage wore a germ-proof suit, something like a featherweight diving regalia, as he came out of the laboratory, and he was throwing back the hood. He had been in the laboratory twelve hours straight, trying to perfect a cure for the common cold.

"Hello, Doc," said Lieutenant Colonel Andrew Blodgett (Monk) Mayfair. "Here's this mornin's crop of mail."

Monk Mayfair would not have to be seen in a very thick jungle to be mistaken for an ape, masculine gender. He was built very wide, and there was no danger of his ever having to stoop for a door. He did not look like one of the world's noted industrial chemists. Monk was one of the five Doc Savage assistants.

Monk asked, "Did you find a cure for colds, Doc?"

Doc Savage looked at Monk and sneezed.

"All I found out," he admitted, "was how to catch one."

"How?"

"Work standing in a draft."

"Ah, so that's what science has come to," Monk chuckled. "Here's the mail."

THE contents of the envelope was ample explanation of the reason for its arrival. There was really another letter inside, and this was accompanied by a note.

The note, addressed to Doc Savage, read:

> The enclosed letter, received from my brother, Tom Idle, will explain itself.
> There is something so incredible and mysterious about the whole thing that I thought it best to mail my brother's letter ahead, and not carry it on my person. Perhaps I am foolish. At any rate, will you hold this letter until my arrival? I am coming to New York by bus.
> And thank you,
>
> Nona Idle

The enclosed letter that the note mentioned was the one in which Tom Idle had explained to his sister exactly what had happened to him, beginning when he was awakened by the exclamation of a bum known as Seedy Smith, in a Salt Lake City park, and ending where he was now, sitting in the Utah penitentiary with the name of Hondo Weatherbee, outlaw.

While they were reading, Colonel John (Renny) Renwick came in. Renny was a tall, bony man with a long face that always wore a my-but-aren't-these-funerals-awful expression. He was famous for two things: One, his boast that he could knock the panel out of any wooden door with the two coconuts which he called fists. Two, he had few superiors in ability as a civil engineer.

"Holy cow!" Renny rumbled, having read the letter.

This was his favorite expression. Also, he had a voice something like a troubled bear in a deep cave.

"Holy cow!" he repeated. "That's fantastic enough to be one of these nut letters like we sometimes get."

"Me, I like it already," Monk said.

"You would!" Renny rumbled. "But you don't know whether she's good-looking."

"I didn't mean the girl," Monk disclaimed.

"You're a liar," Renny assured him. "You like anything that's got a girl connected with it."

"You're gettin' so you ride me as bad as that over-dressed shyster, Ham Brooks," Monk complained. "Some day, I'm gonna bob both your tails off right up next to your ears."

Doc Savage had not joined the discussion. He rarely had much to say. However, he had seated himself at the telephone, put in a call, and was waiting.

Doc sneezed twice.

Monk grinned. The idea of Doc Savage catching a cold while conducting a scientific experiment to find a cure for colds was something Monk found amusing. He knew that Doc Savage was one of the greatest living scientists, and the more remarkable because his knowledge covered a number of lines. He knew more about electricity than Long Tom Roberts, another associate, for instance, and Long Tom was supposed to be a combination of Steinmetz and Marconi. Personally, Monk was sure Doc knew more about chemistry than he himself.

Doc Savage finished that telephone call, and made several others.

"The girl disappeared," he said, "at a highway dining room near Columbus, Ohio."

"Then we'd better investigate!" Monk exploded.

"It might not be a bad idea," Doc admitted.

DOC SAVAGE maintained a combination hangar and boathouse on the bank of the Hudson River, on Manhattan Island. The huge building masqueraded as a warehouse.

Brigadier General Theodore Marley (Ham) Brooks was waiting at the warehouse when they arrived. Ham was another Doc Savage assistant, as well as being a noted Harvard lawyer, and one of the best-dressed men of the twentieth century, as a noted men's magazine had recently dubbed him.

Ham, a thin-waisted man with the large, mobile mouth of an orator—he was a sharp-tongued talker who could stick words into a man as though they were knives—was always correctly dressed for the situation.

Ham wore an extremely natty aviator's outfit for their flight. Monk scowled at the lawyer. Monk considered Ham's attire an unnecessary affectation, since they were to fly in a cabin plane and business suits would be just as appropriate. Moreover, Monk had quarreled with Ham for years.

"You'll probably turn up in the hot place," Monk told Ham unpleasantly, "equipped with an asbestos suit."

Ham scowled and suggestively fingered a sword cane which he always carried.

"Listen, you missing link," he said, "you start anything with me today, and I'll take this sword and sculpture you into something that bears some resemblance to a man!"

Monk glared. "Start any old time! I'll thread you on that sword cane like a fishin' worm on a hook!"

In the past they had risked their lives for each other, and would doubtless do so again.

Doc Savage entered the control cockpit of a large twin-engined, streamlined monoplane. He had scarcely spoken, but that was not unusual since he never did any pointless talking solely to make conversation. As Monk frequently put it, words only came out of Doc when they were jarred out.

Yet it was an undeniable fact that the big bronze man completely dominated any group and every situation. It was not necessary for him to tell anyone who he was to make an impression, and he never appeared to issue an order directly. Yet his quiet presence carried complete power.

They landed—Doc Savage, Monk, Ham and Renny—in a meadow near Columbus, Ohio, less than three hours later. Alighting from the plane, they crossed to the roadside dining room at which Nona Idle had last been seen.

Doc Savage questioned the waitress who had been on duty.

"I remember the girl you mean," the waitress said. "She fainted, or something, and Dr. Joiner took her to a hospital."

"Do you know this Dr. Joiner?" Doc asked.

"Why, no. I never saw him before that night, nor since. But he said his name was Dr. Joiner."

"And the hospital?"

"Why, he never said what hospital."

Doc looked meaningly at Monk, Ham and Renny, who at once got busy on telephones.

"There is no Dr. Joiner," they reported later.

Which was what Doc had expected.

Monk scowled. "This guy turned up and drugged the girl and carried her off."

Ham said, "That was to keep Doc from learning anything about Tom Idle. The fake Dr. Joiner didn't know she'd mailed the letter."

Big-fisted Renny rumbled, "Holy cow! There's somethin' blasted queer behind this."

Doc said quietly, "We will have to do some detective work."

Shortly after this, the bronze man disappeared.

THE vanishing of Doc Savage startled his assistants, but it did not surprise them. Doc had a habit of dropping out of sight when he wished to pursue a private investigation, and he usually turned up again with something accomplished.

The three aides, waiting at the roadside dining room, marked time. Monk and Ham went into a competition, to see who could date up the waitress. The waitress was not good-looking and did not seem overly bright, and neither man really wanted a date.

What they did want was something to quarrel about. Renny got in a corner with a pencil and paper and sketched out a bridge which he was supposed to construct soon across a tide rip between two Florida keys.

They did not discuss the mystery of Tom Idle and his sister Nona, because they had not yet found out enough to make sense.

Two hours later, Johnny and Long Tom turned up. These were the remaining members of Doc's group of five associates.

Johnny was William Harper Littlejohn, one of the tallest and thinnest men alive—you wondered how such a bony man could stay alive—and was also a famous archaeologist and geologist. He could read an ancient Egyptian hieroglyphic as freely as his afternoon newspaper. He could say, without hesitating, what kind of rock was ten thousand feet under Sapulpa, Oklahoma.

Johnny at once went into discussion with Renny, for he was to help on the Florida bridge. He began using big words. "I'll be superamalgamated," he said. "An enigmatical verbal summation precipitated our eventuation."

Big words were Johnny's bad habit. He could have said merely that they were here because they had gotten a call from Doc.

Long Tom was Major Thomas J. Roberts, a scrawny fellow who looked as if he had spent his early life in a mushroom cellar. He was an electrical wizard who knew more about the innards of an electron than the average citizen knows about the construction of his fountain pen.

Long Tom and Johnny had come by plane, and they had brought along Habeas Corpus and Chemistry. Habeas Corpus was a runt pig which was Monk's pet; and Chemistry was, according to his owner Ham, a thoroughbred South American jungle chimpanzee, although Monk had other opinions. Chemistry looked distressingly like Monk.

The five men looked at each other and wondered what Doc Savage was doing. They fell into a discussion.

The waitress, neglected for the moment, made her way to a back room, where there was a telephone.

The waitress put in a call.

"Listen, Dr. Joiner," she said, "do I get that fifty dollars you promised me for information?"

The answer she received evidently reassured her about the fifty.

"Well, you better be sure you mail it to me," she said. "Here's the information: Doc Savage's five assistants are right in this place now. And Doc Savage is out roaming around somewhere."

After she had listened to Dr. Joiner swear for a while, the waitress hung up.

Doc's men had made a mistake about both the moral level and the deceitfulness of that waitress.

Chapter VI
HELL IN OHIO

DOC SAVAGE had been doing some routine detective work, and had finally unearthed a clue. He was talking to a man who wore overalls and had greasy hands.

"And this so-called Dr. Joiner seems to wear black gloves all the time," Doc finished a description.

"That's the guy," said the man, wiping his hands on cotton waste.

Outside the garage, it was late afternoon. Cars were passing at high speed on the highway, making long, windy screaming sounds. In a field nearby, a boy with a stick was chasing a dog which in turn had been chasing some cows. It was a peaceful highway crossroads scene.

"You rented this Dr. Joiner a car?" Doc Savage inquired.

The garage man nodded. "Sure. We rented him the heap right after he landed in his plane."

"The man came by plane?"

"Yep. Left by plane, too."

"Alone?"

"He had a girl when he left. Right pretty, too. One of them kind of long girls. He carried her and put her in the plane. Said she was sick, and he was takin' her to a hospital."

"You didn't," Doc Savage suggested, "get the number of the plane?"

"Nope."

"Can you describe the plane?"

The man scratched his head. "Well, I don't know much about these flying machines. This was one of them kind that only had one wing, whatever you call 'em."

A man who did not know what a monoplane was called was not going to be of much assistance in identifying a plane.

Doc said, "You might show me where the ship landed."

"Sure."

The bronze man's idea was to measure the span of the plane wheel tracks. Different planes had assorted wheel spans, and it was possible he could determine the manufacture of the plane. But in the field, he ran across luck.

"Here was where I cleaned the stuff outa the plane wheels," the garage man said.

Doc looked at him. "You what?"

"Some weeds had got stuck in the wheels and in that skid thing the hind end of the plane drags on," the man explained. "The feller gave me fifty cents to clean 'em off."

"Where did you throw the weeds?" Doc asked.

The garage man squinted at Doc Savage as if he thought the bronze man's interest in weeds might be a sign of mental deficiency.

"Over here," he said.

Doc Savage found the "weeds." He studied them thoughtfully.

The garage man lifted his head and looked about, seeking the source of a sound which had come into being. It was a strange sound. A trilling, low and exotic, mellow and not unpleasant, a note that was as fantastic as the noises of the winds among the ice pinnacles of an arctic waste.

"What's that?" the man demanded.

The sound ceased then, but Doc Savage did not answer, did not explain that the trilling was a small, unconscious habit, a thing which he did in moments of mental or physical stress—and did most frequently when he had discovered something of importance.

Doc made a package of the "weeds" from the plane wheels, wrapping them in paper and placing them in a pocket.

He went back to the roadside dining room.

"What'd you learn, Doc?" Monk asked.

Before Doc Savage could answer, three strangers stood up in the dining room and took guns out of their clothing.

"If one of you guys move," one of the men said, "there'll be quite a party!"

HIS five aides had frequently remarked on Doc Savage's apparent lack of emotion, and it was true that he had trained himself to a point where he could control his feelings. But his training had not overcome his natural instincts, and it is the instinct of a surprised man to give a start.

Doc started. But after that he stood very still, only the animation in his flake-gold eyes showing he was not exactly composed.

"Have they been entertaining you long?" Doc asked.

"Holy cow!" Renny rumbled. "They just came in, sat down and ordered hamburgers. Fifteen minutes ago, maybe. They hadn't said nothin'."

Long, thin Johnny said, "They interlocuted the viand purveyoress infinitesimally."

Ham snapped, "Why not just say they asked the waitress somethin'."

"Probably asked her if we were the guys," Long Tom said. He scowled at the waitress. "So you tipped 'em off we were here?"

The waitress grew nervous and started to back out of the room.

One of the men with guns beckoned her back. "You stick here, sister."

To Long Tom and the others, he said, "And you birds lay off barkin' at her!"

The raiders were organized. One whistled. Promptly, an engine started outside, and a large moving van drew around in front of the dining-room door.

"Get in!"

Monk bowed his thick arms and pulled his big mouth into a fierce shape. Monk wanted to fight. He liked to fight. He always howled and bellowed when he fought, and now he drew air into his lungs and got ready to bellow.

"Too risky!" Doc warned.

Monk subsided. With the others, he went out to the van. The van driver searched each of them hurriedly, and from everyone but Doc Savage, he took one of the machine pistols, very like overgrown automatics, which the bronze man's aides carried. On Doc, the man found no weapon.

The waitress had been trying to sidle away again.

"You too, babe!" a man rapped. "You go along!"

She began to look horrified. She screamed, "But I tipped off your boss that they were here!"

"It was the boss said take you along," a man told her.

"But—"

"Go on and get in that van, hasher!" the man snarled. "You know too much."

They had to toss the screeching waitress into the van, where she at once clamped herself on Monk's arm and demanded that he, "For God's sake, save me!"

Monk steered her toward Ham. "Have him save you. He was makin' passes at you all afternoon."

Ham yelled indignantly, "You made as many passes as I did!"

Big-fisted Renny let out a rumble of disgust. "You two clowns sure got a choice for girl-friends!"

The truck began to roll. The three men with guns rode inside, lined up in the rear, holding their weapons ready and making the prisoners sit on the floor.

There was considerable silence. Monk and Ham were regretting their attentions to the waitress, and she made it no easier by clawing at both of them frenziedly and squalling, "Save me!" incessantly.

Finally, Doc Savage asked, "What is this all about?"

THE bronze man's tone was calm, but the three gunmen stiffened and instantly pointed their weapons at Doc; so it was evident they had heard a good deal about him.

"The less words you use," one of them said, "the longer you'll live!"

"Mind giving a reason for this?" Doc asked.

The man scowled, and finally said, "A girl tried to get in touch with you."

"I know that," Doc said.

The man stuck out his lower lip. "Let's hope that's all you'll ever know."

Renny rumbled, "I don't like the way he said that!"

There was more silence, until one of the men picked up the package which Doc had been carrying, and which he had brought into the van. The man tore the paper apart and contemplated the contents, puzzled.

"What's this?" he wanted to know.

"Weeds," Doc said.

The man used the fingers of his left hand to twist the end of his nose around thoughtfully for a while, after which he wadded the "weeds" up in the paper and hurled them in a corner.

"Hell!" he said.

There was a small barred window in the forward end of the truck van; the sun was now so low that its rays blazed directly through the window, making a large barred patch of light on the van interior. Renny got the attention of their captors and pointed.

"You're liable to see your sunsets with that pattern for a long time," Renny remarked. "Through jail bars, I mean."

"At least, I'll be cooler," one of the men said, "than where you're going."

And all three gun holders showed their teeth with unpleasant satisfaction.

IT is a fact which cannot be disputed that nature is not only the greatest creator, but also the most grim destroyer. Nature can build an ocean like the Atlantic, but Boulder Dam is the best man has been able to do. Nature can wipe out an Ohio valley town with a flood; the best man can do is blow up a few houses at a time with bombs.

The burning coal beds are a case in point. Lightning or natural combustion sets a vein of coal afire, and it burns underground, sometimes for years, and covering areas of thousands of acres.

Where there is a burning coal bed, the earth splits cracks yards wide, the cracks pour forth lurid fumes, and deep in the apertures there is white heat that will promptly melt steel. At night, gory red glow and sulphurous stink comes out of the bowels of the earth. A burning coal bed is a closer imitation of hell than any Hollywood movie mogul will ever create.

The truck stopped on a hill and waited for complete darkness. The spot was a lonesome one, for no one cared to live within miles of the hell-stink of a burning coalfield. At the foot of the hill, the earth glowed red veins, and yellowish smoke crawled upward. Years ago all hope of extinguishing this coalfield fire had vanished.

The prisoners had not been permitted to look out of the van interior.

"I smell sulphur," Monk muttered.

Doc Savage made his small, exotic trilling sound, and it had a startled, uneasy quality, for he understood what the stink of sulphur meant.

The van door opened, and their captors got in. It was so dark that the men were using flashlights.

"Lie down!" one snarled. "We're gonna tie you!"

Doc and his men could either permit themselves to be tied, or get shot. They let the men tie them. The waitress whimpered and screamed; so they gagged her.

"Maybe we better gag 'em all," a man suggested.

Doc and the others were gagged with sleeves torn off their own arms.

"Now there won't be any yellin' when them and the truck go into one of those cracks," a man growled.

The men got out, stood waiting for it to get darker. They contemplated the burning coalfield. The appalling nature of the thing, and its resemblance to Hades, evidently gave each one of them a bad case of red ants on the mind, because they kept talking.

"You sure this will finish 'em, Heek?" one asked.

The man called Heek snorted. "Listen, we drive that truck in one of them cracks, and in five minutes it'll be a puddle of melted iron. The truck, all the bodies, will be gone."

The first man muttered, "It seems kind of a nut way of doing."

"Listen," said Heek, "did you ever try to get rid of a body? By damn, I did one time."

"You did. When was that?"

"The hell with you," Heek said.

There were clouds packed in the sky, and finally it became intensely dark. The men could see each other only as lurid devillike shapes against the crimson fumes of the burning coal bed.

"I'll get in there and make sure they're tied," said Heek, the man who had once tried to dispose of a body.

Heek climbed into the truck. The others stood outside. They kept close together, making their eardrums crack with listening, for they were naturally afraid of being discovered at the last minute. They heard grunting and scraping sounds from inside the truck.

"Heek's doin' a good job of makin' sure they're tied tight," a man mumbled.

It seemed a long time before Heek's voice spoke from the van.

"Don't show any lights," the voice ordered. "Ain't no use takin' chances."

The vicinity of the truck remained black.

"You guys stick here," Heek's voice continued. "I'll drive the truck into a crack."

THERE were no objections to Heek taking care of that part of the job. It was Heek who had known of this place, so it seemed appropriate for him to take care of the dirty work. The other three stood back.

A shadowy form moved around to the front of the truck and disappeared behind the wheel. The engine came to life; the big van lurched toward the inferno at the foot of the hill.

Once the machine paused, and they could hear the engine laboring.

"I hope Heek don't get stuck," a man gasped.

The truck went on after a moment. It moved like a square-backed turtle. Drawing near one of the largest cracks, it seemed to have trouble again. It came to a standstill.

"Hey!" Heek's voice yelled. "I think I'm stuck! C'mon and help!"

The other three men dashed forward.

But before they reached the van, the engine gave a louder roar and the thing leaped. A *leap* was the only way to describe the way it moved. It seemed to jump—into the crack.

There was a crash. A burst of gory red flame as gasoline exploded. Then smoke.

And then screams. Awful, agonized screams. Shrieks of death—in Heek's voice.

The three gunmen stopped as if embedded in invisible ice.

"Heek!"

"Heek didn't get out of the truck!"

The death shrieks took only a short time to come to an end.

A man croaked again, "Heek didn't get out!"

"The door on that side was hard to open," another muttered. "He musta forgot that!"

For moments they were held petrified, the accident having gone off in their faces with the unexpectedness of a gunshot. Then the same idea hit them all at about the same time. Get out of here! Leave the spot before anything else went wrong.

They ran like wolves caught in a sheepfold.

Behind them, red flame and yellow-black smoke continued to boil out of the great fiery crack into which the truck had plunged. There was the smell of burned rubber with the natural sulphur stench of the smoldering coalfields. There was a screaming whistle as the truck spare tire let loose.

But in time, these sights and sounds and smells ceased, and there was nothing to show that a truck had gone into the crack except the tracks of the vehicle, which of course would be plainly discernible with daylight.

Deep in the crack, where the superheated gases came out from smoldering coal that underlay the surroundings, in the very depths of the crack where there were rocks that glowed always white-hot, and other rocks that had melted and become lava, there was a dirty-looking, semi-liquid mess.

Heek had been right. No one would ever recognize that mess as a big van which had contained Doc Savage, his five aides, and a waitress whose fingers itched for money—and Heek himself.

It only looked as if someone had junked an old jalopy by rolling it into the crack.

Chapter VII
TWO TRAILS TO TROUBLE

THE three killers ran until they remembered that their fast pace would seem strange if anyone heard them, after which they walked. There was not much talk. They had seen death, and the sight had taken their words.

Once one of the men cried out in horror. That was when an owl said, *"Huh-huh-hoo-o-o!"* and the sound seemed like nothing that could have been. The night was as black as a bat's idea of Valhalla, and such was the state of their minds that the men used their flashlights sparingly. They were cold with horror. They felt as men always feel when it is too late, particularly too late to do anything about a murder. At this moment, they would have paid high for the chance to live their lives over.

And so they came to a filling station, where they conferred; then one man went ahead into the station, leaving the others behind. He made a telephone call. The man tried to be funny.

"Dr. Joiner's operation," he said, "was a success."

His mirth sounded like a rattle of skeleton bones.

"You sound," growled the voice of the black-gloved man known as Dr. Joiner, "like a buzzard that has just laid a square egg."

"Heek got killed."

If there happened to be a telephone girl listening in on that conversation, she probably never forgot the profanity she heard.

Later, the man who had telephoned went back to the other two.

"The boss blistered the paint about what happened to Heek," he said.

"It wasn't our fault."

"I know. I told 'im that. He finally said he guessed it was worth what happened to Heek to get everything back in running order."

The other two shivered.

"I'd hate to think," one muttered, "that anything was worth my neck."

"They fight wars over nothin'," the other said thoughtfully. "But you take us—we're gonna get more outa this than a lotta people think they're gonna get when they're fightin' their wars."

The third man snorted disgustedly.

"If you two philosophers will follow me," he said, "we'll go find a depot and wait for the first westbound train."

"What about Tom Idle's sister?"

"We pick her up and take her with us. The boss says we'll hold her, on account of we can threaten to hurt the girl and keep Tom Idle quiet."

The three birds of a feather descended the road into a valley and found a village railway station. They sat in the station and waited.

Doc Savage could see the three men through the depot windows.

DOC waited in silence until Renny joined them. The big-fisted engineer had gone to ask train times.

"Holy cow, there's no westbound train for almost two hours," Renny reported. "They'll just sit there for that time."

"Let us get everybody together for a minute," Doc Savage suggested.

They moved away from a sidetracked boxcar, from which concealment they had been watching the depot, and crept silently to a spot in a brush patch a hundred yards away, where a sheep went, *"Ba-a-a-a!"*

"All right, Monk," Doc whispered.

Ham said, "Monk sounds very natural as a goat, don't he?"

"That wasn't a goat," Monk hissed. "It was a sheep."

"You put too much of your own personality into it, then," Ham assured him.

Johnny and Long Tom shushed the pair of perpetual quarrelers. Doc Savage and all five assistants then gathered in a close group.

A few yards away, just out of earshot, lay Heek and the waitress. They were bound and gagged.

Doc said, "There is no need of letting the waitress and Heek overhear plans."

"I'll say not," Monk agreed vehemently. "And we gotta hang onto that waitress. Boy, would she have a story to sell Dr. Joiner now. Whoever the guy is, he'd pay plenty to know we're alive."

Renny chuckled. "I wonder what they'd do to Heek if they found out how Doc got his ropes loose, then knocked Heek senseless when he climbed in the truck," he whispered. He added: "But then, the other three were more to blame than Heek. They didn't know what had happened. They thought it was Heek talkin' when Doc imitated Heek's voice, and volunteered to drive the truck into the crack in that burnin' coalfield. They stood there as trustful as babes while Doc faked gettin' the truck stuck, so we could climb out."

The big-fisted engineer chuckled again. "Holy cow! What a case of creeps they got when Doc faked the last cries of Heek burnin' to death."

Renny's whisper was almost as bull-throated as his voice.

"If you don't want 'em to hear you over in Kentucky," Long Tom breathed, "you'd better tune down."

Doc Savage interrupted to summarize the situation.

"We have done some rushing around, and nearly got ourselves killed," he said. "But we have actually accomplished little."

"Me, I've accomplished something," Monk muttered. "I've dang well proved to my satisfaction that somethin' mysterious is goin' on. Also, that the brains behind it dang well don't overlook any bets. Also that we'd dang well better be careful."

"Maybe you've dang well got some idea what we'd better do next?" the dapper Ham suggested to the homely chemist.

Doc Savage spoke, quiet-voiced.

"Suppose we split," Doc said, "You five trail those three men waiting in the depot. Find Tom Idle's sister, and do whatever else you can."

"What about you, Doc?"

"I'll put Heek and the waitress in college," Doc Savage explained. "Then I'll fly to the Utah State Penitentiary and look into the mystery of how a man named Tom Idle could turn into an outlaw named Hondo Weatherbee."

"We'll keep in touch with each other by radio, as usual?"

"Right."

DOC SAVAGE and his men had referred to the "college" casually. No one else would have been prosaic about the place. But then, very few knew the "college" existed. The newspapers didn't, certainly. Or they would have broken out the type they used for war, earthquakes and the Worlds' Series.

The "college" was a cluster of grim, graystone buildings located in the unpopulated mountainous area of upstate New York, and it was surrounded by several different, high man-proof fences bearing signs that said:

WARNING
GERM RESEARCH INSTITUTION
—YOU MAY CATCH A DISEASE—
KEEP OUT

The warning signs were mildly misleading, for the disease that was treated was not contagious, not by germs. The disease was crime. Such criminals as Doc Savage captured were taken to the place, where they underwent delicate brain operations at the hands of specialists whom Doc Savage himself had trained. The operations wiped out all the patient's memory of the past.

Permanent mental amnesia was created surgically. After this, the patients were trained to hate crime, and were taught trades at which they could earn honest livings. Finally, they were discharged, specialists in some profession, with no knowledge of having been criminals in the past.

As far as the outside world was concerned, existence of the "college" was a secret.

Doc Savage landed his plane—he had taken the small plane, let his associates use the large one—at the "college" while it was still dark. There was a lighted landing field, and after Doc set his ship down, several quiet and efficient young men helped unload Heek and the waitress.

"The girl," Doc said, "will go through in the usual way."

The waitress was not much of a criminal, and she had received such a scare that she would probably reform. But the course of training would benefit her, so Doc was putting her through the place.

"We'll use truth serum on the man, first," Doc announced.

The administration of the truth serum was a success. Sometimes it wasn't. The stuff was given as a gas, the same way a surgeon uses an anaesthetic, and its effect was to stupefy the victim so that he could not consciously refrain from answering incriminating questions.

About Heek, Doc learned:

Heek was a local Ohio hooligan, with a record of two prison terms. Eleven years ago, however, Heek had taken an Idaho vacation to permit the police to forget him, and while in Idaho he had associated himself with an outlaw gang dominated by a man named Jan Hile and another man named Hondo Weatherbee.

Pickings in the wild and woolly West had been thin, however, and Heek had returned to Ohio, where he'd led a typical crook's life—in jail and out, hiding from police, double-crossed by fellow crooks, and suffering from disease—until as recently as yesterday. Yesterday, who should appear but Heek's old Idaho outlaw acquaintance, Jan Hile, who at once hired Heek to take part in the murder of the Doc Savage group and the waitress.

About the mystery, Doc learned:

Nothing. Heek didn't know what was afoot. The total of his knowledge was that he had been hired to commit a murder by an old-time outlaw associate named Jan Hile.

Jan Hile, of course, was the same man as Dr. Joiner.

Having expended six hours in obtaining this negligible information, Doc Savage was not enthusiastic about the progress.

"Go ahead with the treatment," the bronze man said.

So the specialists took Heek into the operation room and prepared to make him forever forget that he had been a crook.

Doc Savage left by plane.

GREAT SALT LAKE glistened in the afternoon sun as Doc Savage slanted his plane down the side of the last black mountain. The salt flats, the same flats which displaced Daytona Beach as the rendezvous of speed demons trying to set world automobile records, were an expanse as flat as a marble table-top. Altogether, it was a very bright, cheerful afternoon as Doc put the plane down between the red-and-white striped poles that bordered the Salt Lake City airport.

He did not alight at once. He used the plane's powerful shortwave radio.

"Monk," he said.

"Yes, Doc," Monk's small squeaky voice answered over the radio.

"Where are you?"

"We're on a westbound passenger train that just pulled out of Marceline, Missouri," Monk explained. "Our three guys are in the car in front. They still don't dream they're being followed. I've got this portable radio in a drawing room."

"Tom Idle's sister?" Doc asked.

"Somewhere ahead, the three men are going to meet someone who is holding the girl. What progress have you made, Doc?"

"Practically none."

This terminated the bronze man's contact with his five associates.

Doc Savage next did something that appeared to be entirely senseless. Something for which there was no apparent reason. One of the last things he might have been expected to do.

His act was a typical example of the kind of thing which later developed in such a way as to give his enemies unpleasant shocks.

Doc went to police headquarters. Since the Salt Lake City police department was very modern, the rogues' gallery contained a picture of Big Eva, and a description which included the huge convict's measurements and weight.

Tom Idle, in his letter to his sister, had mentioned that a convict named Big Eva was his cellmate. Doc Savage examined Big Eva's photograph and description for some time.

"Thank you," he said thoughtfully.

The bronze man now went to a hotel. He took along two articles, the first being the paper which contained the "weeds" that the garage mechanic had removed from the wheels of Dr. Joiner's plane in Ohio.

Doc Savage mailed the package of "weeds" to himself, care of general delivery, the Salt Lake City post office.

The second article which Doc carried was a metal equipment case. In the privacy of his locked hotel room, he opened this. It contained make-up articles, but nothing as conventional as grease paint

and false whiskers.

There was a bottle containing a colorless chemical, and when Doc applied this to his ears and around his mouth, a harmless swelling of considerable degree at once developed, greatly changing the aspect of his face.

Another contained dye which made his bronze hair black, and could only be erased with the proper chemical remover. There were glass eyeball caps, like the "invisible" spectacles which the better opticians supply, and these were dark enough to disguise the flake gold of his eyes. They were made of transparent, nonshatter compound instead of glass, for safety, and could hardly be detected with a magnifying glass.

Doc Savage, walking out of the hotel room, was a man who bore a striking resemblance to the convict called Big Eva.

Chapter VIII
SKOOKUM'S IDEA

SKOOKUM'S lunchroom had changed. It had lately received an addition which had almost doubled its size, and the exterior was bright with a fresh coat of paint, while a new and elaborate neon sign advertised the place. Inside, there was much new equipment, including booths and a hardwood floor on which couples could dance to music that was furnished each evening by an orchestra of four colored gentlemen.

Skookum had spread himself.

Doc Savage said, "Lesh have shervice aroun' hersh!"

He sounded very intoxicated when he said it. He sank in a booth and pounded a table with his fist. The waiters—Skookum himself no longer stooped to anything as undignified as waiting table—frowned at Doc, and decided it would create more commotion if they tried to throw him out than if they served him. They brought him ginger ale. His pockets already bulged with bottles bearing alcoholic labels.

Doc Savage looked as if he had emptied a number of such bottles. His hair, now black, was down in his eyes. His thick-lipped mouth was loose and his expression was stupid. His speech was none too coherent, and it grew worse as he downed drink after drink.

There was nothing alcoholic in anything the bronze man drank, but there was nothing to indicate such a fact. Only one bottle contained genuine spirits, and he spilled some of the contents at intervals to create the proper smell.

He spent an hour deliberately making a noisy nuisance of himself.

Then he slumped forward, buried his head in his arms and emitted a loud snore.

Skookum had been watching for some time. Skookum had taken to wearing striped trousers, lap-over vest and cutaway coat for his daytime working garb. At night, he wore full dress.

It was the hour when Skookum usually changed to his claw-hammer coat, but he was so interested in watching the big drunk who had invaded his place that he had put it off. When Doc apparently went to sleep, Skookum looked elated.

"Carry him in back room heap sudden," Skookum ordered.

The back room of Skookum's lunch stand was also a new addition, and if the police found out about it, there would be trouble. The room was a high-powered gambling establishment which Skookum had started on the side.

As a number of persons had remarked, Skookum had certainly branched out recently.

"Make track," Skookum told his waiters.

The waiters departed and closed the door.

Skookum seated himself at the telephone and made long-distance telephone calls, each to a hotel in a different city. He began with Kansas City and Tulsa, then worked westward past Pueblo, Denver and Cheyenne. In Sheridan, Wyoming, he located the man he was seeking.

"Hello, Jan Hile," he said.

Skookum listened, and his expression showed that he was being abused over the telephone.

"Sure, chief, the name is Dr. Joiner. Heap sorry," he said. "You fan out ear and listen. Me catchum big idea."

Jan Hile, or Dr. Joiner, as he seemed to prefer being called for the time being, evidently told Skookum where he could take his ideas.

"Now you got me wrong, chief," Skookum said desperately. "Listen. A drunk came in my place a while ago and passed out. He's layin' here on the floor by me, heap much asleep."

The other man's angry demand could be heard all over the room.

"What the hell about it?" he yelled.

"This drunk, he look plenty like Big Eva," Skookum explained.

"Eh?"

"Same size. Same thick mouth, thick ear. Same black hair. Heap alike."

THERE was a long silence, but Skookum could hear the other man whistling thoughtfully, so he knew the fellow had not hung up.

"How much, Skookum?"

"Ten thousand dollar," Skookum said.

"Not a chance!"

"Heap cheap."

"Listen, you crazy Indian-talking hotdog merchant, ten thousand is all you got for helping

with the Tom Idle thing. That was different. Five hundred this time. Not a cent more."

There was protracted dickering, during which Skookum was insistent that ten thousand was as cheap as dirt, and the matter was compromised on six hundred dollars, with the added promise that Skookum would get his entrails kicked out if anything went wrong.

Skookum hung up the telephone receiver.

He called, "Hey, Seedy!"

One of the new waiters came in, scowled uneasily and said, "Damned if I don't think you'd better quit callin' me that name."

Tom Idle would have recognized the waiter as that blowsy fellow, later identified as Seedy Smith, whose startled ejaculation had aroused him that incredible morning on the park bench. It was this waiter who had addressed Tom Idle as Hondo Weatherbee, then fled.

Skookum pointed at the limp form of Doc Savage.

"Heap watchum," Skookum said.

The waiter looked puzzled. "Huh?"

"Watchum," Skookum ordered. "Just watchum."

Skookum left the lunchroom and strolled to the neighboring park, where he looked about until he found a young man who was carrying a big broom and pushing a large tin can equipped with wheels.

"How?" Skookum said.

"Not so hot," snarled the young street cleaner. "There must've been twenty picnics in the damn park today, and they all scattered papers. To say nothin' of the fact that a whole blasted regiment of cavalry rode their horses through."

Tom Idle would also have recognized the surly young street cleaner as the man he had thought was Officer Sam Stevens, the park cop. The fellow's name was actually Sam Stevens, but the nearest he had ever come to being a policeman was in wearing the uniform which Skookum had bought him.

Sam Stevens eyed Skookum cunningly.

"You wouldn't have another job for me?" he asked. "Maybe somethin' like playin' cop again."

"Sure," Skookum said. "You bury bottle of stuff we use first on Tom Idle. Show me where."

"Heap betcha," said Sam Stevens.

Skookum and Sam Stevens went on hurrying when they thought no one would notice, until they reached the park bench on which Tom Idle had awakened that ill-fated morning. Skookum was not concerned with the bench, but he was interested in the soft ground behind a patch of shrubs which stood at a short distance. He watched Sam Stevens get on all fours and dig.

The bottle which Sam Stevens unearthed was half emptied of its contents, but tightly corked.

"This is it," Sam Stevens said. "There's enough of the stuff left in the bottle."

"Want help me?" Skookum asked.

"Sure."

"Fifty dollars."

Sam Stevens swore. "That ain't enough, but I'll do it."

They went back to the lunchroom. Doc Savage still lay on the floor, breathing in what they took for a drunken stupor, and watched by the waiter who had taken the part of Seedy Smith in the Tom Idle melodrama.

"This heap easy," Skookum said.

He poured some of the liquid from the bottle on his handkerchief. He was careful to avert his head, so as not to inhale the pungent fumes, and the others did likewise.

Skookum had held the handkerchief under Doc Savage's nose for hardly a minute before the bronze man became unconscious.

Chapter IX
LIFER

THE storm rumbled and crashed. Lightning jumped in jagged streaks and impaled clouds, stood in white heat and shook; it stabbed straight down out of the sky with gunshot reports. Thunder made the sound of cannons, and the roaring was all mixed with echoes that came bouncing back from the mountains, so that the night was a hideous, cackling bedlam and a flame-flushed inferno.

The penitentiary was like a grimy gray goat crouching near the mountains; there were two towers at the gate, these sticking up like the goat's horns. Bolt lightning suddenly came down out of the sky, touched one horn tower with a sizzle and a bang, and in the penitentiary cells a hundred convicts lay rigid while fear chills walked their spines. They hoped with all their minds that it was not too late to begin better lives.

The lightning glare came in through the bars and licked the cells with ethereal red tongues. Thunder shock made iron cot legs tremble grittingly on concrete floor.

Doc Savage awakened in all that; he sat up with the feeling that he had aroused because of the uproar. But he pushed this idea out of his mind, for he knew the anaesthetic he had been given in Salt Lake City had finally worn off. The last thing he remembered was Skookum bending over him. Skookum with a handkerchief wet with stuff that had come from a bottle. Skookum saying, "This heap easy."

Now the bronze man ached, his stomach wanted to rebel, and there was uneasiness in his mind as well.

"Hello," he said.

There was another cot in the cell; on it a form in a blanket. The form stirred.

"They never had lightning like this on Bear Creek," a voice said.

Bear Creek was near Sue City, the Missouri home of Tom Idle. Doc lay very still and thought about that.

He asked, "How long have you been asleep, Tom Idle?"

The other man bolted up in his cot. Hearing the name—Tom Idle—had torn him loose from his control. His glare was mad in the red flush of lightning.

"Stop it!" he snarled. "Don't begin callin' me Tom Idle! I'll go nuts!" He shook both fists in a frenzy. "Cut it! I can't stand it, Big Eva!"

Doc Savage knew that he was looking at a man who had been under a fantastic strain for weeks, and who could not stand much more.

Doc got up and went to the cell mirror that was of stainless steel—convicts have been known to break glass mirrors and use the fragments on each other or themselves. There was no light in the cell except the lightning, but that was sufficient.

Doc Savage was looking at Big Eva, the convict. He showed the mirror his teeth, and it was as if Big Eva had snarled.

THE likeness shocked the bronze man. He had gone into this deliberately while holding in his mind the suspicion of what would happen, and hoping it would happen. But suddenly he doubted himself. His confidence slipped.

He gripped the cell bars with both hands. He exerted force. Was this really *his* body? He had to know that. The sinews stood out in his arms and shoulders. His temples pounded with effort—and the cell bars slowly gave.

"Great grief!" Tom Idle croaked.

Doc Savage released the bars, his uncertainty gone. He knew now. His body was still his own body.

Tom Idle was ogling the distorted cell bars.

"For the love of mud," he muttered, "I didn't think any man was strong enough to do that."

Doc Savage went back to the cot and lay down. He thought for a while.

"Idle."

"Yes?"

"A while ago, I asked how long you had slept."

"I went off like a log right after supper," Tom Idle said. "Darnedest thing, too. I haven't been sleeping worth a toot. But tonight I sure made up for it."

"So they drugged you."

"Eh?"

"Drugs. They had to be sure you would sleep through it."

During the next few moments, the roar of thunder was pounded into insignificance by the abrupt coming of hailstones, some as large as bantam eggs, which struck by the millions in a hammering avalanche that beat pits in roofing and frayed edges of fence posts out on the range.

Unexpectedly, the lightning revealed Tom Idle, leaning over Doc Savage.

"I thought so!" Tom Idle muttered. "You look different."

"I am not Big Eva," Doc said.

"Huh?"

"I am Doc Savage," Doc explained. "You wrote your sister to get in touch with me. Remember?"

It must have been a minute before Tom Idle said anything. He sank back on his cot and just sat there.

"I guess I'm crazy after all," he said.

He sat with his head in his hands for a while longer.

"It's kind of a relief at that," he muttered finally, "to know that I'm nuts, and there really ain't any explanation for what happened, on account of it didn't happen."

He lay back on his bunk and pulled the blanket up around his chin.

"I wonder what booby hatch they've really got me in?" he pondered gravely. "I wonder if it's the one at St. Joe?"

He began to laugh hysterically.

THE warden of the penitentiary returned from his cow ranch the following afternoon. The ranch was located near the prison, so the warden had ridden a horse. He still wore his cowboy boots and was turning a five-gallon hat thoughtfully in his lean hands as two guards led in Doc Savage.

The warden looked at Doc Savage and recognized him only as Big Eva, whom he did not like. He lost no time making known his impatience.

"As a hardened criminal, you're second only to that cellmate of yours, Hondo Weatherbee!" the warden said grimly. "If this is some kind of a trick, you'll land in solitary confinement so fast you won't know it!"

Doc Savage spoke in a calm voice. He said that his name was Doc Savage, and that he was certainly not the convict known as Big Eva. He made this statement with conviction.

The prison warden put on his cowboy hat, then took it off again. "I'm a son of a gun!" He sat down behind his desk. But he jumped up almost at once in a rage.

"What the Hades is this?" he yelled. "Hondo Weatherbee tried to pull the same trick!"

"My cellmate is named Tom Idle—not Hondo Weatherbee," Doc Savage said.

The warden snorted.

"And you're Doc Savage—instead of Big Eva?"

"Yes."

"You two stir-bugs must have been eating loco weed from the same patch," the warden said angrily. "I know both Hondo Weatherbee and Big Eva by sight. I ought to. They've made me enough trouble. You're Big Eva. And your cellmate is Hondo Weatherbee."

"There may be a physical resemblance," Doc said. "But the whole thing is a trick to get Hondo Weatherbee and Big Eva out of the penitentiary."

The warden jammed his hat on his head. "I'm going to be reasonable." He lifted his voice and yelled for a clerk to bring the fingerprint identification file.

Doc Savage looked at Big Eva's fingerprint card when it was put before him. Doc knew his own fingerprints by sight, and did not need to compare to know that the prints on Big Eva's card were his own.

"They're your prints, ain't they?" the warden asked. "Just the same way the prints on Hondo Weatherbee's card are the prints of the man you've got for a cellmate now."

There was a magnifying glass on the desk. Doc Savage put the fingerprint card under this for an examination. He held the card up to the light. He rubbed the print to test the dryness of the ink, until the warden angrily ordered him not to smudge them.

Doc said, "According to the date, the card went in the file three years ago."

"Sure. When you were committed to this institution."

"But the card," Doc said, "was manufactured less than a year ago. And the fingerprints have not been inked on it more than twelve hours. Doesn't that strike you as strange?"

The warden scowled and picked up the card.

"I'll have an expert look at this. You go back to a cell, meantime."

It was five hours before the warden visited Doc Savage.

"Expert says you're crazy," the warden growled. "This card is three years old, and the fingerprints on it are three years old, too."

"What expert?"

"Our fingerprint expert right here in the penitentiary. He takes care of all the prints, and these cards."

"That explains it."

"Explains what?"

"He is probably the man they hired to switch cards."

The warden was doubtless justified in considering the whole thing a ruse on the part of two prisoners. There were clever prisoners in this penitentiary, and the devices they tried were strange.

"You're not going to get out of this penitentiary with a trick," the warden snapped. "You serve out your sentence."

"And how long is Big Eva's sentence?" Doc asked.

"Life," the warden growled. "Furthermore, you get two weeks in solitary for trying to pull a phony story."

"May I send a telegram to a man named Monk Mayfair?" Doc asked.

The warden shook his head.

"You don't send or receive anything. It'll be a hot day when I trust Big Eva."

THE solitary cells were three feet wide, so an inmate could always get plenty of exercise by bracing his feet against one wall and pushing with his back on the other, a form of exercise that had a depressing effect because it brought a full understanding of how close and how hard the walls were. There was no light, a small barred aperture in the door being closed by a lid on the outside. Ventilation was through a pipe, there was practically no sound, and it was an excellent surrounding for deep thought.

Doc Savage, being a giant of a man, was cramped for space. He leaned against one cold stone wall in the utter blackness for which a solitary cell is famous, and his thoughts were not cheerful.

No doubt every visitor going through a penitentiary has stopped at least once and thought, "What if they don't let me out of here?"

Doc Savage was no exception. Here was the predicament come to life.

It was obvious that Hondo Weatherbee had been taken out of the penitentiary and Tom Idle substituted in his place, Tom Idle being selected simply because he looked something like Hondo Weatherbee. Doc Savage had surmised this when he disguised himself to look like Big Eva. He'd suspected Big Eva of knowing of the hoax, and helping it along by claiming Tom Idle was Hondo Weatherbee. The man would have known Tom Idle wasn't his cellmate.

Because there was a chance that Big Eva was also slated for release from the penitentiary, since he had once been a bandit associate of Hondo Weatherbee, Doc had disguised himself to resemble Big Eva and offered himself as a sacrifice to see if he was guessing right.

So he was in the penitentiary—in a great deal more solidly than he had anticipated. Still, it should be only a question of time until he could manage to get word out to Monk or another of his five aides. After that, it would not take long for them to extricate him.

His only hope of getting out of the penitentiary was undeniably through the aid of his five assistants. Without outside help, he might easily become a permanent fixture.

The outlook could have been more cheerful. Disgusted, Doc Savage finally went to sleep.

IT was well after midnight when the man in the gray suit crept into the section of the prison containing the solitary cells.

The man in the gray suit was pale with strain, and desperate, for he was the prison fingerprint expert who had switched fingerprint file cards of Big Eva and Hondo Weatherbee for cards holding the fingerprints of Doc and Tom Idle—prints placed there while the latter were drugged, just prior to being spirited into the penitentiary.

He drew a blackjack from his pocket, and creeping forward, managed to slug the solitary cell-block guard. The guard collapsed without knowing what had hit him.

The grim-faced fingerprint man then skulked toward Doc Savage's cell.

"They killed Doc Savage in Ohio," he muttered. "So this guy can't be him."

He took from his clothing a bottle that contained one of the most deadly poison gas mixtures ever contrived for modern warfare. It was a gas against which there was no known defense. Its fumes would kill through the skin pores. Days afterward, if a man handled an object which the stuff had touched, death would come almost instantaneously.

Holding the bottle ready to throw into the cell, he fumbled with the fastening of the lid over the barred opening in the door of the solitary cell which Doc Savage occupied.

Chapter X
SUITCASE TRICK

THE passenger train pulled slowly into Salt Lake City, the wheels clicking over rail joints, and stopped in the station, where the air brakes emitted tired hisses; the porters swung down with their little steps, and the cars began to spew luggage and passengers.

Two of the porters were short men, although one of these was much wider than the other, and had arms fully as long as his legs. Both porters were as black and shiny as Concord grapes, and each carried a load of suitcases that would have dismayed a mountain burro.

Ten yards behind the two porters walked a feeble-looking old lady who wore colored spectacles and hobbled with a cane. She had stringy white hair, and her face looked bony and unhealthy. This old lady had gotten on at St. Louis, and she was a confirmed train-prowler. That is, she had made innumerable trips from one end of the train to the other. She carried a cheap brown suitcase.

Another ten yards back came a very tall, very thin man with flowing white whiskers, and who walked with a pronounced stoop.

Still farther back, and bringing up the rear of the procession, was a huge news butcher with a bundle of magazines under his arm and a tray containing candy, cigars, cigarettes and toys slung around his neck by a strap. He was also as black as a Concord grape.

In the middle of this parade walked the three men who thought they had killed Doc Savage in a burning coal bed in Ohio. They did not know they were the center of a parade, any more than they knew they had not killed Doc in Ohio.

At the station exit, the three rascals became six when they were joined by Skookum, Seedy Smith and Sam Stevens. There was enough handshaking all around to show that they knew each other.

"How's it go?" Skookum asked.

"Swell. And with you?"

"The same."

"Did they get here with the girl all right?"

"Sure," Skookum said. "Everything heap good. We pick her up later."

The men hurried over to swear at the porters who had their luggage. The porters were in some kind of a mixup. It was the short, thin-waisted porter and the one who had arms as long as his legs—the pair that were as black as Concord grapes.

Unnoticed, the porters had already switched a bag belonging to the three men for the one the feeble-looking old lady was carrying.

The three men were not aware of the swap, and loaded themselves into the new sedan which Skookum had recently bought. The six men and the bags made quite a crowd, and it ended up by one of the men having to hold a bag on his lap. The bag was the one the porters had switched.

Skookum and his companions drove away, unaware that any manipulating had occurred.

AT the station, there was at once a furious scramble, and the two porters, the old lady, the bony man with the white whiskers, and the big black news butcher all landed in a taxicab.

"Follow that car ahead."

The huge news butcher gave the order, then settled back on the cushions and contemplated his companions.

"Holy cow!" he rumbled. "We sure make a freaky collection for one taxicab!"

"You haven't got these skirts to fuss with, Renny," snapped the little old lady in a voice that belonged to Long Tom Roberts, the electrical wizard. "You should kick."

The two porters—Monk and Ham—were already scowling at each other.

The bony old man picked up the ends of his white whiskers and contemplated them distastefully.

"A hirsute incongruity," he remarked.

Renny, the news butcher, looked puzzled.

"Johnny means," Long Tom translated, "that his whiskers get in his soup."

Renny sighed, blocked his huge hands into fists and eyed them thoughtfully, then shrugged.

"We've gone to a lot of old-fashioned gumshoe detective trouble; and trailed those three guys so close that we know how many breaths they took between here and Columbus, Ohio," he rumbled disgustedly. "And what's it got us?"

Monk said, "Well, whoever had the girl brought her on ahead to Salt Lake City."

"You … always thinking about a girl!" Renny thumped. "That's another thing!"

The taxi rolled swiftly through the midsection of the town, stopping frequently for the rather unusual Salt Lake City traffic lights, each of which was connected to some kind of a gadget that emitted a shrill policelike whistle each time the lights changed.

Doc Savage's five aides were silent. They were tired. Long Tom, as the old lady train-prowler, had kept close touch on their quarry. Monk and Ham, as porters, and Renny, as news butcher, had eavesdropped. Johnny, as a white-whiskered old gentleman, had occupied a seat in the car with the trio they were trailing. But the sum total of their success was that they had trailed the men as far as Salt Lake City.

Furthermore, there had been no word from Doc Savage for some time.

Renny rumbled, "Maybe our last gag will get some kind of results."

He lifted a small equipment case onto his knees, opened it and disclosed dials and loudspeaker aperture of a portable radio receiver.

"Bet it don't work," Monk muttered.

Long Tom, the electrical wizard, flared up with, "Sure, it'll work! You switched suitcases, didn't you? And one of the men is holding the case on his lap, isn't he?"

"Yeah," Monk admitted.

"Well, there's a shortwave radio transmitter in that case, isn't there? And the microphone is mounted behind a label on the suitcase, where it'll pick up anything said, isn't it?"

JAN HILE

"Um-m-m," Monk said. "What if they open the suit case?"

"I took care of that when I made the device!" Long Tom snapped.

Long Tom always had confidence in his electrical work. He had mounted this transmitter in a suitcase which they had managed to buy en route, a suitcase that was an exact imitation of the cheap one carried by one of their quarry. He was sure the device would function.

They listened to what was said in Skookum's car.

SKOOKUM drove with his shoulders back, proud of himself. Obviously he considered that he was getting along in the world.

"Ugh!" he remarked. "Heap no profit in goin' straight."

The others looked at him, wondering what had brought that out.

"Long time ago, I belong to bandit gang with Hondo Weatherbee and Jan Hile," Skookum explained. "Hondo Weatherbee kill a man he was prospecting with, and the gang split up!" Skookum scowled. "Me, I turn heap honest and run lunchroom. Ten years, I run him. Ugh! What he get me?"

"Well, what'd it get you?" a man asked indifferently.

"Headache," Skookum said. "Heap headache."

He puffed his chest until the big imitation diamond in his tie pin scratched his chin. He patted the steering wheel of the shiny car as if it were a new pup.

"A few weeks ago, I have talk with Jan Hile, and decide to turn bandit again. Now look at me! New car. Almost new lunchroom. Heap wampum."

"Wampum?" One of the men was puzzled.

"Money. Dough and spondulicks to you, paleface."

Skookum peered at himself in the mirror as if he were observing the acme in wit, wisdom and worldly goods. Anyone else would have seen a greasy brown fat man with the eyes of a cow pony and jowls which appeared packed full of hickory nuts, gopher fashion.

"Where was Jan Hile," a man asked, "all these years?"

Skookum looked at the other belittlingly.

"Hile go to Chicago," he said. "Got to be heap famous lawyer."

In the trailing taxicab that was some distance behind, Brigadier General Theodore Marley (Ham) Brooks, the pride of Harvard law college, gave a violent start.

"Whew!" Ham exploded. "I didn't dream *that* Jan Hile was the man behind this!"

Monk frowned. "What about *that* Jan Hile?"

"Haven't you heard of him?" Ham demanded. "He's one of the sharpest criminal lawyers in America. He's saved more killers from the gallows than any other four lawyers put together. He should've been hung years ago!"

"Hung along with all the rest of the lawyers," Monk suggested.

Ham ignored the inference. "I wonder," he pondered, "what is back of this? That Jan Hile is a millionaire. He doesn't touch anything small."

Renny held up one of his big hands.

"Sh-h-h!" he said. "That Skookum is bragging again!"

Skookum was speaking in a tone of deep-throated resonance which—little did he dream—made an excellent radio voice.

"I'm in charge of this," he said. "I'm running it. Get that heap clear."

The men in the car eyed him, not greatly impressed.

"If you know so much," one said, "suppose you tell us what is going on?"

"Why," said Skookum grandly, "Jan Hile wanted Hondo Weatherbee and Big Eva out of penitentiary. I get 'em out with heap good trick."

The man snorted. "I don't mean that. I mean—Why? What's in the wind?"

"Yeah," another man echoed. "What's going on around Mad Mesa?"

Skookum opened his mouth, then shut it. His

expression showed that he knew no more than the others, if as much. He shoved out his jaw belligerently.

"I ain't tellin' what I know!" he snapped.

He at least knew that the safest refuge for a dunce is an air of mystery.

WHEN Skookum entered the back room of his lunch stand, he gave a violent start.

"Ugh!" he said. "Me think you in Wyoming."

Jan Hile said, "There's such thing as an airplane."

Hile did not move from the chair where he was seated. He nodded to each man, spoke in a way that showed he had known all of them in the past. He wore his inevitable black gloves, and there was about him a fierce predatory air. Men usually grew uneasy in his presence, and these men were no exception. They did not look at him any more than they had to. They could not have explained why.

"You three"—he eyed the trio who had arrived by train—"tell me what happened in Ohio."

"Well, we got Doc Savage, his five men, and the waitress who knew too much," one of the men said. "And we put 'em in a truck and ran 'em into a crack in a burning coalfield. Heek couldn't get out of the truck, and he was burned up, too."

Jan Hile's black-gloved hands made an impatient gesture. "Details! I want details! I want to know every damned move you made that night, no matter how inconsequential!"

They told him. When one of them overlooked something, the others broke in with the omission. One thing was evident when they had finished. That night in Ohio was printed in their minds with red ink.

Once Jan Hile interrupted.

"You say," he snapped, "that the truck seemed to get stuck just before it went into the crack?"

"Yes."

"Was it dark? Could you *see* the truck then?"

"Well, not exactly. No."

Jan Hile scowled at his black-gloved hands grimly.

"That comes under the head of supporting evidence," he said with sudden furiousness.

The man who'd had the suitcase switched on him had brought his suitcase inside, and was sitting with it between his knees. The label—it was one which advertised a gaudy Colorado Springs summer hotel—was turned outward, but there was no evidence that behind the label reposed the microphone of a radio transmitter.

Doc Savage's five men, in a taxi parked in the street nearby, were looking at each other dubiously.

"That Jan Hile is a clever devil," Ham muttered disgustedly. "He's guessed that we didn't die in Ohio."

Jan Hile's harsh voice came to them again from the radio loudspeaker.

"It's lucky," he said grimly, "that I ordered the guy who took Big Eva's place in the penitentiary killed."

Monk scratched his nubbin of a head.

"Now I wonder who he's talkin' about?" the homely chemist pondered.

JAN HILE was still scowling at his hands, which looked so sinister in the murky gloves. He seemed in deep thought, and none of them interrupted him. Abruptly, he stood up.

He went to a steamer trunk which he had evidently brought with him. He opened this, and disclosed firearms, bulletproof vests and gas masks.

"Stock up," he ordered. "We've got one of those nights ahead of us. I don't think it'll get tough, but it might."

The men clustered around the steamer trunk, selecting weapons which suited their fancy, taking off their outer clothing and donning the bulletproof vests.

The man with the suitcase grinned.

"Them new guns is all right," he said, "but I got Old Reliable in my suitcase here. I think I'll get her out and strap her on."

In the parked taxi nearby, Monk clenched his furry fists and looked apprehensive.

"He's openin' his suitcase!" Monk blurted. "Now we're sunk!"

Long Tom—the suitcase was his idea and creation—said, "Hold your horses."

They held their breaths as well, for a good two minutes, after which they heard a disgusted grunt come over the radio.

"I can't get the dang thing open," complained the man with the suitcase. "The lock seems to be out of order."

Long Tom cocked an eye at Monk. "You see, I jimmied the lock."

The man with the suitcase spent some more time trying to make his key function, then gave it up in defeat.

"I guess I pack one of the new rods," he said. "Later on, I'll take a hammer to this lock."

He placed the suitcase on the table, selected himself a gun from the steamer trunk, then followed the example of the others in putting on a bulletproof vest under his outer clothing.

Jan Hile got up, sauntered idly to the suitcase and scrutinized the thing. He ran his hands over it. His fingers seemed sensitive in spite of the gloves, for they came to the label—and dwelled there, exploring.

Jan Hile did not say anything.

He went into the front of the lunchroom, looked

out of each of the windows in turn. He whistled disgustedly, for he could discern nothing suspicious.

Suddenly he went to a telephone—and not one in the rear room where the suitcase was located.

"Big Eva?" he asked.

"Yeah," said Big Eva's ugly voice.

"You got the men all set?" Jan Hile demanded.

"They'll be spread all over that freight train when it pulls out."

Jan Hile made an ugly, satisfied noise.

"Doc Savage's men are here in town and have been eavesdropping on us with a radio gadget," he said. "We'll have to take care of them. Think you can do?"

"If they're alive in the morning," Big Eva said, "you can send me back to that penitentiary."

Chapter XI
PHANTOM FREIGHT

THE driver of the taxicab which Doc Savage's five aides occupied was a good Mormon who attended to his own business and did not usually inquire into the affairs of his passengers. But the crew he had aboard at the present time obviously had him puzzled.

His passengers had identified themselves as being associated with Doc Savage, but that meant nothing to the driver, since he had never heard of the Man of Bronze. The fares seemed a daffy crowd. They were jammed in the back seat now, listening to squeaks, scratches and—at rare intervals— understandable words that came out of a portable radio set. They were very serious about this.

Furthermore, they were three black men, a white-haired old lady and a tall skinny fellow with snowy whiskers. A circus assortment.

The black one who looked like an ape said, "I wonder who that was in the penitentiary they ordered killed?"

This made several times the fellow had wondered aloud about that killing.

The taxi driver made a mental resolution to report this business to the police as soon as he got rid of his passengers.

"Holy cow!" one of his passengers rumbled. "There they go!"

A moment later, the hackman was ordered to follow the same car which he had trailed to this spot, and also an additional machine which had been pressed into use by the men his strange assortment of fares seemed to be following. The driver obeyed. After all, he had a wife and four children who would get hungry if anything happened to him.

"I wonder what's become of Doc?" the black ape passenger growled.

"An enigmatically obfuscated interrogation," stated another.

There's a sample, thought the driver. You couldn't understand that one if you did know what he was talking about.

It got dark suddenly, the way it does in clear, dry countries. A bank of clouds pushing up in the west to shut off the twilight made the coming of night doubly swift, like a curtain being drawn.

The pursuit wound its way to the railroad yards, where the two cars ahead discharged their passengers, who promptly disappeared into the thicket of railroad sidetracks with obvious furtiveness.

"As soon as we find that girl," growled the black ape of a passenger, "I'm gonna start in bustin' necks!"

The taxi driver shuddered and resolved to buy some life insurance. He had never believed in insurance.

His fares alighted.

"You wait here," one of them ordered.

The five men moved away as silently as ghosts, and were swallowed by the darkness. The driver peered after them, but saw no sign that any of them had lingered near. It was now quite dark.

The taxi driver decided to leave the spot, call the police, and be rid of a bad job.

He started the motor, meshed gears, and the cab began to move.

A man came out of the darkness and landed on the cab running board.

"Going some place?" the man snarled.

The driver realized the man was a stranger. The fellow had the kind of face that interests policemen.

"I was just driving off," the driver mumbled.

"You're wrong. You're walking!"

The stranger had a gun, and the driver went with him into the darkness of the railroad yard, without argument.

"I'm a straight guy!" protested the driver.

"Sure," agreed the stranger. "I could see the I'm-gonna-tell-a-cop in your eye."

SOMEWHAT to the bewilderment of Doc Savage's five assistants, the men they were following gathered in the shadow of a pile of ties and proceeded to do nothing for some minutes. This was puzzling, and aggravating. Doc's aides intended to trail the men only until the gang led them to Nona Idle, after which they were going to close in.

Near by, an engine coupled onto a line of freight cars with a crash. It was a short train, no more than twelve cars.

There was more silence. Then the engine whistled a highball, and a peal of thunder ran down the string of a dozen freights as the train began to move.

Jan Hile, Skookum and the others suddenly dashed for the freight and scrambled into an empty box car.

"Holy cow!" Renny thumped. "Come on!"

There seemed to be only one empty box car on the rear portion of the train, and they climbed into that, Monk and Renny, who were most agile, going first, and helping Johnny and Ham, and particularly Long Tom, who was hampered by his skirts.

There was a little hay on the floor of the box car. They crouched down in that, all except Johnny, who prowled around and explored the car with as much interest as he would have devoted to the tomb of a Pharaoh.

"A superimpregnable—"

"Whoa!" requested Long Tom. "Bob the tails off them words."

Johnny sighed and said, "This box car is one of those modern things made out of steel, and there is some baled hay in the other end that we can use for chairs."

Renny rumbled. "Holy cow! He does know little words!"

They dragged hay bales around and made themselves comfortable, except for Monk and Ham. The latter two kept a lookout from the one open door. The other was closed and locked.

"We don't want them guys droppin' off without us seein' 'em!" Monk said grimly.

The night was dark, the wheels roared and pounded over rail joints, and the engine whistle howled at intervals.

The inactivity began to pall on Renny.

"I think I'll climb out of this car and have a look around," he said. "There's a kind of hatch here at one end."

"I'll go along," offered Monk, who was acrobatic by nature. "We can mosey along the tops of the cars."

The two skinned off their coats, preparatory to beginning their trip.

"What if you meet somebody?" Ham demanded.

"We'll say we're brakemen."

"And what if it's a brakeman you meet?"

"To you," Monk said, "the fruit of the peanut bush."

He leaped and knocked at the underside of the hatch in the roof of the car. "Hey! This thing seems to be locked!"

"We'll go out of the door, then," Renny advised. "You lift me up, and I'll grab the roof, then pull you up."

The open boxcar door rolled shut as they approached it.

Both men stopped.

"That's danged funny," Monk muttered.

Ham called, "The motion of the train probably rolled it shut."

Monk tried vainly to open the door, then said, "Well, the motion of the train'll never roll it open again."

They unconsciously held their breaths. The thing had been a little spooky. It did not help any when Long Tom let out a gulp.

"The hatch!" he croaked.

Long Tom's croaks were always effective. Generally, they were reminiscent of a crow caught in a bear trap, and this time was no exception. Everyone looked at the car roof.

They could see a vague square of dark slate which indicated the trapdoor in the top of the car had opened.

A moment later, two heavy objects were shoved through the hatch and thumped on the car floor.

Then the hatch started to close.

Monk took a running jump and clamped fingers onto the hatch rim.

MONK considered that he had gone far too long without action. He intended to have some. He hung to the hatch edge with one hand, grabbed with the other. He got something. A man's arms, he always thought. It did him no good. A hard article landed on his head.

The article was very hard, and it struck his head with force. A rifle stock, he reflected, and saw stars. He hung on. He tried to jerk his victim down into the box car. Failing in that, he did his best to jerk the man's arm off. He was not successful there, either. The rifle stock hit him again.

Monk landed, flat-backed, on the two objects which had been tumbled down through the hatch.

The hatch slid shut with a sound like a bowling ball going down an alley.

Johnny said, "I'll be superamalgamated!"

Monk got air back in his lungs, felt around with his hands, and gave a hiss of astonishment.

"Hey!" he exploded. "Man and girl!"

"Well, what did they throw in here?" demanded Ham, who thought Monk was swearing a new oath.

"I told you," Monk snapped, "a man and a girl!"

They made several ineffectual attacks on the top hatch, and as many futile attempts on the door. Then Long Tom gave the spring-motor generator of his flashlight a twist, and they had light on the individuals who had been dropped through the roof lid.

A man and girl, as Monk had said.

The girl they recognized instantly.

"Nona Idle!" Renny rumbled.

"Man," Monk breathed in an aside to Ham, "is she a looker!"

Monk took a running jump and clamped fingers onto the hatch rim.

They had heard Nona Idle described at the lunchroom in Ohio with sufficient detail that they were sure of the identity of this girl. As Monk was whispering, she was a looker. Much more so than they had expected.

They got her loose.

"What's happening?" Renny thumped. "Why'd they throw you in here?"

The girl's breath had been knocked out by the fall.

"Let me … get … wind back!" she gasped.

Long Tom got down beside the other man with his light and said, "Who's this guy? Blazes! He's our taxi driver!"

The hackman was gagged with tire tape and tied with copper wire which had not treated his wrists kindly. He was relieved of these handicaps.

"What're you doing here?" Monk asked him reasonably.

"Why do the worst things always happen to honest people like me?" the taxi driver demanded wildly.

Monk said, "Listen, you're not the only honest guy around here. Answer my question!"

The taxi driver began to shake.

"There's somethin' gonna happen to this train!" he groaned. Then he fell to making sounds and rattling his teeth.

Monk grabbed the taxi driver and began shaking him and demanding to know what the fellow meant, and the cabby recovered enough to start calling Monk words that even Ham had never dared apply to the homely chemist.

In the middle of the uproar, Nona Idle began speaking. What she said silenced them all as suddenly as if their throats had been cut.

"I do not understand it," she said, "because I know only what I overheard. But as the man says, something is going to happen to this train. And that isn't the worst."

"Worst?" Monk muttered. "What do you mean?"

The girl's face looked stark in the flashlight glare.

"I'm going to tell you something that doesn't sound reasonable," she said. "I'm going to tell you that thousands of people are soon to die. I don't know how. Nor why. But a lot of people are going to lose their lives before this is over with."

The horror in her voice was a hammer that made her words drive like nails.

They stood there in the locked, rumbling boxcar, each man with a blank feeling.

Finally, Monk muttered, "A train is a pretty big article for anything to happen to it."

"They may plan to wreck it," Renny rumbled.

IT wasn't a wreck.

At first, the railroad officials decided it was nothing more mysterious than a coincidence. First an engineer, fireman and brakies—a whole train crew—had simultaneously gotten tired of their jobs and decided to quit railroading and had disappeared. Second, a dispatcher had made a remarkable error and showed a train running on his division when there wasn't any train. Not even a short one of a dozen cars.

These two coincidences were farfetched.

But not as farfetched as trying to believe an entire train had disappeared.

The train dispatcher got red in the face when the freight was not reported past a little way station, and he called the operator, accused him of sleeping while the freight went past, and gave him hell for not sending in an "OS" report. The telegrapher swore up and down that there was no more wide-awake brass-pounder on the system, and that no freight train had passed.

It began to look as if no freight train had passed anywhere.

They called the superintendent out of bed. He listened, then howled his disbelief.

"Who the hell do you think you're talking to?" he yelled. "A freight train can't disappear!"

But one had. It had vanished thoroughly, without a trace. An engine, eleven boxcars and a caboose.

The initial suspicion was that they would find the freight piled up in a canyon somewhere. Or maybe it had run off on a siding.

The roadmaster went over the track; then section crews, trackwalkers, and platoons of railroad detectives who had been told that if they didn't find this missing freight train, goodbye jobs.

There was no wrecked freight train in any canyon.

There was no freight train standing on a sidetrack anywhere, and for a very good reason. There was no sidetrack at any point along that line.

There were no spur tracks running to abandoned mines, or anything of the kind.

In substance, the freight train couldn't have disappeared.

The president of the railroad, the superintendent, and numerous lesser officials boarded "go-devils" and went over the section where the train had vanished.

There was a stretch of about a hundred miles in which the train must have disappeared. Half of this was arid, semidesert prairie, and the other half mountains. There were no train tracks on the prairie, and a train off the rails could not have gotten far in those mountains.

The railroad men on their go-devils gave the track an intense inspection, devoting particular thoroughness to the point where it ran along the edge of Stone Mountain Dam.

Stone Mountain Dam seemed a likely point at first.

STONE MOUNTAIN DAM was a great and worthwhile project, in spite of the fact that it had chopped the political heads off a number of politicians. It had obviously been a great undertaking from the first—it was one of the highest dams in the world, and also one of the most expensive. It was the expense that had done the political head-lopping, all the politicians who had voted for the dam having been defeated at the next election.

Now that Stone Mountain Dam had been completed for two years, it was proving to be a better investment of the public's money than some others the politicians had made. The dam supplied water which was piped three hundred miles to one of the largest cities in the West. It also furnished irrigation canals with water, and numerous millions of volts of electricity were generated in the powerhouse at the dam.

The railroad tracks followed the highwater line of the dam for about two miles. The dam lake itself was almost seventy miles long. A newspaper reporter had once taken a ride on the lake, then written that it reminded him of what he had always thought the Grand Canyon would be like if it were dammed.

The railroad tracks ran, at some points, in a groove cut in the sheer stone walls of Stone Mountain Canyon. From the groove, there was a sheer drop to the water, only a few yards away.

But the railway officials decided no train had left the track at that point, because: first, there were no broken rails; second, a train could not jump a track and plunge into a reservoir without leaving some trace; third, and clinching the impossibility, the telegraph operator at Stone Mountain Station, just a little beyond the point where the track ran close to the water, had reported the freight train as passing his station on schedule.

The mystery of the vanished freight train got into the newspapers.

It crowded from the front pages the matter of the man who had died mysteriously in a solitary cell in the Utah State Penitentiary.

Chapter XII
DEATH IN THE SOLITARY BLOCK

THE warden of the penitentiary took his job seriously, so he had insisted on the institution's board of inquiry going into session over the mystery of the murder in the solitary-cell block.

The inquiry board had nine long-jawed members who, had they lived three centuries ago, would doubtless have been in the front row at all witch burnings. They sat in all particularly serious cases concerning prisoners. They were sitting now, listening with pinched-lip attention as the warden explained the circumstances leading up to the murder in the solitary-cell block.

"Prisoner No. 09983, known outside as Big Eva, unexpectedly claimed to be another person named Doc Savage, of whom you have doubtless heard," the warden was saying. "Several days prior to that, his cellmate, Hondo Weatherbee, had told a similar story, claiming to be a man named Tom Idle. As a result of this story, I confined Big Eva to the solitary-cell block. And on the night of the murder—"

One of the inquiry board interrupted, "Why was prisoner No. 09983 called Big Eva?"

The warden considered the point irrelevant, but he explained patiently. "The man's real name happened to be Everett Houndchased, so the nickname was inevitable." He took a deep breath and tried to go back to his story. "On the night of the murder—"

"Pardon me," interposed another board member, "but was the Doc Savage whom Big Eva claimed himself to be the famous scientist?"

"The point is irrelevant," said the warden. "On the night of the murder—"

"I don't consider it irrelevant!" said the board member. "In fact, I consider it mighty blasted important. I happen to know the real Doc Savage personally. Met him once in New York."

The warden thought that over. His board had been aggravating him by asking such questions as how Big Eva got his nickname, queries which the warden thought amounted to straying after mice when they should be chasing the rat. But if one of them knew Doc Savage by sight, that was different.

"Yes," he said. "Big Eva claimed to be that Doc Savage."

"That Doc Savage," said the board member in a tight-lipped way, "happens to be a very noted man. If the man you refused to believe was really Doc Savage, you're going to be out of a job so fast your head will swim, Mr. Warden!"

The warden folded his lips in and looked at the other. The board member was a squat brown man with a hooked nose. He somewhat resembled one of the owls that live in prairie dog holes. The warden had never particularly liked him.

One of the other board members hastily poured oil on the troubled waters.

"We are investigating a murder," he said.

The warden nodded.

"Yeah," he growled. "A murder committed by Big Eva. The murder of the penitentiary finger-print expert."

THE warden was wearing his high-heeled riding

boots, and also spurs today. He shoved his legs out before him and contemplated the spur rowels with wintry eyes.

Suddenly, he stood up.

"I'm going to let you hear the murder story from Big Eva"—the warden frowned at the prairie-owl board member—"or Doc Savage, if you're gullible enough to think that's who he is."

"I resent your tone!" snapped the "owl."

The warden turned around angrily and yelled at a flunky, "Bring in the murderer!"

His yell frightened a coyote investigating an old jackrabbit squatting place half a mile distant, and it carried plainly to Doc Savage, who was waiting in a windowless, stone anteroom. Doc was handcuffed. Two guards with large pistols kept their eyes on him.

He looked around calmly when he was in the presence of the board. He had removed the trick color-changing caps from his eyes, and the unusual character of his flake gold eyes had an effect.

"Listen!" growled a board member. "Big Eva never had eyes like that!"

The warden ran fingers through his hair. He felt like pulling it all out by the roots, because this whole thing was beginning to get his goat.

"Tell your story!" he ordered Doc Savage.

The bronze man's voice was pitched low and had an utterly convincing quality.

"There was a sound outside the door of the solitary cell," he explained. "It was furtive enough to make me suspicious. Someone was opening the little lid which covered the barred grating in the door to make it dark in the cell."

The bronze man paused. He knew the need of timing to make an explanation convincing, the necessity for a pause now and then to let facts soak in.

"When the lid opened," he continued, "my hand clutched the fingers of a man who was outside. The fingers were against the bars. The man was startled. He dropped a bottle he was carrying. It broke. The sound of glass shattering aroused my suspicions further, and I was able to get the lid closed. That was fortunate, and it was also lucky that the cell door was airtight, having been made so to keep out sound and assure that absolute quiet which is one of the disagreeable things about solitary confinement."

The bronze man hesitated briefly.

"There was poison gas in the bottle which the man dropped," he said. "It killed the fellow."

Doc Savage's attitude showed that this concluded his statement.

The warden was hard, but he was also fair. He cleared his throat.

"You might tell the rest of it," he said gruffly.

"Tell how you opened the lid a crack and endangered your own life to yell a warning for the guards not to come near."

Doc said, "That has nothing to do with whether or not I committed a murder."

The warden snorted. "The hell it hasn't. You saved the lives of the guards." The warden faced the board members. "This man also shouted what type of gas it was, and told what kind of chemicals to use to make the stuff harmless. Whether or not he murdered the fingerprint expert, it is a sure thing he saved the lives of some of my guards. My own, as well. I was one of the first men on the spot."

"I don't believe this man is Big Eva!" a board member snapped.

The board member who resembled an owl stood erect.

"I will talk to the man in private," he said importantly. "I can soon settle the whole question of whether or not he is Doc Savage."

The warden eyed him narrowly. "Why the privacy?"

The other bit his lips. "I'm sure I can better persuade him to tell the truth," he said, "if we talk it over in private."

The warden gave in. "O. K."

Doc Savage was escorted to a neighboring room. This chamber was small, and windowless like the others.

The door was of steel, heavy. The owlish man closed it.

"Now," he said, "we settle this damn quick!"

The owlish man took a revolver out of his clothing and pointed it at Doc Savage.

"You're gonna die sudden," he advised. "And they're gonna think you are Big Eva, you jumped me, and I shot you in self-defense!"

DOC SAVAGE kept his control level, although it got a bad jerking. He saw that the man intended to shoot.

"If it's money," the bronze man said, "maybe there is more in it for you if you do it another way."

The guess was good. Money was magic that loosened the man's finger on the trigger.

"Eh?" he said.

"You know I'm Doc Savage. You never saw me before, but you know who I am."

"Sure. So what?"

"So we understand each other. You have been hired to dispose of me. You might do the job, and you may get paid for it, although that last is doubtful."

The other man showed a set of gopher's teeth. "I'll get paid!"

"How much?"

"Fifty thousand dollars," the man said impressively.

Doc, watching him, figured it was considerably less than that.

"Got a fountain pen and paper?" the bronze man asked.

The other, keeping his gun alert, produced a pen and a blank sheet which he tore from a notebook. He passed these over.

The room contained a small table, and Doc went to that, seated himself, and made some marks on the paper. The marks were meaningless.

He said, "You can get a check for a hundred thousand cashed before I ever get out of here, you know."

The other man had a money mania. The sum mentioned set his mouth to working as though he were tasting something good.

Doc said, "Here."

The man reached for the paper.

He didn't get it; but Doc got his gun. Then they got down on the floor. Doc, a hand over the man's mouth, kept the fellow from crying out. They struggled silently, but after the first few moments the animation consisted mostly of the bronze man's corded fingers inflicting agony. The other man burst out sweating in an incredibly short time.

"Don't yell!" the bronze man warned.

After Doc released him, the other lay quiet, except for such fright twitchings as he could not help.

Doc said, "The only chance you have of walking out of here is to talk fast."

The man went through enough of a convulsion to show that he had never heard of the fact that Doc Savage and his aides had made it a policy never to take a human life themselves. When enemies had died, it had been through unavoidable accident. The owl of a man thought he was to be killed on the spot. He ogled his gun, which Doc now held.

He began to get words out as if he had a mouthful of them, and they were red-hot rivets.

THE man's explanation was clear, brief and earnest enough that Doc Savage knew it was the truth.

"A man named Jan Hile called on me today and offered me twenty thousand dollars to kill you," he said wildly. "He paid ten thousand down. We made a deal. I was to get the rest later."

For a moment there was in existence the low, exotic trilling, the note that was as fantastic as the song of some strange bird in a tropical forest, the sound which Doc Savage made in moments of mental stress.

"Where were you to collect the rest of the money?"

"This guy—Jan Hile—was to deliver it."

"Had you known Hile previously?"

"No."

Doc Savage described the Dr. Joiner who had seized Nona Idle in Ohio.

"That's the man," the owl of a fellow gasped. "That's Jan Hile."

Doc Savage's metallic features were grim. "You didn't know that Jan Hile is an infamous criminal lawyer around Chicago?"

"No."

That seemed to be the substance of what the man knew.

Doc said, "Now we'll go into the other room, and you can repeat this."

Doc shoved him. The man's shoulders fell, and he shuffled into the adjoining room which held the prison warden, the other members of the board and the guards.

The moment he was inside, the owl of a man leaped and snatched a revolver from the nearest guard.

"Watch out!" he screeched. "The man is Big Eva! He's got my gun!"

The gun was there in Doc Savage's hand for all of them to see.

The owl of a man lifted the guard's weapon and fired at Doc Savage.

Chapter XIII
MELEE IN A PENITENTIARY

INERTIA is the unwillingness of things to move. The scientific explanation is more technical, but no more descriptive. Inertia is the natural law that makes a wagon want to stand still when you give it the first shove. Inertia seems to apply generally to other things. Everything seems to need a little time to start moving, men's minds being no exception.

The minds of the men in the room did not start acting instantly.

The exception was Doc Savage, who was on edge and half expecting what had happened. He went to one side. He was all set to do that. And the bullet missed him.

The gun in his hand coughed lead and noise. He never carried a gun, but he could use one. He had spent hundreds of hours in intensive practice—and not with the special target weapons used in matches, for his shooting was never the match kind. He practiced snap work, firing from difficult positions.

The owl of a man howled. His gun was gone, and his hand was mangled. When he screeched, and threw up both arms, his hand showered scarlet over the ceiling.

Doc kept going. His objective was the door.

There were a dozen men in the room, all of them probably armed. It was no place for a pitched battle, particularly when the bronze man had none of the gadgets on which he depended to make his fights effective and bloodless.

He gained the door, pitched through. Then he slammed the door. All the doors in this part of the penitentiary were sheathed with steel and equipped to be locked from either side. Doc locked this one.

Bullets began slamming the other side of the panel as the warden and his men endeavored to shoot out the lock.

Doc went down a passage. He passed a number of doors, gained the one he wanted. He knew the penitentiary layout. This door led up to one of the watch towers, where a guard was stationed with a submachine gun.

The stairs were a gloomy corkscrew. The door at the top was kept always locked. Only the warden could order it opened. But there was a peephole, and the guard was pressing an eye to this.

Doc imitated the warden's voice.

"There's a man escaping!" he shouted. "Watch the outside."

The guard's eye went away from the slit.

Doc reached the tower door. Shooting downstairs had stopped. It was very still. The bronze man slipped the empty cartridge out of the revolver, tapped and scraped it on the floor to make the sound of the warden's spurs.

He imitated the warden's voice again.

"Let me in!" he ordered.

The deceived and unsuspecting guard unlocked the door and opened it.

Doc took him by the neck. The man held his machine gun. He tried to retain his grip on the weapon, to use it, which was a mistake.

The neck pressure which the bronze man used to make him senseless was harmless, but would be effective several hours.

Doc donned the guard's cap and coat. He leaned from the tower window with the submachine gun, aimed at a harmless clump of sagebrush, and opened fire. The sub gun made enough sound for a battle all by itself.

"There he goes!" Doc yelled between bursts. "That way! South!"

Later, after he had watched armed guards scattering through the sagebrush, the bronze man finished changing clothes with the guard.

PENITENTIARY procedure in event of an escape does not vary greatly. If it occurs during daytime, all normal activity in the shops and garment factories at once ceases and the prisoners are marched slowly and under close guard to their cells where they are locked in, the purpose being to prevent a general break, and to obtain a check on the inmates to ascertain how many have made the break. The only reliable checkup is the one made when the convicts are locked in their cells.

It required no more than twenty minutes, in the present instance, to get all prisoners in their cells. The check-up showed, in addition to Big Eva, one other man missing; but this latter convict was soon routed out of the laundry basket into which he had crawled undercover of the excitement, hoping that he might get his chance at a break.

It was near dark. So the prisoners were kept locked up; and for the psychological effect, denied of their evening meal. The warden was fair, but if he was bitten, he bit back in a large, general way.

There was some grumbling and an outbreak of beating of cell doors with shoes, but two guards made a trip down the cell-house corridor with a fire hose and put a stop to that. No man wants to go to bed hungry, and on a water-soaked cot as well.

The night settled down darkly, and the prison was quiet. In the distance, motor cars could be heard carrying searchers, and occasionally a bloodhound broke loose in baying.

Tom Idle was lying on his bunk feeling extremely low, when a key rattled in his cell lock. He sat up, saw two husky guards.

"Warden wants to talk to you," one of the guards growled.

"What … what about?" Tom Idle asked uncertainly.

"You're Big Eva's cellmate, aren't you? And he escaped, didn't he?"

That seemed to answer the question, and Tom Idle followed the guards. They reached the warden's office and stopped outside.

"You go in," one guard growled. "I think the warden is ready to lay eggs, the way he snarled at us and told us not to come in, but to fetch you."

Tom Idle entered the warden's office.

Doc Savage said, "Give me a natural greeting."

TOM IDLE demonstrated that he was not without wits.

"Good evening, warden," he said in a loud voice. "What did you want with me?"

His tone was not exactly natural, but then a convict called before the warden might not be expected to speak calmly.

Doc Savage went over, said in a voice that was so like the warden's that Tom Idle jumped, "You two guards can go on about your duties. I'll take care of this man."

There was the faint sound of the guards moving away.

Tom Idle breathed, "I thought you escaped!"

"Not completely," Doc admitted.

"But what are you doing here?"

"Two things," the bronze man said, and explained what they were: "First, everyone was looking for a prisoner outside the penitentiary, not in it. Second, I wanted to free Tom Idle."

"But why take so much trouble about me?" Tom Idle demanded.

"Suppose something happened to me?" Doc suggested. "No one else has any evidence of the rather incredible chain of circumstances that got you in here. My five assistants do not even know. Something seems to have happened to them, because they have made no attempt to get in touch with me."

Tom Idle subsided.

"How do we get out of here?" he wanted to know.

Doc said, "The warden is out directing the search, and some of the guards do not know it. We'll see if he took his private car."

A bit of graft connected with the wardenship of the State penitentiary was the fine limousine supplied for the warden's personal use. This warden, however, preferred an ancient jalopy of his own, a car of uncertain vintage with high wheels adapted to hurdling the local sagebrush. He often boasted that his car could go anywhere that a jackrabbit could travel. He was using the jalopy now, and the fine limousine stood in the garage.

The garage, opening off the warden's office, was unguarded. There was a chauffeur's cap and a dark raincoat, evidently used by the trustee who did the warden's driving, hanging on a hook.

"Put these on," Doc directed.

Tom Idle attired himself in the cap and coat, and got behind the car wheel.

"What if this don't fool 'em?" he asked anxiously.

"By thinking things won't work," Doc said, "you just give yourself an unnecessary advance scare."

This bit of philosophy, as a matter of fact, was opposite that which the bronze man practiced. He always acted on the mental theory that everything conceivable would go wrong with anything he attempted, a conviction that impelled him to prepare against all possibilities. It probably accounted for his high average success in attempting the apparently impossible.

The warden's limousine rolled to the gate. From the gloom of the rear seat, Doc imitated the warden's voice once more and said, "Open the gate, please."

The guard saluted and began opening the gate. The gate was a sliding steel affair which operated by turning a wheel. Having opened it, the guard stepped back and saluted.

Then another guard walked out of the shadows, said, "Who's in that car?"

"The warden."

"Like hell!" barked the second guard. "The warden's out with the searchers!"

The man carried a sawed-off shotgun, probably one of the most mangling short-range weapons ever devised by man. He lifted the gun.

Chapter XIV
SAGEBRUSH TRAIL

DOC SAVAGE had rolled down both rear windows against such an emergency. He was all set with a monkey wrench he had taken from a rack in the garage.

The wrench, thrown hard, took the shotgun-wielder just above the belt buckle. The wrench was heavy. The man doubled, dropped his gun.

"Drive!" Doc rapped.

Tom Idle shaved the edge of the gate, barely missed the warden's private horse-hitching rack in the graveled parking area outside, and got on the road beyond. The road was a full eighteen-foot concrete slab, but Tom Idle had trouble keeping on it.

"Something wrong with the steering gear?" Doc asked.

"It's me. I'm a better hand with a team of mules."

Doc climbed over into the front seat and took the wheel.

Back at the prison gate, the sawed-off shotgun began banging, and shot spanked the rear of the car. But the distance was great enough that the missiles had lost their force by the time they arrived.

"Sorry about my driving," Tom Idle said. "But you see, I'm poor folks and never had a car."

The limousine had a big, well-tuned engine, and it settled down to running with the whine of a high-speed electric motor. The road changed from concrete to blacktop, and there was nothing alongside but telephone poles, and these began going past considerably faster than heartbeats.

Tom Idle settled back. He shuddered.

"The last time I had a fast car ride," he said, "things went black right in the middle of it, and I woke up in that penitentiary."

"You were probably struck over the head when you were not looking."

"I know. I thought a bullet had hit me. The driver, that devil in the black gloves, had said cops were after us. I guess that was to get me to turn around so he could hit me."

**The car bumped the barricade,
upset it.**

"The man in the black gloves," Doc said, "seems to be a criminal lawyer named Jan Hile. The man is abnormally clever, and has no scruples."

"What is he up to? What is back of all this?"

Doc Savage did not seem to hear. Tom Idle, being unfamiliar with the bronze man's habit of apparently going deaf at questions which he did not wish to answer, repeated his inquiry. Again getting no response, he clenched his teeth.

"What happened to my sister?" he asked hoarsely.

"Jan Hile has her," Doc said.

Tom Idle made a hoarse sound. "Maybe that devil's killed her!"

"No."

"What makes you so sure?"

"He was undoubtedly keeping your sister alive to use the threat of harming her to keep you from talking. Now that you are out of the penitentiary, he has more need than ever for a club to hold over you."

The bronze man lifted an arm, pointed ahead.

"They have this road barricaded," he said. "And there seems to be a military machine gun planted alongside the road."

Tom Idle turned his head. He groaned.

"There's a whole string of cars chasing us!" he croaked.

DOC slowed the limousine. The barricade

ahead was looming up, and appeared to be a gate they had taken from some ranch. It was painted green, propped up with two-by-fours.

The road was ditched deeply on either side, but the car possibly might hurdle those. The machine was equipped with a spotlight controlled by an inside handle, and Doc raked its beam over the adjacent terrain. It picked up rocky hills, a dozen washes that would hold small houses.

"No use!" Tom Idle gulped. "Road's the only way out! And they've got it blocked."

Doc said, "How high can you pitch your voice?"

"Eh?"

"Like this." The bronze man brought his voice up and emitted a shrill, girlish scream.

Tom Idle said, "How's this?" and did very well.

Doc headed the limousine for the barricade. He rolled down the driver's window, shoved his head out, blinked the car lights to compel attention, then lifted his natural voice to crashing volume that made the words easily understood by the men manning the barricade.

"Don't shoot!" he roared. "You want to kill the warden's wife?"

He jerked his head back.

"Don't!" screeched Tom Idle in a high voice. "Don't shoot! You'll hit us!"

He had the idea. Doc Savage added his own high voice, screaming, then changed to his normal tone and shouted threats.

The car bumped the barricade, upset it. The boards broke under the wheels.

The men manning the barricade yelled profanely, but did not fire for fear of injuring the women they thought were in the car.

Part of the barricade was dragging under the limousine with a loud grinding. Doc swayed the car from side to side, and lost the impediment. He put weight on the accelerator.

The car picked up speed, went away from the barricade.

Tom Idle said, "Danged if I ever thought that'd work!"

Doc Savage drove with grim, furious silence, and when he had gained a little on the machine ahead, suddenly braked to a stop; and with the gun he had taken from the owllike inquiry-board member, he shot twice at the insulator on a telephone pole, limned brightly in the illumination of the car spotlight. The insulator shattered; the telephone wire fell in two parts. There was only the one wire.

"Keep them from telephoning to head us off," he said.

He drove on.

The clouds parted and let moonlight through; the whole western rangeland and desert and mountain became bathed in soft silver, with Great Salt Lake finally coming into view, a pale mirror with its far edge buried in the haze of what seemed infinite distance.

Tom Idle spoke in a puzzled voice. "What gets me is this: How did they get you and me into the penitentiary, and get Big Eva and Hondo Weatherbee out?"

"Jan Hile had a number of men around the penitentiary bought off," Doc reminded. "Probably others besides the fingerprint man who got killed in his own trap, and the crooked board member. They probably worked out a plan. It is possible."

"After seeing the way we got out tonight," Tom Idle grunted, "I'd say anything was possible."

There was traffic around them now, and they joined it, traveled the way most of the cars seemed to be traveling. Later, they turned into the wide parking area at the swimming pavilion and amusement part on the shore of Great Salt Lake.

Tom Idle said, "The last thing I need right now is a swim."

Doc Savage indicated their garb—his own prison-guard uniform, Tom Idle's convict dungarees.

"Clothes," he said, "are more necessary."

"Huh?"

"People usually drive out to lakes wearing bathing suits under their clothing," Doc reminded. "They leave their clothing on the beach. We might do some borrowing."

"That's stealing."

"Technically. Not if we later pay the owners well for the stuff."

They left the car and began haunting shadows.

DOC SAVAGE and his five assistants had operated together long enough that they had worked out definite methods of procedure. They had agreed upon a hotel, for instance, in each large city, which they would use for headquarters, where they would leave messages in case they became separated.

The Salt Lake City rendezvous hotel was the Lake Palace, a hostelry of good reputation; and to this Monk and the others had forwarded baggage from Columbus, Ohio, the baggage containing such stuff as they would not need in their immediate job of following the three burning-coal-mine killers westward. The Lake Palace clerk was a pleasant young man.

"Why, yes," he said. "We have been holding some baggage for Andrew Blodgett Mayfair and party for several days, but they have not appeared."

Doc Savage's metallic features did not change expression.

"You have had no word from them?"

"None," the clerk assured him.

"Their baggage is still here?"

"Oh, yes. In Suite 13."

Doc said. "We'll take rooms, if you please."

The bronze man's personality was impelling enough that the clerk overlooked the formality of having guests without baggage pay in advance. This in spite of the ill fit of the suit which Doc had purloined on the beach. The suit was much too tight. A notebook in the pocket had contained the owner's name, so there would be no difficulty about remunerating him later for the suit.

They were shown to a room.

As soon as they were alone, Doc stood on the radiator, which was under the window, removed the window shade, and dissecting it, secured a length off the stiff spring which the roller mechanism contained.

They went to Suite 13, made sure the corridor was deserted. Doc began operating on the lock.

"Sure appropriate," Tom Idle muttered, eyeing the number on the door.

Doc got the door open shortly, and they went inside. The baggage was there, just as it had arrived from the East. The bronze man removed a portable radio transmitter-receiver from a case, switched it on, and spent some time vainly trying to raise his aides.

He took the radio and two other cases to his room. There was also money in the baggage, and he took part of that. Back in his room, he folded a hundred dollar bill in each of two envelopes and addressed these to the owners of the suits which he and Tom Idle had filched.

Tom Idle said, "I wonder what the newspapers are printing about the penitentiary break?"

"You might have a paper sent up and see."

When Tom Idle got the newspaper and opened it, he emitted a grunt.

"Heck!" he said. "I guess it just seemed important because we were mixed up in it ourselves. They only gave the prison break a couple of paragraphs. The rest of the front page is about the vanished train."

Doc looked interested. "What vanished train?"

He took the newspaper and read. He noted the date of the train disappearance and consulted the tags on the luggage which his men had shipped. The duffel had arrived in Salt Lake City the same night the freight train disappeared.

But there was nothing else that seemed to connect the vanished train with the mystery of why Hondo Weatherbee and Big Eva had been spirited out of the penitentiary.

"What do we do now?" Tom Idle asked.

"We have one clue," Doc told him, "but we'll have to wait until the general-delivery window opens to get it."

Chapter XV
TROUBLE, GENERAL DELIVERY

THE post office general-delivery window regularly opened at eight o'clock in the morning.

It was fifteen minutes until eight when Tom Idle put on his hat in the hotel room which he and Doc Savage occupied.

"I'll get the package," Tom Idle said. He looked disgusted. "You say it's one you mailed to yourself when you first got to Salt Lake City?"

"Yes."

"And you say it's got some weeds in it?"

"Right."

"What I want to know is how the blazes weeds are going to help us find my sister and your five helpers."

"You get the package," Doc Savage said patiently, "and we will see what happens."

It was one minute until eight when Tom Idle entered the post office, put his elbows on the general-delivery window ledge, and waited. The window slid open on time.

"Clark Savage," Tom Idle said, as Doc had directed him. "You should be holding at least one package."

The package was passed out to Tom Idle. The young man tucked it under his arm, walked out of the post office. He was in a cheerful frame of mind, and he almost whistled. Personally, he didn't see how a package full of weeds would solve anything, but he had confidence in Doc Savage.

When the squat, bowlegged man stepped up to Tom Idle, it was entirely unexpected.

The man held a lumpishly folded newspaper under Tom Idle's nose.

"Can you recognize a guy inside a newspaper?" he asked.

Tom Idle swallowed. "I ... uh—"

"In case you can't"—the man showed the muzzle of the gun in the paper briefly—"this ought to satisfy you."

Tom Idle got hold of his wits. "There must be some mistake!"

"If there is, it ain't mine," the bowlegged man said. He had chewing tobacco stain on his lips, and leashed ferocity in his blue eyes. "Where's the bronze guy?"

"Huh?"

"You heard me! Where's Doc Savage?"

Tom Idle countered, "Who are you, anyway?"

"A Fed."

"You mean—agent of the Federal Bureau of Investigation?"

"That's right. But if you want to talk, suppose we go out in the car and do it."

The words were no suggestion, but command.

Slight motion of the paper containing the gun made that evident.

The car was a touring model, but the curtains were up and enclosed the rear. The machine was dust-coated, and there was a fan-shaped rust stain on the hood where water had been boiled out of the radiator by hard mountain driving.

Three men sat in the car. Tom Idle did not like their looks.

"Listen," he said suddenly, "if you're genuine Feds, you can tell me who is head of the Bureau of Investigation for the Missouri district."

Tom Idle happened to know the answer to that question.

They laughed at him.

"Jan Hile is the head of the only bureau you're interested in," one said.

REALIZING he had been tricked, Tom Idle made a sudden effort to fling the post-office package into a nearby store. The bowlegged man stopped that, seized the package, then crowded Tom Idle into the car.

"Careful, stupid!" one man gritted. "We don't need you so much that you can afford to get funny!"

The car began moving, working its way through traffic. Tom Idle sat rigid, feeling about as useful as a rock.

"Let's take him to the mountains to work him over," one man suggested.

"Maybe he'll tell us where Doc Savage is, without a lot of trouble," said another.

"Not him." The man scowled at Tom Idle. "He's a heroic sap. You can see it in his face."

Tom Idle said, "I don't know about that, but if you think I'm going to tell you anything, you're crazy."

The car left the city and began to climb a mountain road. The same road, Tom Idle realized with a start, up which Jan Hile had driven furiously on that strange morning weeks ago.

"How'd you know I'd turn up at the post office?" Tom Idle asked.

"Didn't. Thought it would be Doc Savage." The man chuckled grimly. "Hell, if that bronze guy is so smart, I'd think he would've realized that we'd check on all the time he spent in Salt Lake City. We did, and found out he'd mailed a package to himself at the post office. He bought the stamps and envelope off the hotel clerk, and the clerk saw him address it. Twenty dollars got that out of the clerk."

Tom Idle said nothing more.

The men knew this mountain road, and the reason for that was evident when they turned off on a narrow trail which looked impassable, but afforded smooth although steep going, until they eventually stopped before a cabin.

The cabin was old, and so long unused that a small pine tree had grown up through the porch. But the thing had been built substantially, with huge logs, stout rafters, and a roof of slabs that had withstood the test of time. The windows were thin and narrow, and spaced around the building in a manner that puzzled Tom Idle until he realized that they were intended as loopholes. The door was at least four inches thick, and also equipped with a loophole.

They shoved Tom Idle inside.

"Remember it?" one asked.

Tom Idle looked startled. "Why, I've never been here before!"

"The hell you haven't!" the man told him. "You were brought here after Jan Hile cracked you over the head, and it was here that you were doped up and your appearance changed so you looked more like Hondo."

Tom Idle thought back. "That time in the park—I must have been drugged while I slept, and my clothes changed."

"Remember the ham and eggs Skookum gave you?"

"But that was the morning before."

"Slow-acting drug. Made you sleep sound enough that we could give you an anaesthetic the next night."

One of the men looked around the cabin, then went over to one corner, struck a match for light, and examined what proved to be an ancient bullet hole.

"Haw, haw!" he said. "Here's where Jan Hile told Hondo to shoot at that Piute fifteen years ago, and Hondo missed him! Boy, don't this bring back the old outlaw times?"

Tom Idle gathered that they had once belonged to a gang of bandits to which Jan Hile and Hondo Weatherbee had also belonged.

He asked, "Why did you use such an elaborate scheme to get Hondo Weatherbee out of the pen? Why not just stage a break? It would have been simpler."

The man who had been doing all the informing leered at him.

"Hondo's gonna get a few million dollars," he said. "Hondo wanted to enjoy it. He couldn't with the cops hunting him. As long as cops figured he was still in the pen, they wouldn't hunt. See? Simple, eh? In a few months, we'd have slipped you a shot of strychnine, and the law would've thought they'd buried old Hondo. He'd have been safe, see."

"You were going to poison me, too!" Tom Idle gasped in horror.

Another man interrupted, "That ain't nothin' to what we're gonna do to you now if you don't tell us where Doc Savage is."

The next development had about the same effect as the Empire State Building would create if it upset.

Doc Savage, from the door, said, "You should have looked backward more often as you drove up here."

THESE men had been taken by surprise before. They lost no time in going into action. Weapons came out with the adeptness of old-time gun fighters. They scattered instinctively, no two men close together, so as to make too general a target for effective shooting. One upended a heavy table. A second slid into the disused fireplace. The two others took opposite corners.

The cabin quaked with gun roars.

But Doc Savage had jumped back outside, yanked the door shut.

The man in the fireplace swore and came out, showering ashes, and dashed for the door, aiming at the lock as he came. He got perhaps half across the room before he seemed to lose interest in trying to point his gun at the lock. Then he dropped the gun, pounded the palms of both hands against his forehead as if to jar out a dizziness. Finally, he lay down on the floor, limp.

Tom Idle stared in astonishment, and looking around, saw that the other men were likewise lying down. He had been holding his breath. He drew in a gasp of relief.

When he took in the breath, the effect was almost instant. His head swam, his breathing apparatus seemed afflicted with sleepy numbness, and the sensation spread through his body with lazy languor. He felt like yawning, always thought he did yawn while he was falling to the floor.

It must have been much later when he awakened. The sun was higher. He turned over, saw the four men who had seized him at the post office.

The quartet were bound hand and foot now. But they appeared still asleep.

"You have a strong constitution to come out of it so quickly."

Tom Idle turned his head at Doc Savage's voice. The bronze man stood at the table, which he had set on its legs again, and was doing something. Tom Idle lifted his head, felt like lying down again, but forced himself to get up.

He saw that Doc Savage had recovered the package of weeds and was examining the contents with what was evidently a powerful magnifying glass.

"What—" He held his head. "What happened?"

"I broke several small glass anaesthetic bombs in the cabin just before appearing in the door," the bronze man explained.

Tom Idle pointed confusedly at the weeds. "I mean—what earthly help are those things going to be?"

Before Doc Savage could answer, one of the bound men began swearing. He had revived.

AN hour later, Doc Savage stepped back from the four bound men and put on his coat. His face was grim.

"You do not often find four men in a group who cannot be scared into talking," he said quietly.

"They haven't told us a thing!" Tom Idle said desperately.

"No. And unfortunately I have no truth serum."

Tom Idle's hair was disheveled, and there was a wild expression on his face. He had been thinking about his sister, and the more his mind dwelled on the fact that it was men like these holding her prisoner, the more desperate he became.

"Damn 'em!" he yelled furiously. "I'll make 'em talk!"

He lunged and seized one of the revolvers which they had taken from the captives.

Doc Savage got in his path, the two men struggled for a moment, and Doc took the gun.

"Killing men keeps you awake at night," the bronze man said. "Even men like these."

"And what do you believe thinking about my sister will do?" Tom Idle screamed.

Doc Savage made a quieting gesture.

"We have another clue."

"You mean those weeds?"

"Yes."

Tom Idle shuddered, backed outside and sank on the doorstep. "I hate to think you're crazy," he said angrily. "But if your weeds don't pan out, I'm going to beat all four of those men to death if they won't talk."

"We can get truth serum from New York in two days, and try it as a last resort."

"Two days!"

Tom Idle shuddered.

He watched the bronze man lift the prisoners and place them in their own car. The machine in which Doc Savage had followed the trail to this spot, a rented coupé, was down the mountain trail a short distance where it had been parked.

"You drive the other car," Doc directed.

Tom Idle followed in the coupé, and two miles outside of Salt Lake City he overhauled Doc, who had stopped the bandit car. To Tom Idle's astonishment, Doc left the other car and got in the coupé.

"You're not turning those four devils loose!" Tom Idle yelled.

"They are drugged now," Doc explained patiently. "They cannot possibly be revived for a day. They will be found and taken to a hospital. When we want them, we can go get them. In the meantime, they are off our hands."

Tom Idle did not favor the procedure.

"What do we do in the meantime?" he asked anxiously.

"See what we can develop from the weeds."

They drove on into the city, the bronze man driving boldly, stopping with the traffic lights, sometimes almost within arm's reach of the policemen who were supposed to be on the look-out for them. Tom Idle felt as if he were sitting with his feet in a pail of ice water each time this happened. He could not quite accommodate his mind to the fact that, since Doc Savage had resort-ed to their natural appearance, they did not so nearly resemble Big Eva and Hondo Weatherbee.

Tom Idle's cheeks and lips were still thick. Doc had explained that Jan Hile had effected this by injecting paraffin, and that the stuff had best be removed later with a slight surgical operation.

Tom Idle waited without much patience for their destination.

Chapter XVI
WEED CLUE

IT is a popular supposition that the Antarctic regions and the great desert of Rub-Al-Khali in Arabia are the only unexplored sections left on the face of the earth.

That probably depends on the point of view. There is exploring, and exploring. One kind of explorer takes a trek across a stretch of unknown territory and calls it exploring.

There is another kind of explorer, the scientific type, who spends as much as several months on a few square miles of territory; and when he has finished, there is not much left to be known about the district. The species of plants, the chemical make-up of the soil, the exact type of rock, and probably the type of rock at any given depth up to thousands of feet are all known, and made a matter of record which go into files.

By this last standard, there are many unex-plored areas in the United States. But there are many sections that have been explored, and the data made a matter of record in the States and in Washington.

Doc Savage finished four consecutive hours at the long-distance telephone, and hung up.

"That does it," he said.

Tom Idle rubbed his forehead. "I don't get this."

"Those weeds," Doc Savage explained, "were caught in the wheels of Jan Hile's airplane, and torn out by the roots."

"Sure. And Hile hired a mechanic in Ohio to clean them out of the wheels. You told me that."

"When you pull up a weed, dirt clings to the roots."

"Sure."

"In this case, roots were jammed in the wheels, dirt and all, so that the soil was still on the roots when they were dug out in Ohio."

"Um-m-m."

"Sagebrush was mixed with the weeds," Doc said. "That indicated the plane had been landing in one of the western States, where sagebrush grows. Furthermore, it was a type of sagebrush which only grows in one section."

Tom Idle nodded.

"I can understand it that far," he admitted.

"The earth on the roots was filled with sand and rock particles which must have been eroded from surrounding rock formation." The bronze man indicated the telephone. "The checking by telephone was to compare the sand with data from geological and engineering surveys in the govern-ment files. The sand checked with the sagebrush source exactly."

"Eh?"

"Both came from the vicinity of the arm of Stone Mountain reservoir that extends around Mad Mesa."

Tom Idle gave a jerk of astonishment.

"Stone Mountain Dam," he exploded, "is where that freight train disappeared!"

DOC SAVAGE had originally flown to Salt Lake City in his own plane, and the craft had been hangared outside the city. It was still there, fully fueled, ready to take the air as soon as it was wheeled out of the hangar.

Doc Savage finished looking over the vicinity of the hangar.

"Either Jan Hile's men did not locate the ship," he told Tom Idle, "or they do not have anyone watching it. There seems to be nobody suspicious around."

"Let's get going!" Tom Idle said impatiently.

The bronze man did not take the ship off the ground at once, but went over it with what seemed to his companion to be aggravating slowness, examining and tapping the metal fittings with a hammer and chisel. Tom Idle finished loading two equipment cases in the craft, then paced impa-tiently. He was almost insane with anxiety over his sister, so much so that Doc Savage had flatly forbidden him to carry a gun, lest the young man start shooting the moment he saw any of the Hile crew.

"Clever," Doc Savage said unexpectedly.

"Eh?" Tom Idle came over to stare.

"Hile's men found this plane, all right."

The bronze man put the cold chisel against one of the metal attachments which held the left wing to the fuselage, and tapped with the hammer.

"Well, the chisel made a nick," Tom Idle said.

"Exactly. And that fitting is supposed to be the toughest steel. Nothing short of a diamond should scratch it."

Tom Idle looked, startled and puzzled.

"They took the fitting off, drew the temper, then replaced it," Doc explained. "It would have sheared off, and we would have lost a wing the first time we hit hard going."

Tom Idle made no more comments about their progress being slow. He was beginning to understand how this strange bronze man had managed to live a long time while following a highly dangerous avocation.

When Doc had retempered the fitting, and they were finally in the air, progress was fast enough to satisfy even Tom Idle. Doc flew low, and the incredible fanged buttes and knife-slash canyons which rutted the landscape around Stone Mountain Dam seemed to lunge past the plane with flashing speed.

The plane, like all the craft used by Doc Savage and his associates, could operate from land or water, and if necessary, snow. This one, when landing gear was retracted, became a seaplane.

Doc set down on Stone Mountain reservoir late in the afternoon.

They had come onto the reservoir through one of its canyon arms at a height which Tom Idle had mistaken for only a few hundred feet, which, he realized now, must have been an altitude of at least three thousand feet. Nothing else would have made the canyons look so small. They were incredible. The walls of stone shot up so sheer they appeared to overhang.

The water, in the evening shadows, was as black as ink. The lake was no more than half a mile wide, but it had at this point close to the dam, a depth approaching a thousand feet. It extended back for seventy-five miles as the crow flew, but there were hundreds of miles of shore line; for the shape of the lake, as photographed from the air, made it resemble a great gnarled tree of naked branches.

"Is that Mad Mesa?" Tom Idle asked, and pointed.

"Mad Mesa is fifty miles from here."

"Then what—"

"Yonder," Doc said, "is where the railroad parallels the lake. We're interested in that point."

AFTER Doc Savage taxied the plane close to the steep cliff, in the perpendicular stone of which was the chiseled groove in which the railroad ran, Tom Idle failed to climb to the railway itself. He was disgusted with himself, and dumbfounded as he watched his companion make the ascent where there seemed no possible handhold.

Doc gave attention to the rails, to the ties, to the gravel roadbed. He made note of a number of things, among which was a scar in the stone roof of the groove, as if it had been struck a hard blow by some very large piece of machinery. At one spot, he found a bit of steel which had been snapped off the underside of a boxcar; and in various places he found wood splinters and scattered rust.

He climbed back down to the plane. The wind was pushing the craft toward the cliff, and Tom Idle had only to fend off to keep it in place.

"Find anything?"

Doc Savage appeared not to hear the question.

He examined the lake waterline below the railroad. He seemed much interested in several long, fuzzy strings which he found clinging to the rough stone. These were brown.

Tom Idle said, "But the train couldn't have disappeared here. It was reported as passing the station at the dam, beyond this point."

Doc taxied the ship down the lake to the dam and tied up at a motorboat dock. He left Tom Idle to stare in awe at the giant spillway and speculate on their chances if the plane motor should stop while they were taxiing, and they were swept over.

The railroad crossed the river on the dam.

The young telegrapher at the "OS" station below the dam obviously considered his job as serious as being president. He was copying a train order when Doc arrived, and he broke the dispatcher with repeat requests often enough to show that this was probably his first assignment.

"This is only my second day here," he said. "I really don't know anything about the missing freight, except what I've heard."

"What happened to the other operator?" Doc asked.

"He was drowned," the brass-pounder explained. "Nobody knows how the accident happened. They found his body inside one of the power turbines at the dam. He was a mess, I guess."

Doc returned to the plane.

"It is getting lighter," he said.

Tom Idle looked around in the increasing dusk. "Looks like it's getting darker to me."

"I was not referring to the weather."

MAD MESA was no-telling-how-many-million-years old. The scientists had never been able to get on the top to find out; they could only use their telescopes and make guesses. The name—Mad Mesa—was less than two years old, the name being the result of the efforts of a half-cracked explorer to climb the butte and find out what was on top.

He had spent all his money, and finally gone crazy without succeeding. There was some opinion that he had been insane to begin with, because there was probably not five dollars' worth of scientific information to be had on top of the butte.

Mad Mesa was four thousand feet high, most of it straight up. It was not flat on top, although it appeared so from a distance. Nor was it a symmetrically shaped butte; its sides were as grooved with canyons as if a titanic bear had clawed them. In the smaller of these canyons the *Queen Mary* could have been hidden, and the larger ones were a mile deep.

Mad Mesa was an island; the building of Stone Mountain Dam had backed water up around it and made it so.

It was three o'clock in the morning when Doc Savage gave his paddle a flip and brought the folding canvas boat around a headland with sufficient speed and silence that it was not likely to be seen.

The boat had been in the plane. The plane itself was some four miles away, fastened by spring-lines to the sides of a narrow canyon.

Having eased the boat into the intense black shadows close to the cliffs, Doc breathed, "You might paddle now."

Tom Idle's boating experience had been limited to pond paddling in Missouri, so he took over cautiously. He knew the need for silence.

He was puzzled. This was the fourth or fifth canyon in the side of Mad Mesa that they had investigated. And Doc Savage had not been going more than a few hundred feet into the harborlike canyons.

How the bronze man could ascertain anything in the pitch blackness was a mystery.

It was so black that Tom Idle could not see Doc Savage place before his eyes a strange pair of spectacles which had can-shaped contrivances for lenses. This device was almost as bulky as binoculars. Doc also lifted a contraption which resembled a large, old-fashioned magic lantern, and pointed it at the surroundings. He was using it like a searchlight, but it was apparently giving out no light.

Had Tom Idle been able to see what Doc was doing, he wouldn't have been greatly enlightened. He was no specialist in electricity.

He would have known that there are wavelengths of light which the human eye does not perceive, X-rays being an example, as well as wavelengths of ultraviolet light and infrared.

With a little explanation, he might have been made to understand how wavelengths of infralight could be sent out by a portable projector resembling an old-time magic lantern, and he probably could have conceived how the infralight was made visible, just as X-rays are made visible by a fluoroscopic screen, by a device not as large as a pair of binoculars, complicated though the contrivance might be. After all, watches are made, and keep good time, and are hardly larger than pencil erasers.

They did not find anything that night.

They camped under a ledge in a canyon that day, and did not show themselves.

At two o'clock the following morning, they heard three shots in quick succession.

Chapter XVII
MADNESS ON THE MESA

THE shots were not close. A mile distant, possibly. But it was hard to judge, particularly after the echoes began jumping among the canyons, thumping and grumbling and going off in the distance, then coming back as if they were answers being returned.

"What'll we do?" Tom Idle gulped.

"Keep quiet and investigate."

Doc paddled toward the spot where the shots had sounded. The folding boat was constructed of waterproofed silk over a duralumin framework, and had the lines of an Eskimo kayak, a type of craft which looks absolutely unsafe to the uninitiated, but in which the Eskimos frequently paddle fifty miles offshore in some of the most stormy waters in the world.

The craft was fast, and Doc, using a double paddle, sent it at its best speed. Now and then he paused to use the infralight-scanner device which enabled him to "see" in the intense darkness.

Then Doc saw the swimming man.

The man, at first, resembled a beaver. The water had slicked down his hair until his head resembled a beaver's bow-works, and he was swimming with a careful mud crawl, only his head out, making practically no splash.

The man was going along the sheer stone face of Mad Mesa.

He disappeared so suddenly that it seemed he must have sunk.

Doc Savage paddled silently to the spot, and found a mouth that was like a knife slash. It was hardly fifty feet wide, but the canyon spread out inside.

Before Doc could overhaul the swimming man, the fellow climbed out of the water. He was mysteriously silent about it.

He had a long knife in his teeth.

The man disappeared over a ledge.

"Hondo!" a voice exploded in frightened astonishment.

"Yeah! Stand still, damn you!"

This second voice was breathless, so it was evidently the swimmer speaking.

"Listen, Hondo, I'm all for you." The first man was terrified. "I'll take your orders."

"I know!" gritted the voice that must belong to Hondo Weatherbee. "You'll take 'em till my back is turned!"

"Hondo, you got me wrong!"

"Yeah?"

"Honest, Hondo."

"Suppose you tell me what Jan Hile is figuring on, then."

It was not hard for Doc Savage and Tom Idle, crouched in the folding boat below the ledge, to visualize Hondo Weatherbee standing above, holding the point of his knife against the other man's ribs. The second man, judging from his post here at the mouth of the canyon, must be a lookout. The sentry paused long enough to show that he was reluctant to answer Hondo Weatherbee's question.

"C'mon!" Hondo snarled. "What's Hile up to?"

The lookout spoke in a voice hoarse with fright.

"Hondo, they're gonna double-cross you for your share," he explained. "They're going out tonight with diving suits and check to make sure. If it's there, like you said, they're going to get rid of you."

"It's all Jan Hile's idea?"

"Uh-huh. Him an' Big Eva."

"I shoulda put a knife in that Big Eva while I was his cellmate!" Hondo Weatherbee gritted. He was silent a moment. "After they gun me, what're they gonna do?"

"Go ahead as planned," the other explained.

"Use the stuff in the boxcars?"

"Sure."

"That's liable to kill six or seven hundred people," Hondo Weatherbee growled.

The other man's teeth rattled.

"Hondo, that Jan Hile only needs horns and a tail to be the devil," he croaked.

Hondo Weatherbee made a growling.

"Then somebody oughta go ahead an' tell 'em down in hell what a great guy is gonna join 'em!" he snarled.

There were several sickening sounds above, then the body of the lookout, the knife sticking in his chest, toppled over the ledge, barely missing the boat in which Doc and Tom Idle sat.

THE most intense shocks are the unexpected ones, and somehow neither Doc Savage nor Tom Idle had expected Hondo Weatherbee to murder the lookout. They sat petrified with grisly astonishment, while their little boat rocked on the waves thrown by the body of the dead man. Doc Savage, recovering, reached back and gripped Tom Idle's face to prevent the young man, in the amazement of the moment, from making a sound.

They waited to see if Hondo Weatherbee would climb down to investigate his handiwork. He did not. They could hear him climbing cautiously along the ledge.

"Going to follow him?" Tom Idle breathed.

"No."

"But—"

"We would only be helping Hile," Doc pointed out.

The bronze man stroked with the double paddle and sent the boat back out of the canyon. A few moments later they were lying against the stone cliff, waiting.

Tom Idle said, "I don't understand this at all."

"Jan Hile is double-crossing Hondo Weatherbee for his share of the loot," Doc reminded, "and Hondo has found out."

"Share of what loot?"

Instead of answering that, Doc stated, "There was something said about Jan Hile going out with diving suits tonight to make sure. We'll wait for that. We might as well get this all cleared up."

When the huge tunnels, the tunnels which had diverted the river while Stone Mountain Dam was being constructed, had been closed, and the giant dam had backed the spring floods up to make this strange lake, and the water had surrounded and isolated Mad Mesa, a number of coyotes must have been trapped. Their forlorn, hungry howling was audible at intervals, an eerie and shrill bedlam that might have been silly girls giggling.

The motor that silenced the coyotes was a huge one. The exhaust must have been cut out of the mufflers, because there was profanity, then the motor sound became muffled. But it was still a powerful throbbing, a slow, mighty pulse,

"Look!" Tom Idle gasped.

A flashlight had blinked briefly, and because of the intense darkness, seemed to throw out an astonishing amount of light. The glow revealed a strange horned monster crawling on the water.

A strange horned monster was what it appeared to be in that brief instant. More than a hundred feet long. Blunt and wide. Black. The horns were four, in two pairs, and they stuck up at either end;

of each pair one was larger and standing straight, the other smaller and coupled to the straight one at the base.

The black monster crawled out onto the lake.

Doc Savage said, "You know what it is?"

"How'd they get it here?" his companion breathed. "They must have trucked it in by pieces and assembled it secretly." Tom Idle made a low mutter of astonishment. "Say, they've been preparing for this thing for months."

"Then you know what it is?"

"A big barge with cranes on it."

Doc suggested, "And now you know what happened to the freight train. The freight had only a dozen cars, remember?"

Tom Idle thought for a moment, getting his mind to accept what he realized must have happened.

"They laid the barge alongside the tracks and lifted the train off with the cranes, one car at a time," he surmised. "I remember them strings you found hanging to the rocks. They must have been off the fenders they put between the barge and the cliff, so there wouldn't be any marks. That nick above the track must've been made by one of the cranes. And the pieces of metal you found were broken off the cars by the lifting chains."

"Something like that," Doc admitted.

"But the missing freight was reported as going past the railway station at the dam!"

"The operator was bribed," Doc decided. "Later, they murdered him so that he would never be able to tell. Made it look like a drowning."

The two were grimly silent as they paddled in the wake of the huge barge, which was making its way beneath the towering stone sides of Mad Mesa.

THE barge went through an interesting procession of maneuvers to find its destination. It started off by cruising first one way, then the other, moving slower and slower.

"Look," Tom Idle breathed. "I can see four lights at four different places. They seem to be on surrounding buttes."

"Bearing points."

"Huh?"

"Jan Hile is on the deck of the barge," explained Doc Savage, who had been using the infralight scanner. "He has a surveyor's transit, and is locating a spot on the lake by taking bearings on the lights, which are being held by some of his men who must have been dispatched earlier to the bearing points."

"Oh."

Later, a hoarse grumbling of chain indicated the barge was being anchored. The amount of chain that went out showed the water was deep.

Preparations to dive began.

They used modern suits, all-metal, not unlike armor. Suits so heavy that the divers, two of them, had to be put over the side with the crane. A motor-operated pump supplied air.

The diving continued for an hour. The men on the barge put up canvas screens to hide the lights by which they worked, and the effort to maintain silence was continuous.

Twice, the divers were hauled up in haste, following which there were explosions under the surface, great shocking blasts followed by an uprush of water, bubbles and smoke. After the blasts, the divers went down immediately.

"They're hauling something up in buckets," Tom Idle breathed.

Doc Savage had handed him the infralight scanner so he could get an idea of what was going on. They were holding their small boat at a considerable distance from the point where the diving operations were going on.

Tom Idle scratched his head and mumbled his bewilderment.

"They're after something down there," he decided. "But what on earth could it be? There couldn't be any sunken pirate treasure ships or nothin' like that."

Doc picked up the paddle and sent the light boat back toward the canyon from which the big derrick barge had come. The barge had hauled anchor. The distance bearing lights on the buttes had gone out. The night's diving seemed to be over.

Waiting just outside the canyon mouth, Doc watched the barge approach. When it was abreast, he began paddling, and entered the canyon mouth silently, and almost alongside the huge, panting barge.

"There is just a chance they might have a black-light burglar-alarm beam across the mouth of the canyon," he explained in a whisper.

The intense darkness made their furtive entrance possible. The barge was showing no lights, but steering was being done by two range lights on shore. These ranges appeared to be flashlights with red and green paper held over the lenses.

They got into the canyon harbor without incident.

Chapter XVIII
THE DOUBLE-CROSSED MAN

DOC SAVAGE worked quickly, so as to get ashore under cover of the excitement. He found a spot which was not too steep for landing, put Tom Idle on the beach, then quickly hauled the boat out and collapsed it so that it became a package not quite as large as a golf bag. He gave this to Tom Idle to carry. Doc himself handled the two equipment cases, both of which were heavy.

He found a niche in the stone, and posted Tom Idle there.

"You understand how to unfold that boat?" he whispered.

"Yes."

"As soon as it gets near daylight, put the boat in the water, clear out and notify the police—in case I do not return," Doc advised.

The bronze man left Tom Idle, somewhat disgruntled, hiding in the niche.

Tom Idle had been under mental strain for so long that he was beginning to feel that he had to have action to keep things from snapping inside him. They had found nothing to indicate that his sister might be here on the island, but the possibility was enough to get him worked up.

Waiting in the rock crack, he found that time dragged incredibly. He felt of the rough stone, tried to visualize what it would look like from its broken-glass feel to his fingers. He fingered around in the sand. He untied his shoes and tied them tighter. He stood up and sat down half a dozen times.

Finally, he boiled over.

It wouldn't hurt to do a bit of cautious exploring on his own. After all, he had a lot at stake. His sister.

Doc Savage had told him to wait here. Well, he'd come back.

He took off the shoes, which he had earlier tied so tight. The rock was sharp, cut his feet through his socks. He managed, with a pocketknife which had been in the suit he purloined on the beach of Great Salt Lake, to cut the sleeves from his coat, and put one of those on either foot and tied it. This made the going more comfortable.

Shortly, he discovered a light. It was in a tent, he saw, when he had crawled nearer. Men seemed to be in the tent, and he could hear a voice mutter.

He could not resist the impulse to crawl close enough to listen.

Jan Hile was thumbing through a sheaf of papers, and stopping now and then to set down some figures. Finally he totaled what he had written.

He took the papers.

"These," he said, "are copies of the Federal engineers' report of the cubic-foot water capacity of Stone Mountain Dam."

He waved the papers again.

"Also here," he added, "I have the reports of chemists on the amount of the chemical it takes to cause illness and eventual death. Also the chemists have certified that the poison cannot be removed from water by any processes of filtering that could be applied to a city water system without prohibitive expense."

He looked around at his men. Several of them were there, among these being Big Eva, Skookum and the trio who had failed to commit a murder at the burning coal field in Ohio.

JAN HILE took a drink of water, then grinned thinly and said, "That ain't lake water."

"You're going right ahead with it?" a man asked uneasily.

"Why not?"

"There's a hell of a smell about that disappeared train."

"Let it smell."

"What about Doc Savage? He's charging around somewhere."

Jan Hile scowled. "I've got Doc Savage's men right here, and if he gets too close, we can keep him off by threatening to kill them. The same thing goes for that Idle kid and his sister."

Skookum said, "Hondo heap no like see them guys get out of pen. Cops look for Hondo now."

Jan Hile looked around cautiously.

"Hondo," he said, "doesn't figure in this any longer." He frowned at Big Eva. "How about you? The scheme to leave a stooge in your place in the penitentiary has flopped. You got any kick?"

Big Eva shook his head hastily. "I'm outa the big house. Hell, that satisfies me. Anyway, maybe we can catch the stooge later and turn him back over to the law."

Jan Hile nodded. "That's sensible."

The head schemer now folded the papers, touched a match to them, and watched them burn. Tom Idle flatted close to the ground, fearful lest the additional light would show his presence. But his suspense subsided when Jan Hile ground his heel on the ashes.

Hile eyed his men. "Now, I'm going over this once again."

"Hell, we've got it all clear," one muttered.

"You never get a plan too clear," Hile snapped. "We'll hash it over again. First, we've got six carloads of poisonous chemical, and nobody knows that we've got it. The stuff was loaded into the boxcars marked as common flour, and nobody is going to kick about losing the flour. Because we were shipping it to ourselves in Frisco."

"What about the stink over the missing train?" asked the man who was worried about the train. "Seems like we could have worked a better gag than stealing a whole train."

Hile shook his head. "That was the easy way. We lift the train off the track and drop the engine and all the cars in deep water. Nobody knows. Nobody, that is, who's gonna tell anything."

He laughed grimly.

"The boxcar doors are open and the sacks of poison are ripped, and they're bein' dissolved by the lake water," he continued. "In two weeks more, the lake water will be poison enough that people in the city drinkin' it will begin to get sick."

He shrugged. "What'll naturally be next?"

"A chemical analysis by experts," a man said dutifully.

"Sure," Hile agreed. "And it will show poison. But what kind of poison?"

"One that the lake water could have absorbed by dissolving a natural vein of the stuff somewhere that the water has covered since the dam raised it," said the dutiful man.

"Exactly. Then they'll drain the dam. The water won't be fit to use."

A man started to say something, and Hile lifted a hand and stopped him.

"I know. We'll have our own geologist turn up and locate the vein that is doing the poisoning. I've got the geologist all arranged for. He says we can doctor the vein so samples will show the poison."

The worried-about-the-train man changed his worrying to the dam.

"I been thinking," he said. "Suppose they don't destroy the dam and drain the lake? After all, it's a power dam as well as a water supply."

"The main purpose of the dam is water supply," Jan Hile said. "If they don't drain the lake, we'll dynamite the dam and make it look like a nut did it to get even about the poisoned water. Sure thing they wouldn't rebuild it for only power purposes. You know how much political fuss was raised about the building of such a dam in the first place. No, it won't be rebuilt."

TOM IDLE had lain in something close to a physical trance as he listened to the scheme being unfolded. His first impression was that the thing was too fantastic to be true. But he had seen enough evidence of the vicious cleverness of Jan Hile's mind to realize that the man would attempt something this incredible.

But what was the whole thing about? That mystery plagued him.

Jan Hile answered the question a few moments later. He gestured with both black-gloved hands, gave an order, and some of the men dumped buckets of material on the tent table.

It was the stuff that had been hauled up from the lake bottom by the divers. Shattered rock fragments.

Jan Hile examined the rock samples with a magnifying glass, then took a hammer and chisel, worked on one of the rocks, and finally burst out in a wildly triumphant laugh.

"Look!" he chortled. "There's wire gold in this stuff as thick as shingle nails. The stuff will run twenty thousand dollars a ton! After they drain the lake, all we gotta do is buy the land, then start mining!"

One of the men said, "Hondo sure made a strike eleven years ago, didn't he?"

Jan Hile laughed. "He sure did. You begin to see why he killed his partner to keep the partner from sharing in it."

"Hondo went to the pen for that, didn't he?" asked a man who evidently had not belonged to the old-time outlaw gang.

Jan Hile nodded. "Yes. Hondo was smart enough, though, not to tell why he'd murdered the partner. He thought they'd pardon him in a few years, but he got into so much trouble in prison that he saw he would never get out. So he got in touch with me, and we cooked up this whole thing."

Jan Hile looked around at the men.

"I was to get Hondo Weatherbee out of prison," he said. "And Hondo was to show me the exact location of the gold lode. Hondo knew they'd built this dam in the meantime. That was a bad break. We had to go to all this trouble to get the dam drained."

"Where's Hondo now?"

"I don't know. He may know I plan to shut him out. If he does, we'll have to gun him."

The discussion now turned into one of methods of getting rid of Hondo Weatherbee. Apparently they had not yet discovered that Hondo had murdered the lookout.

It dawned on Tom Idle that he had been away from his hiding place a long time. Moreover, he realized suddenly that there were traces of dawn in the east.

He crept away from the tent hurriedly and crawled into the stony crack where Doc Savage had hidden him.

He had been there no more than two minutes when, without the slightest warning, a gun muzzle pressed against his face.

"All right," growled Hondo Weatherbee's harsh voice. "You're dealing with an old Indian fighter now. I been watchin' you layin' by that tent and listenin'!"

Tom Idle blurted something which he would not have said had he taken time to think.

"Where's Doc Savage?" he gasped.

The instant the words were out, he knew that he had betrayed the fact that Doc Savage was on Mad Mesa. He started to groan, but even that died unpleasantly at the other's next words.

"I happened onto Savage a little earlier!" And the man chuckled.

Chapter XIX
MELEE ON MAD MESA

A FOG had lifted from the lake during the night, and now that there was a faint red flush of dawn on the topmost pinnacle of Mad Mesa, the fog either had thickened, or the presence of the slight light made it more noticeable. Visibility had not improved.

Jan Hile was in his tent, and he had extinguished the lantern which had furnished light. His men were stationed at strategic points in the neighborhood. Hile was afraid of Hondo Weatherbee, for he knew the man was a hardened killer. If Hondo suspected he was being double-crossed, Hile realized the outlaw would be a bad customer. Hile knew very well that it would take only one small lead slug from a gun to decide whether Hondo Weatherbee or himself secured the major share of that lakebed gold, which they were doing such elaborate scheming to get.

So Jan Hile nearly jerked his hands out of his black gloves when one of his sentries cracked a harsh challenge in the murk.

"What is it?" he yelled nervously.

"Hondo," the sentry called. "And he's got the Idle kid."

"What?" Hile screamed.

Hile was a nervous man. He naturally associated the presence of Tom Idle with the nearness of Doc Savage, because the two had escaped the penitentiary together, and he was suddenly frantic with anxiety. He had spent a great deal of his own money in assembling the barge, buying the huge cargo of poison, and in paying the numerous itching palms that had to be paid. There was a great deal at stake. Millions. And there were few men who ever craved money more than Jan Hile, or would go to such lengths to get it.

He had intended to shoot Hondo Weatherbee, or have him shot, on sight. He changed his mind.

"Bring them here," he ordered.

He sat down behind the table, took a small black derringer out of his pocket, and held it cupped in his black-gloved hands, where it was not very noticeable.

A man came in carrying another man.

Jan Hile had seen Hondo Weatherbee and Tom Idle together once before, on the night that he had personally engineered the substitution of Idle for the convict in the penitentiary; but there had been hurry and tension that night, so that he had not noticed what he saw now—the startling physical resemblance of the two men.

Skookum had selected Tom Idle as a man who looked like Hondo. Skookum had done an excellent job. No movie stand-in ever resembled his star more closely.

Had one of the men not been unconscious, and the other attired in the clothing which Hondo Weatherbee had worn that night—and draped with Hondo Weatherbee's gun belts—Hile knew he would have had difficulty telling which was which.

Hile tried to keep his eyes from Hondo's guns, but they had a grim fascination.

"Where did you find him, Hondo?" Hile asked, and had trouble keeping his voice from shaking.

THE other man did not answer. He dropped the unconscious form he had been dragging, made his stance a little more wide-legged, and frowned.

"I'm not some kinds of a fool, Hile," he said.

Jan Hile decided Hondo Weatherbee's voice was changed, and he grew more uneasy. He kept thinking of the two or three times in the past when he had seen Hondo kill a man, and how Hondo had always seemed to change, to assume a calm that was deadly, just before he committed the deeds.

"What do you mean, Hondo?"

"You been planning to get rid of me for my share." When Jan Hile would have spoken, the other man lifted his hand to command silence. "Oh, don't bother to lie about it. I know."

Jan Hile thought how young Hondo Weatherbee was, really, to have lived the life he had led. The man seemed hardly in his thirties, in spite of the eleven years he had spent in the penitentiary. He was older, of course, but he seemed younger. If a life of crime, and prison, is supposed to age a man, Hondo Weatherbee was an exception.

Then Jan Hile jerked his thoughts to the present, for the other man was speaking.

"I'll make you a proposition, Hile."

"What kind, Hondo?"

"I take a fourth of the gold, instead of a half. I know how rich that lode is. A fourth will do me."

"And in return?" Jan Hile asked from a dry throat.

"Wait, I ain't finished. I take a fourth. I turn this Idle fellow over to you, and we hand him back to the law. And I also turn over Doc Savage."

"What?"

Hile was dumbfounded. He knew that this would be his biggest surprise, no matter how long he lived.

"What?" he repeated incredulously.

"In return," the other man said, "you let up on me, Hile. And to make sure you let up on me, you write out a confession to this whole mess. I'll put the confession where it will go into the hands of the law if anything happens to me."

Jan Hile wet his lips. "And if I don't?"

"I'm going to kill you!" The other man's voice was suddenly guttural with emotion. "And if I don't kill you, Doc Savage is layin' out there in the rocks unconscious. He's where you won't find him. But he'll regain consciousness, and go on, and he'll get you as sure as I don't. Because I've told him everything."

There was enough conviction in the other man's voice that Hile knew he was not bluffing. The man meant it. And he didn't care much whether Hile accepted, or refused and elected to shoot it out. This also showed in his voice. His hate for Hile was utter and complete.

Hile was weighted with the conviction that he was whipped. He had to give in. If not because of fear of Hondo, because seeing Doc Savage out of the way was worth whatever sacrifices he must make.

"All right," he said.

"Before you say it's all right," the other answered grimly, "you better know I put a knife in the lookout at the canyon mouth. He was one of your best pups. And I was starting out to clean house."

Jan Hile felt cold pinpricks on his skin. He was glad he had capitulated.

"If you can smooth it over with his friends," Hile said, "I'll forget about the man."

The other slapped his gun. "This will smooth it over." He scowled at Jan Hile. "Go ahead and write out that confession. Sign it and fingerprint it, and we'll have the men sign it and print it as witnesses."

AS Jan Hile had known, Hondo Weatherbee was no fool in many ways. He had, for instance, an animal kind of cunning, as shown by the men he picked to witness the confession which Jan Hile composed. The men were those without police records, the men whose testimony would best stand up in a court.

Another move of typical Hondo slyness was the man's act in dispatching one of the men to mail the envelope containing the confession. The messenger did not know the envelope contents, and there was no doubt that he would mail it, thus putting Jan Hile's confession where he could not recover it.

"We understand each other now, eh?"

"Yes," Hile admitted. "We do. Where is Doc Savage?"

Hile was led into the brush and boulders in a nearby gully and confronted with the prone, motionless form of the giant bronze man.

Hile snarled and drew his gun. It was in his mind to end the Savage menace there.

"Hold it," interrupted Hondo Weatherbee's voice.

Hile frowned at the other man in the dull gloom. The smoky dawn-lights and twilights at the base of Mad Mesa had the peculiarity of seeming to last for hours because of the number of peaks and buttes around about. It was like dawn coming in a forest.

"He's got to be killed, Hondo!" Hile snapped.

The other nodded. "Who said different? What I mean is that I'm doing you a favor."

"Favor?"

"Take Savage and the Idle guy to the rest of the prisoners," the other said fiercely. "And I'll put them all out of the way."

"Oh!" Hile said.

He was satisfied. Pleased. In his old outlaw days, he had been a bloodthirsty man, but his interval as a lawyer had been one of comparative peace, and these late killings had given him some twinges. He was willing for Hondo to do the murdering. He even felt himself warming toward Hondo. The man, after all, was a valuable associate.

"Right," Hile said.

Doc Savage was lifted and carried, along with Tom Idle, to a shallow, natural cavern in the cliffs. The big bronze figure of Doc Savage was completely limp. There was no visible wound, so Hile presumed the bronze man had been struck on the head and his hair hid the spot.

The other prisoners were stiff and weak. Monk and Renny not as much as the others, although they showed the effects; for they had been tied tightly since their capture, and fed only twice. They stared in hollow-eyed horror as Doc Savage and Tom Idle were dumped among them. Doc Savage's five men had not before seen Tom Idle and did not know him. But Idle's sister emitted a low cry.

There were several other prisoners—the crew of the railroad train and the Salt Lake City taxi driver. They stared listlessly. They had given up.

Hile's men withdrew hastily. Mass murder was too much for their stomachs. Only Hile remained.

"You want to watch it?"

Hile nodded. He didn't want to. But he did not wish, either, for Hondo Weatherbee to get the idea he had a weak stomach. Men such as these would only follow a leader who they thought was unafraid of anything.

"I'll stay," Hile said.

"Too bad," the other growled. "I hoped you wouldn't."

He drew both his guns and pointed them at Hile. Hile blanched. "Hondo—"

"Don't move!" the other gritted.

"Hondo!" Hile croaked. "You're not double-crossing—"

The man with the guns showed his teeth fiercely.

"You don't get it!" he snarled. "I'm not Hondo! Damn you, if you've harmed my sister—"

Doc Savage got up off the cave floor.

"Careful, Idle!" he warned. "You can see your sister is all right!"

IMPACT had followed impact for Jan Hile, until he held his self-control barely pinched between his fingertips. And now he lost it.

The man he had thought was Hondo Weatherbee was Tom Idle. The semidarkness accounted for his being fooled, that and the way the man had talked.

Jan Hile became entirely rattled. He spun, pitched backward. There was a ledge below the cave, and he went over that, almost headfirst.

Tom Idle would have killed him, had Doc Savage not lunged and knocked the gun up. With his aim distracted, Idle had presence of mind to hold his bullet, and there was no shot sound to spread alarm.

Hile landed, with crashing of boughs, in small pine trees directly below the ledge. The crash was long, small boughs breaking first, then larger ones. Then silence. The fall had stunned the man.

One of Hile's men shouted an inquiry.

"Hey! What happened?" he wanted to know.

Doc Savage had flung to the prisoners. "No noise!" he warned.

He began freeing them, slashing the knots and saying, "Get up and move around, to limber your muscles!"

He freed his own men first, and as best they could with their stiffened muscles, they helped loosen the others. The cave became crowded with grim-faced men trying to get their arms and legs in condition to move dependably.

Tom Idle clasped his sister in his arms and listened to her incoherent assurance that she had not been harmed.

Monk jumped up and down apishly and swung his arms.

"I got a whole book of scores to settle with these yahoos!" he gritted.

Long, bony Johnny was also trying to unlimber.

"I'll be superamalgamated!" he muttered.

Renny said, "Holy cow, Doc! How'd you manage that trick?"

The bronze man either did not hear, or was too busy to answer.

Tom Idle replied.

"Mr. Savage found Hondo Weatherbee and over-powered him," he explained. "In the meantime, I had been left hiding, but had crawled away to listen to Hile's men. When I came back, Mr. Savage took a very effective means of fixing in my mind what Hondo Weatherbee's voice sounded like."

"Whatcha mean—effective?" Renny asked.

"Mr. Savage imitated Hondo Weatherbee's voice as he would sound if he had captured us," Idle explained. "It was kind of a trick, and it scared ten years off my growth. But it fixed Hondo Weatherbee's voice in my mind. I'll never forget it. In fact, I don't think I could have carried out that imitation without the scare."

Tom Idle shivered, remembering the frightening moment when he had returned to his niche in the rocks, and thought that he had been captured by Hondo Weatherbee, who had also taken Doc Savage.

Doc said, "This may be tough."

Below the cave mouth, Jan Hile regained his senses and began screaming an alarm.

"That won't help any!" decided Long Tom disgustedly.

Chapter XX
DAM DEATH

TOM IDLE had Hondo Weatherbee's two six-guns. At Doc's suggestion, he gave one of them to Ham, who was unlikely to do any unnecessary shooting, in contrast to Monk and Renny, who had been known to let their enthusiasm get the better of them.

They crouched at the cave mouth. It was still too dark for accurate shooting, because of the fog. They fired a few times to make the enemy cautious.

Doc Savage left the cave. He moved rapidly, scaling the sheer wall of stone, then turned to the right. He had concealed the two equipment cases which he had brought ashore; hidden them on a ridge where they were not hard to find.

One case contained the machine pistols which Doc Savage had developed for the use of his men. These unusual weapons, which were like oversized automatics, fired various types of missiles.

The case held an assortment of ammunition—mercy bullets causing unconsciousness, smoke slugs, and little explosive bullets which looked harmless, but anyone of which could tear a small-size house to pieces.

There was shooting now, back at the cave. The bronze man hurried, came in sight of the spot, stopped and used one of the machine pistols loaded with a drum of explosives.

The gun made a deep bullfiddle sound, so rapidly did it discharge. He fanned the muzzle, spreading the slugs.

The bullets hit, exploded. The roar was deafening. The ground trembled. Rock fragments swirled high in the air. Loosened boulders tumbled down the canyon sides.

After that unexpected bedlam, there was an abysmal silence. A single six-gun whanged. The bullet smacked a rock near Doc, climbed away with a bullfiddle moan. He fired another explosive. The gunman yelled, could be heard running.

Doc hailed the cave, using the ancient Mayan tongue, an almost unknown language which he and his men spoke and used to communicate without being understood by others.

He warned them that he was coming back to the cave. He did not want to get shot by accident.

He gained the cave without trouble.

While distributing the machine pistols, he said, "Spread and keep them down from the canyon sides. Try to herd them together."

Numerically, they were still outmatched. But the machine pistols gave them infinite superiority. The little guns, the ripping, demolishing blasts of the explosive bullets, struck terror. The firing was sporadic, now and then a six-shooter, more often bursts from the rapid-firers.

It got a little lighter.

Jan Hile could be heard shouting. Then the big motor of the crane-barge started.

"Blast it!" Monk howled. "They're pulling out that barge!"

A few minutes later, the unwieldly barge nosed out of the narrow canyon mouth.

"We might sink it!" Ham suggested.

Doc Savage had what he considered a better plan. He called Monk and Renny, the two physically strongest, to assist.

They unfolded the collapsible boat and put it in the water.

"Have they got a rowboat here?" Doc asked.

"I think so," Long Tom said.

"See if they smashed it."

They had not. It was a slow, clumsy punt of a craft. The oars were gone.

Doc indicated planks which had formed a floor in one of the tents.

"Use those for paddles." He described the location of the spot where he and Tom Idle had hidden the plane. "Get to the plane. It has a radio. Have plenty of State police waiting at the dock above the dam. We'll try to herd Hile and his men down there."

THE slowness of the crane barge made the bronze man's plan feasible. It was no more than three quarters of a mile distant when Doc Savage, Monk and Renny put off in the folding boat. There was an extra paddle, and Monk and Renny furnished propelling power.

Doc sat in the bow. When the barge headed for shore, he elevated the muzzle of a machine pistol, using the weapon like a field piece, and dropped explosive slugs ahead of the larger craft. It changed its course almost at once.

A few high-powered rifle slugs came skipping over the water. They were low, kept the kayaklike folding boat head-on to offer as small a target as possible.

The sun came from behind the buttes suddenly, and was hot. A few birds sailed above the lake, dodging wildly whenever there was shooting, but for some reason not going away.

Back in the distance they could see the punt. Ham, Long Tom, Johnny and Tom Idle were in the craft, propelling it clumsily with boards. It took them fully two hours to disappear behind a headland. Later the plane flew into view.

The plane circled very high, out of rifle shot, and sent explosive slugs to aid harassing operations of the men in the folding boat.

It was almost noon when the big barge chugged up to the boat landing not more than a hundred yards above the great dam with its booming spillways.

Renny groaned.

"Holy cow!" he croaked. "There's not a cop around the place!"

Jan Hile, Skookum and the others must have thought the same thing. They slammed the heavy barge against the boat dock, crumbling some of the piling. The men, carrying guns, piled onto the dock.

THE police appeared then. There were plenty of them. More than enough. They had placed machine guns. These cackled a warning burst.

Doc and his two men, waiting offshore, could hear the command that was sent to Hile.

"Lay 'em down, you guys! You haven't got a chance!"

Hile must have figured they didn't have a chance if they did surrender. He screamed at his men. They would run the barge back on the lake, try to hold out until nightfall, or reach the shore at some other point.

The men fell back onto the barge, shooting. Three of them went down, were dragged aboard by the others.

The barge backed away from the half-demolished dock. It backed for all of two hundred feet.

Then Doc Savage, who had been watching intently, was startled by the abrupt, thundering moan of a machine pistol behind his head. He whirled.

Monk said, "Well, blast it! We couldn't let 'em get away!"

To the homely chemist's credit, he had endeavored only to disable the barge. His slugs had ripped open the side of the heavy craft near the stern, where he reasoned the engine would be. And he had stopped the motor.

But he had not stopped to think what would happen if the barge motor ceased turning. His horrified gasp proved that he hadn't.

"I never thought of that!" he croaked hollowly.

The barge turned around four times slowly in the interval that it took to reach the spillway. For there was current here, more current than was apparent. The barge, by the time it reached the spillway, must have been going several miles an hour. And it weighed hundreds of tons.

The spillway was one of the breathtaking sights of the dam. It was not the tunnel spill—there were four of those; but this was the high-water season, and water, hundreds of thousands of tons of it an hour, was going over the dam itself in a Niagara roar that could be heard for miles.

There were steel gates that could be lowered to cut the volume of the flood. If they had held, the men on the barge would still have lived.

The spillway crushed when the barge hit it. The barge nosed over. It hung, like a boat on a reef, for moments.

Some of the men, who had jumped earlier and tried to swim for it, were swept over while the barge hung there—in the hugeness of the flood, like half-drowned flies.

With a long, shuddering grunt, the barge took the plunge, took with it to demolition and death all the men who were aboard.

LATE that evening, Doc Savage himself supervised the blasting open of the huge drainage tunnels through which the river had been diverted while the dam was constructed, and which later had been sealed with concrete.

It took three weeks to drain the dam.

Another two weeks were required to locate the freight train and raise it, remove the poison—such as had not been dissolved.

Jan Hile had been clever, and had dropped the cars in the channel of the old river, where, even after the dam was drained, they were still submerged.

Johnny, the geologist, checked on Hondo Weatherbee's gold lode.

"They did not underestimate its value," he said, for once using small words.

Renny, the engineer, having conferred with Doc Savage, busied himself making surveys.

Hondo Weatherbee, the one man who had survived the affair, was back in the penitentiary.

Renny reported results of his survey. "That gold," he said, "isn't so deep. With a little reconstruction, the water level of that dam can be kept down when it is refilled, so the gold vein will not be covered. It can be worked. The dam will still furnish enough power and water. It was too high in the first place, as a matter of fact."

That arrangement was agreed upon. There were no objections from politicians, the politicians having gotten their fill of that dam much earlier. Ham took care of the legal details.

Nona Idle seemed to be seeing a good deal of Ham, which disturbed Monk, who was busy with the muddy job of getting a freight train out of a river.

"I can't savvy what you see in that guy!" Monk told the young lady.

"Mr. Brooks," the young lady responded, "is a very clever man."

Monk was disgusted.

"Ham is a big bluff!" he said. "Nothin' to 'im. You open his front door, and you're in his back yard!"

THE END

Battling an enemy you can see is one thing; fighting an invisible menace is another. No man who has ever lived could down the Man of Bronze and his Iron Men in a battle of wits or fists. But if they cannot see an enemy, how can they fight it? How can Doc Savage outwit

THE SPOOK LEGION

when he doesn't know where or what the enemy is? Then, it has the United States Navy baffled; it stumps the United States government; it has the world wondering what will happen next ...

THE SUBMARINE MYSTERY

It might be a gigantic hoax—but there was no hoax in the bloodshed that accompanied it. It might be only a crackpot scheme—but the people who lost their lives would not believe that.

What is the strange mystery that so baffles everyone, and requires all the skills and abilities of Doc Savage and his brain trust?

Don't miss these two action-packed novels in DOC SAVAGE #5!

POSTSCRIPT

There's an interesting story behind *Mad Mesa*. Its unusual penitentiary background prefigured Lester Dent landing in prison not once but twice in 1938, and it was the only Doc novel Lester Dent wrote during his European "vacation" that year.

As his Street & Smith colleague, Steve Fisher, told the tale:

> About this time Lester Dent arrived in town, looking as much like his character Doc Savage as ever. Les announced that he and his wife were going abroad in three days, leaving on the *Queen Mary*.
>
> That night I consulted Edythe. When the *Queen Mary* sailed, Ede, our young son, and my Great Dane "Johnny" were all on board. I stood against the rail with Les Dent and waved goodbye to all the editors.
>
> Les and his wife toured Europe, but Ede and I settled in a small chateau just outside of Paris, and there we stayed. It was the first rest I had. I was in love with beautiful France, and I was happier there than I had ever been in all my life.

Another writer, Ken Crossen, recalled:

> Steve, naturally, didn't have enough money with him and when they arrived he told Les to take care of the advance rent money on the house that Steve wanted. Les did and wrote it down in a little book. But the same thing happened with everything else that required money. Steve kept telling him that he was expecting a check from *Collier's* and would settle everything. As was to be expected, Steve never did get that check until after they were back in NYC.

Dent was forced to banged out a flock of pulp stories while in Paris that April, to finance further travels. From Vienna in May, he mailed *Mad Mesa* from the Hotel Erzherzog Karl.

There were other problems along the way. High in the Swiss Alps, they climbed Mount Pilatus. From its snowy summit, Lester peered down from his dizzying perch. As Norma Dent later recounted:

> Les picked up two rocks. His face had a strange expression. He threw one of the stones over the edge, then listened. The rock landed somewhere, doubtless, but it was so far below that no sound came back. Les said, "I've changed my mind." I knew what he meant—for a couple of years he'd had a yen to try climbing Mount Everest in Asia, which in round figures was about four times as high as the spot where we were now standing. Eureka! He'd just given up that notion.

Dent next landed in hot water while visiting Prague. It was June. Since the annexing of Austria by Germany three months earlier, war jitters had gripped Europe. Bordering both, Czechoslovakia was especially tense. "We went to Czechoslovakia with the vague idea of watching a war start," Dent reported at the time. "We're managing to tough it out less than two weeks. I still cannot tell whether there will be a war in Europe soon."

Scaling a shack attached to a stadium in order to get a better camera angle, Dent was accosted by Czech police. Unbeknownst to the writer, the "shack" concealed an anti-aircraft battery emplacement. Dent found himself at a local jail.

"I remembered all the times that Doc had been imprisoned, and what means he had used to escape, but found calling up the local Associated Press was the most practical course to follow."

In his pre-writing days, Dent had been an A.P. telegrapher.

After his release, Norma asked Lester, "Could this be one time we're too far from home?" He agreed. They trained back to England, and took the *Queen Mary* home. Three months later, the Nazis began dismembering Czechoslovakia, paving the path to World War II.

Was there a real-life analogue for Mad Mesa? The Stone Mountain Dam was undoubtedly based on Utah's Pine View Dam at Weber Canon, which was completed in 1936, amid considerable political controversy.

Mad Mesa itself was inspired by a giant artifact of Dent's childhood. As a boy, he lived on a ranch near Pumpkin Buttes, Wyoming. Miles away in the badlands where dinosaur bones and petrified shellfish abounded, reared a thousand-foot high volcanic plug whose rugged physical description matches Mad Mesa in several respects—particularly its "bear-clawed" sides. Lester often played at the base of Devil's Tower National Monument, cracking open fossilized oyster shells left over from the age when Wyoming lay on the floor of a forgotten ocean.

Before 1938 was over, Lester had another prison experience. Street & Smith editor John L. Nanovic valued authenticity. In November, he organized a field trip to Ossining Prison—better known as "Sing Sing"—for his top writers. Among them were Dent, *The Shadow*'s Walter B. Gibson and Laurence Donovan, another Doc Savage ghost.

Out of that visit came a first-hand view of the inner workings of a large penitentiary. Each writer eventually wrote a prison story. But with his usual uncanny foresight, Dent had turned in *Mad Mesa* six months before. With its maddening mystery and murky motives, it's a foray into Shadow territory, replete with a classic Shadow-style proxy hero in Tom Idle. *Mad Mesa* represents one of the most inventive Doc adventures ever.

—Will Murray

Lester Dent (1904-1959) could be called the father of the superhero. Writing under the house name "Kenneth Robeson," Dent was the principal writer of *Doc Savage,* producing more than 150 of the Man of Bronze's thrilling pulp adventures.

A lonely childhood as a rancher's son paved the way for his future success as a professional storyteller. "I had no playmates," Dent recalled. "I lived a completely distorted youth. My only playmate was my imagination, and that period of intense imaginative creation which kids generally get over at the age of five or six, I carried till I was twelve or thirteen. My imaginary voyages and accomplishments were extremely real."

Dent began his professional writing career while working as an Associated Press telegrapher in Tulsa, Oklahoma. Learning that one of his coworkers had sold a story to the pulps, Dent decided to try his hand at similarly lucrative moonlighting. He pounded out thirteen unsold stories during the slow night shift before making his first sale to Street & Smith's *Top-Notch* in 1929. The following year, he received a telegram from the Dell Publishing Company offering him moving expenses and a $500-a-month drawing account if he'd relocate to New York and write exclusively for the publishing house.

Dent soon left Dell to pursue a freelance career, and in 1932 won the contract to write the lead novels in Street & Smith's new *Doc Savage Magazine.* From 1933-1949, Dent produced Doc Savage thrillers while continuing his busy freelance writing career and eventually adding Airviews, an aerial photography business.

Dent was also a significant contributor to the legendary *Black Mask* during its golden age, for which he created Miami waterfront detective Oscar Sail. A real-life adventurer, world traveler and member of the Explorers Club, Dent wrote in a variety of genres for magazines ranging from pulps like *Argosy, Adventure* and *Ten Detective Aces* to prestigious slick magazines including *The Saturday Evening Post* and *Collier's.* His mystery novels include *Dead at the Take-off* and *Lady Afraid.* In the pioneering days of radio drama, Dent scripted *Scotland Yard* and the 1934 *Doc Savage* series.

Walter Ryerson Johnson (1901-1995) worked in Illinois coal mines before embarking upon a life of joyful wandering. Dropping out of medical school, he hoboed around until the writing bug bit him. Very soon, he was writing for top titles like *Adventure,* producing coal mine and Royal Canadian Mounted Police yarns during the 1920s pulp boom. When those genres faded, he took up Westerns, becoming a prolific wordsmith for the Street & Smith, Clayton and Popular chains. His gun-fanning heroes like Len Siringo, Chop-Chop Charlie and Guncat Bodman are still fondly remembered.

Johnson wrote two Doc Savage novels, *Land of Always-Night* and *The Fantastic Island,* which *Time* magazine suggested was the model for Ian Fleming's *Dr. No.* He plotted a third, *The Motion Menace,* but bowed out of the project, leaving Lester Dent to complete the story himself.

In the mid-1930s, Johnny had an opportunity to journey to Brazil with a group that included pulp author Arthur J Burks bent on locating the missing flyer, Scotty Redfern. Instead, he married his wife of 60 years, artist Lois Lignell.

Over a writing career that encompassed seven decades, Johnson penned numerous stories and articles for markets as diverse as *Esquire* and *Wild West Weekly.* His suspense novels include *Lady in Dread* and *Naked in the Streets.* In addition to Doc Savage, he ghosted the adventures of the Phantom Detective and Mike Shayne, and briefly edited *The Spider* for Popular Publications. His comic book career involved scripting *Batman, The Wyoming Kid, Dale Evans* and other titles. Johnson also wrote many children's books and television scripts.